SECRETS
OF THE BIG ISLAND

Linda B. Myers

About This Book

Secrets of the Big Island is a work of fiction. Names, characters, places and happenings are from the author's imagination. Any resemblance to actual persons – living or dead – events, or locales is entirely coincidental.

No part of this book may be used without written permission, except in the case of brief quotations in critical articles and reviews. Email inquiries to myerslindab@gmail.com

Published by Mycomm One as *A Time of Secrets*. Edited and retitled 2018.

For updates, news, blog and chatter:

www.LindaBMyers.com

Facebook.com/lindabmyers.author

myerslindab@gmail.com

Dedication

For Sondra AhSam and Claudia Mulder

The Best of the Aloha Spirit

I wasn't always *lolo*, you know. People didn't think I was crazy. Keeping silent is where I went so wrong. And nothing was ever right again.

- My Book of Revelation
Excerpt from the Year 2012

CHAPTER ONE

Tattooist Found Guilty of 'Ass-inine'
Crime
By Jackson O'Reilly
Excerpt from the *Keawalani Voice*, 2015

Kaleo Palea, proprietor of the Tat Joint, has been sentenced to thirty days in the Hamakua District jail. The judge also closed his tattoo shop for six months, a little extra punishment to dissuade him from vandalizing the backsides of others in the future.

In the opinion of most villagers, including this reporter, Kaleo Palea does not deserve his fate. "He's not a bad guy," his sister Nani Palea said in his defense. "Just a little unrestrained in anger management."

The blonde muscle man who was his 'victim' is a locally-known blowhard from California. Everything is better in Pismo Beach, according to him, so everyone here on the Big Island wondered why he didn't just go back home. Apparently he has now done just that. Surfer Dude made bail and skipped town, but Kaleo will serve his time. For the next thirty days, prison tats received in the Hamakua jail will no doubt be of a distinctly higher grade.

Nani Palea was philosophical about the temporary closure of her brother's tattoo shop. She figured business would have been bad anyway. Even though the town did think he'd done the right thing, who'd trust her brother with their skin now?

Kaleo had told her – and the rest of Keawalani – all about it. Surfer Dude had swaggered into his shop, interrupting him in the midst of sketching a delicate hibiscus. The Californian had demanded a tattoo on the small of his back.

"What you want in such a hurry, *haole*?" Kaleo had asked using the not-necessarily-flattering term for a Caucasian mainlander.

Surfer Dude explained he wanted a naked chick who would bump and grind when he flexed his butt muscles. Wouldn't that be 'fuckin' awesome' undulating above his Speedo? He pointed out a girlie pattern he liked from the designs tacked to the Tat Joint's wall. For the next three hours, Kaleo worked. When at last he finished, he said, "Some of my best work, *haole*."

"I gotta see it."

"Not yet. Leave this bandage on it 'til you get to the beach then remove it and lie in the sun. Bright rays bring out the colors. Them beach babes gonna love it."

Kaleo was right. The women did love it when Surfer Dude unveiled his body art. They pointed and laughed. They made fun of his ass. That's how Surfer Dude discovered his tattoo was actually Kamapua'a, the Hawaiian Pig God, a porker best known for vulgar conduct.

When Surfer Dude busted in to confront the tattooist, a waiting customer called 911 before Kaleo could beat the snot out of the idiot. Police arrived and arrested them both.

Today, thirty days later, Kaleo was getting out, so Nani was anxious to get to the Hamakua District jail. If she were late he'd start thumbing, and he'd be cranky enough as it was. But she couldn't rush Bethie Kalapana's feet. Bethie's tongue relaxed right along with her arthritic toes as Nani worked to loosen them. The brittle-boned woman was on the massage table, fussing about the new people who'd purchased the house just downhill from her own.

"She move da bonsai wikiwiki. Even before Martina Martin stay gone." Bethie used the pidgin English that was Hawaii's unofficial language, a rich stew from the immigrant populations who had settled the islands. Nani translated in silence. *She moved her bonsai plants in fast, even before Martina Martin moved out.*

Bethie's eyes were shut tight as Nani's talented hands manipulated hot stones to release the hammer toe. "Thirty da kine bonsai all over da lanai. Jacaranda ... shower tree ... all kine." The buyer of the Martin home came each day to water, prune and talk with her plants.

Nani understood that new neighbors were big news and no small cause for alarm, but she hurried the session as much as she could while still giving her client more than her money's worth. She believed in the art of touch, that all humans benefit from contact with others. Through massage or reflexology, she helped those around her with their physical woes.

What surprised her early in her career was the amount of emotional woes that also came her way. Clients told her the most remarkable tales. Through no intent of her own, Nani Palea became the Big Island secret keeper: secrets she kept and sometimes even acted on.

Bethie finally climbed down from the table, slid into her *slippahs*, and wrote her check to Keawalani Hands.

"You know you need better support for your feet, Auntie," Nani said, using the respectful title for older women whether they were relatives or not. She said it well aware that flip flops were the only footwear Bethie would ever consider.

"*You* da support fo dese feet," the old woman said, stretching up to kiss Nani's cheek. Bethie was actually up on her toes. She could barely hobble before her session.

At last, Nani closed down her massage salon which was once the front bedroom of her house. She hurried out back and started up her Vespa. A car would have been better today, but the scooter was her only vehicle. It could just barely carry two when one was the size of her brother, Kaleo. He had customized her bike with a surrey top made from woven palm, and as long as she kept under 40 mph, the top stayed in place protecting her from sun or rain.

Nani putted through the village then accelerated out the other side. Keawalani was far enough off the Big Island's beaten path that the air was still perfumed by plumeria more than by exhaust. Few tourists made it up the secondary road from Highway 19 to the village perched on the shoulder of Mauna Kea, the highest peak in the Pacific. If they did, they might stop for a pineapple shave ice at Halemano's Heavenly Treats or even a loco moco at the Big Island Girl, a diner whose signmaker had misheard the word *grill*. The islander attitude was "no worries" so Girl it remained.

After filling their bellies and maybe their fuel tanks, tourists moved on. There was no Hilo Hattie or Walmart to keep them or their money in the village. They traveled back down the road through cattle pastures to the highway and turned left toward Kona or right toward Hilo. It was the road that Nani took now, turning to the right to pick up her little brother, the convict. Kaleo had been in the slammer for thirty days sitting out his sentence. He'd been released to the custody of his big sister who was widely known to be the more dependable of the two.

Nani saw him walking along the side of the road and knew she was late. His boardshorts and tee-shirt looked a smidge tight. Prison food must have appealed to him. She'd get him off the fried rice and back on fresh fruit and mahi mahi.

"Aloha, bruddah," she said after she u-turned and pulled up next to him. They exchanged the Hawaiian embrace, kissing cheek to cheek. Then she placed a lei around his neck. "Welcome home." She'd made it from brown kukui nuts because they symbolized knowledge. Maybe some would actually rub off on her little brother.

"You're late," Kaleo griped. "I was released hours ago."

Okay, maybe knowledge will never rub off on him.

"You're welcome for picking you up at all."

Kaleo climbed aboard the Vespa behind her, grabbed hold of her waist and said, "You can drop me at the Tat Joint. I guess I'll stay there until I find someone to rent it. Hit it, *sistah*."

"No you don't, *bruddah*. According to the judge, you're coming home with me."

CHAPTER TWO

The Great Loco Moco Debate
By Jackson O'Reilly
Excerpt from the *Keawalani Voice,* 2015

This reporter was hanging with the boys down at Sunny Daze barber shop, awaiting a bi-monthly scalping. The conversation turned to loco mocos. Rumor has it this Big Island comfort food was invented in Hilo after WWII to keep the cholesterol of hungry guys climbing sky high.

"You gots to start with da good ground beef," Sunny claimed. "Not dat low fat crap." There was general agreement except from Motorhead who claimed to prefer his loco moco with pork or fish.

"But that ain't right," Sunny snapped back, snipping the air with his scissors. *Note to readers: you don't want to make Sunny mad just before you get your haircut.* "A real loco moco got da big scoop white rice under da burger patty, eggs sunny side and plenty brown gravy. No onions, mushrooms, kim chee, dat kine stuffs."

Vincent Moy revealed that his family's secret for a superior loco moco was bacon fat in the gravy, but others shouted him down using an unprintable phrase implying he didn't know poop from polish.

The battle raged over long or medium grain rice, Worcestershire in the gravy or chili pepper water, Maui onion or daikon pickles as a condiment. But everyone agreed on two things:

First, the proper way to eat a loco moco is to break the eggs and blend with a bit of the meat, rice and gravy on your fork, then devour together in one *ono* bite after another.

Second, the best loco moco on the island can be had at the Big Island Girl. Asked later for a comment, Daya the Waitress said their secret ingredient was safe with her. She followed up with her enigmatic smile before gliding away to serve another round of Kona coffee to her happy customers.

"Got any ice cream?" Nani's little brother asked. 'Little' was misleading for Kaleo. True, he was twenty-six which made him three years younger than Nani. But at six foot four, he was ten inches taller. While he had the size of his Hawaiian ancestors, she'd inherited the slighter height of their Filipina great-grandmother or maybe the

Chinese plantation worker even farther back on their family tree. The Palea family, like most Hawaiians, was a mixed bag of backgrounds. *Chop suey* as the local slang went or *poi dogs* which meant mongrels.

Nani was a little brown dove of a woman who could best be called curvaceous. Her body wanted to be as lush as the island greenery, and it required as much maintenance to keep it trim. She wasn't crippled by body shame issues like so many of her *haole* sisters on the mainland, but she felt better when fit. It was easier to perform her job when her hands and arms were in peak condition.

Nani's smile was easy and infectuous. Her almond shaped brown eyes were as dark and welcoming as Kona coffee. She looked happy and yet an empathic spirit might divine the sadness always there, just behind the smile.

At long last, Nani's shiny black hair had outgrown the oddball slant created by Sunny Daze, the Keawalani barber. He disliked it when someone called him a stylist. Nani wouldn't make that mistake again. Snipping at the ends a bit at a time, she'd finally been able to even out the cut until her hair once again draped straight down to the middle of her back.

"There's frozen yogurt, non-fat vanilla," she said to her brother.

"Wailelenani. That is unfit food for a big man." Kaleo used her full name when she annoyed him. It meant *beautiful waterfall*. Her nickname, Nani, was common in the islands and simply meant *beautiful*.

"That man better not get any bigger if he doesn't want to look like a certain Pig Man himself." She believed he'd been making a few too many loco moco runs to the Big Island Girl.

Kaleo was out of the slammer and had been living in Nani's house for a couple weeks. He'd claimed the lanai so he would have his own back entrance without bothering Nani's clients who came through the front door. After framing and screening its open walls, he moved his bed into one end and reassembled his sound equipment along the other. Soon the entire residence – including Nani's massage table – vibrated with its volume. Kaleo agreed to use headphones whenever clients were in the house.

He took on the job of doing all her spa sheets and towels since the washer and dryer were also on the lanai. The old machines seemed to dance along with him as music pounded through buds directly into his eardrums. He kept fresh coffee brewing all day for her clientele, made sure there were plenty of water bottles in the fridge, chatted with clients who had to wait while Nani finished up a session, and took to answering Nani's phone to schedule appointments. He also launched into household maintenance, fixing the wobbly handrail out front, replacing a faucet washer and cutting the tough centipede grass with her hand mower.

Nani knew he was trying to earn his keep, and she appreciated most of his help. But she just never knew what change in routine awaited her each time she finished with a client. She was not pleased when he rearranged her kitchen cabinets to suit himself and updated her bookkeeping program. Now she could no longer find a frying pan or call up a balance sheet for Keawalani Hands Massage and Reflexology.

Today, Bethie Kalapana was back for her second appointment of the month. She was filled with news about the new neighbors soon to move in next door. "Martina Martin yard sale tomorrow den she goin' afta. Da peoples moving in wid all the bonsai name stay Yohay. I finally seen him first time oddah night. Now I get big problem, I tell you."

Bethie had begun to gesticulate with both hands while Nani decoded the pidgin: *Martina Martin was leaving right after she held a yard sale. The Yohays, who owned the bonsai plants, would then be moving in. Bethie had finally seen Mr. Yohay the other night, and now she had a problem.*

"You must keep still, Auntie Bethie," said Nani. She was trying to loosen the joints in the old woman's arthritic fingers. "Your hands are fluttering like 'i'iwi birds."

Bethie stopped her waving but continued her story. She had recognized Mr. Yohay as the boyfriend of her best friend, Likolani, who'd shown her a lovey-dovey photo of them together at the beach. "How you figgah? How he be husband of dis Miz Yohay *and* boyfriend of Likolani? I tink somethin' not right, yeah?"

"Hmmm. Sounds like one too many women to me," said Nani.

"How I tell my friend Liko? *Do* I tell her? She hate me for telling? For not telling? Auweeee." Bethie had worked herself into a snit again.

Nani knew her massage efforts would go to waste if the old woman didn't settle down. She thought about the problem for a moment then said, "I'll tell you what we will do, Auntie."

✦ ✦ ✦

After Bethie departed, Nani had a half hour before her next client. She padded barefoot to her kitchen for a cup of coffee. She was humming as she bent down in front of the fridge to get the low fat milk from the bottom shelf. While she was down there, she opened the crisper and rummaged around for one of the carrots she had cleaned. They had to be there. Kaleo wouldn't have touched them.

Now let's see ...

"Nani? We have a guest." Kaleo's voice was right behind her.

She shot straight up, slammed the refrigerator door on the gaping crisper drawer, opened it enough to shove the drawer back in, then whirled around as she kicked the door shut. Kaleo was sitting at the table in the breakfast nook with a smirk on his face and a stranger in a deep blue uniform sitting across from him. A stranger who'd just received a view of her blue jeaned butt gyrating to the Lady Gaga tune she was humming.

"Oh!" she said. "I didn't see you!" She glared at her brother who should have warned her.

The officer had a wide smile on his face as if he'd seen plenty of her. He stood and offered his hand. "I'm Officer Lindsey. You can call me Hank."

The handshake was a good one. Not the bone crusher she'd found common among men with a little authority. But not limp either. Firm and warm. She felt like the tropical temperature was rising. His face was all chiseled planes and sun-browned skin and his pumped-up arms were ...

Maybe I better open the fridge again for a shot of cold air.

"It's the long arm of the law checking up on me," Kaleo said. "Hank here is the one who arrested me."

Nani bristled, tender thoughts of the cop dispersing. Any cop might bring back memories of that bad time years ago, of course. And this one had recently busted Kaleo. Her brother might be a pest, but he was family which made him *her* pest. "I assure you my brother is here all day long with me, helping run my business. He will be no further trouble to the law, Officer Lindsey."

"Glad to hear it, Ms. Palea. So you do massages here?"

Not the kind you're picturing, Officer Friendly. In a haughty tone she replied, "I am certified in Swedish, cranio-sacral and sports massage. As well as Thai, Danish and American reflexology."

The doorbell rang.

"Excuse me, officer, my next client is here. If you are through with my brother, he has work to do. I'll show you out." She turned to go then whipped back around. She wasn't giving him another rear view. "Please, after you."

Hank Lindsey must have substantial *haole* blood for his eyes to be that pure blue. They sparkled at her as if he saw right through the 'stick up her butt' routine.

Of course he would. He's a cop. He pries truth out of suspects.

His only parting shot was a smile that added laugh lines to those ocean blues. He went out the screen door as the village librarian scuttled in for her session. Nani watched him go, thinking this cop was the most intriguing Big Island scenery she'd seen since cancelling her wedding two years ago.

Fo' shua!

CHAPTER THREE

My Book of Revelation
Excerpt from the Year 2003

Tomorrow I'll be fifteen. But a birthday party for me? That's totally not happening. I have to babysit for the dentist's kiddies. And give Father all the money.

He says it's for my education fund. Yeah, right. How much does home schooling by Ma cost, anyway? It's not like he's ever going to send me to college or anything. I'll never be out of his sight long enough to do anything but work my butt off.

I'm sure most missionaries who came to the Big Island in the olden days were well-intentioned. But my parents are descendants from the other sort, the ones who turned the good in the Good Book into something unrecognizable. They're stone cold unforgivers, teaching the golden rule with a golden ruler across our backsides. I've learned such fear of damnation from them that it feels safer to never utter a word.

Criminy.

My BF begged me to come outside after the kiddies I'm babysitting go to sleep tonight. To meet him on the lawn behind the dentist's house. He says he'll give me my birthday present then. As if I don't know what kind of present he has in mind.

I shouldn't go. Ma will kill me if she ever finds out. Father will kill my boyfriend if he ever finds out his name. I can never tell, so BF will have to do. And nobody but he will give me anything. Nobody else will even remember. So I will go.

My Book of Revelation
Excerpt from the Year 2003

Oh my God!!! Oh shit. Maile Palea is hurt, really really hurt. And we did it. My BF and me.

Jesus help me now.

It happened so fast. My heart was flying high, then *wham!* it plunged like a bird shot from the sky.

I was lying in the tall grass, gasping. But he was pinching my nipple again even though he was still soaked with sweat, and so was I. We stank of it. There was that other smell, too. Not just the sweet grass or the flowers. That sex smell. Boys are so messy. At least if they're all like my BF.

We could hear a kids' birthday party next door. Children were hunting some sort of prizes that Mrs. Lopaka had hidden in the yard. Flashlight beams danced. Little girls laughed, sounding so happy. The way kids are supposed to sound if their parents aren't shitheads.

BF whispered that the children were celebrating *my* birthday, too. I don't like his tongue in my ear. It makes me shiver, but he thinks it turns girls on so I let him do it.

Or maybe the shiver is because I'm always scared what will happen if anyone finds out about us. I said, "No they're not. They know nothing about me. Nobody can ever know about this. That I'm here with you." I put my hand around his penis and felt the life surge inside. I squeezed. "Promise me."

He promised. But he's a boy. What does he stand to lose?

My need for him frightens me. He's the only one who cares if I live or die. I know that sounds all over-the-top and shit, but it's the truth for real. Does he need me as much as I need him? Won't all the boys at his school laugh if he scrawls that I suck cock on the locker room wall?

He climbed on me again. That's when we heard footsteps. Coming nearer. Nearer. We froze. His naked ass was a second moon in the night.

"Oh!" said a little voice. "I was just looking for these. I'm sorry." Maile Palea held out one of the little prize boxes. She began to back away. Her eyes locked on our nakedness.

Then, I don't know. I think I screamed something about stopping her. BF leaped up and pounced. Maile fell backwards. She dropped her prize box and her flashlight. Its beam went out. She started crabbing backwards, out of his reach. I grabbed her arm, pulled her up and pushed her back toward him. Between us, she turned like a rabbit looking for a bolt hole. She tried to scream but somebody, BF or me, told her to shut up. We jumped her again, both of us, I think. I grabbed for her mouth, but she fell again. A slushy thump like a muskmelon split with a mallet. A little cry. Then quiet. This time she stayed still.

I think I cried my boy friend's name over and over. He shook Maile but couldn't rouse her. He turned on her flashlight, and we saw lava rubble in the grass where she fell. Jagged shards. One rock had blood on it. She'd hit her head on the sharp edges.

Together, we wrapped her and the rock and the prize box in our beach towel, the one we'd been making love on. I couldn't stop tears flooding from my eyes.

"I better get someone. Mrs. Lopaka," BF said, his skin looking pasty and his body shivering now as much as mine. He snapped off the flashlight and began to cover his nakedness.

"Jesus, no! The questions. We can't." I pulled my muumuu on over my head, his semen sticky between my legs. Hide it, hide the evidence.

My brain couldn't go forward, couldn't go back. Stuck in neutral. We continued to dress. In the moonlight, I saw him forcing his shirt buttons into the wrong buttonholes. I pulled my panties on backwards.

Then we heard another little girl. "Maile? Maile, where are you?" she called.

No time for more talk. No time to figure what to do. Just time for panic.

BF picked Maile up. Gently, gently, but she groaned. Rolled in the towel, her little body was limp as bread dough. "I'll take her to my place. You go back inside. Meet me when you can."

Then he was gone. My knees didn't work right, but I wobbled up onto the dentist's lanai. It was dark there behind the screens. I stood in the shadows, shivering in the hot night from the cold in my soul. This wasn't real. A horror movie. Not real. But it kept on.

I heard the child call for Maile again. I saw her flashlight beam approach the yard. Then she saw something on the ground. She picked it up and turned on its beam – it was the flashlight that Maile had been using. She aimed it at herself like she was seeing if the bulb was getting dim. I saw the child was Lynn Martin. But I don't think she saw me.

Nobody ever really sees me.

My brain feels paralyzed. But in my gut I know the world changed forever.

CHAPTER FOUR

The Last Martin Flies Away to Honolulu
By Jackson O'Reilly
Excerpt from the *Keawalani Voice*, 2015

Next week, long time Keawalani resident Martina Martin will follow her children to Oahu. Her daughter, Lynn, attends beauty school in Honolulu, and her son, Martin, is an insurance claims adjuster there. Mrs. Martin (widow of Martin Martin, Sr.) is moving to be closer to her kids as well as to medical specialists that are too far from Keawalani for her to reach easily.

She is hosting a yard sale this coming Sunday afternoon and extends an invitation to all bargain hunters as well as any villager who just cares to come by and wish her Aloha.

The day was cloudy and humid but promised to clear as the afternoon progressed. Kaleo and Nani walked down the lane that meandered behind many of the village houses under the wide spreading branches of candlenut trees. It had been trampled by decades of cattle, wild hogs and people. Follow it far enough downhill and a hiker came to the high coastal cliffs above the Pacific. Take it uphill and it climbed toward the peak of Mauna Kea.

In the village, the path cut behind Bethie's home. From there, Nani and Kaleo crossed to the street out front. Sure enough, Martina Martin's yard sale was in full swing next door. It was the village's opportunity to buy and to snoop. What would Martina leave behind? What would she have to say about the new people? Who had need of what? A yard sale of this magnitude was fair-like entertainment for the afternoon.

Because it was Sunday, many people were arriving after church. The older women had flowers in their hair, blossoms they had picked that morning in their own backyards. Some arrangements soared to such heights that the women could not sit in their sedans without bending their heads to the side. Nani smiled as she watched one such group arrive. These ladies in their good muumuus made as colorful a patch as a tropical garden. But their game faces were stern. These were the serious shoppers, wending their way between sale items on folding tables and overturned boxes, ferreting out the best bargains. Around them buzzed a crowd of children playing tag, young couples feathering their nests, teen boys eying teen girls who preened under their appraisal.

Old Man Hookano across the street was not one to miss a profitable chance like this. He'd dragged a battered grill out to the sidewalk and was selling BBQ pork loin sandwiches with fresh pineapple on taro buns.

"Looks like a wild pig must have rooted up Old Man's garden once too often," Kaleo said. He wandered over to sample Old Man's wares.

Nani saw the newspaper editor Jack O'Reilly chatting with several other men. He was the palest of them by far, his fair Irish skin protected from the Big Island sun by his battered wide brimmed hat, woven many years ago from *hale* fiber. It was one of the editor's trademarks. A love of fermented grain was another. Find O'Reilly at a gathering, and you'd find where a bottle was being passed. She waved as she walked by to take a look at the merchandise on display.

Martina was using this sale to offload goods for her son and daughter as well as herself. Nani saw piles of boardshorts, Aloha shirts, *slippahs*, swim fins and boogie boards, none of which suited Mrs. Martin herself. Her belongings must be the piles of needlework projects. Mrs. Martin had long been known as a first rate craftswoman, but her aging fingers could no longer stitch together delicate materials. It saddened Nani that Martina had never come to her for help, that not everyone believed in reflexology.

Amazing.

Nani joined Maggie Wilson in looking through a collection of colorful feathers and felt strips used to make leis for hat bands. Maggie was the village seamstress as well as a laundry service. She made lovely creations for others, but often tossed together a haphazard selection for herself, clothes as ill-fitting as they were drab. Only her wild bouncing curls softened her look at all.

Nani was glad to see her because she wanted Maggie to know why she'd stopped sending out her spa linens. "Kaleo's home," she explained. "He's helping out by doing the laundry."

"Yes, I'd heard he'd moved in with you." Maggie dipped her head up and down quickly, a tell of shyness more than an actual nod.

"As soon as he finds work, I'll be sending the laundry back to you." Nani lowered her voice and added, "You do a much better job."

"Thank you, Nani. No worries." The news that the Keawalani Hands business wasn't gone for good produced a timid smile from Maggie. After the seamstress moved on, Nani turned back to the sale tables to paw through the piles of partially completed Hawaiian quilts.

The new owners of the Martin house – people named Yohay – weren't at the yard sale, but their bonsai plants had been moved up on the lanai out of reach of the bargain hunters. Other house plants, though, were arranged on the front stoop awaiting new owners. Nani was heading that way past a stack of toys when Kaleo joined her.

"*Ono,*" he said downing the final delicious bite of a pork sandwich. "Now you don't have to feed me."

"Yeah? Well you still have to take me to the Big Island Girl, *bruddah.*"

"Speaking of which ..." he said, reaching out to the toys piled high in a green plastic bin shaped like a cartoon sea turtle. He picked up a figurine that resembled a plastic Kewpie doll in a hula skirt. "Here's one of the flashlights the restaurant used to give away."

A cloud darkened Nani's sunny mood. "I remember. Maile had one."

Kaleo nodded. "She woke me up once by lifting my eyelid and flashing its beams at me."

"She took it with her that night." Nani knew they were both thinking about the loss of their little sister.

Kaleo turned the doll in his hands and his brown face paled. "Oh my God."

Nani pulled his enormous fingers out of the way and looked closer at the toy. She gasped. Her heart began to race. Her skin felt suddenly clammy as she began to tremble. "Kaleo, this *is* Maile's flashlight."

✦   ✦   ✦

When Nani called the police station, Hank Lindsey was off duty. He was in the hangar he rented, up to his elbows in airplane wire, diagrams and mysterious instructions. Dispatch reached him and said Nani Palea sounded anxious to connect with him.

He went directly to her house in his jeans and tee-shirt. If she was eager to get together, he was delighted. He'd thought about her more than once since he met her. How could a guy as meaty as Kaleo have such a delicate sister? The brother's features were the broad soft surfaces of the original islanders. Hers were modified with the hint of Asian blood. She made Hank think of wildflowers from foreign lands that now populated the Big Island hills.

He'd detected interest on her side, too. Or so he thought. But you never knew about women. His instinct had been wrong before regarding that half of the population, so now he avoided making first moves. But she'd called him.

Game on.

Hank was surprised to find Kaleo there with Nani. Okay, not surprised. Disappointed. This wasn't a social call after all.

Guess there'll be no action on her massage table tonight.

He sobered the moment he saw the despair on the siblings' faces. Cop instincts went on alert; Officer Hank Lindsey was no longer off duty. "I hadn't expected to see you again so soon, Ms. Palea," he said as he seated himself in the breakfast nook along with Nani and Kaleo. Kaleo looked as happy as a thunderhead cloud.

"Please, call me Nani." She'd placed a tray of sliced fruit and cheese on the table along with coffee. He'd like to think it was a sign of her interest in him. But Hank knew it was island custom that any guest – even a cop – should be offered food.

"Okay, if you call me Hank. What can I do for you? What's happened?"

Neither sister nor brother answered immediately. Kaleo leaned back, focused on something – or nothing – miles away. The bulk of him monopolized the bench on one side of the table, its brightly colored cushion a counterpoint to his dark mood. Nani looked tiny tucked up next to her brother, her hands tightly grasping her coffee cup as if it would levitate if she let it go. Hank felt an impulse to clasp those hands in a gesture of comfort.

To serve and protect doesn't mean to gawk. Get to work, asshole.

He gave them a second prompt. "What's going on, you two?"

"It was her big idea to call you. Not mine." Kaleo jerked a large thumb at his sister. To Hank, he looked even more upset than the day he'd been sentenced to jail.

Nani raised her face to Hank. She was an artist's portrait of sadness, the kind with big liquid eyes and pouting lips.

"I'm going to have to beat up whoever made you feel this way." Hank smiled, hoping to reassure. "It's a service we cops offer. So you have to tell me."

When she started to speak, he thought her voice would tremble, but it was soft and steady. "Martina Martin sold her house and is leaving for a condo in Honolulu. It's hard to imagine such a thing since she's lived here all her life, but her children are there. Besides, she needs to be closer to medical specialists."

Hank knew that much from the *Voice*. But people reporting distressing events often had trouble getting to the point. He waited patiently.

But Kaleo didn't. "We went to Martina's yard sale today, and we found this." He opened one big mitt and set a plastic figurine down on the table. It was a chubby girl in a hula skirt. Kaleo turned it to show Hank the button in the center of its back. "Its eyes would light up if the batteries were fresh. Years ago, the Big Island Girl gave these flashlights away to birthday kids whose families came in to celebrate."

Hank picked it up and turned it around in his hand. "Okay. But what does it mean to you?"

"It belonged to our little sister, Maile. She had it the night she disappeared twelve years ago." While Nani's eyes looked near tears, Kaleo's were cold dark agates.

Nani reached out and tipped the doll in the cop's hand so he could see the bottom of its plastic feet. "I know it was hers because I let her play with my nail polish the day she got it. It was her eighth birthday." Painted in bright red, in a child's scrawl, was the name Maile.

Hank gingerly set the figurine on the tabletop, hoping to leave no more fingerprints than it already had. He'd heard bits of the old story from the other cops at the station and from his captain, Frank Lono. But it hadn't hit home. He hadn't been a Hamakua District cop back then, in fact would have still been a teenager.

"Tell me about your sister," he said to the siblings. They'd clearly been rattled by the discovery of this toy. If they could start by just talking about their sister, he could lead them around to her disappearance. Cop Interview Technique 101.

Nani smiled as some memory danced before her eyes. Softly, she began. "Maile was a child who wormed her way into even the stoniest hearts. She was always curious. Down right nosey, in fact. Could get anyone to talk about themselves."

"Funny, too," Kaleo said. He looked sideways at his sister. "Remember the contest she won with her drawing of a jet covered with pineapples and papayas?"

Nani grinned, then explained to Hank. "She labeled it 'Above the Fruited Plane.'"

"When she was seven, the *Keawalani Voice* hired her to write a

weekly column because she was such a rich source of village news."
Kaleo made air quotes as he said *hired* and *news*. "The whole village knew her. She'd ride her Huffy around town, pink streamers flapping in the breeze and bike bell ringing. She waved a *shaka* at everyone she met." Kaleo created the traditional Hawaiian greeting with extended thumb and pinkie, as if he were seeing his little sister pedaling by. He clenched his teeth.

Hank understood that a guy didn't cry in front of his big sister and a cop.

Nani said, "She chatted with shopkeepers and their customers, asking who was sick and whose cat had kittens and whether the macadamia crop looked good this year." She rose to get a small album from the kitchen counter and handed it carefully to Hank. On its cover was a clear pocket with a dog eared school photo. "She wasn't a picture perfect child. But she was beautiful to everyone who knew her. Those are her articles from the *Voice* inside."

Hank grinned at the eight-year-old with frizzy braids and a smile so big it revealed a missing tooth. He held the treasured album and thumbed through it. While Nani poured more coffee for each of them, he scanned a couple of the clippings inside.

Big Bird Drops In
By Maile Palea
Cub Reporter for the *Keawalani Voice*

Our class went to the Discovery Center in Hilo to learn about reefs. It is called Mokupapapa but I can't spell that so Mr. O'Reilly will have to correct it. That is what an editor does. Fixes things. Thank you, Mr. O'Reilly.

I liked the fish tank the best with all the fish. Cool. Many colors like my brother's paintings.

But most fun was when the wild turkey landed by the mynah birds out front right in town. That's a very big bird. Teacher said an English sailor brought the first ones to Hawaii to give to our king. She didn't say what we gave him to take home to his king. Maybe a hula DVD, yeah?

— — —

Cats and Dogs
By Maile Palea
Cub Reporter for the *Keawalani Voice*

My sister took me to see the movie about the Dalmatians. They were real cute with all their spots. You should take your little sister if you have one.

Old Man Hookano has puppies, too, but they are mostly brown. His beagle Sadie is their mama. He says their daddy is some poi dog who can jump a very tall fence.

Maybe I'll get a puppy for Christmas. But I would rather have a kitty. Are you reading this, Mom and Dad?

Hank closed the album with a sad smile, and put it down on the table. "Tell me about her disappearance."

Nani said, "The Lopakas' daughter invited Maile to her birthday party along with the other nine girls in her grade school class. They had cake and candy, played games, ate a picnic. Mrs. Lopaka said later how happy they all had seemed. When it started to get dark, the girls played with the flashlights they'd brought. Mrs. Lopaka had extras for those who'd forgotten. Maile had her Big Island Girl flashlight. This one."

Nani gently tapped the hula girl on the table. "The girls said they were pretending to be friends of Pele's little sister, helping the god dess stamp out man-eating sharks and evil spirits. They were looking for little tin boxes that the Lopakas had hidden in their shrubbery and trees. A 'magic spell' was broken when a kid opened a tin and found a trinket inside. You know, like a beaded bracelet or pack of gum. It got dark enough that all the Lopakas could see were the dancing flashlight beams, and all they could hear was the giggling of the girls. And then Maile was gone."

Hank heard a catch in Kaleo's breath before the big man said, "By the time I went to pick her up from the party, she'd disappeared." His soft features looked haunted. "I was fifteen and had the car. My girlfriend had chosen that night to finally say yes. It was the first time for both of us so it didn't take long to christen the back seat. Still, I didn't arrive at the Lopakas right on schedule. By then, Maile was gone."

Hank read Kaleo's guilt as clearly as if it were printed on his tee-shirt. He cast his eyes over to Nani who looked impatient with Kaleo's confession.

"Kaleo, she was already gone by the pick-up time. The Lopakas had started looking for her. We've discussed that before. It's not your fault."

"Still ..."

She waved him off and continued with the story. "I came running as soon as Kaleo called me. Nobody had seen her go. We searched the house, the yard, the neighborhood. The cops arrived and so did neighbors. Search parties spread out to every yard, fence row, lava pile, pasture. Nobody remembered seeing a stranger or an unknown vehicle. Nobody heard a child's cry. That was twelve years ago. And we've never heard another word."

Silence settled on them like a shroud. Hank had heard a lot of sad stories in his job, but a dozen years of not knowing? People had to have answers even if those answers weren't the ones they hoped for. And it was a cop's job to find them.

These two seemed protective of each other. Was it just natural with siblings? Or did they have reason to be? Were they hiding anything? Surely their grief was genuine. But you never know. Relatives were always leading suspects, but the thought that Nani might have any part in this, well, it just seemed insane. Finally Hank asked, "How old were you then, Nani? Where were your parents?"

"I was seventeen. I'd been left in charge. If anyone was guilty of losing her, it was me. Mom and Dad were at a craft show in Hilo, with her jewelry and his leather work."

Hank nodded. He could double check all of their whereabouts in the old file that must still exist on the case. "So how did the Big Island Girl flashlight get to Martina Martin's yard sale?"

"Exactly," Kaleo muttered.

Nani added, "*Your kokua* is desperately needed, officer."

Hank looked into those dark eyes and saw the sadness that was imploring him, and he knew he'd do damn near anything to provide the help she'd just asked of him.

CHAPTER FIVE

Haoles Have Hula All Wrong
By Jackson O'Reilly
Excerpt from the Keawalani Voice, 2015

The first thing most haoles learn about hula has virtually nothing to do with hula. I know because that describes my state of mind when I moved here from the mainland many years ago. I expected to see skimpy grass skirts and bodacious breasts overflowing coconut bras on women gyrating like strippers gone wild. I'd even worn gear like that to a Halloween party, I'm ashamed to say.

Speaking of shame, many island hotels *do* give tourists the titillating shows they seek, helping to promote the false image. Fortunately, others aren't so crass.

It takes a little education from the locals to get the real skinny. Islanders are practically born into a particular hula school called a halau. Boys and girls may stay for years, learning island legends from a venerated instructor called a kumu. The dance is the unwritten language of all the generations.

It is passionate, to be sure. Stories are told through the sensual, graceful movements of hands, hips, face and most every other body part. It's all about strong bodies with even stronger emotions which are more often about love or war or loss than about sex.

If the hula were no more than bumps and grinds, it would have never endured through the centuries, even outlasting the missionaries who tried to kill it off. The good news for islanders and haoles alike is that new hulas are still being composed to join forces with the old. Dance is very much alive. And as long as it is, Hawaiian traditions, gods, history and language live on.

The day after finding the flashlight, Nani made a pilgrimage to her hula halau. The school was outside the village, on the road to Kona. It was a long bouncy ride on a Vespa through the green cattle country and down the arid highway past black lava fields dotted with memorials made from white coral.

Nani did not visit her halau often any more. In part, it was because her kumu, the halau teacher, was still frustrated with her. Hakumele Silva had been terribly upset when Nani quit the professional circuit over a decade ago, and her resentment – like Pele's – lasted a very long time. As a student, Nani had lived with Hakumele for weeks on end, practicing at all hours. Hakumele was her aunt – her father's sister – as well as her teacher. They had grown very close. Nani knew she shouldn't question her kumu who seemed to have the ear of the gods. Veneration was her due.

Nani had won a soloist award at the Merrie Monarch Festival, the super bowl of hula competitions. She was the best Hakumele had ever taught, and Nani knew her skill brought great honor to Hakumele's school and reputation as a teacher. But there was more to it than that. Nani wasn't just a prize pony for her kumu.

"When you do not dance, the ancients cannot speak," the teacher said the day Nani walked away.

It happened soon after the disappearance of her little sister. The joyful hulas became too painful for Nani to perform. She could no longer celebrate the kindness of the gods and the wonders that enrich the world, flora to fauna, mountains to ocean. Or maybe she was giving up something she loved in order to punish herself for not protecting someone she loved. Or maybe, even back then, she had known that dance would never pay the bills and that her magic hands were better employed in massage and reflexology. How could she expect Hakumele to understand when she didn't understand it herself?

From the day Maile disappeared, Nani was infected by the sadness others saw in her eyes. It lived on like a virus. Now when Nani danced it was from grief. She favored the stories of longing for loved ones, of sorrow over deaths. She occasionally biked to the school, went into the studio with the key she still had, started a chant on a CD, and danced to the tales of loss. She went at off hours when no class was in session. She wanted to express her sorrow in solitude.

She thought she was alone. But she rarely was. Hakumele was often there in the dark, her broad shoulders slumped while she watched the beautiful young woman bend and sway with an artistry that was nearly unbearable. The very air around the dancer seemed heavy as though sadness had physical weight and dimension. Hakumele stood and watched as her own heart broke for what might have been.

The village thought only one sister had been lost. But Hakumele knew the older one was lost, as well.

CHAPTER SIX

Newcomers Get Big Lift from Tiny Trees
By Jackson O'Reilly
Excerpt from the *Keawalani Voice*, 2015

Silas and Takara Yohay have moved into the Keawalani home they purchased from Martina Martin, who has recently moved to Honolulu. Bethie Kalapana, their neighbor just up the hill, reported that the couple has now joined their bonsai family.

Bethie is referring to the three dozen bonsai plants that Mrs. Yohay has maintained for many years. She moved them from Kona to the premises even before the couple themselves could move in, visiting at least once a day to water and chat with her little green friends. While she spoke with this reporter, she was pruning one with the care you'd like to expect in a haircut from Sunny Daze Barber Shop.

"You must prune to maintain the desired

design and to keep the leaves from growing big again. It's your will against nature," she said. In case you didn't know, the art of bonsai is all about capturing a living tree in miniature. According to Mrs. Yohay, it requires a special pot, special soil, summer shade and winter sun, a chopstick to settle the soil around the roots, and tweezers to remove weeds without disturbing the tiny plant.

While Mrs. Yohay busied herself with daily care of her garden, Mr. Yohay rested in a hammock nearby. He has recently retired from stocking shelves in a Kona Safeway which allowed for their move to Keawalani. "Life is easier here," he said. "And some of the villagers have been extremely friendly."

Silas Yohay lay back on the massage table as the gorgeous girl manipulated his legs, ankles and feet. *This is the effin' life.* Who'd have thought Bethie Kalapana, that scrawny biddy next door, would come up with such a housewarming gift as a certificate for two at the local massage parlor? Too bad half the therapist's time had to be spent on his wife.

Nani could tell that the stringy little man, puckered as dried fruit, was totally relaxed. It was time. "Hmm," she said, going over his left ankle once more. "Hmmm."

"Something wrong?" he said from far away as if he were nearly asleep or being recalled from the dead.

"Well ..." Poke, prod, rub. "Well, sometimes a man's ankle tells me something not too good. Of course, I may be wrong. But ..." Nani shook her head and gave an exaggerated sigh.

"But what?" Mr. Yohay opened one eye and lifted his head enough to stare at the reflexologist.

Nani did her best to look innocent as a lamb. She stared wide eyed back at him. "When a man of a certain age, um, pleasures a woman too often – or too *many* women – his libido may suffer precipitous deterioration. If this happens, his reed could become prematurely – possibly even permanently – shriveled from excessive growth." Dig, punch. "The outer nerves in your ankle are telling me there is impending danger of such a calamity."

"What? What do ankles have to do with my ... my *reed*?" Mr. Yohay was fully awake now.

"What I am doing is called reflexology. The extremities reflect the woes in the rest of the body."

"Pshaw. I never heard such a thing." He'd had no problems below the belt. Had he? Still, there had been that night ... now he was worried.

"No, sir, you would not have heard of such a problem. This is a secret that wives in long term marriages share. These wives can feel when their husbands change, when the libido shifts as surely as the tides. Wives then know their men are spilling their seed in other fields." Jab, elbow, nudge. "I am told that some wives keep the secret to themselves hoping to spare their old men the embarrassment of knowing performance is flagging." Nani shrugged. "Of course, other wives poison these misters."

Mr. Yohay sat up, done with his free session. "Nonsense. You are a foolish girl to talk such stink."

But Nani could see the concern in his frown lines, grooves as deep as plow furrows. She bit her cheeks to stifle a giggle and appeared contrite while he replaced his slippahs. "I'm so sorry that my work has not pleased you. I'll add your unused minutes to your wife's session. Please send her in."

Looking worried, Silas Yohay pulled himself up to his full five foot two height and stomped out.

Mrs. Yohay's first impression of Nani was of a likable woman with a beautiful grin. *What a friendly place*, the older lady thought. She was very grateful for the lovely back and shoulder massage that Nani gave her. She felt a gentle release of the stiff neck that had haunted her for weeks. And she was sincerely pleased with the neighborly warning Nani shared.

"We who love Keawalani warn our newcomers of a slight problem our village has. There is one woman who fancies all new men, whether they are the territory of other ladies or not. I doubt you have problems with Mr. Yohay responding to good time girls like her, but you might keep an eye out for inappropriate moves in his direction."

Keep an eye out, indeed. Mrs. Yohay thought it was wonderful that the village ladies took care of each other in such a way. She'd certainly take care of Mr. Yohay if a volunteer flower should take root in his backyard. She was so pleased with her massage that she made an appointment for a full hour the next time.

So Nani Palea gained a new client. And the next time Bethie saw her, she said that her friend Likolani no longer heard from Mr. Yohay. In fact, Liko had moved on to someone who didn't mind being seen with her in public places around the village.

"Tings mo bettah," Bethie said with a queen sized smile that revealed teeth as sparse as a jack-o'-lantern grin.

Nani was tickled. The Big Island secret keeper had succeeded again. And if the Yohays didn't live in the Martins' house, the very same place where she had found the Big Island Girl flashlight, Nani's fun wouldn't have been marred by thoughts of her little sister at all.

✦ ✦ ✦

"So I treat it like a cold case even with this new evidence?" Hank asked Police Captain Frank Lono who was leaning back in an ancient office chair that listed dangerously to the left. Lono was cleaning his nails on the edge of an attorney's business card. He didn't much like anybody but other cops and could have been doing a lot worse with the card. Several on his wall had been skewered there with X-acto knives.

The captain's pit bull temperament was the biggest reason he wasn't higher in the police department structure. He simply had no use for politics. He was widely regarded as a good investigator, but he'd been busted down nearly as often as promoted up. That's why there weren't any layers between the aging veteran and his young officer.

Lono's scruffy size thirteens were crossed on his desktop. Even shoes that size could do the government-issue furniture no more harm than had already been done by raving addicts and violent thugs through the years. The guest side of the desk even had a bullet hole through the gray metal center panel. Hank suspected the captain had shot it himself late one night when the higher ups were giving him grief.

"Not sure a flashlight that's been lost for twelve years could be called *evidence*. Dust it and you'll find prints from everyone in the Martin household if not all of Keawalani."

"I had it dusted, and you're wrong. Only half of Keawalani." Hank stared at the Big Island Girl hula figurine in its plastic evidence bag.

"Shows-to-go you," the captain said, crumpling the business card and tossing it into the circular file. "It's a cold case, *cuz*."

"It's gotta be at least lukewarm, Cap. I won't pester Allison to dig it out. I'll find it in the store room myself." The police department's receptionist/dispatcher, Allison Costello, had all the officers cowed about requesting things she considered unnecessary additions to her work load.

"Quityerbitchin'," said Lono as he got up and banged open the bottom drawer of his own filing cabinet. "I keep it here. You can work on it if you want, but it's not a priority."

"A cold case? Why do you keep it here?"

Lono dug out a thick manila folder. It had scribbles from a variety of pencils and pens on the outside, and its tab was nearly worn away with age. "Never could bear to think of that little girl as cold."

"It's been twelve years," Hank said. "Chances aren't good that she's still alive."

Lono tossed the folder across the desk to Hank. "Don't you think I know that? Twelve fucking years. Dreadful, that long with no answers. It's always spooked me that the perp might not be a stranger. Might be one of us villagers." He leaned back in the ac-cident-about-to-happen chair. "Or maybe she *is* alive. She was only eight, Hank. That's young for her to be able to find her way back home if she did manage to escape. You read about kids sticking with abductors. Like that 14-year-old in Salt Lake. Probably too confused or too scared to reach out for help. Never gave up hope that we'd find Maile one day, maybe a happy twenty year old now with a kid of her own and no memory of the past."

"You believe that?"

"Nope. Don't believe in Santa Claus either."

✦   ✦   ✦

Hank stopped by Keawalani Hands and helped Kaleo replace bright white fluorescent tubes in a bathroom while waiting for Nani to get out of a massage session. When she appeared at the bathroom door, the little room was brilliant as a sunspot.

"Not sure my clients will want to see every blemish quite so clearly," she said, putting a hand above her eyes like a visor and squinting.

Kaleo, folding the stepladder, said, "The truth isn't always pretty."

"Hey, Nani," Hank said with a grin.

His smile warmed her. His worth had doubled since they first met. He was the one and only lawman now looking for her sister. He'd taken her loss onto his shoulders. Without this man, Maile could be lost for all time in some old file cabinet in the police department bowels. "What's up, Hank? How can we help?" she asked as they all left the bathroom together.

"I wanted to let you both know that we didn't find usable prints on the flashlight. Just a mishmash of images. But I'll be interviewing Mrs. Martin to see what she knows about it."

"Her daughter Lynn was one of the children at the party," Nani said, consulting the invitation list that was on permanent record in her memory. All the other known facts were tucked in there, too.

"I have the case file now, and I'll talk with everyone again."

"What you expect them to know now that they didn't know twelve years ago?" Kaleo said as he stored the stepladder in the hall closet.

"You never know," Hank said. "Frank Lono interviewed them all back then. But people's perspective can change. Won't hurt to ask again."

Nani followed him out to his Honda Pilot. It was white like most Big Island cop cars which were privately owned by the officers.

"Nani, I don't think you should get your hopes up," Hank said.

"Kaleo is right. Anything now is a long shot."

"I know that, Hank. But we can't live with a story that just stops, you know? Even if it's a sad ending, I could handle it better than no ending at all."

"I get that."

"It's been twelve years. Kaleo and I don't grieve all the time, but it's never very far from mind. The littlest thing can set it off. A child that laughs like her ... a news story about another missing kid ... a silly flashlight. Brings it all back, you know?"

"Maybe fresh eyes can help. Can't promise success. But I promise to try."

She'd thought he was on the verge of more, the way he looked at her sort of shy-like.

Maybe getting ready to ask me out.

Instead, after a second of hesitation, he touched the brim of his hat, got into the car and backed out of the drive.

Maybe I should ask him out.

But she was not that independent of the old ways. Besides it was best to forget a personal relationship while a professional one was in the works. That's what most people would say. But maybe that wasn't always true. Hank might be more willing to work on the mystery if he was involved with her, if he had that kind of vested interest in solving it. She realized it wasn't the main event on his desk these days. There were newer cases demanding his time.

Hell, Maile, I don't know. A little guidance from the spirit world would be welcome any time.

Nani returned to the house. She had other things to do than think about Hank. She gathered her portable massage table, oils, stones, warmer, and towels just in time for Mrs. Cunningham's limo to come pick her up. Taking the Keawalani Hands show on the road didn't work well when you only had a Vespa.

✦ ✦ ✦

Nani watched the scenery from the backseat of Mrs. Cunningham's limousine as she rode toward the mansion. The highway past Puako Bay cut through ancient flows from Mauna Kea. Scientists had managed to convince most people that the volcano was now defunct. That didn't keep Nani from listening to the daily lava flow reports. No islander, regardless of how cynical about the spiritual world, ever really lacked respect for Pele. The Fire Goddess could go ballistic any time. The volcano currently active was Kilauea on the other side of the Big Island so it was not a threat to Nani's plans today.

But you just never know.

The narrow strip of million dollar land between the road and the island's northwest coast had been coaxed, dozed, irrigated, sodded and seeded until the black ribs of lava cradled an intensely private resort. White sand beaches, turquoise water and lush greenery surrounded the mansions and golf course hidden from the view of lesser mortals who drove on by, never knowing that the golden life glittered just out of their reach.

Many people from Nani's village worked at Puako Bay as landscapers, guards, housekeepers, wait staff. A bus brought them in from Keawalani every morning and returned them to their village every night. The workers were carefully vetted and hesitantly trusted. Nonetheless, the stink eye turned on them first if the least thing went wrong.

Mrs. Cunningham was far less judgmental of the locals than other residents were because she was one. Her family had lived on the island since her grandfather managed land back in the Parker Ranch heydays. She was as Hawaiian as a haole could get, proud of her roots and wealthy beyond words. Everyone in Keawalani considered it an honor to work for her. That included Nani. This one client had raised her stature and fueled her business from touch-and-go to waiting-list success.

Of course, it wasn't exactly one client. Mrs. Cunningham also had Nani work on her maid, Emelina. They tipped her well in addition to the session fee. These two monthly afternoons were Nani's richest days. But even without the money, Nani would have made the trip to the mansion from a deep sense of loyalty to her empire builder.

The puffy cloud of snow white hair over Mrs. Cunningham's slender body usually reminded Nani of a dandelion gone to seed, but today the old woman was far too stiff to resemble any kind of bloom. She was obviously troubled and in pain.

"What's been going on since I last saw you, Auntie?" Nani asked, carefully assessing Mrs. C's facial expressions. She modified her session to suit a client's current pain level, so her question was more than chitchat. She needed the personal information.

"Maybe surgery is in store for me after all," Mrs. Cunningham said as she clambered onto the portable massage table. For ages this game old girl had refused back operations, preferring to live with arthritic pain just as long as she could.

Nani watched in concern, then began the session by gently reflexing Mrs. C's ears with jasmine-scented oil, listening to her client talk about who had visited and what they'd said. For a while after that they were both quiet. Nani rubbed a rich lotion on Mrs. Cunningham's hands, covered them with plastic bags and placed heated mitts over them. She warmed hands before reflexing arthritic fingers.

Silently, Mrs. Cunningham began to cry as if her misery was so full it was spilling over. Nani had seen people through times like this before. She quietly continued to work on Mrs. C's feet, leaving it up to the client whether she wished to talk or not.

"I apologize. I don't know what to do," Mrs. Cunningham said.

"No apologies necessary, Auntie. You know that."

"It's about Emelina."

Emelina had been with her for decades. She was still called a maid, but Mrs. Cunningham now employed a younger woman for most of the housework. Emelina was friend and companion. Both women had outlasted husbands, had raised children and now had grandchildren. Among the secrets that Nani kept from the world at large was that Emelina had also become Mrs. C's lover back in the days before such a thing was openly discussed. Whatever sort of physical relationship they still maintained, their emotional commitment was one of unconditional trust. So Nani was astonished when Mrs. Cunningham said, "I think she's stealing from me."

"No! Impossible."

"I would have said the same thing," her client said, tears channeling through her wrinkles to plop onto the massage table. "But a while ago, I missed some money from my purse. I assumed I'd just lost it. Then last month, more was missing. I thought it was the new girl so when she quit, I was glad. But it happened again yesterday."

"I can't believe it. Emelina loves you more than life itself."

"Emilena *is* life itself to me."

"You should just ask her about it." This misunderstanding needed cleared up, a secret that must be revealed.

"Oh no. I can't accuse her after all these years. Isn't the maid always the scapegoat? No, I couldn't. I won't."

Nani managed to calm Mrs. Cunningham and continue the session. She removed the heated mitts and worked on fingers and palms, carefully manipulating nerve and muscle. Through her own steady hands, she could feel knuckles begin to loosen and flexibility increase.

"Maybe I just don't want to know for sure, Nani, because the option is even worse. If she isn't taking the money, I must be using it myself. And I don't remember it. I know what that means. My father had Alzheimer's, you know. And maybe I ..."

Nani took firm hold of the gnarled old hands. "Now you listen to me, Auntie. Emelina is not stealing, and you are not losing your mind. I know you both too well. Your bodies would confess to me if such a thing was happening to either of you." At the moment, fact wasn't as important as comforting her client. "There must be a simple explanation, and we'll find it."

She worked longer than usual, providing Mrs. Cunningham all the solace she could. Her next client would be Emelina, and she'd straighten things out.

But what if it turned out Emelina *was* guilty? Could she break Mrs. Cunningham's big old heart? Anything really was possible. Nani had suffered enough sorrow in her own life to know that – her sister's disappearance, her father leaving home for good, her mother fading away from what everyone knew was grief.

Still, Nani wanted to believe that you could always depend on the people you love. And if anyone had that kind of trust, this old gay couple did. She tried to forget that nothing was ever guaranteed.

✦　✦　✦

Hank Lindsey knew George Lopaka, or at least who he was. He worked at the Big Island Bank, locally known as BIB. He was a quiet little man, a backroom bean counter who appeared far too unimaginative to perpetrate a crime. But from the file, Hank knew that George Lopaka had been a key suspect in Maile Palea's disappearance. Sad but true, all men who had known the child were looked at by the law twelve years ago. It was a price the innocent paid for the misdeeds of their brothers.

Twelve years ago, Mr. Lopaka and his wife appeared to be in shock throughout the taped interviews that Hank played. All they'd done was host a child's birthday party. No evidence of wrongdoing was found against them. But it was a cloud they would live under forever after. Today, the village rumor was that Mr. Lopaka never spoke unless spoken to, and Mrs. Lopaka had gone irrevocably insane. Hank discovered this rumor, like most, had a basis in truth when he went to see her at home.

She opened the door only a crack to peer at him as he waited on the rickety porch. The Lopaka house had received no care for a very long time. Mrs. Lopaka was rarely seen outside anymore, a hermit in her own home.

She let him in only after he pleaded that he needed her help to set the record straight. Eying him with fright, she finally allowed him a seat on the stained and butt-sprung chair in the living room. Then she scurried off and returned with cookies and tea. The china cup was dirty and the Oreos were limp from the heat and humidity. The hot dark room felt as confining as an incubator to Hank.

"People say I'm *lolo*," Mrs. Lopaka said, using the Hawaiian word for crazy. She hunched forward on a straight back chair next to an old console TV. Hank thought there was a pretty good chance that she had been driven insane. Her hair was curled and fussed with in the front but an untouched rat's nest in the back as though she couldn't bear to look behind her.

He tried for a sensible interview but stopped asking questions when he realized she either couldn't or wouldn't tell her story with any flow of logic. Instead, he allowed her to ramble.

"I let the girls play an evil game, tempt the spirits. Mo'o ate her.

The lizard dragon lives in me now eating my insides. To punish me. I am *kapu*. I stay in here." Hank understood why she now believed in evil, especially the legendary mo'o that lured people into the sea to devour them. She considered herself taboo.

Hank's heart softened for George Lopaka at the bank who only had this addled woman to come home to. But then, how could she not believe in such malignance when a child in her care was gone without a trace?

Both the Lopakas were ruined people.

CHAPTER SEVEN

My Book of Revelation
Excerpt from the Year 2003

When little Lynn Martin ran back to the Lopakas to rejoin the party, I went into the dentist's home to check on his kiddies. It felt like I was moving in slow motion, slogging through a tub of Vasoline. The babies were still asleep. I checked them once then checked again. Poor little shits if I'm the best the dentist can find to take care of them.

Criminy.

I've hurt a child. A sweet child, this Maile. She's alive because I heard her groan when my BF carried her away. But maybe now she's crippled. Blind. Paralyzed.

Jesus protect her and have mercy on me, Your sinner.

I've wondered before how it would feel to injure a child, the way people do never meaning to at all. You know? Like to be driving and hit one in the street. Or maybe your dog attacks one. Or if you give one candy, and she chokes. I never thought it would really happen, though. Not to me.

You feel sick is how you feel. I know that now. Head rushing dizziness, black dots in front of your eyes. Your gut wants to hurl, and you piss down your own legs. Everything distorts like those fun house mirrors. Fun house is bullshit. I hate those spooky things.

My parents will shun me if they ever find out. I hate my Father, sure, but where else will I go? BF will leave me. God will get me. I guess maybe He already has. If these sleeping dentist babies only knew, they'd wake up wikiwiki and go screaming away from the monster.

Me. A monster. Shit. That's the doorbell.

Answer it.

And lie, God help me.

My Book of Revelation
Excerpt from the Year 2003

They're gone. Mr. O'Reilly, Old Man Hookano, Kaleo and the rest of a search party looking for Maile. I know them all. Maile's brother is my age, but big enough to play soccer with my BF at the public school. He told them who I am ... they looked nervous to be talking with one of those nut jobs who might start levitating in front of them or speaking in tongues. The whole village thinks our church is a cult of wackos. Not sure they're wrong.

Or maybe these villagers were just worried about what happened to Maile, too. Maybe that's why they all looked so fucking agonized.

I told them I hadn't seen or heard anything. That it had been quiet. Quiet enough that the kiddies were still asleep. I blinked, all innocent like. A preacher kid wouldn't lie. It must have worked because they left.

It was very late before the dentist and his wife came home. They'd been searching, too, but nobody found anything. I'd cleaned myself up. To remove the stink of dirt and fornication and fear.

As the dentist drove me home, I thanked God that BF got away. Apparently, he disappeared with Maile without a trace.

Jesus help that little child.

Now if I could just disappear, too. I'm home in bed, under the covers writing this. It is dangerous to record these words, I know. Prying eyes are everywhere. But I have to do it. I have to record every tiny thing that has happened. Nothing else important has ever happened to me, but I think this will be big forever. It will change my life, it will change BF's. I'm pretty sure shame and guilt can do that. So I want to remember then the way it really happened now. It is a revelation of the truth to myself, when I become an adult.

I'll hide this notebook in my backpack so my nosey little brother and sister won't find it. They know I will trounce them for touching it. If Ma notices that it is missing, I'll tell her I left it at the dentist's house.

If they ever find out what really happened, Father will say I brought it all on myself, that I am surely the whore of Babylon offering up a cup of filth. And since *"the inhabitants of the earth have been made drunk with the wine of her fornication,"* it's probably deep shit time for BF, too.

If you ask me, this God is as much of a flame-thrower as Pele could ever be.

CHAPTER EIGHT

Fly High With Halemano's Spiked Shaves
By Jackson O'Reilly
Excerpt from the *Keawalani Voice*, 2015

For this month only at Heavenly Treats, two Big Island favorites have joined forces to give you a double buzz … coffee and shave ice. Proprietor Alakai Halemano calls his new creation Spiked Shaves.

He starts with a big scoop of his hand-made dark roast Kona coffee ice cream in the bottom of a cup. Next comes Heavenly Treat's fluffy shave ice. "My Japanese great-grandfather made shave ice," said Halemano. "Back in the twenties, plantation workers chipped away at blocks of ice with machetes and sucked the shavings to beat the heat. Today, I use a machine with a razor-sharp blade to shave the ice block. I can make hundreds of shave ices every hour." Halemano shrugged his shoulders then added, "At least I could if the tour buses stopped in Keawalani."

The end product is as fluffy as new fallen snow atop Mauna Kea. Its fine, soft texture allows flavorings to saturate the ice instead of drain to the bottom of the cup, making it a far more delectable treat than a mainlander's snow cone.

For Spiked Shaves Month, Halemano is featuring coffee flavorings such as Irish Crème, Amaretto, Blue Curacao, Kahlua, Crème de Menthe and Crème de Cacao. On top of that he sprinkles ground coffee beans and a dash of cream.

With a wink, Halemano said that the double buzz of caffeine and liqueur flavoring is definitely For Adults Only. But no worries. He still features all his regular family-rated fruity flavors along with such toppings as mochi, tapioca boba balls, and sweet azuki beans.

"So what you think?" Halemano asked after this reporter sampled the Coffee Blue Curacao Spiked Shave. Well, it may not keep me out of the Suck'en'em Up Saloon on a Friday night. But it certainly should send me off to Weight Watchers before the month is through.

Nani and Kaleo ate dinner at the Big Island Girl. The little restaurant was older than most villagers, offering breakfast through dinner for generations. There were no booths, under the theory that Big Island bellies were often too big to tuck in comfortably. Every wide chair was at a table, and all the tables were placed around the room seemingly at random. It promoted conversation group to group, and since almost everybody knew almost everybody else, the Big Island Girl was the village place to socialize as well as chow down.

There was air conditioning but it often didn't work. Tonight, a soft scented breeze wafted between open north and south facing windows. Island tunes from the restaurant's sound system floated on that breeze. Even Daya the Waitress and her busboy Akela Onekea managed to appear unrushed although they kept the service moving with the precision of a military strike force.

"Mrs. Cunningham thinks Emelina may be stealing money from her," Nani said to Kaleo, keeping her voice low to avoid being overheard. He had a mouthful of loco moco. The serving was so big it hung over the rim of the plate, too gluey to drip. To Nani it smelled rich with forbidden calories. She had selected a salad with grilled chicken on a bed of field greens.

A nicer name for weeds.

"Impossible," Kaleo said after swallowing his shark-sized bite.

"I agree. Emelina is pretty sure the culprit is Auntie's grandson. He comes to visit on occasion, and Emelina has found him sniffing around the house in places he doesn't belong. She doesn't trust him." It had taken the loyal Emelina until the middle of her session to whisper even this much to Nani.

Kaleo washed down his meal with Liquid Fire from Keawalani's Volcanic Brewery. While he scrubbed his mouth with his napkin, Nani asked, "You knew him, didn't you? Patrick Cunningham?"

"Knew him, and know him. He was in my class all through school 'til he dropped out. We called him Packer even back then."

"Packer?"

"Short for *pakalolo*. He could get it for all the kids whenever we wanted. I mean whenever they wanted. I gave him a marijuana leaf tattoo a couple years ago, so I guess he's still in the business."

Kaleo put a hand to his mouth trying to stifle an appreciative belch. He held off further comment while the busboy removed their dirty dishes. Nani smiled, but Akela was not known for friendliness. After he finished with a swipe of his rag across the spilled gravy, he did nod at Kaleo before moving away. The two had played sports together when they were kids.

Kaleo asked Nani, "If Emelina knows the truth about him, why doesn't she just tell Mrs. C?"

"She can't get herself to say that Patrick, er, Packer is the culprit. It would hurt a doting grandma far too much. On the other hand, Mrs. Cunningham won't ask Emelina if she's taking the money, because she's afraid that her friend would never get over being accused. Check and checkmate."

"That's shitty. Someone should do something."

"I was hoping you'd say that."

Nani was explaining to Kaleo what she had in mind when a voice behind her said, "Evening, you two. Mind if I join you for a few minutes?"

Nani hadn't heard him coming. She stiffened, hoping that Hank Lindsey hadn't overheard their conversation. He might frown on her plan for Packer, the weed boy. Kaleo did a far better job of hiding his concern, assuming he was concerned at all. "Howzit, brah? Free country. Grab a seat."

Daya glided over to the table jangling from the dozens of charms on her bracelet. She was plump enough to be the original Big Island Girl. Hank grinned and said, "Evening, Daya. I'll take one of those." He pointed at Kaleo's ale.

"On its way," Daya replied, sailing away at the graceful pace of an ocean liner. In the meantime, Akela provided Nani a refill on her coffee. This time, he actually nodded at her, too.

Nani observed Hank through her thick eye lashes as she sipped it. She wondered if that bronzed skin would feel like silk or satin. She also noticed an intriguing old scar that trickled down his forehead and bisected an eyebrow. Of course he had a scar. All the best romance heroes had them from sword duels or knife fights in their mysterious pasts. All the best heroines swooned over these badges of honor. Nani was surprised to discover she fit that mold perfectly.

"I talked with Martina Martin," Hank said after Daya delivered his ale. "I caught her as she was cleaning up her yard from the sale. She was making one pile of leftovers for Big Island Charities and another for the dump. She says she has no memory of Maile's flashlight or how it came into her possession. But she admits that her daughter Lynn was jealous of Maile's popularity back then."

"And she was at the birthday party," Nani said. "Maybe she took it."

"A little kid might do that, sure, but it doesn't mean she had anything to do with Maile's disappearance," Kaleo said.

"True. But I'm more interested in Mrs. Martin's son, Martin," Hank said then took a sip of his brew.

"Martin Martin?" Kaleo raised his eyebrows.

"The third. Named for dad and granddad Martin." Laugh lines crinkled around Hank's blue eyes. "Martina must have enjoyed the name game to marry into that family."

"I knew Martin, or at least of him. He graduated from high school a couple years ahead of me," Nani said. "Big Buddha looking guy."

"Apparently known as a bully."

"That's what I heard. All I remember is that our football team actually won a game or two with him on the defensive line."

"Captain Lono interviewed him back then. His notes indicate nobody much liked the kid other than his own mother."

"And he's in Honolulu now?" Kaleo asked.

"Both siblings are. He's a claims adjustor, and she's a student. I'm flying over to talk with them tomorrow. Wondered if you'd like to come. I have no official reason to interview them, so having a be-reaved family member along might grease the skids." He looked at them both.

"Hawaiin Air costs too much for me," Kaleo said.

"Oh, it's not a sanctioned trip. Lono wouldn't agree to that. But tomorrow is my day off. And I fly a Mooney."

"Aren't Moonies those wack jobs from that old cult?" Kaleo asked.

"Not that kind of Moonie. A Mooney is a private aircraft."

"You mean a little plane?" Kaleo signaled Daya for another brew. "Then not just no. *Hell* no. If Pele meant us to have wings, she'd have provided them."

Nani had never seen her brother look that apprehensive before.

Fear of heights? Fear of flying? Fear of lawmen?

Whatever, she wanted to know everything she could about her sister's disappearance. "I'll go," she said. "I'll rebook my clients to make time for the trip." The power of Hank's smile warmed her head to toe. The trip was about Maile, of course. Seriously. But she might as well enjoy the company on the way.

"Good," he said standing up and leaving cash on the table for Daya. "I'll pick you up in the morning unless I hear otherwise. The plane's hangared at Waimea-Kohala field."

Nani was so pleased to be invited, to have the chance to talk with a girl who might know more about Maile on that fateful night, that she allowed herself the treat of a third cup of coffee, this time with real cream.

✦ ✦ ✦

Nani had never flown in a small plane before. When she saw the Mooney tied down at the airport, she thought it looked about the size of a large dragonfly. "Is it a baby? Does it have a real engine?"

Hank gave her such a look that she knew she'd trampled on his ego.

"I mean, it's really beautiful. Looks very fast. And it's yours?" she asked as he performed what he called the walk around inspection.

"Only in part. A syndicate of eight owns it. Like a time share. That's the only way I can afford a bird like this."

"Is it safe?" She asked as he stepped on the wing walk and scrambled into the cockpit, crossing the passenger seat and settling into the pilot's. There was no door on his side.

"Well, she's been flying for more than fifty years. Come on. Step where I did."

"Fifty? Doesn't that make her an antique?" Nani's sweaty palms made her appreciate Kaleo's apprehension. It grew worse when she considered how much the little bird could carry.

Jeez. He better not ask how much I weigh.

To her relief, he didn't. Nani stepped onto the wing, then down to the floor of the little plane and lowered herself into the seat.

"Fifty isn't ancient in airplane years. Most private planes are old soldiers these days. Too expensive to buy otherwise. But don't worry. She passes all inspections with flying colors." As if he thought Nani didn't look convinced, Hank added, "A single engine plane has so many back-up systems, it's damn near a twin. When something goes wrong, something else takes over."

Yeah, sure. That's why you never ever hear of little planes going down.

But Hank's confidence helped calm Nani's nerves, and she gave him a weak smile. Nervous or not, she had to go if there was even the smallest chance to learn something new about Maile. He reached across her to lock the door. This near to him she could smell laundry soap, and maybe that muskier odor was shampoo. He wasn't in uniform having explained he wanted to look less threatening to the Martins. He'd opted for a red pullover and tan shorts. Big Island business casual.

Hank was all pilot now, ignoring Nani as he worked his way through the preflight checklist, priming the engine, hitting the master switch, and clearing the prop before starting the plane. He turned on the radios, giving Nani a headset. After that he and ground control spoke a weird language with numbers like niner and words like foxtrot. He taxied to the end of the runway. Then the tower took over and cleared him for take-off.

When Hank pushed the throttle to the firewall, the little plane roared, shuddered, then leaped forward. Nani's stomach leaped right along with it, and her hands clenched tight on the edges of her seat cushion. The plane lifted into the air with the grace and ease of a flying dolphin. Hank turned almost immediately toward the northwest, dipping one wing low enough for Nani to see the emerald that was Keawalani and the slopes of Mauna Kea towering sternly over it. Greenery gave way to white sand and ebony lava along the coast. Then all land was gone as the Mooney headed out to sea.

"You're going to have to breathe," Hank said into her headset. She realized she'd been holding her breath and took down a great gulp of air. She looked at him and laughed for the sheer joy of it, letting go of her seat cushion to flash him two thumbs up. Everywhere was a fairy tale of sparkling aquamarine ocean sprinkled with outcroppings of deserted rock and verdant islands. There were more than 130 of them in Hawaii, and Nani imagined she could just about count them all.

This was her home as she'd never seen it before. The beauty stunned her. It was the best thing she'd ever done other than commune with spirits when she danced, and she owed it to the man sitting calmly next to her, concentrating on his job.

"I'm in love," she trilled into the headset's microphone, staring at the panorama below.

Hank looked sideways at her. He touched her arm then ran his fingers gently down to the back of her hand, enfolding her fingers with a gentle squeeze before letting her go. "Yes. Everything seems much clearer up here."

She didn't think it could get much better, but it did. They saw humpback whales breaching the water as the Mooney neared land. Kalaeloa Airport was Oahu's general aviation field near Honolulu. By the time they landed, Nani had experienced a very literal sea change. If she'd ever dreamed of moving to the mainland for greater adventure and wealth, that fantasy ended today. She now knew she would never abandon her Big Island home.

Hank had given her this wonderful gift. Plus, he was looking for Maile. She was nearly overwhelmed with gratitude, but he was now involved with the radios, switches and whoever was broadcasting from the tower. Her desire to shower him with hugs and kisses would be out of place at the moment.

Besides, it would probably be interpreted as more than a simple gesture of affection. Not that she'd really care. It was getting damn hard to keep a proper distance in such a tiny cockpit.

✦ ✦ ✦

Nani never thought she'd play the role of good cop. But Hank had gone all stern and superior. He actually looked down that might-have-been-broken-once nose as he inspected Lynn and Marty Martin.

Nani felt the need to soften his approach. It wasn't just that she believed in honey vs. vinegar. Lynn was a direct link to Maile's last known moments. The girl just had to be coaxed into telling anything she knew about the night Maile disappeared. Nani had been irritated with Lynn Martin ever since finding the flashlight at the yard sale. But that was unfair. Even if Lynn had taken it, that was twelve years back when she was only an eight year old.

Lynn and Marty Martin had chosen the time and location for this meeting to coincide with their lunch breaks. A food truck always parked in a strip mall half way between his office and her beauty school. Fish tacos were the specialty of the day along with a grilled Spam and cheese. Lynn and Marty ate while Hank had a passion fruit shave ice. Nani chose a strawberry, banana, vanilla rainbow shave, the combo that had been Maile's favorite. It felt important to represent her little sister here today.

Hank thought Lynn Martin looked more like a pagan fertility fetish than a girl who must be only nineteen or so. Her ponderous breasts and thighs might not have been so eye popping if she'd opted for anything other than those shorts and that tee. He understood enough about young women to know that Lynn wanted to dress like the rest of her pack, regardless of size. Hawaiian girls had little issue with exposing skin to sun.

But still...

"We want to talk about the disappearance of Maile Palea," he said after the introductions. All four were seated at the uncomfortable chairs that appeared to be refugees from some long ago ice cream parlor. The swirling loops in the metal chair backs and seats were painful enough on his slender ass to keep this interview short. "You were on the scene twelve years ago, Lynn."

"Ancient history. Surely there are better things to talk about," Lynn purred, leaning forward and touching his hand before he could snatch it away. She'd been tossing her hair and batting her eyes and nipping at her lower lip as though she'd read a training manual called *The Mating Game for Dummies*. He found it embarrassing to be her target, making him chillier than the shave ice he'd ordered.

By the set of his jaw, Nani saw Hank's distress with Lynn's clumsy skills. Her behavior was totally inappropriate, far too juvenile for a woman who must be nearly twenty. Why? Something was definitely wrong here.

"Shut up and stop it, Lynn." Marty Martin gave his sister a disgusted look.

So big brother might still be a bully, at least to little sister. Nani decided to speak up. She smiled at the girl and said, "I'm Maile's sister, Lynn. It broke my heart when she disappeared. She was your friend. I need your help. Maybe we can still find her." The emotion in her voice wasn't forced; it was there for anyone to hear. Anyone who cared at all.

Nani saw the glance from Hank. Had she overstepped her bounds by cutting in?

If he doesn't want me to talk, he shouldn't have invited me.

Lynn turned her focus from Hank to Nani. Her flirtatiousness drained away. Maybe Nani's distress had reached some soft spot deep inside her soul. Now she just looked pouty, like most teenagers when confronted by adults. Nani had seen this kind of quick change before, in the privacy of her massage salon. It happened when a stressed out woman felt safe to remember her past. Something bad had happened to Lynn. What went on here?

Solemnly Lynn asked, "What do you want to know? Not that I remember much. I was just a little kid then, too. Right, Marty?"

Marty was conservative in both dress and demeanor, an opposite from his sister. His Aloha shirt was monotonal browns instead of the riotous colors of most, probably in accord with the dictates of the insurance office where he worked. He was a big man, but one who had not gone to seed the way linebackers easily could. He'd reminded her of a Buddha when he was a kid. But now, other than the fleshiness in his cheeks and chin he carried his size well. Nani found him attractive in a bad boy sort of way.

"*You* were an annoying kid," he huffed at his sister. "Always into something. I had to get you out of one mess after another."

"Oh, I don't know, Marty," Hank said, flipping through a pocket size spiral notebook. "You were the annoying kid. You're the one with the record. Drugs ... vandalism ... auto theft. And the rep as a bully. Did you really get off extorting money from schoolmates?"

Marty smiled and raised his hands in an I-give-up gesture. "All too true, Officer. You got me. But they were all juvie offenses. Nothing anymore. I've changed. I'm a businessman now."

"Yeah? What made you see the light?"

"I grew up. Met Jesus along the way. He helped me learn the error of my ways." He flashed another smile.

Hank had heard this 'found religion' con from crooks before. He doubted he'd ever believe it. "No more picking on kids, huh? Even little girls in party dresses?"

Nani sucked in her breath at Hank's crass remark. But she understood that cops sometimes had to shock. She just wished it hadn't been her right along with Marty.

Marty turned icy as his smile evaporated. "So this is an official police investigation then? Should I call a lawyer?"

Nani recovered enough to interrupt, hoping to keep the peace. "Not at all, Marty. We're just questioning the past now that new evidence has turned up. To see if it spurs any memories for the people who were there. If this were official, Hank wouldn't have me here, would he? I know you're upset. So am I. I understand how siblings want to take care of each other. It's like that with my little brother and me. He gets in messes all the time, too."

Marty wasn't buying her good cop act. "I was hounded about this twelve years ago," he said. "Lynn was, too. We've got nothing more to say." He started to stand until Hank put a hand on his arm. Nani figured it was quite a hold because Marty sat back down.

"That was before we found Maile Palea's flashlight with your other possessions," Hank said.

Nani thought Lynn and Marty would look surprised. Neither did.

"Yeah, Ma told us about that," Lynn said. She looked at Nani. "That must have been a terrible shock for you. Seeing it after so long."

"How do you explain it?" Hank asked.

Marty snapped, "She doesn't have to. Isn't it up to you to figure it out?"

"It's okay, Marty. Time I told the truth, at least as I remember it." Now that Lynn wasn't playing the flirt, she sounded like a lot of young women with bad memories. "I found it in the grass behind the houses. Under the biggest candlewood tree. We were looking for hidden prizes, and I thought some might be out there. Maile's flashlight was so much cuter than mine. Like a little hula girl. So I picked it up and kept it."

"You just *took* it?" Nani asked. She was so insensed that she wasn't sure she could maintain the good cop crap. She was back to wanting to throttle the girl.

"She was only a kid, Nani. Kids do stuff like that," Marty said.

Nani knew he was right. It sounded just like something a jealous youngster might do. But it still rankled.

"Did you see anything else?" asked Hank.

"No."

"Any*one* else?"

"No ... but I heard something. It sounded like someone running away through the grass. And there was crying. But not like a kid. More like a wounded animal wailing. I couldn't tell for sure. Then I thought it might be a ghost howling. I got really scared. So I ran back to the Lopakas and started playing again. I was too frightened to say anything."

Hank was upset. "You didn't tell anyone what happened? I mean, I know you were just a kid, but you didn't *tell* anyone?" What might the searchers have found if she'd only spoken up? Lono was smart ... what could he have done with information like that?

Nani only managed to ask, "Didn't you realize that someone might have rescued her? If you would have talked? There might have been time."

Lynn cringed, tears beginning to plop onto the taco remains on her paper plate. Marty interrupted with heat. "She told *me* the next day. Okay? She did tell. Thought I'd be proud of her for stealing and getting away with it. Like I always did as a kid. But instead, I told her to keep her yap shut. If she told anyone else she'd stolen that damn flashlight, everyone would think she knew more than she did about who took Maile. Better to keep it a secret."

"So you let someone kidnap a little girl and never said a word." Hank had experience with using shame. Suspects often cracked from it more than from anger.

"That's right, cop. I had to protect another little girl." Marty cocked his head toward Lynn. "Besides, you and I both know whoever took Maile had killed her by then. Uh, sorry Nani."

"That's cold, Marty," Hank said.

"Cold describes our life, *brah*. I was afraid the culprit might be someone we knew. That gave us another reason to keep it quiet."

Lynn gasped and stared at her brother. "Please. You're not going to tell, are you?"

"Another kid? Someone older? Who did you suspect?" Hank asked, leaning closer.

But brother and sister went silent, Lynn staring at her plate and Marty at something deep inside. From the way he grimaced, Hank knew it was ugly.

Finally, Lynn spoke. She sniffed back snot and wiped away her tears. She sounded small and tragic, like she'd regressed in age once more. "He liked little girls. Liked to show them secret places. Make them do bad things."

And now Hank knew what Nani had guessed. Lynn was an abuse survivor. He felt fury rise like bile. "Who, Lynn? Who are you afraid of? Did Marty do things to you?"

Marty bared his teeth. "You son of a -"

Nani cut him off. "Did your daddy hurt you, Lynn?" If the man abused Lynn then maybe he took Maile and ...

Lynn winced. "Marty wasn't the real bully in our family."

"We can't tell you any more about that. It would kill our mother to know the truth, and our dad is dead," Marty said, looking more sorry than angry.

"I could charge you with obstructing an investigation."

"You do that, officer. Hell, I've been beaten and Lynn's been screwed by everyone else in authority. You think I care about obstruction? And with all the jurisdictional paperwork you have to file, I'll be home before you will. Come on, Lynn. Lunch is over."

"You'll hear from me again, Marty," Hank said as the siblings stood to go. Marty took Lynn's fleshy upper arm to urge her away like a tug boat pushing a barge.

Lynn turned back for a final look at Nani. "I'm sorry about Maile.

I was jealous of her because she was always so happy. I wanted to be like her. I hope you find out what happened to her."

Hank and Nani sat in silence. Tears filled Nani's eyes. She'd been so hopeful that new information would be helpful. She'd never considered it would be hurtful, too. Thinking about what happened to Maile had always felt abstract ... she didn't have to picture it too realistically until she knew the truth. Now her mind was filled with images that were too dreadful to bear.

Hank put an arm around her shoulders. They stayed still as the other tables emptied, lunch hour a thing of the past. The truck crew gathered up their used paper plates, bundled the trash, and finally moved Hank and Nani along so they could pack up their two chairs along with all the others. As the breeze scattered the last odors of salt and fried grease, Hank and Nani walked toward an intersection to hail a cab.

Nani was subdued on the flight home, no longer as exhilarated as she'd been that morning. Hank must have been downcast, too. At least they were in the air before he finally spoke about the interview. "Well. We make a pretty good team. I've needed a bad cop partner."

"Bad? I thought I was the good cop."

"Oh. I'll try to keep that straight from now on."

It was strange to converse through headsets. There they were side by side in an intimate space, but they needed the thick padded gear to hear each other well. Nani said, "Those two were abused as kids, Hank. And, at least for Lynn, it was sexual. That's what all that flirting was about. She thinks sex is the only thing she's good for. She doesn't know any other way to relate to a man."

"No wonder they didn't tell anyone about the flashlight. Lynn was where she shouldn't have been, stealing something that wasn't hers. Doesn't sound like their dear old dad – or whoever the son of a bitch is – would have been very understanding. Wouldn't want the cops sniffing around. He'd have punished them both. I see more of that kind of thing on the job than I care to. Domestic abuse is too gentle a term for it." He clenched his teeth for a moment before going on. "If the bastard wasn't their father, I'll find out who it was. Whether he had anything to do with Maile or not, he may still be a danger to other island kids now."

Nani agreed. "So what all did we learn?"

"That the culprit was strong enough to escape the scene with Maile. That someone was crying. That the perp knew the territory well enough to avoid all witnesses and make good an escape. That Lynn and Marty have an abusive adult they're shielding. And, I don't think either of them is the culprit."

"Even if Marty found religion? Wouldn't that fit with a guilty conscience?"

"Possible, but doubtful. I'll try to keep an open mind."

For the rest of the journey Nani was quiet. All of her anger at Lynn was vanquished. The fragile teenager had at last told her secret about that night she took a flashlight. And breaking that silence had brought Nani one step closer to what happened to her lost sister. Even if that step had been a very hurtful one to take.

✦   ✦   ✦

Kaleo painted. He wanted more than anything to make a living with his art, but he failed for two reasons. First, while his colors and lines were endemic to his island home, the compositions were abstract. Most tourists wanted realistic interpretations of the beaches and rainforests as memories of their island dream long after they'd returned to the frigid snow storms of Chicago or Minneapolis. So Kaleo's art was for island people, and island people could rarely afford fine art.

The second reason – and the one that frustrated Nani – was that Kaleo wouldn't exhibit his canvasses. He was shy of public scrutiny. Almost nobody knew of his remarkable talent unless they were close enough to visit Nani's home. Her walls were slowly but surely being covered with Kaleo's murals. After a client session she might emerge from her salon to find a new blast of yellow or streak of blue shooting across a room.

When she got home from Honolulu, eager to tell Kaleo everything she'd learned, the house appeared dark out front. But the minute she opened the front door, Mannheim Steamroller music greeted her arrival. She crossed the shadowy living room, following beams of light from the kitchen. As her eyes adjusted to the brightness, she could see Kaleo suspended in the air like an oversized angel. No, not suspended. Standing on her kitchen counter, working on a mural above her cabinets.

"Kaleo!" she said, ready to scold him for covering one more surface without her permission. But then she looked at the mural. It stopped her speechless.

It was breathtaking. Colors swept in swirls of motion, curving and spiraling around each other. Oranges, yellows, reds all raced across the wall, one dominating then dissolving into the other. As she looked closer, she realized these colors were actually wings, an abstraction of birds lifting in flight. It was beautiful and joyous, capturing the way she had felt in Hank's Mooney just that morning.

But like so many of Kaleo's works, sadness was there, too. For viewers who knew their ornithology well, these were the brilliant wings of island varieties of honeycreepers, flycatchers, thrushes and more, all of them now extinct. This beauty would never fly again on this earth. And that's when Nani realized that Kaleo, whether he understood it or not, was actually painting a portrait of Maile.

CHAPTER NINE

High Spirits at the Suck'en'em Up Saloon
By Jackson O'Reilly
Excerpt from the *Keawalani Voice,* 2015

This reporter was on his way home last Friday night after a Pau Hana celebration when a user-about-town went flying by, hell bent for leather. He, and let's just call him Weed Boy, was running from a startling sight that followed him out of the darkness.

Maybe he thought headless horsemen were in pursuit. Banshees or Valkyries. Or maybe the pakalolo was bad seed that night. Whatever, he looked too frightened for the two jolly ghost riders on a Vespa, who were snickering their way toward home. They seemed friendly enough to be siblings. I'm just saying.

Any of you insomniacs may have heard the ruckus. It looked like good clean fun to this reporter. But it must have been hard for Weed Boy to sleep it off. Or to figure it all out come Saturday morning.

Nani put down the paper with a sigh. She hadn't seen the editor, but apparently Jack O'Reilly had seen them. She could only hope that Mrs. Cunningham or Emelina wouldn't recognize the cast of characters from the article. She folded the paper so Kaleo would see the story when he awoke. As she finished her coffee, she thought about the evening before ...

It was Pau Hana Friday at the Suck'en'em Up Saloon. A raucous happy hour celebrating the end of the work week was rocking deep into the night. The only light in the gravel parking lot came from a dozen neon beer signs across the front of the bar. In the glow, Nani could see one car bouncing as the occupants performed couples aerobics.

"This isn't the kind of place for a Vespa," Kaleo muttered as she aimed the scooter between the Harleys.

"I'll park it over there under the banyan tree. Like we planned. Now get off."

Kaleo dismounted from behind her. "I still think your script sounds like a grade B movie."

"He'll be high on heaven knows what. He won't notice bad dialog. We just have to scare him a little."

"You got it, *sistah*. I been practicing my scowl." Kaleo stretched his soft cheeks and heavy jaw into a monster face, flashing her his version of the stink eye. Then he returned to normal and walked toward the saloon's front door.

The banyan in the little park next door was one of the largest on the Big Island, a spreading tangle of thick trunks and dangling vines. Three picnic tables nestled beneath the enormous limbs which were shorn up with timbers. Nearby, a fountain splashed musically into a cement pool. During the day, the park was alive with shouts and giggles. But on the back side of midnight, it was deserted. Or so Nani thought.

She drove the Vespa under the tree and cut the engine. Raucous snoring overwhelmed the fountain and the thunderous music from the bar. In the pale moonlight, Nani could see that someone who'd sucked up a few too many passed out on a picnic table.

She approached and cleared her throat.

Sleeping Beauty didn't move.

She *ahemed* loudly.

He didn't hear.

She shook his shoulder, at first gently then with vigor.

He remained dead to the world.

She left him to it. Otherwise the park was empty. Nani stripped down to the black wetsuit under her clothes. She wanted to blend into the darkness as long as she could. Mrs. Cunningham's thieving grandson, Packer, already knew Kaleo, but it would be better if he couldn't identify Nani. She'd rather Mrs. C never know anything about this.

She stuffed her shirt and jeans into one of the Vespa's saddlebags. Then, from another, she took out a plastic eye mask. Unfortunately, it was white and sprinkled with glitter, a feathered leftover from a Mardi Gras party. Even in the low light of the half moon, it sparkled in hues brighter than the beer signs. She'd prefer something scarier like maybe a zombie, but this was the only mask she had.

Nani leaned against a tree limb, killing time until Kaleo returned. She was unafraid to be alone in the balmy tropical night. If anyone should feel threatened tonight, it wasn't her. To her surprise, the drunk was the first person she frightened. He awakened himself with a mighty snort, sat up on his tabletop and stretched. He took a look around as if trying to get his bearings. With one sight of the masked demon in front of him, looming bodiless out of the dark, he yelped and scuttled away. Nani thought she heard him promise some deity that he'd return to AA in the morning.

Nani the Demon continued her watch on the front door of the saloon. She waited five minutes. Ten.

When Kaleo came out he was accompanied by a shorter man. Of course, most men looked short beside Kaleo. Packer was cave-chested and round shouldered. His upper body slanted forward as if his spine were too wobbly to hold him upright. Like a mongoose trying to balance on its back legs.

Nani stood silent and still. She hoped Packer wouldn't notice her until he got close. As he approached, she could see he was still just a boy, one who needed a lecture on personal hygiene. His stringy blonde hair fell down to his shoulders in matted strands. The *Legalize Ganja* tee-shirt was sweat-stained and his boardshorts perched precariously on his slender hips.

Nani glided forward in a smooth hula move, appearing to float out of the darkness.

"Holy crap!" Packer's unfocused and dilated eyes blinked wildly as he stared at Nani's slick black profile and sparkly head. Whatever wild spirit the stoned boy thought he saw, it must be working. He looked as thunderstruck as the drunk had been.

Packer stuttered. "Y-you some kind of spook? Didn't know spirits used. The man here says you got a brick to sell."

"You have the money?' Nani growled in her best bad ass voice.

"No worries. I can get it from an old lady I know."

"Your grandmother, right?"

"Steal from your *tutu*, yeah?" Kaleo said. He donned the monster face he'd been practicing.

With a "Fuck you," Packer turned to scramble back to the bar. But Kaleo grabbed a hank of his hair in one massive paw and the back of his shorts in the other.

"What the fuck?" Packer yelped as he took flight.

Nani said, "Shut your mouth if you know what's good for you."

Kaleo carried the wriggling body to the fountain and dumped Packer into the cement pond, holding him underwater for two seconds, then a third for good measure. He let go of the hair long enough for Packer to bob to the surface, spitting and gagging. The boy gathered breath to scream for help, but Kaleo ordered, "Close your yap and listen very, very closely to what the Demon has to say."

Nani leaned over the pool and placed her lips near Packer's ear. "Your *tutu* is a great lady, respected by all of Keawalani. If you ever steal from her again, we will tell the entire village. You will be dead to us. Every back will turn on you. Again, Kaleo."

Splash. The big man held the boy under another three seconds then released his head. Now Packer was blubbering.

"If you squeal, no one will believe an addict's story. Kaleo will deny it. He'll tell the authorities about your thieving. They'll find other thefts to blame on you."

"I won't squeal, not to nobody," Packer sniveled.

"Say nothing to your grandmother about this. She is never to know that you stole from her. From now on you will be a good little grandson who makes his *tutu* proud. Got it?"

"Yes, ma'am. I got it."

"Stop stealing and we'll keep quiet. Break your word, and we'll visit you again. We won't be so forgiving the next time."

Kaleo finally released the kid. "Get out of here."

Packer clambered out of the pool. Sopping wet and holding up his sagging boardshorts, he disappeared into the night.

✦ ✦ ✦

Police Captain Frank Lono was slurping the last of the sweet caramel macchiato that only the receptionist Allison Costello knew he loved. She brought him one each afternoon when she picked up a mocha grande at the Brewed Awakening for herself. He'd once said to her, "You ever tell anyone this ain't just black coffee, I'll stop buying these concoctions for us both. A guy can't be caught with a girlie drink."

Hank had just given the captain the weekly update on his official caseload. Everything seemed temporarily calm. He'd even nabbed two guys who'd been selling hot electronics out of a minivan. "And I might have something on the cold case ... the Palea girl."

Lono leaned forward. "Yeah? What you got?"

Hank could tell Maile was still a priority for his boss, officially or not. "We may have a new lead." He eagerly shared the results of his interview with Lynn and Marty Martin. "They don't admit that their abuser was their father. But Allison is looking up some info on him for me. He's passed away now, but I want to know about his life twelve years back. If it wasn't him, it was somebody who could still be around."

Lono made two points with a free throw when his paper cup hit the circular file. He took his feet off his desk, stood and put on his hat. His eyes took on a steely look, the kind a shark has when it devours prey. "There's one place around here that knows most every story."

Sunny Daze Barber Shop had a traditional red and white pole out front, but it had given up revolving years ago. The handpainted gold letters on the storefront window were faded to illegibility by the Big Island sun. Lono knew that the owner didn't care. Sunny had told him if you were from Keawalani you knew where the shop was. If you weren't from Keawalani, he didn't give a shit what you knew or what you didn't.

Sunny was a tiny Chinese immigrant, one who'd worked in the sugar cane fields for *haoles* and cut Chinese hair in the camps many years ago. He eventually saved enough to open his shop. Now he was on his third generation of customers. He started on kids who were kicking and screaming over the injustice of shorn locks. When they grew old enough to be picky about their cuts, they often disappeared to trendy salons in nearby towns and only returned when they were approaching their senior years.

When Lono and Hank walked in, Hank felt out of place. He was the youngest person there. Apparently the children of Keawalani had been given a reprieve for the day.

Two cops in the small shop stopped conversation dead in its tracks. "Howzit, Sunny," Lono said, removing his cap.

Hank saw three villagers give them the once over while a fourth slunk out the back. Lono asked Sunny for a trim, maybe because the barber had just lost a customer. Or maybe because his hair cut was nothing special to begin with. Hank, far fussier about his own chestnut curls, took the remaining seat in the waiting area and hoped to go unnoticed by the barber.

"What you lawmen up to?" Sunny asked as he finished a razor clean-up around the neck, sides and hairline of the man currently in his chair. Hank recognized the customer as a cashier from the Ono Grinds Market.

Lono explained it had been a dozen years since the disappearance of the child, Maile Palea. They were seeing if anyone knew anything new, remembered or heard any rumors through the years. He spoke loudly enough for all the customers to hear.

Meanwhile, Hank's gaze wandered around the shop. The entrance had two dusty shelves behind a miniscule front counter, one holding a collection of funky old lamps with surfers, geckos, palm trees and hula girls as bases. The other shelf held several *maneki-ne-ko*, the beckoning ceramic cats found in every island business. They were gifts to the owners for good luck and wealth. From the looks of the place, Hank doubted whether Sunny had much of either.

There were two old Emil J. Paidar barber chairs but only the one old barber. If Sunny ever had a partner he was long gone, probably sick of the sour old man's company. There was no flat screen TV for waiting customers, but a radio was tuned to a local talk show, currently discussing anthurium blight. Sunny had a selection of hair oils, tonics and shampoos, but nothing as swanky as skin care products for sale. Hand written signs made it clear he offered no manicures, pedicures, detox face treatments or other such nonsense. Cuts and shaves only. The counter held a sign saying "No Credit, No Credit Cards, No Checks."

Considering the temperament of the owner and the lack of services, Sunny Daze Barber Shop did not attract many outsiders. But Hank knew why the shop was popular with the village men. The regulars talked sports, cars and investments with each other. They could safely discuss a local woman's ass or a man's sexual orientation without anyone calling them misogynistic or homophobic.

And with the barber himself? This was where a man could come for fifteen minutes every few weeks. He could spill his guts. At such infrequent intervals, he didn't sweat the small shit. He talked about weighty matters in his life. It was free therapy. Sunny knew a lot about a lot of the men in Keawalani. And he was known to keep it to himself. He would never reveal a word of anything said in confidence.

But Martin Martin Jr. was dead now. Hank knew Captain Lono hoped it would free Sunny up to talk about the past. That's the real reason he had stepped into the barber chair after the Ono Grinds cashier left the shop. Sunny was about half through the buzz cut he was giving the captain.

Lono said, "Not quite so short around the ears, Sunny ... or okay, that works, too."

"I remember the daddy of that little girl Maile. He leave town after she disappear. Before her mama die. Broke his heart," Sunny said.

"Broke Keawalani's heart. We all missed her," agreed Jackson O'Reilly, editor of the *Keawalani Voice*. Hank saw enough curly red snippets on the floor to know the Irishman had just had his cut. Plus, it didn't take a trained detective to see the newsman's head was as naked as a shorn sheep.

"She was the best reporter *you* ever had. Paper's gone downhill ever since," sniped the owner of the WikiWiki Fix Garage, shaking his head over the decline in quality journalism.

O'Reilly said, "Must be too many assholes among the subscribers these days to recognize real Pulitzer stuff."

"We all searched for her. Never found anything," said the dentist who was still the Lopaka's next door neighbor. "Poor George and his wife have all but died of shame."

"You were new flatfoot in those days, captain. Too bad you could not solve case." Sunny observed. "Might be a big deal by now. Star of *Hawaii* 5-0, maybe. Making big bucks."

The dentist seemed to want détente. "Everyone felt bad. You hear about too many kids abused by sick men these days. Never heard such crap when we were kids."

"Just because people didn't talk doesn't mean it didn't happen." The garage owner was flipping through a year old *Popular Mechanics,* the only thing Sunny had for customers to read.

O'Reilly nodded. "Now I feel guilty for just enjoying kids, watching little ones play, leading a scout troop."

The dentist agreed. "Those bastards give the rest of us men a bad name. It's wrong having to avoid kids in case we're accused of threatening them."

The customers continued to mull over the problems with being a man in modern society. Hank had to strain to hear over the dentist, editor and garage owner when Lono quietly asked Sunny, "You knew Martin Martin? He was a regular wasn't he?"

"He was. He dead now." Sunny removed Lono's cape and brushed off his neck.

"He ever tell you much about himself?"

Sunny's mouth clamped shut in a tight little moue. But as Hank watched, the barber seemed to reach a decision. He finally said, "That man a bully. Like his father. Like his son. I did not like that man."

Lono asked, "You think he could have had something to do with Maile's disappearance? Was he more than just a bully?"

Sunny busied himself sweeping up fallen hair and placing combs in a sterilizer. Sadly he said, "I think with no ransom asked, no contact made, that little girl was snatched for terrible purpose. Mr. Martin, he had diabetes. He could no longer get stiff. You know. Do it."

Hank glanced up from his notebook as Lono asked, "So ... with Martin then, sexual abuse – at least penetration – would not have happened."

"He said to me he impotent. Tell me that while crying into hot towel on his face." Sunny put the broom away and stood arms akimbo in front of the captain. "Better you know that than think he fuck a child."

Hank was surprised. So her father wasn't the one who violated Lynn. And that meant there was no reason to believe he had taken Maile, either. There must be someone else still in the weeds.

Sunny interrupted his thoughts. "You done now, Captain. That twelve dollar."

It was a cheap cut but then, Lono got what he paid for. Hank planned to tease him all the way back to the department. Allison would take it from there. In the meantime, it sounded like the Martins were in the clear. Unless there was someone else in the family who'd abused Lynn and preyed on other little girls.

Sunny broke into his thoughts saying, "Now you, young cop."

"But I was just waiting ..."

"You come into my shop, you get haircut."

Oh shit.

CHAPTER TEN

Come Out, Come Out, Wherever You Are
By Jackson O'Reilly
Excerpt from the *Keawalani Voice*, 2015

Have you ever wanted to make like a bird and fly away? Escape your troubles, your beleaguered life and prest-o change-o, vanish into thin air?

The idea of disappearance *on purpose* intrigues me. Maybe it's just not possible nowadays, not with computers to hunt you down. So I walked over to the police department to chat with Captain Frank Lono. Deputy Hank Lindsey was on hand as well.

Lono confirmed that there was a time not long ago that cutting up your credit cards, throwing away your license and getting a phony social security number made disappearance easier than it is today. I asked the officers under what circumstances people wanted to run away.

Lono: You mean other than criminals and deadbeat dads and people changing identities? That's illegal, by the way. But there are several other reasons to leave an old life behind.

Lindsey: People being stalked by abusive exes. Or looking to escape heavy obligations or reputations that may be unfair. Or people who've come into money and want to drop off the grid.

Lono: CEOs or other rich and famous types who might be taken for ransom. Of course, that's not a big worry around here.

Lindsey: Yeah, how many people want to disappear *from* an island instead of *to* one?

Then I asked about disappearance in the digital age.

Lono: Certainly the internet and social media as a whole have made footprints easier to follow. These days, it sort of comes down to a person's desire to disappear being greater than another person's desire to find him or her.

Lindsey: There are companies that will help you build multiple identities around one name. If you know how, you can do it yourself. You create confusion around your name, like maybe several Facebook pages, and you flood the social media with inaccuracies. Whoever's looking for you may give up before they can work their way through the confusion.

> Bottom line, disappearing without a trace
> sounds attractive from time to time. Espe-
> cially with throw-away phones and internet
> cafes to reach out to friends if you ever
> still want to.
>
> But I don't think I'll try it. After all,
> I'd hate to find out that nobody missed me
> at all.

Nani wouldn't think of laughing at how a person looked. But her brother would. "Been to see Sunny, huh?" Kaleo asked when Hank finally took off his POLICE ballcap. "You look like a mushroom head, *brah*."

Nani saw Hank wince when he lowered his arm, hat in hand. She didn't think it was just at Kaleo's jibe. She'd noticed him favoring one shoulder since he sat in the breakfast nook and downed half the coffee she poured for him. More than the haircut was hurting him.

The three of them were sharing the box of malasadas that Hank had brought still warm from the bakery that was two doors down from the cop shop. The sweet fried dough oozed with a cinnamon cream filling. Nobody but the baker knew the exact recipe, a family secret brought to the Big Island during the Portuguese immigration in the late 1800s. The treat made Nani's stomach gurgle with joy over a breakfast that didn't involve Special K.

"Sunny was living up to his shop's name," Hank said, running his hand through what hair remained. "Either he was in a daze when he did this, or I was."

Hank's haircut wasn't really *that* bad. A little short on the sides maybe, and long on top. A touch uneven. It would grow. "I think you look very nice," Nani the Diplomat said. "Very, um, professional."

Kaleo popped another malasada into his mouth and munched

it down. "*Ono!*" he said of the delicious bite. "Now why you here, Hank? I got things to do on a fine Sunday like this."

Nani, sitting next to him, saw his boardshorts and bare hairy legs sprawled under the table. "The beach real busy, is it? Gotta rush to catch a wave?"

"Be busy when I get there. Lots of chicks needing surf lessons."

"Before you go, Lover Boy," Hank said, "I wanted to ask you both about your parents."

Nani could feel her brother's body tighten next to her on the bench seat.

"It's all in the file, man. Manuku Palea disappeared. Kina Palea died. End of story," Kaleo said.

"Events and dates are all there, sure. But I want to know the reasons behind those facts. Do you remember why your Dad left town?"

"We never really knew the *why*," Nani replied. "In some ways, Mom and Dad are both still mysteries. They were artists. They first met at a craft show. Mom made jewelry from beach glass and gold wire. Beautiful things." She fingered the piece of soft edged, sand-etched glass she wore on a gold chain. The bottle green ornament, decorated with tiny gold beads and wire, nestled in the hollow of her throat. It had been a gift from her mother. "Dad worked with leather. He made saddles for the cowboys on the Parker ranch. He'd get over a thousand bucks on a custom order. Made furniture and satchels, too, for the shows."

"They were both talented, I have to give them that," Kaleo said.

"Like their son," Nani said, pointing up at the beautiful mural now complete over her kitchen cabinets.

"And their daughter," Kaleo said. He looked at Hank. "You should see her dance trophies."

Hank's eyes met Nani's. "Trophies? What kind of competitions?"

"Hula, *brah*. Big Sister was a national champion. She could make the gods smile."

"I'd like to see you dance," Hank said, his eyes holding hers.

"Not gonna happen. She quit the circuit," Kaleo said, sounding like the injured party.

"Enough, Kaleo. Old history." Nani knew her brother was proud of her and wanted her to dance again. But she couldn't. No matter how much she missed the way she had expressed her own artistic soul, she'd given up competition dancing as a sacrifice to Maile's memory. And that was that. "We're talking about Maile."

Hank said, "All the talent in your family makes me wonder what art form Maile would have chosen."

"We like to think she *has* chosen. That she's practicing some art right now. Somewhere. Writing, probably, if Jackson O'Reilly was right about her talent. We have to hope. Sometimes, hope is all there is." She sipped her coffee and looked back in time. "Our mother Kina was never strong, but she was a good mom. Dad was loud, moody. But Mom was always there in the background, quiet and calm. She helped with our homework, made cupcakes for school events, went to PTA meetings. She explored the island with us, walking in the woods and pastures, telling us about flowers and birds. I don't know, Hank. I mean, all kids think they're the only important things in a parent's life, so maybe I'm wrong, but I think she was content. Even happy when Dad was off the sauce. Don't you, Kaleo?"

He nodded. "But after Maile disappeared, she withdrew into some kind of shell. Despondent, yeah? Wouldn't go out anymore. Didn't seem to notice Dad was boozing more and more."

"She still took care of us, at least our physical needs, but she did nothing for herself. Didn't eat, didn't sleep. Dad couldn't take it. After a few months he left, and she just sort of languished like women do in old fashioned stories. Doctors gave her pep talks and antidepressants. We tried to get her out, but she fought us. Just told us to go on without her. She stopped playing games or reading or watching

TV. Spent most of her time in Maile's room. Waiting."

"Waiting?" Hank asked.

"She was waiting for Maile to come home." Nani said. She remembered it all too well. How she, just seventeen, had been hurt by her mother enough to cry out in anger, "I'm still here, Mom. I still need you." Now she wished she hadn't added that guilt to her mother's overwhelming load. "Maybe I could have done more for her. But we were teenagers, consumed by our own lives. It got to the point where we could only be happy when we left the house. So we spent a lot of time away. Then one day she was just gone. She died curled up in a rocker in Maile's room."

"Any idea why your Dad didn't come home then? Or get in touch?" Hank asked.

"Who knows? Maybe he still doesn't know she died."

"Nani and I weren't enough for him, pure and simple," Kaleo said.

Nani heard the anger in his voice. With a touch of loyalty toward her father, she said, "At least before he left, he wrote himself out of their will, so we inherited the house directly from Mom. Our kumu Hakumele was the executor. She's also Dad's sister, our aunt. She made sure I was allowed to live here when I felt strong enough to be on my own. Kaleo didn't want to be here at first. He stayed with Hakumele for a while. Went away to school. He really just moved back in after getting out of jail. Well, you already know that part of the story."

"Any idea where your father is now?"

"Don't know, don't care," said Kaleo. "Wherever he is, Manuku Palea is an asshole."

"I've looked for him online," Nani admitted. "Not a real serious search or anything. He knows where we are if he wants to find us." She wasn't as bitter as Kaleo, but she did believe it was up to her father to contact them. Not the other way around.

"According to the file, he had an air tight alibi when Maile disappeared. Dozens of people saw him at that Hilo craft fair."

"I know close relatives are the likeliest suspects, Hank. But I never believed he'd hurt her. Not Maile. Hell, he was so torn up about that one child, he turned his back on his other two." Kaleo slid out of the booth and picked up his sunglasses from the counter. "Every guy who ever knew Maile was interviewed, including me. And I was just a kid. My girlfriend had to come forward to give me an alibi. Which ended that romance PDQ. If we're done here, I'm on my way."

"Thanks, Kaleo. We're done," Hank said. "Enjoy the board lessons."

Kaleo waved a shaka and headed out the back door. Nani knew he would grab up his boogie board and thumb a ride to the beach.

Hank stood to refill their coffee from the carafe on the kitchen counter. Nani noticed him wince again. "How about letting me even up that haircut a little bit? I've had to even out Sunny's work before on my own head."

"Sure, if you're willing to," he said with a delighted smile that revealed fine-looking pearly whites.

Oh my.

"Come sit on my massage table. It's high enough for me to get a good angle on your neckline."

They left the kitchen through the hall that lead toward the front of the house. Nani opened a door to what had once been her parents' bedroom. It was now completely changed into a secluded hideaway. At the far end, floor-to-ceiling glass panels slid back on themselves, opening to an exterior room with a hot tub, a riot of tropical flowers, and an outdoor shower. A wall of lava rock surrounded the area to keep it private from the neighbors, and an enclosed fountain trickled constantly, heightening the feel of a personal paradise. Nani's clients could use the shower before or after their sessions if they wished, and they could rent the hot tub for themselves or guests. Nani used it herself in the early mornings to prepare her own muscles and nerves for a day of working on others.

Inside the room, surrounding a sturdy massage table, rattan storage bins hid piles of fluffy white cotton towels, sheets and jugs of essential oils. Lavender, sandalwood, patchouli, rose ... she tried to keep all the aroma therapy favorites on hand.

Next to a small sink, a shelf held Nani's massage stones, two stone heaters and all the other equipment she needed. She didn't have built-in speakers – although it was on Kaleo's list of chores – so a stack of discs with titles like "Tropical Mood" and "Sounds of the Pacific" piled next to an old CD player. "Enchanted Pools" was playing now.

Hank looked around the room as he sat at the end of the massage table, dangling his long legs. "It's beautiful in here, Nani. Like a resort."

"Thank you. I like to keep it special for my clients. Helps them relax, like a short get-away. Everybody needs a little pampering now and then." Nani pulled a slim pair of scissors from one of the rattan drawers and turned back toward him. If she wasn't mistaken, he'd been looking at her ass again. She gave no visible reaction but hoped he liked what he saw.

"Lean forward just a little." She circled behind him and began to snip along his hairline, evening out the cut.

"I thought Sunny only did men's hair," Hank said.

Nani snickered. "That was one of the Big Island secrets I didn't know. Turns out it's not that he won't do women ... it's that women won't go there. I'd been too busy to get to my own stylist in Kona, and my hair was so long it was dipping into the body oil while I worked. One day I caught it between a couple of the hot stones and pulled a chunk out. I needed a rush job, and Sunny complied. Took me a while to get rid of the way it slanted across my back."

She came around to the front to stare at him, her eyes squinting as she mentally measured. "And speaking of slants, your shoulders aren't straight today."

"The right one is sore," he admitted stretching it up and down in a circular motion.

"Stop that," she ordered. Nani the Therapist was in the house. "What did you do to it?"

"I'm building a plane – "

"You're building a Mooney?"

"Not a Mooney. A homebuilt called a Velocity. It's the only way I'll ever have a plane that's all my own. Anyway, I was glassing in the shelf that supports the top of the instrument panel. To do it, I had to lie on my back in the fuselage and work over my head. I felt something give. Not on the plane, but on me."

"Mind if I touch your shoulder? I might be able to tell what's going on."

"How?"

She felt her feathers ruffle just a little. He wasn't the only professional in the room. "Well it's what I *do*, Hank. Help people with pain. I've trained for it, and I've done it for years. Need to see my references?"

"Oh, no ... be my guest ... just remember, it's sore."

"Alright then. I'll just finish this cut ..." Snip, snip, snip. "Okay, it's short but even." She put the scissors back in the drawer and walked behind him. "Lean your head down and a little to the left."

Nani put her right hand on his neck, above the dark collar of his police shirt. She patted the area for a moment, then began a gentle stroke downward following the line of muscles to his bicep. While she worked, she said, "I'm trying to determine whether the damage is to the soft tissue or bone structure."

His muscles were tight under his sun browned skin. She had to loosen them so she began to dig a little deeper.

Hank sighed. It morphed into a slight groan. It must have been a groan of pleasure because Nani felt his shoulder relax a bit.

"Feel okay?"

"I think I'm purring." His eyes were shut and his upper body was slumping forward.

"That's good. It probably isn't the bones or it wouldn't feel quite that comfy." She stroked again, searching and exploring. "Hank, I think it might be a pulled rotator cuff. If so, it's going to hurt for a while yet. But that's all I can tell like this. If you want, I can give you a therapeutic massage to find out more."

"I ... I've never had one."

Nani felt him tense again. Most people were nervous the first time they had body work. They should be. Between the different kinds of acupuncture, reflexology, massage and chiropractic – along with varieties of just plain woo-woo – there were a lot of ways to hurt instead of help.

She came around to face him. "It's up to you. At best, I can relieve your pain. If not, I can give you advice about what to do next." She'd be disappointed if he said no. She wanted to show him the quality of work she could do. And, she had to admit to herself, that smooth brown skin felt as good to her as the massage did to him.

Hank looked into her eyes. "I'd be very glad to have you try. I'm tired of feeling like this."

For a longer beat than necessary, she met his gaze. *Blue ice.* Then she pulled away. "Right, then. Strip down to your shorts, and cover yourself with this sheet."

"Strip?"

"I need to work more than the shoulder because of the way muscle lines up and down. For instance, it can take massage to a hip to release a shoulder."

"Ah, sure. Okay."

"Cover up with the sheet, and lie with your face in the cradle."

"This donut-y looking thing?" He looked at the padded ring at one end of the table.

"Yep. I'll give you some privacy and be back."

Nani went to her narrow galley kitchen, cleaned up the malasada crumbs, brewed more coffee. It had been fun to ogle Hank, sure. He was a damn fine specimen. But it was time to quit playing around. Most therapists had experienced arousal with a client at some point in their lives, and it was considered a professional taboo if you couldn't get it under control.

When she thought enough time had passed, she knocked on the door to her spa. "Ready?"

"Come on in."

The room was warm with a pleasant breeze blowing in from the grotto. The music was soft. The oils scented the air.

"If you get cold, I can shut the door. Just let me know," Nani said.

"I'm good," Hank replied, his voice muffled from the padded donut that held his face.

Since this massage was exploratory, Nani didn't think she'd need hot stones, but she turned on a warmer anyway. She'd certainly need oil. A male client could be a problem if he was too hairy because it matted the delicate lubricants. Nani had learned to add olive oil to keep it from knotting.

When she rolled down the sheet enough to expose Hank's back, her first view was pure pleasure. Hair was not an issue. He had beautiful skin. Unblemished and smooth over well-developed muscles. Not a muscle man, but long lean power. Like a race horse. He was beautiful, and she caught herself staring. Her own skin began to tingle in response.

This is no way for a professional to think ... feel ... act!

Maybe her offer to assess his anatomy hadn't been such a smart idea. She changed her mind about which oil to use. Sandalwood was popular with men, but it was too sensual. She chose lemongrass and eucalyptus, both for their clean outdoorsy scents. Medicinal. Nothing passionate. Nani started with a gentle stroking to the shoulder muscles and gradually began to work across Hank's neck to the other shoulder, then down his back. After a few moments, she said, "Your muscles are very tight. People with stressful jobs often feel denser. Cops probably qualify near the top of the list."

"Mmmmm," he mumbled.

Dense tissue was harder on a therapist's hands. She was working hard, and the room suddenly felt too warm. She could feel her heart begin to beat faster. Her breath quickened. The repetition of her moves, stroking again and again, was softening his muscle tissue, but it was having quite another effect on hers. Her nipples hardened, and she felt that insistent tingle begin deep inside her own core.

Professional, hell. Nothing professional about it. I'm hot.

The feel and the visual pleasure of his beautiful body not only unleashed her desire but was now sending it into the danger zone. And she hadn't even gotten to the territory below his waist. She'd thought she'd been doing massages long enough that she had it under control. But she'd been wrong. It had been a long time since she'd wanted a man the way she wanted this one, right this second. She wanted to lean into him, to rub her breasts against his nakedness and run her tongue along his spine.

Stop!

This was all wrong. Nani pulled her hands away. "I have to stop now. I can't ..."

Hank lifted his head out of the cradle, propping himself up on an elbow. Now Nani could clearly hear his accelerated breath. His face was just inches from hers, his lips so close she could nearly taste them.

"Don't stop." Hank reached out toward her and began to push himself off the table. She was sure he was going to pull her into his arms and press her against his naked chest. It was exactly what she wanted. It was exactly what she didn't want.

"No!" she gasped, taking a step backwards just as his fingers reached her upper arm. She put her hands on her cheeks to hide the blush that she knew was there. "I'm ... so sorry. I think I'm getting too into this. I've overstepped my bounds."

"But, Nani ... I ..."

She moved further away and busied herself with putting the caps back on the oils. "I think your spine is out in the upper thoracic. You need a chiropractor or ... or a doctor for muscle relaxants. Not me. I can recommend someone, but you have to get dressed now."

She spun around and scooted from the room, hoping he hadn't smelled her body heat rising.

✦ ✦ ✦

Hands shaking, Hank dressed quickly, shoving his hard-on into his uniform pants. "Shit," he muttered to himself. She wasn't the only one out of bounds. "A man should make it through a professional massage without a fucking boner." He hoped Nani didn't think of him as Kamapua'a the Pig Man.

And the damn thing wasn't retreating either, not with the images dancing before his brain. Her breasts tight against her blouse. The feel of them on his arm when she reached across him to massage his opposite shoulder. He shivered with the recollection as he struggled back into his ten pound utility belt, complete with gun, cuffs, nightstick, flashlight and radio.

Goddammit.

She was the crime victim's family, and *he* was the cop. That was all there was to it. He should be more in control of himself.

✦ ✦ ✦

After Hank left, Nani needed physical work to replace physical longing. She washed the kitchen floor and cleaned the oven. It wasn't enough. So she scoured the downstairs bathroom sink, tub and toilet. She moved on to the front porch and worked until she was at last exhausted. That's when she finally allowed herself to think about what the hell had just happened.

Okay, he was an attractive guy. Sure. If this was just about sex, well, she could control that. But these particular waters were not so easy to navigate. This wasn't as simple as sex.

There was something about Hank that had all the earmarks of a relationship in the works. Fondness, longing, trust, or OMG, maybe even commitment. The last time *commitment* had gotten involved it had led to the disastrous break up with her fiancé.

More important than that, Hank was the cop and she was the victim's sister. Their roles were very clear and should not be clouded by other emotion. She needed him to find Maile more than she needed to find love.

Nani sighed. Then she started to defrost the freezer.

CHAPTER ELEVEN

Reflexology: Treatment or Just a Treat?
By Jackson O'Reilly
Excerpt from the *Keawalani Voice,* 2015

When this reporter takes his two dogs for a walk, they yelp. Yep. During interviews or investigations, my feet hurt.

I'd heard of reflexology, but it sounded bizarre. Besides, I'm ticklish. But desperation took me to Keawalani Hands Massage and Reflexology. If Nani Palea couldn't help my feet, she'd at least be easy on my eyes.

"So what is reflexology?" I asked removing my slippahs. Everything else stayed on, unlike a massage. A good thing since there are body types that shouldn't be sprung on a young woman.

Palea said, "When I use my thumbs and fingers on specific areas of your feet, hands, and ears, I can help relieve stress in different body organs and systems as well."

Huh?

"Conditions like asthma, anxiety, diabetes, headaches, sinusitis can all benefit."

"But what if I'm ticklish?" I said, afraid that the second she touched me, I might kick her in the nose.

"Lots of people are. But as you relax into the work I do, the toxins that cause that ticklish sensation can be released."

I clenched my teeth as she placed her hands on my feet and rubbed in scented oil. And you know what? It didn't tickle. Nor did it hurt. It felt good. The more she worked, the better I felt. I was soon wasting away in reflexology-ville.

"Massage manipulates muscles and fascia to release tension. Reflexology stimulates the nervous system to release tension. The two therapies work independently or together."

Palea doesn't claim to diagnose or cure. But she told me she could feel bone spurs in my feet. "I'm releasing the tension in the fascia now."

After my session, I considered whether there is really anything to it. After all, reflexology has been around for thousands of years in dozens of cultures. I strolled up the street, relaxed as a noodle. My dogs were happy, and even my sinuses felt clear.

I can hardly wait for my next appointment.

The door screeched as Nani opened it to enter the main hall. She caught it before it slammed shut. Experience had taught her to ease it closed gently, or it banged like a rifle shot. It was at least sixty years since the old building had been a school house, but Nani could still hear the ghostly sounds of school bells and small scuffling feet and chalk on blackboards. A chorus of little ones singing pagents or shouting at pep rallies echoed from the large room to the left that had once been the school auditorium.

Children no longer came to this school to have *Fun with Dick and Jane* or to practice penmanship. Now they came to learn who they were through the musical language of their culture. Nani's aunt and *kumu*, Hakumele, had acquired the abandoned school three decades ago and transformed it into her hula *halau* dance studio. Parents sought her out for her renowned mastery of the dance.

Ghostly clamor had been replaced with the real thing. Nani followed the recorded sound of *ipu heke* gourd drums and chanting into the main studio, the one-time auditorium. Hakumele had transformed this room from somber to brilliant. One wall was all mirrors, and a mural painted by Kaleo in his childhood splashed across another. It was an abstract that captured the essence of Hawaiian dance – dazzling costumes swirling around brown bodies in a frenzy of color and emotion. Nani had seen this sample of Kaleo's early talent when she danced here every day. Now she missed it.

The smell of boys sweating was not quite so pleasant to her senses. Her nose wrinkled. Eight boys, ages ten through fifteen, were dancing along with an assistant to Hakumele. They swaggered and leaped, pounded the floor, thrust their hips, shouted in response to the recording. Their practice shorts and tee-shirts were soaked with the effort. This was a *kahiko* dance for warriors, one that featured the power of the male body as much as its grace. This hula was preserved from a time before the missionaries, when masculine beauty was celebrated instead of concealed.

Nani sat in one of three metal folding chairs near the doorway. She watched the boys practice, concentrating on one who was – to someone who knew hula as intimately as she – clearly superior to the rest. The movements of his body were powerful, mesmerizing. She could not keep her feet still as her own body responded to the cadence of the drums and the drive of the chant.

Hakumele stood before the group, calling to one boy or another over the music, a drill sergeant perfecting her troops. A knee wasn't perfectly positioned ... a fist pounded the floor a fraction of a beat too soon ... a foot was too flat. The boys responded as though to the voice of God, hastily resetting the offending knee, fist or foot. Hakumele was taller than any of them and certainly broader. Her size alone would have cowed them. But Nani knew it was far more than that. Hakumele not only spoke of the island spirits, she spoke *to* them. She communicated with essences the rest of them couldn't see. The boys in this room – and the villagers in general – held this *kumu* in awe.

Hakumele stalked an invisible line in front of the boys, her enormous scarlet muumuu billowing gracefully as she swayed back and forth. Nani imagined an oversized cat on the hunt in a forest of blooming *'ohi'a* trees. She sobered, though, when she noticed the gray now in her aunt's tight topknot of braids, not a single hair daring to escape. Aunt Hakumele was no longer young, but still the two had not buried the hard feelings between them.

At last, Hakumele held up a hand, and her assistant scurried to turn off the music. The *kumu* allowed the dancers to drop to the floor, and there they sprawled, no longer warriors but smelly, exhausted boys. The kumu let them rest, but she continued to pace before them, round face stern with wrinkles embedded from five decades in the Big Island sun. "Boys! This hula is the story of the god Maui battling with Death. He is terrified and alone in a volcanic hell, driven on by duty to mankind. A trusted bird betrays him, awakening the Guardian of Life, a reptile woman who snaps Maui in two with her ragged sharp teeth, then swallows him. Maui never returns, leaving his wife and children to grieve. And so, to this day, death goes unconquered."

She paused, hands on hips, staring from boy to boy. "This is a story of battle and loss, struggle and sorrow. You must feel the courage and fear of the warrior Maui and the grief of his family. If you do not feel the story, you will never tell it properly. And we'll never understand why men must die. Now go home. And do nothing but practice."

The boys scrambled up and said their mahalos and alohas to their *kumu*. When the boy that Nani had particularly noticed approached Hakumele, she said, "Kala, you will stay a moment."

The rest left, and the room fell silent. Nani stood to come forward and let Hakumele know she was there. But somehow, having never looked her way, the kumu already knew.

She always knew everything when I was a kid. Why should anything be different now?

"Mahalo for coming," the *kumu* said meeting Nani eye to eye, but not with a customary hug and kiss. Hakumele had left a message with Kaleo that Nani was to come at this specific time. Not to come if she *could* ... just to come.

"Of course," Nani said. "I will always answer your call." Of course Nani would comply. Hakumele had been a beloved authority in her life for many years, both as teacher and aunt. Nani would do nearly anything to clear the stormy weather between them – nearly anything but the one thing Hakumele wanted. Nani would no longer perform the joyous hulas that had made her a champion once and could do it again. That elation had disappeared with Maile.

"You saw this boy, Kala, dance, yes? Kala, this is the famed Wailelenani Palea," Hakumele said.

The boy's dark eyes widened in delight. "You were the great champion of this halau."

Nani smiled but shook her head. "The great champion was Hakumele. I was just the next champion."

"And I will be the third," the boy claimed with a thirteen-year-old's surety that his dream would come true.

Nani knew it could. It had for her. From what she had seen, he was still far from perfect, but he had the fluid lines, an innate grasp of the island rhythm, and was already drawing the eye from others to himself. One day, this boy could be a champion. "Then you must work hard and listen to your *kumu*," she said to him.

"Yes, ma'am," Kala answered, staring at her with obvious awe. It must be her dancing reputation or a thirteen-year-old's crush. Either was charming.

"You may go now, Kala. Aloha," Hakumele said with a face that softened almost to a smile. Nani assumed all the *kumu's* students knew that, beneath her gruff exterior, a big heart beat for them as resolutely as the gourd drums.

With a slight bow toward each woman and one last long look at Nani, the boy ran from the room yelling for the others to wait for him.

Hakumele sat gingerly on one of the folding chairs and indicated to Nani that she should take another. "You are well? You and Kaleo?"

"We are very well, Auntie. And you?"

But Hakumele ignored the inquiry and went right to business. "I need your expertise with Kala. Not as a dancer since you refuse me that, but as a therapist."

The grudge saddened Nani because she loved this old woman, but it pissed her off, too. Neither of them seemed able to give in. Like aunt, like niece. Like teacher, like student.

"What therapy does the boy require?" Nani asked.

"You have seen in just the moments you watched that Kala is special. He will be my masterpiece before I die."

Guess I've been written out of history.

"But lately, something's not right. I sense it." Alarm clouded Hakumele's full moon face. "Something about his hands and feet, eating from within. Threatening his movements. This frightens me."

Nothing much frightened Hakumele. This was serious, and Nani the Therapist went to the rescue. "What can I do?"

"See the boy. Examine his limbs. Tell me he will be well. Or if he will not, fix him."

"Of course, Auntie." Nani pulled out her phone and called up her schedule. "His parents can bring him ... ah ... a week from today, in the afternoon."

The older woman stood. "I will bring him tomorrow before your day with other clients begins. We'll be there at seven. Mahalo." With that, Hakumele swayed toward the door to her office at the back of the studio. She paused, turned, nodded royally to Nani, and disappeared into the inner sanctum.

Nani sighed. Her aunt was opinionated, unreasonable, irritating. But she had made Nani a champion. And long before that, she had taught Nani and Kaleo about Hawaiian spirits and the connectedness of all things. Her message of balance between intuition, intellect and emotion lived within Nani.

When Maile disappeared, this auntie had been their only source of comfort. After their father disappeared and their mother died, it was Hakumele who had stepped in. She'd fought for Nani's claim on the house, promising to oversee the young woman's safety, and she'd taken care of Kaleo until he was old enough to fly solo. Hakumele was the only true family the siblings had left.

And yet, Nani had dealt her a deep blow by refusing the hulas that expressed her kumu's beliefs. How could she restore their relationship? Nani felt capable of most things, but it seemed to her that this was too high an obstacle to see the other side.

She stood to go. This time she allowed the front door to bang. Nani motored away on her Vespa, her long skirt floating in the breeze. She knew she'd never again deny her aunt another thing, so she would see the boy Kala tomorrow. But she wondered how Kaleo would feel about preparing breakfast by 6:30 in the morning.

✦   ✦   ✦

Hank hadn't pulled into Nani's driveway. He'd parked across the street when he saw her leave home on that damn Vespa. He worried that she wasn't safe. He worried that another man might also be enjoying the flash of her smooth brown legs. He just had to figure out exactly what to say, how to act in order to get their relationship back on track.

Thoughts of Nani had been heating up his nights, ever since that day in her massage room. It kept him from sleep. During the day he took it out on the criminals who looked at him cross-eyed. He was hard on his co-workers, too, apparently, since Captain Lono told him to either back off or fuck off.

He wanted things the way they had been with Nani. He wanted to be someone she was comfortable with, someone dependable. Someone to trust. She was the kind of woman that could make him be that kind of man. She was the kind of woman who would accept nothing less.

But he'd been a dick-for-brains screw up moving too fast. What was his best approach now? Ignore what had happened in that massage room? Apologize? Tell her what he was beginning to feel? Would it scare her? It scared him. There were so many ways to play the scene he was goddamn guaranteed to choose the wrong one. With a sigh, he powered up the Honda and eased out of the neighborhood, looking for any raggedy-assed criminal to bust.

CHAPTER TWELVE

My Book of Revelation
Excerpt from the Year 2003

The *Keawalani Voice* hadn't arrived when I came down for breakfast this morning, but the whole village would already know that Maile Palea disappeared. Gossip here moves at tsunami speed. The walls have eyes and see all. Just try to get away with something in Keawalani, and you'll know what I mean. You have to be very, very careful if you plan to so much as cross against a light.

Ma was frying Spam for Father and us kids. The scent of food made me want to hurl, but I had to gag it down. Father can spot unusual behavior as easy as a mongoose spots a rat. He'd drag the whole story out of me if I made one false step. Now more than ever, the innocent me must hide the guilty me. I've had practice lying, but I am terrified that I'll blubber like a baby.

I need Ma now. Can I trust her? Would she help me or just tell the Bad Ass what I've done? What should I do?

Oh, Jesus be kind. Jesus be gentle. Tell me who to trust.

Father knows that the dentist's place where I babysat last night is next door to the Lopaka's. He demanded to know what happened. He's given us kids the stink eye so often that his face is stuck in a permanent scowl. Mooshed up like a fat fist. He always assumes I'm a know-nothing so it was no surprise to him when I said I knew nothing about Maile, only what the search party had said. I flew under his radar. Phew.

I'm dying to talk with my BF. It's making me crazy. Okay, crazier. He can't come here or even call. Not only is he a *boy*, he's a boy tainted with Filipino blood. It would spoil the reputation of a lily white girl like me to be seen with him. They're such bigots, my parents. Upstanding members of a church at the ass end of the word of God. And Father is the biggest Bad Ass of all.

I had to get through my home lessons. Ma didn't even notice I'd started a new notebook. She won't ask about this one now. Another bullet dodged.

It felt like a century, waiting until I could get away. Finally, I left to do the laundry for the Keawalani Inn. They hire Ma to do it. But it's mostly me – she told them I'm sixteen. The Bad Ass believes if I'm working, nobody's getting in my pants. Ha ha.

It takes all afternoon, washing and drying and folding in the Inn's laundry room. I mend things, too, like their sheets and pillowcases. I sew really good. By early evening, I deliver tidy loads to the housekeeper's closet before I go home. I always smell like jacaranda by then from the flowery soap they use. I hate it. BF likes it, though. He touches my skin and says it is soft as petals. He usually meets me after my shift and walks me as close to home as is safe. That's how he gets his nightly feel under my blouse.

Today, I called him from the laundry room as soon as the maids delivered the last of the dirty linens. Sometimes, if they come up short on maids, the Inn gives me a few bucks to clean rooms, too. I like it because the Bad Ass doesn't know about that cash so I keep it. I'm building my own little stash.

It's lucky the Inn didn't need extra hours from me today. BF told me to come to his place NOW! He has Maile hidden there. He said she didn't look good. He sounded really scared.

I started up the two industrial washers. Normally, I'd sit and mend until the wet sheets are ready for the dryers. But today, I ran over to the WikiWiki Fix garage. I'd have to catch up on the mending later.

BF's place is above the garage. The owner knows he's up there, but told him to keep quiet about it since it isn't a real living space. In exchange, BF keeps an eye on the shop overnight. And they teach him about cars a couple hours after school on days when there's no soccer practice. He wants to be an ASE mechanic when he graduates. He has a future, not that my parents would care.

To get up there unseen, I have to stay outside the fence that goes around the back of the building – plastic strips woven thru the chainlink mostly hide me. I climb up the fire stairs between the dumpster and oil recycling tanks. The steps are rickety old metal, and BF's door is at the top. It's really just a storage area, but he's made it okay. He uses the shop's bathroom downstairs at night when he does rounds. Nobody ever sees me go up there. We always wait 'til everyone else is gone for the night.

But not today. I had to take the chance that some busybody would see me since the shop was open and working. At least, I didn't have to worry about being heard. It was too noisy for anybody to hear anything upstairs. Nobody could hear me climb the stairs no matter how much they rattled. Nobody could hear a little kid cry either.

Oh, Maile, I am so sorry.

My boyfriend grabbed me when I got there, pulled me in and slammed the door behind me. He should be in school but they don't know where he lives, not since his brother blew himself up cooking meth, and his parents left town. His folks don't like him any more than mine like me. We're a matched set that way. I really, really love him.

But that's not what I mean to be writing about. I'm writing about Maile. She was on an air mattress, the one BF usually uses. He'd covered her with a sheet I stole once upon a time from the laundry, one too worn for them to use anymore.

I asked him what she had said.

"Not a fucking thing." His voice sounded tight, plucked like a guitar string. "She's never woke up."

What does that mean? How could she still be asleep almost a whole day after it happened?

Criminy.

"We need a doctor." He sounded close to losing it.

I put my hands on his face, one on each cheek. "We can't, my love. Now let me look." I crouched beside her and saw he'd made an effort to patch her head with garage rags. It wasn't bleeding anymore anyway. There was some gooey stuff caked there but nothing oozy and fresh. She should be better then, yeah?

I patted her cheek. It felt cold. "Wake up now, Maile." I gently shook her, coaxed her. Nothing.

"Maybe we should take her home. Just leave her in front of her house and then run away." BF sounded even more scared than I am.

I told him no. "We'd be seen. They'd accuse us of hurting her on purpose. We'd go to jail. Let me see what I can do. I take care of my little brother and sister lots of the time."

Maybe she should sit up. Maybe her head needed to be higher than her feet so stuff could drain. Snot and stuff. I pulled Maile up by her arms, but she just slumped against me.

"She feels cold." And she stank of piss. Her shorts were wet.

BF stopped saying anything. Maybe he was mad at me. But he brought me clean garage rags, hot with water he heated on his hot plate. He had hand wash powder, too. I put Maile back down and began to clean her, top to bottom. So little, so delicate. Sacred flower.

She seemed to relax with the warmth from the rags. I felt her muscles loosen. Her eyelashes fluttered.

"It's helping, yeah?" BF finally spoke. He sounded excited.

But then I smelled shit. Maile's shallow breathing stopped. With a tiny gasp, it started again. Then it stopped once more.

I waited. One beat, two, ten. But there was no more. That was all. *Oh merciful God, no. No.*

"She's gone. Maile has passed." I felt sick with sorrow. And guilt. And dread. We sat stone still on the air mattress, staring at Maile's fragile body. No sound but the impact wrenches, hammering, grinding, and awful music from the shop below.

Dear Jesus. Be with this sweet broken bird on her journey home to You.

CHAPTER THIRTEEN

Beach Board Bingo: It's Bitchin'!
By Jackson O'Reilly
Excerpt from the *Keawalani Voice*, 2015

A surfer may have a wide variety of boards in his quiver. Longboards and short, paddleboards, fish-, boogie-, or bodyboards. And a surfer may be an old grey belly, a gidget, a shark biscuit, a shubie who has equipment but never really surfs, a paddlepuss who stays in the waves along the beach, or a hang eleven if a male surfs in the nude.

A surfer may perform aerial tricks, shoveits, turtle rolls, duck dives, and slashes on rollers that are barrellers, ankle busters, or party waves where everyone gets aboard. And when the day is done, there'll be plenty of bad backs, sprained ankles and noodle arms to go around.

Surfing started in Hawaii long before Captain Cook claimed the islands. One thing fo' shua … as long as we ride the waves, the language of surfing will roll on and on.

And another sure thing? On primo Big Island days with offshore winds, a certain Keawalani tattoo artist will be there on the beach, offering the babes lessons on the boards … and, I suppose, on all kinds of smooth rides.

Nani awoke to the scent of rich Kona coffee. She quickly showered, wound herself in a floral sarong and knotted her damp hair in a bright lavender scrunchie. Then she followed the life-giving aroma to the kitchen. Kaleo had bellyached about it last night, but he'd gotten up in time to make breakfast before her seven o'clock appointment with Auntie Hakumele.

When she padded barefoot into the bright little galley, there was coffee but no Kaleo. The only sign of breakfast was an empty bowl and spoon on the breakfast nook table. No cut fruit, no toast, hell, not even the jug of milk and box of Special K. Nani deduced her Brother the Louse had merely set the timer on the coffee pot and put out the bowl the night before. She marched out the kitchen door onto the lanai.

"Rise and shine!" she burst cheerfully to the bear-sized mound under the covers on Kaleo's bed. Looking around for a weapon, she trilled, "Face the new day!"

"Mrhpygt?"

"Why? Because *you* will entertain Auntie Hakumele while I work on the boy." Nani spotted the houseplant spray bottle on the sill below a window screen. That would do.

"Uptgtjo …"

"She will *too* want to see you. You know you're her favorite." Nani grabbed up the bottle.

"Pkduwy!"

"Such language!" She pulled back the covers and sprayed water directly into her brother's face. "Now haul ass."

"You ... you ..." Kaleo rose up, drying his face on his sheet.

"You know you love me, little brother."

"It ain't easy, big sister."

By the time Hakumele arrived with Kala, Nani was still not fed, but she had dressed. Her cap-sleeved purple tee revealed the firm muscles in her tawny arms. Physical bodywork on others kept her strong.

She gave her aunt a two-page form to fill out for Kala and escorted her to the kitchen where Kaleo would make her breakfast. He hadn't visited his aunt for a while, and Nani saw no reason for them to grow apart just because Hakumele and she were at odds.

Besides, it'll keep him from going back to bed. Heh.

Then she took Kala to the salon for a short, evaluative session. He was more standoffish than he had been in the dance studio. Nani knew why. "You can leave all your clothes on except your *slippahs*. And nothing will hurt. We're just exploring today."

Knowing he would not be hurt – and not be nude – did the trick. Kala stopped chewing his lip and gave her a faint smile. But something else was bothering the boy. She was sure of it.

"First, soak your feet in this." Nani filled a basin with warm water and scented Epsom salts. The mixture quickly hydrated Kala's feet so his skin would more readily absorb oil during his session. Nani started all her reflexology clients this way. It softened their feet so they were receptive to her work. Softening their skin also helped protect her own sensitive hands.

"Now hop up on this table and lie on your back." For the next half hour Nani reflexed Kala's feet and ankles, asking a few questions and changing this move or that based on his answers. She then moved on to his hands.

"I like it," Kala said, relaxing into the work. But Nani heard the apprehension in his voice. "My *kumu* is worried. That makes *me* worry. Will I have to give up dance?"

For a child with dreams of becoming a champion, this must be terrifying. Nani patted his shoulder and looked him steadily in his eyes. "No, sir. Not if I have any say in the matter. That's a promise from one champion to the next."

His relieved smile was a sunbeam. She could only hope she'd told him the truth. The brief session had revealed a mystery to her, one that she needed to solve. But she didn't tell him about it.

When they were done, Nani and Kala went out to the kitchen to find their *kumu*. There she was, nearly overwhelming the narrow galley with her mass, serving up a platter of Hawaiian sweet bread french toast to Kaleo. She'd made enough for Kala, Nani and half of Keawalani, as well.

"Kaleo," Nani said sternly. "I thought you were going to host Auntie, not the other way around."

"I don't know, Nani. She just didn't seem all that interested in Special K. So I told her that her french toast would be okay." His dark eyes sparkled with humor as he poured the lilikoi syrup he loved.

Hakumele gave Nani a cold glance. "Cereal is not a proper breakfast for a man."

Nani silently groaned. *Once again, I'm below expectations.*

When Kala finished his second piece of sweet bread, Hakumele sent him out to the car to wait for her. She told him she had to pay for his session. As soon as he was out of earshot, she turned to Nani, worry lines cut deep into her brow. "Tell me what you have found. Tell me the boy will dance."

"I feel hostile activity in his feet, but not much. In fact, I am amazed, Auntie, that you sensed it when there is as yet no visual clue." A little soft soap was never a bad idea. "To my hands, it feels like those air pockets in bubble wrap. Only miniscule. Tiny globules of toxic substance that should be worked out."

"You can do this?"

"Yes, with a little time, but – "

"And he will be a champion?"

Nani was careful how she answered. Soft soap yes, false hopes no. "There are toxins in his body, Auntie, more than usual for such a young boy. It is not bad enough to think in terms of liver or lung problems. But it could worsen. I can help stop it, but we need to discover why the toxins are there to begin with."

She picked up the papers that Hakumele had completed on Kala's behalf and skimmed through them. She stopped when she read his full name. "Kala Nawahine," she said looking up. "Is he related to John Nawahine?"

"Yes. John is his grandfather. Kala lives with him."

Nani frowned. "I will need weekly appointments for a while. Can you arrange that with Mr. Nawahine?"

"John Nawahine counts on me to make his grandson a champion. If you need to see Kala, Kala will be here."

Nani and Hakumele set up a schedule while Kaleo cleared the table and loaded the dishwasher. Even though their aunt neglected to pay for the session after all, Nani was glad she'd be working with the boy. She needed to do a little research on her own before telling Hakumele any more, but she thought she knew just what was wrong with him. If so, she could help him. But only if his family did, too.

✦ ✦ ✦

Nani's mother Kina had taught her all about plumeria, also known as the lei flower or frangipani. Years ago, they would stand beneath a shower of petals as the gnarled little trees dropped their blossoms in the early mornings. Before going inside, Kina would twine the velvety blossoms in Nani's hair over her right ear. The flower rain was one of the happy memories from before Maile's disappearance.

The propeller-shaped blossoms flourished all over the island lowlands clustered on trees with shiny dark leaves. They were especially fragrant at night. Nani's mom said they liked the thicker, cooler air. The oils that produced the sweet scent on the petals didn't evaporate as quickly then, so they perfumed the air more pungently. Their intoxicating aroma invaded the heads of *haoles*, following them back to the mainland as one of the most exotic reminders of paradise.

No matter how much she knew, Nani wasn't as expert about plumeria as John Nawahine, the man who grew more varieties than any other Big Islander. He was something of a local hero, employing many Keawalani villagers. One of them was a Keawalani Hands client.

Tiny Vincent Moi had told Nani all about the grower's operation in his sessions. Mr. Nawahine started his plants in well ventilated sunny greenhouses, using a mix of top soil, clay, organic compost, and crushed lava rock. His goal was to create plumeria hybrids hardy enough to live in higher altitudes so that *haoles* could buy the starts to take home. In the meantime, he sold his blossoms through the most popular Big Island gardens.

Vincent Moi came to Nani monthly, often with a bouquet of blossoms in some radical new bittersweet orange or unique star shape, smelling unexpectedly of spice or citrus. Nani took them gratefully, because all women love flowers. Unless they have allergies. But, in truth, she preferred the traditional, less experimental varieties. The kind her sister Maile had also loved.

Vincent Moi spent his days lifting bags of slow release fertilizer or bending over to hand groom fragile seedlings. His back, knees and feet showed the stress of such arduous work for so many years. Nani and a chiropractor maintained his body so he could continue with his job. Nani wished he could come more frequently than once a month, but she knew he could barely afford his maintenance program as it was.

During sessions in the last three months, his problems had taken a new turn. It started with nausea that didn't seem to go away. Chronic congestion was causing him to wheeze. Reflexing his feet, Nani had begun to feel tiny bubble wrap globules ... the same kind she had discovered in Kala's feet but far more advanced.

Kala and Moi were both denizens of John Nawahine's plumeria farm.

Nani's best work for Kala might be a serious conversation with Vincent Moi. She would have called him right away, but the old man would be at work. Besides, his next appointment was already set for tomorrow. It could wait until then.

In the meantime, the limo arrived to take Nani to her afternoon appointment with Mrs. Cunningham and Emelina. They were in far better moods than the last time she'd seen them.

Weed Boy must have stopped his thieving.

Nani was tickled about that, and she enjoyed a good gossip with Mrs. C and Emelina about the comings and goings in the village, good fortunes and bad.

"You know Akela Onekea?" asked Mrs. Cunningham. "Maggie Wilson's man."

It took Nani a moment because she hadn't heard his last name aloud before. "Akela. You mean the one who buses dishes nights at the Big Island Girl?"

"That's him," Emelina answered. "Been there for donkey's years. But that's not his main job."

"Just listen to what's happened now." Mrs. Cunningham explained that many of the gardeners who raked, mowed, watered and tweezed the grounds at Puako Bay planted a few of their own vegetables under remote shrubs where the residents wouldn't see or be bothered by them. It might be the only land they had available to raise a little food for their families.

"Who are they hurting?" Emelina interjected with a frown.

"Akela got caught weeding a yellow squash vine he had hidden, and the management made an example of him. Fired him on the spot."

"Bad business," Emelina said. "Man works hard all day then picks up dishes at night? He and his family need the food, or he wouldn't be doing it. It's a shame."

Nani agreed. Why couldn't people with so much cut some slack for a guy with so little? They chatted on into the afternoon as Nani worked first on Mrs. Cunningham then on Emelina. Each client in her turn told Nani the good news that absolutely no money had gone missing since they'd seen her last. Mrs. Cunningham was no longer worried about Alzheimer's; Emelina thought she must have been wrong about the grandson.

Nani was eager to tell Kaleo that they'd solved the women's problem. At least she was tickled until Mrs. Cunningham walked her out to the limousine. Just at that second, Packer came slouching around the side of the magnificent home. He must have been sunning by the pool out back because he was only wearing a bathing suit. She'd know that scrawny chest anywhere.

His *tutu* introduced them. "Nani's done so much for me, Patrick," Mrs. Cunningham said. "She keeps me walking."

Packer stared squinty-eyed at Nani. "You look real familiar."

"Oh, I imagine everyone in Keawalani has seen each other many times before," Nani said with a nervous little laugh.

"No, it's more than that ... it's ..." His eyes narrowed into slits. "You hang with a big guy named Kaleo?"

"Kaleo is Nani's brother," said Mrs. Cunningham amiably.

Busted! Packer, drug addled or not, had remembered where he'd seen her before.

Oh well. He won't tell or he'll give himself away. She said her good-byes and ducked into the limousine. By the time the driver dropped her at home, she'd quit worrying. She found her brother, and they clinked glasses of Fire Rock Pale Ale to toast their success.

Then she began to think about Akela Onekea.

✦　✦　✦

Kaleo didn't own a car. He saw no reason to. Nearly anywhere he wanted to go was just a walk or a Vespa or a thumb away. But sometimes he was toting his longboard, and not many people stopped to pick up a huge hitchhiker with a nine foot six inch carry-on.

When he needed one, Kaleo rented a beater from the WikiWiki Fix Garage. Sometimes he'd take the upper road over to Honolii Beach north of Hilo for a couple days of surfing. Where the ocean met the river was one of his favorite spots for experienced boarders only, crowded with sharp rocks and tiger sharks more than with tourists. If he couldn't find a crib for the night with a local cutie, then the car would do. He always parked as close as he could to the cliff that overlooked the beach.

It wasn't Honolii that was calling him today. He had work to do that required wheels. The judge who had closed down his Tat Joint for a few months hadn't exactly said that Kaleo couldn't ink elsewhere. He'd decided to set up shop on Nani's lanai. He'd bring over his so-called portable tattoo kit. The plain aluminum case looked lean and mean, like it might hold a hitman's AK47. It was loaded with Kaleo's tat guns, needles, inks, power supply and various grips, trays and stencils. He'd also need enough space to load his tat chair, magnifying glass lamp and body art bed.

When he walked into the garage, he saw Hank's patrol car up on a lift. A local high school dropout nicknamed Motorhead was working under it, on what appeared to Kaleo to be the exhaust system. Motorhead wasn't a mechanic certified by anyone's association, but he was widely known as a car whisperer, nearly magic at keeping old vehicles humming.

Kaleo waved a shaka then went through to the office in search of the WikiWiki Fix owner. "For just one day," he said holding up an index finger. Kaleo did this so often, no more conversation was necessary. The owner knew he needed something big enough for his board so he went out back to find whatever gas hog would start that morning.

While he waited, Kaleo turned and put his back against the counter, resting on his elbows. He stared at Hank who was sitting in one of the knife-sliced-and-duct-taped chairs, waiting for his car.

"Howzit?" Kaleo said. "Haven't seen so much of you lately."

"Busy with bad guys," Hank replied. "No news on Maile to report."

"Sort of thought it was my other sister holding your attention these days."

Hank looked surprised. "So you've noticed."

Kaleo snorted. "Hell, Hank, I've noticed volcanoes around here, too. An ocean ... blue sky ..."

Hank shut the *Motor Trend* and tossed it back on the stack of tires that served as an end table. "Not so sure she wants me around anymore."

Kaleo leaned toward a little wooden counter dispenser with the slogan, "When you pick, pick WikiWiki Fix!" He twisted a knob and doled out a toothpick, then chewed on it for a while, rolling it from one side of his mouth to the other. Nani wasn't always predictable but one thing he knew *fo' shua* ... she'd boil over at him like Kilauea for nosing around her private territory. So he merely nodded sagely. "Hard to read a woman, *bruddah*."

"Yep. You think you'll be glad when they're not around. But then you miss them." Hank looked sad as a basset.

"True story." Kaleo munched on the pick for a while longer then couldn't help himself. Hank may be a cop, but he seemed like a good guy. He had to offer some kind of hope so he said, "Nani's like a guy, you know? You can mostly say what you mean with her. She'll tell you what she's thinking flat out."

Hank raised an eyebrow, appearing to tuck away Kaleo's pearl of wisdom. Then he changed the subject to safer territory. "What are you here for today?"

"Renting a car. Gonna move some stuff over to the house." He didn't get more specific because the deputy might just question whether his plan was compliant with the judge's wishes.

"Nani know you're adding more clutter to your domain?" Hank asked.

"No. And don't tell her."

"Thought you could just say what you mean."

"Maybe. But with all women? Usually best to tell them as little as possible."

The WikiWiki Fix owner pulled a 1992 red – now sun faded to pink – Volvo station wagon to the front of the shop.

"Ah," Kaleo said. "Pink Floyd." He'd rented the clunker before, often enough to name it. It didn't have air, it didn't have power anything, and its exterior was littered with rusty dents like a bad case of acne. But like everything else maintained by Motorhead, it went from point A to B reliably. And there was plenty of cargo room to move his office equipment.

✦ ✦ ✦

According to Nani's hands, Vincent Moi's condition hadn't gotten worse. But it wasn't any better. As if it were the most natural topic in the world, she asked, "Are plumeria susceptible to lots of insects?"

"Insects ... fungus ... all kine," the little man said, his eyes squeezed shut as Nani worked to clear the toxins from his system. His expressive face told her exactly which move felt good and which created pain. Most clients were unaware that body workers read faces for valuable clues.

"Tell me more about it."

"You like da cooties?" Vincent asked, perhaps beginning to wonder about Nani's sudden interest.

No, Nani didn't like bugs, but she had to find the truth. "Oh, just curious, uncle. Always interested in other people's jobs."

"Eh! We fight scale and spider mites all da time. Big job. Wash under all da leaf wid insecticide soap. Or mites kill new growth at tips."

"Interesting. Anything else bother the plumeria?"

"Plenty udda bugs. Borers, white flies, thrips. Everyting wants grind our plants. And now, the worst! Orange spore fungus called plumeria rust. *Plants* against plants. Very bad. Tough to kill. Take away infected leaves from ground to stop infection. If that fails, gotta use strong fungicide or tree could die."

"Has there been any change lately? I mean in how you treat the plants?"

Vincent Moi pursed his lips. He opened one eye to peer at her. "Fo' what you ask this, Nani?"

"Uncle, it's important."

He stretched his eyebrows up and the corners of his mouth down. He squeezed his eyes shut again. Finally, he spoke. "Mr. Nawahine, he buys a new fungicide. Cheaper. Some ingredients come from China."

"Do you think there is something wrong with it, uncle? Are your co-workers getting skin rashes? Eyes tearing?"

Moi was silent.

"Uncle, you must tell me. It could be poisoning you."

"No complain, Nani. We lose our jobs. What we can do?"

"But what if it is poison? You could be in danger."

"No can, Nani! Need work."

"But Mr. Nawahine may not know what's happening. You could tell him – "

"But he *may*. We stop talk now. You work."

He was the client. Nani honored his request to hush and continued working his ankles, the only sound the "Kona Interlude" CD playing slack key guitar softly in the background. But her thoughts were loud in her head.

CHAPTER FOURTEEN

Birds of a Feather Craft Together
By Jackson O'Reilly
Excerpt from the *Keawalani Voice*, 2015

Clara and Clea Fern look as alike as two o'o birds. They're both slender as reeds, they both wear glasses worthy of Elton John, and they both have mastered creating feather leis, a dying art that far predates flower leis.

This reporter saw the sisters recently in the village park under the banyan tree. Piles of thread, long strips of fabric, a selection of needles, and small tubs of feathers littered the picnic table in front of the two like a colorful fortress.

"How are you, aunties?" I asked. One was cutting individual feathers into the proper shape as the other sewed them onto a velvet band. "That must take the patience of Job."

"This is nothing," said Clea who may or

may not be the older of the two. "The one with real patience was the poor SOB who was the feather gatherer for royalty."

"That's right," Clara added. "Kings and queens who wore feather capes centuries ago had designated bird catchers."

"So our birds are now as extinct as our royalty?" I asked.

"Jackson O'Reilly. Haven't you learned anything in all your years here?" Clea was the touchier of the two. "The birds weren't killed, you nincompoop. Birds are power. They reach the heavens and see farther than the likes of us. Who'd kill that?"

Clara the Sweeter said, "The bird catcher had to be ever so patient. He put sap on tree limbs to capture a bird during its molting season when its feathers were loose. He removed just a few that would soon grow back, cleaned the bird's feet and released it. A renewable resource like wool on a sheep."

"It wasn't Hawaiians that made songbirds extinct," Clea harrumphed. "Imported diseases and habitat loss did that."

"We don't kill them just for feathers now, either. The feathers we use are from domestic and game birds killed to eat, or raised in aviaries, or dead of natural causes."

It takes many hours to make a feather lei or hatband. And what do the sisters do with the leis they create?

"We sell to tourists at craft shows for hundreds of dollars each," said Clea the Touchy.

Clara the Sweeter added, "We sometimes give them to our friends." With that she placed a splendid Kalij pheasant feather into what little hair I have left.

An unsolved mystery made Hank uneasy. He worried one like a tongue on a sore tooth, poking, poking, poking. It didn't have to be a big unknown. If he had nothing else immediately pressing, he could even indulge in free floating fretting. About killer bees. Or where that other sock goes. Or how you can eat an ounce of beer nuts but gain a pound.

But today, Hank had something far more significant on his mind. He sat in Frank Lono's office, mulling over Maile and the Martin family. Shutters over the only window allowed the breeze in but filtered out the afternoon sun. Here on the flank of Mauna Kea the heat was rarely as intense as lower down the hillsides, so there were many afternoons that needed no air conditioning. That was fortunate because the AC unit in the police station belched more racket than cold air.

Lono was pretending to be too busy with current crime to concentrate on a cold case, thumbing through file folders and requisitions and junk mail that littered his desk. Hank knew that, despite his captain's attempt to appear disinterested, he'd been listening to every word. Lono hated an unsolved mystery, too. That's what made them good cops.

"When we were at the barber shop, Sunny told us Lynn and Marty Martin's father was impotent by the time of Maile's disappearance. And Allison has confirmed that he's dead. Lost a battle with diabetes."

Lono nodded, flipping through a catalog of exorbitant snacks from Big Island Candies, goodies that few locals could afford. Hank didn't think Lono's girth could afford it either, not that he would say it out loud.

"But somebody hurt those two when they were kids. If it wasn't their father, the perp could still be around. We have to find him whether he had anything to do with Maile or not, in case other kids are in danger. I need to talk to Mrs. Martin again, see if she might suspect anyone else."

Lono tossed the catalog into the circular file.

"Neither of us thinks Lynn and Marty had anything to do with Maile's disappearance."

"Us?" Lono asked, looking up from the clutter. His craggy face was handsome enough with its high cheek bones, but it looked too big under the short fringe of hair Sonny had left. "Who's us?"

"Did I say us?" *Shit.* Hank cringed. That was a mistake.

"Yeah, you did. And since you and *I* didn't interview them, I assume you and somebody else is *us.* I'm a trained detective, you know."

Hank's skin reddened under his tan. "Ah, when I flew over to Oahu, I took Nani Palea with me. On my day off. Not wasting work time on a cold case, no sir. Thought she'd have a lot to offer."

Lono grinned at him hugely.

"I mean a lot to offer in terms of ... enhancing the interview. What with being family of the missing and all."

Lono continued to smirk, apparently content to let his officer wallow.

"Martina Martin is gone now, moved to Honolulu. But I want to talk with her again to find out – "

"Hey, *cuz,*" Lono said, finally holding up his hand in a cop's stop gesture. "Can't see why any man wouldn't want a shot at Nani Palea. The girl's a sweetheart with great tits. She return your affection?"

"Yeah. Is she interested in catching a cop?" Allison strolled into Lono's office with the day's mail. She dumped it on the rest of the debris.

"- to find out more about Martina's husband," Hank finished, unable to bury the heat in his voice any better than in his face.

Damn it. Does everyone know how I feel about Nani? Everyone except Nani?

"Officer Lindsey's got a crush," Allison said with a wink to Lono.

Jesus.

Hank stood. "The hell with you both." He stalked toward the door.

"Hold on, hold on," Lono said as Allison slipped out of his office, her head just passing beneath Hank's chin. "Village folks will miss Martina Martin now she's gone to Honolulu. But as a consolation prize, they'll enjoy a good gossip about her. Talk to her old neighbors. You'll get more out of them than her. And Hank?"

"Sir?" Hank said, still irritated at his boss.

"Nani Palea is good people. I admire how she's juggled a peck of lemons life has thrown at her. Losing Maile, her mom, her dad running off ... and hell, without her influence, we'd be seeing a lot more of that brother of hers. You couldn't do much better than Nani."

Hank considered telling him to mind his own business. But what he really wanted was to prattle on and on about her. About the atmospheric changes when she walked toward him, how everything earthly around her went soft focus while she stood out crystal clear. About how her spirit seemed contained and still as she concentrated on what you had to say as though you were the wisest man on earth. About her unfettered joy when they had flown in his Mooney. About the sorrow he was desperate to eradicate from her eyes when she spoke of her lost sister. About the strength of her lovely warm hands as she stroked his sore back.

Instead, he walked past the short row of fellow officers to his own desk and Googled the number for the Mauna Kea Meeting Hall.

✦ ✦ ✦

Keawalani was too small to have separate locations for senior and community centers, non-denominational churches, Elk and Mason lodges. So the Mauna Kea Meeting Hall was the clubhouse for one and all.

The senior citizens met there on the first Tuesday of every month. A stilt-thin woman in the front banged the lectern mightily with her gavel as the gray haired gathering finished with one agenda item and moved on to the next. Hank patiently waited through plans for a bus outing to Walmart in Hilo and an update from the craft committee on goods promised for an upcoming library fundraiser. As he marked time, Hank sensed the glances his uniform was drawing from the aunties and uncles in the audience. He also noticed Jack O'Reilly there, covering the meeting for the *Voice*.

Bang went the gavel. Hank jumped again. The Stilt said, "We have a visitor this afternoon. Hamakua District Policeman Hank Lindsey would like a word with us. Officer?" She bobbed away graceful as a cattle egret to perch on the plastic chair designated for her in the first row.

Hank walked to the front and stood next to the lectern. He held his hat in his hands. Public speaking was his idea of life in hell. And envisioning these oldsters in their underwear, well, that just made it scarier. Finally, one kindly old soul piped up with a "Welcome, Officer Hank," and started a small round of applause.

Hank flashed a grin, the crooked one that made one cheek dimple. He'd found it useful before. The ice broken, he began. "The Keawalani police need the help of you folks who have lived in the village long enough to have known the Martin Martin family for a long time. Martina and her kids are now in Honolulu, and as far as we know, life is happy for them. They are not in any trouble with the police.

"We are focusing only on events from the past. If any of you were close to Martina, maybe even before she married Martin, would you speak with me after your meeting?" A gentle wave of whispering began in the room. Hank knew these seniors would never speak to him in a group this big about anything personal. So he added, "If you can help, I will be across the street at the Big Island Girl. Coffee is on me. Thanks for your attention, and thank you for being such good citizens as to aid in an official police inquiry."

As he walked toward the back of the room to leave, the Stilt called after him, "Thank you, Officer Hank. Please help yourself to one of Haloke Hale's coconut macadamia cookies. We all love it when it's Haloke's turn for refreshments." The cookie platter was on a table next to the door. Hank took two that had been dipped in dark chocolate.

Well, that wasn't so bad.

Hank congratulated himself with his public speaking, munching on the cookies as he left the meeting hall. He crossed the street and went into the Big Island Girl, selecting a table for two toward the back of the room. It would be cooler there, maybe a little more private, next to an open window shaded by a stand of ironwood and canary date palm trees.

Daya the Waitress glided toward his table, jingling with the ever present music of her charm bracelet. Today she'd added chandelier earrings with clusters of tiny bells. She was darn near an entire rhythm section. She carried herself with a sedate sort of confidence not often found in a woman of Daya's proportions. Her dark eyes were deep pools that promised sensual secrets and safe havens. The local joke might be that she was the original Big Island Girl, but Hank knew a lot of guys who'd like to come ashore that particular island and nestle between those mountainous thighs. Daya had broken many a heart in her time.

"Morning, Hank. Early for lunch, aren't you?" Daya asked, automatically filling a coffee cup for this regular.

"Just coffee today, Daya. I'm hoping someone will be joining me."

"Nani?"

Damn it all anyway. Does the whole freakin' island know? Was it announced in the Voice?

Hank was hoping to hear gossip about Martina, not about himself. "No, not Nani. Someone from the senior meeting across the street."

Daya gave him a knowing smile and drifted away.

In time, two hippies scuffled through the door with the *squeak kachunk squeak kachunk* of identical walkers. Fly-away grey wisps, baggy jeans and loose tops pegged them as refugees from some long ago production of *Hair*. They had apparently uniformed themselves for the senior meeting. One wore a "Young at Heart, Older Elsewhere" tee-shirt and the other proclaimed on a hot pink visor, "Age Means Wisdom. And Discounts." Both wore vibrant feather leis, real beauties. Hank hoped one day to afford a hatband crafted like that.

The women peered around the restaurant with rheumy eyes behind huge eyeglass frames. The way they squinted, Hank realized they were having trouble adjusting from brilliant sun to indoor light. Once they zeroed in on him, they flashed identical smiles and tottered on over. Hank wondered if they were aware of the old man who'd entered behind them and was dogging their footsteps.

Success!

He'd hoped for one fish, but he'd reeled in three. Quickly, he moved from the two-top to a table for four. Each woman accepted his help as he stood holding a chair back while they seated themselves, first one then the other. It turned out they were sisters, Clea and Clara. After initial introductions, Hank never kept them straight again.

Meanwhile, the old man made a try for the fourth chair, but Clea – *or was it Clara?* – lashed out at him. "Harvey, you didn't know Martina in the old days. Go away."

Sister Two scoffed, as well. "You weren't even on the island when we were young."

"When *you* were young, Captain Cook hadn't arrived yet," the old man sniped back. Then, pointing at Hank, he added, "This jamoke offered free coffee, and I walked all this way to avoid that dishwater they hand out at the meeting hall."

Hank ordered Harvey a cup to go. The old swindler carried it away, cackling happily over his con.

Meanwhile, Clea and Clara settled themselves. They rummaged in their oversized satchels until they located identical little clamps, each monogrammed with a mother of pearl C. They hooked the clamps to the table edge, then suspended their bags above the floor. Next they spread their napkins over bony knees. "Now then. We're ready for the inquisition, Officer Lindsey," one of the sisters said, peering at Hank.

Clara or Clea?

Both old girls charmed him. This was not like interviewing street-hardened felons. "Please, call me Hank. Coffee for you, ladies?"

"Oh, no, Officer Hank. We never drink coffee. Just herbal tea."

"Daya keeps Hawaiian Mamaki in stock for us."

Sure enough, the waitress appeared with a full tea service, a ritual that was pretty much another inexplicable mystery to Hank. He hadn't even known that the Big Island Girl had china cups and saucers. A mug was more his cup of, well ... he sipped his refill of coffee.

"Herbal tea has no caffeine, young man," said Clara or Clea.

"Cleanses the liver."

"Better for the bowels."

"Lowers your blood pressure."

Hank speculated whether the medical community was aware of this wonder drug. He watched Clara/Clea top off the cups with liquid from a vial she rummaged out of her satchel.

"Dark rum," she said, smiling at him. "Adds the flavor this shit is missing."

"No use being good for you if you can't get it down."

The sisters each took a sip, smacked their lips and one asked, "Now then. What's all this about Martina?"

He explained that the police were taking a new look at some old cases. He wasn't free to share all the details with them – *hell, I don't know any details* – but there was indication that someone from Martina's past may have endangered her and, worse yet, her kids. It would have happened many years ago. And the culprit may still be at large.

The sisters tsk-tsked over such a dreadful thing.

Hank asked, "What was your connection to Martina?"

"We lived up the hill from the Lee family when we were kids."

"We still live there, but they're all gone."

"Lee. That was Martina's maiden name."

"I'm eight years older than Martina, and Sis is three years older than that."

"Anything more about our age is not the concern of the Hamakua District police."

"We babysat Martina and her baby brother, Jeffery. Off and on from the time he was a toddler until she was old enough to do the babysitting herself. I'd say for six or seven years."

"That's about right. We watched them grow up."

"Martina was a quiet little thing, docile and sweet. She surely loved her baby brother. Took care of him even when that's what we were paid to do. Changed his diapers, fed him. Cuddled him like he was her own."

Clara and Clea came to a full stop and sipped their tea in unison.

They had travelled back in time together, and Hank could tell when good memories became bad just by watching the movie on their faces.

"Jeff was an adorable little boy, like a dark haired angel. But he had an ornery streak. He'd pull Martina's hair and refuse to do what she asked. He took his Dad's razor to her kitty one day when he was maybe five."

"Poor little cat ran away after that. Broke Martina's heart."

"But she went right on loving Jeff."

"We grew apart when we stopped babysitting her. Life went on. But we knew when she and Martin Martin got engaged. We were even invited to the wedding."

"We neither of us liked Martin very much. He was our age, and we remember what a bully he was in school. But after they were married, Martina never said a peep against him. And Jeff seemed to adore him. He followed Martin around like a puppy dog until they had some sort of falling out."

"That was after Martina's kids were born. Maybe Martin didn't want her brother around anymore. Another mouth to feed. Whatever the reason, he kicked the kid out of the house."

"Jeff stayed around, though. Last I heard he was a baggage handler at the airport."

"I'd be surprised if Martina didn't stay in touch with him."

"Martin Martin was a pain in the rear, Officer Hank. But he was mostly just a blowhard. He could have given Martina and their kids a bad time – "

" – but we'd be inclined to think that Jeff might have been more of a problem if it was serious."

Hank had said little and written much in his notebook. He was grateful to Clara and Clea, regardless of who was saying what. It should always be this easy to gather information. Truth was he didn't mind keeping his yap shut. Holes in the conversation made many suspects or witnesses nervous. They rushed ahead to fill in the blanks, often saying more than they intended.

Besides, in his experience, most women thought most guys didn't listen to them, so he was willing to play the quiet man. It got him further, not only in interviews, but in personal relationships he'd had in the past. Listen to a gal jabber away, and he'd get to have sex.

Somehow he doubted it would be all that simple with Nani. Those waters ran a whole lot deeper.

✦ ✦ ✦

Nani thought she saw Hank's patrol car pull away as she entered the Big Island Girl. But her aunt arrived moments later so she turned her attention to the business of Kala and John Nawahini. Nani had asked Hakumele to join her for lunch so they could talk about it.

Daya seated them at a table for two next to the window. Nani handed her a note she had written. "Could you give this to Akela when his shift begins? He doesn't seem to have a home phone or I'd call him." She had come up with a plan for gardening which could help him now that Puako Bay had fired him for growing vegetables. And it would serve her own purposes as well.

"Sure thing," the waitress said. Then she added, "Hank was just here."

Nani was startled.

Now why on earth would she think I'd want to know that?

Hakumele nodded a greeting to two old hippies at the next table. They looked like twins to Nani. They were gathering their possessions to leave, but stopped to chirp at the *kumu.*

"A handsome young man just bought us a lovely cup of tea," said

SECRETS OF THE BIG ISLAND

Clara or Clea.

"Officer Hank told us we'd been a big help."

"And all we did was tell him about Martina Martin's background."

"He said he wished all citizens were as helpful as we've been. What a charming fellow."

The two shuffled off behind their walkers, neither having any idea that their words were now butterflies fluttering in Nani's stomach. Hank must still be working on Maile's disappearance.

What has he found out? Why hasn't he told me he's still investigating the Martin family?

He'd acted so receptive to her ideas when they flew home from Oahu. But he'd probably called it quits with her after the massage fiasco. The story of Hank and Nani had never really gotten off the ground, but it was already in a nosedive. She longed to find him and pin him down right now.

But Hakumele came first.

Nani waited until they had ordered lunch. Then she said, "Whether he knows it or not, John Nawahine is poisoning his employees and his grandson, Kala. We need to get it stopped."

CHAPTER FIFTEEN

My Book of Revelation
Excerpt from the Year 2003

This secret is too heavy for us, this passing of Mailea Palea. We're only just kids. It is crushing us. We didn't mean it to happen.

But we have to act like nothing has, like everything's cool. We have to.

We wrapped Maile's little body in two beach towels and left her on the air mattress until we could hatch a plan. I had to get back to work at the Inn, and BF was due to help downstairs in the garage.

We have to act normal. BF scares me because I don't know if he can. He's terrified and not as good an actor as me. Since he doesn't have parents around, he hasn't learned to lie as well as I have. Not that I'm super proud of that or anything. But I told him it is way important that he makes it through the next hours with our secret safe. He promised.

When I got back to the Inn, I pulled sheets from the dryer. Their warmth helped me stop shaking. I went on with the washing and drying as if the world hadn't turned upside down. The repetitive noise of the machines helped me through my own repetitive actions. Detergent and spot removers, bleach and fabric softeners. Clean it away, clean it away.

The problem with Maile began to feel unreal, like it never happened. Maybe it didn't. Maybe the whole thing would evaporate the way even a really bad dream does once you finally wake up.

Like that could happen. The dream just got worse for me when Officer Lono appeared in the doorway of the laundry room. He's big and so covered with radios and guns and badges and shit that he clinks when he walks. His shadow was broad enough to cover me like an eclipse. I'm sure my temperature dropped a zillion degrees even though the washers and dryers were still pumping out heat.

"I'm Captain Frank Lono," he said and smiled at me.

OMG. This man is the enemy. He could bury us. Why is he here? Maybe BF squealed?

But no. The scary bastard had come to question me about babysitting last night. Nothing more. He looked tired, his eyes red and his jaw covered with whiskers. In the bright jacaranda-scented laundry room, his uniform looked wrinkled and he smelled of sweat and muddy shoes. He said the search parties had worked all night. He looked the part.

I told him the same thing I told the search party, that I'd heard nothing except kids playing next door. I didn't see any strangers or anyone out in the backyard. I told him I never left the dentist's kids alone. He wrote it down and left. He bought it because he has no reason to think a bible-toting good girl like me could possibly be involved. Besides, what kid doesn't sound nervous when she's talking to a cop?

I have to admit. It was kind of a kick to fool one.

I waited 'til Ma and the Bad Ass would be at evening services then ran home and stuffed some things in my backpack along side this notebook. Mostly food and candles from the pantry. It'll be days until Ma notices. After that, I hurried back to the WikiWiki Fix.

BF was slumped in a massive old wicker chair when I topped the stairs and opened his door. His face was red like he'd been crying. Maile's body was still tightly wrapped in the towels so I didn't really have to look at her. Her presence filled the room anyway. It felt, I don't know, like maybe her spirit was there, giving me orders. And it was pulling my eyes toward that sad little bundle in order to shame me.

As I shrugged off my backpack, BF said, "We shoulda told. Now what the fuck will we do? Nobody will believe that we didn't mean to hurt her if we don't tell."

I know he is grieving. He is a gentle boy who means nobody harm. This accident is as dreadful for him as for me. Maybe more so. The law would blame him more than me. It's the price of being the boy. He needs to keep silent to protect himself, to stay safe. It's too late for forgiveness. Besides, I can't lose him now, I can't. What would I do on my own?

He sounded angry with me. I could see the heat in his face. I've seen it in Father's, too. If Ma has taught me anything it's that angry men are a fact of life for women. We have to learn to control them, or they damage us. So I distracted him.

I stood directly in front of him, slowly lifting my tee-shirt. I shimmied out of my slacks. I leaned into that wicker chair so he had to smell the jacaranda and my own body heat.

He told me to quit it, that he had to think. He lifted his hands to push me away, but I grabbed them and held them against my breasts until they stayed there without any help from me. I unhooked my bra and slid my panties down and off.

What can I say? He's a seventeen year old guy, yeah? By the time I opened his shorts to take his penis in my hand, he'd already swelled up. I turned around, got on my hands and knees, and offered myself like no missionary ever saw. It hurt, sure. But I let him pump away his rage. In time he was moaning in pleasure, not crying in shame.

To keep him with me, I have to keep him happy. Give him what he won't get anywhere else. I'm no good girl anymore.

Afterwards, we curled together in the old wicker chair. I told him I love him and will always try to do what is best for him. I whispered softly in his ear why nobody would believe us anymore, and what we would have to do now. I'd had the whole day to think it through.

At first, he didn't want to accept. His body vibrated with the misery that was eating his insides, and I held him as tight as I could. I wanted to reach in and extract his guilt, but I guess we each have to carry a share of the load.

Finally he agreed to the plan. We'll do it tomorrow night.

I left him there alone with Maile. It would be a horrible vigil for him, but I had to get home before Ma and the Bad Ass got back from church. I had to get their dinner underway.

My Book of Revelation
Excerpt from the Year 2003

This morning, after another night of nearly no sleep, I went to work at the laundry as usual. In the afternoon, I got ahold of Ma to say a maid called in sick so the Inn needed me to clean rooms tonight. I wouldn't get home until late. It's a lie, but I have to be away from the house for most of the night. I'll take money from my stash to give to Father tomorrow, and tell him it's what they paid me.

The search parties have been out looking for two days and two nights. They've been everywhere. Cops have been stopping cars, questioning strangers and locals. Of course, they've all found nothing.

I give thanks to you, most merciful Savior.

Everybody I met today was talking about the disappearance of Maile Palea. Villagers are distraught to lose one of our own. Worse, I think, is the dreadful idea that another one of our own may be the guilty party. And, of course, they're right about that. I am guilty. And it is dreadful.

Lynn Martin didn't tell about finding the flashlight. Maybe she has her own secrets to hide. Or maybe she just doesn't want to admit she kept Maile's flashlight. Whatever, she didn't tell anyone that she saw me so I guess she didn't. Another thing to be thankful for.

Talking with the maids, I heard about the many places the search parties looked. A few of the girls and their husbands have been out looking, too. I already know what we'll do, where we'll hide Maile's body. It's the one place where nobody wants to look, not even once and not very well.

It will be hell for us. BF has to carry the body all that way down, and I'll take along everything else we need to tell her good-bye. It has to be done deep into darkness when nobody but evil spirits walk. The forbidden time. *Kapu.*

When you're burying a disaster like this, no wonder it's called the *dead* of night.

CHAPTER SIXTEEN

Tat Chat
By Jackson O'Reilly
Excerpt from the *Keawalani Voice*, 2015

The only thing that covers more Big Island bodies than swimwear may be tattoos. It's a performance art appearing live all around us.

Well over a third of Americans 18-36 have at least one tat, and that includes nearly as many women as men. Since time out of mind, it has been a part of Polynesian culture so estimates place that figure closer to forty percent here in Hawai'i. Polynesians introduced the art to the Western world when European sailors returned home with tats in the sixteenth century. *Tatau* is, in fact, the Samoan word for the tattoo.

We are fortunate enough to have one of the leading tattooists right here in Keawalani. Kaleo Palea is sought by many who want a new image or to refine an old. But finding the

artist these days is harder than it once
was; a judge closed the Tat Joint for sixty
days when Kaleo was found to be a little too
free with creative license.

But a rumor has reached the ears of this
reporter. A little bird close to the source
tells me that if you're looking for a new
tattoo, you might just find it at the back
door of a certain massage parlor in town.
I'm just saying. Don't quote me on this.

By shoving surf gear, piles of clothes and the rest of his possessions
up against the walls beneath the screened windows of Nani's lanai,
Kaleo created enough room for his work area and portable recliner/
bed. The blue vinyl padded bed was actually a medical exam table
from some prehistoric clinic. Kaleo would have preferred the hy-
draulic dentist chair that was in his shop, the one he'd picked up at
a Hilo flea market when he first opened the Tat Joint. But dragging
it in and out of Pink Floyd and onto the lanai would have required a
hand truck, two buddies promised many brews at the Suck'en'em Up
Saloon, several hours to dis- then re-assemble, and bolts anchoring
it to Nani's floor. All in all, Kaleo thought better of that. Easy tear
down was the key here.

When he finished, he surveyed his new work station. A wide selection of drill-like tattoo machines, each of which fit within his bear-
sized clutch, was displayed on the rolling cart that held his power
supply which was about the same dimensions as a Bose base unit.
Its foot pedal was in easy reach of his work stool. Other shelves held
dozens of disposable needles, bottles of ink, dispensers of tiny cups
for every conceivable color, disposable tubes and the rest of the arcane equipment needed to decorate his customers.

Kaleo had been tattooing for half a dozen years. The job had selected him, not the other way around. He'd still been living with Auntie Hakumele after his dad took off and his mom died, when his artwork had come to the notice of Scratcher Cruz. *Scratcher* is the word tattooists use for amateur inkers; Scratcher used it tongue in cheek, the way a fat man might be called Tiny.

An exhibit of high school students' art had been hanging at the Mauna Kea Meeting Hall. Kaleo, then a senior, had several drawings in the exhibit, each with the startling frozen motion that would become a hallmark of all his artwork in the future. Scratcher, a miserable old son of a bitch, wasn't there to see pretty pictures. He was looking for an apprentice to work cheap in his shop down the road in Kailua. After staring at this boy Kaleo's work, he tracked the student down. One week after graduation, Kaleo moved to Scratcher's Palace. If a representative from a pricey Kona gallery had seen the exhibit, Kaleo's future would have taken a very different course.

The seventeen-year-old was given a bed in the back of the shop plus a few bucks each day for food. His first duty was to be Scratcher's cleaning crew. A tat shop has lots of equipment to disinfect and surfaces to sanitize between customers. Kaleo was also allowed to fill the ink cups and set the needles and ink tubes in the tattoo machines. If he was quiet, he could observe Scratcher at work. And sometimes his mentor told him tales about the ancient Hawaiians who used whale bone needles and dye from the kukui plant.

Money left by his mother for his education supported him during the three years he apprenticed. Kaleo worked hard to make nothing, but he sucked up knowledge all along the way. His first tattoos were done on grapefruits, but they didn't really approximate human skin. He was fascinated how designs that looked good on paper had to change for the bends and surface of human skin. He found the art to be more like sculpting than painting.

Scratcher eventually allowed Kaleo to practice on his own heavily inked body, telling the apprentice when he was applying too much pressure, moving too fast, shading incorrectly. Kaleo also worked free on people who didn't care a lot what the end product looked like. These were often people in rehab, hoping to transfer a crack or heroin addiction to a less destructive obsession for body art.

Kaleo finally repaired homemade work or prison tats inked by inmates from concoctions like ash, water and toothpaste. He had no idea how some people survived the shit they were willing to inject under their skin. Kaleo learned how to create a steady outline from these repair jobs, keeping it an even width and intensity. He then became proficient at shading, feathering in colors from dark to light. The day came when he turned a sailor's poorly inked nude into a married man's angel with a new wife's name. Kaleo had gone from tattooist to tattoo artist.

That was when he felt ready to tattoo his own body. His first ink was on his right leg, just above his ankle. It was the word Maile. His baby sister had been named for the vine with a spicy vanilla fragrance that was used in special ceremonial hulas. Every year, on her birthday, he added another cluster of shiny leaves until the tattoo became a lei winding around his leg. He laced in red iiwi birds, pink plumeria and white pikake blossoms, three of the child's favorites. Kaleo would never complete the tattoo, not until she was found.

He was trying to figure how to say good-bye to Scratcher's Palace when the boss figured it out for him. Scratcher ran his Harley into the side of a Mack truck, dying the way he lived, at top speed.

Kaleo moved back to Keawalani and opened his Tat Joint. He had to do body piercing to begin because it took no time and was pure profit. And for clients with limited imagination, he had to work with flash sheets, the pre-designed stencils that tattooists can purchase. But his own artistic bent was what won him a certain amount of fame in body art circles. People came to him with a rough idea which he sketched and augmented. His design work as well as his technique made him a legend. The brilliant talent that he was afraid to exhibit in shows of his canvasses burst free in his tattoos.

Word spread through the village that Kaleo was back in action. All anyone had to do was go to the back door of Keawalani Hands instead of the front. And bring cash. The woman he was working on now had come by in the evening while Nani was out to dinner with Mrs. Cunningham and Emelina. Kaleo was shading in the outline of a delicate hibiscus next to the woman's pelvic bone.

Later, he realized that if the front of the house hadn't been so dark, or his music so loud, or his attention so focused on the soft skin this close to a bikini bottom, maybe he would have heard the window opening, its old wooden frame screeching in alarm.

✦ ✦ ✦

Mrs. Cunningham and Emelina had invited Nani to dinner for a little celebration. All three women were in a festive mood. The old couple had decided it was time their family and friends all understood their relationship.

"We're engaged!" Emelina said as she and Mrs. Cunningham held up their arthritic left ring fingers, each with an enormous black pearl set in a golden crown circled by diamonds.

Later Nani realized that if she hadn't been out having fun with two of her favorites, the front of her house would not have been dark. The break-in would not have occurred. And her head would never have had the goose egg that throbbed for several days.

✦ ✦ ✦

Hank was feeling the effects of a long day. After the interview with the sisters, he'd spent an afternoon in court, testifying against one man who'd been caught breaking into a car and another who'd been found in unlawful possession of a gun while out on parole. Next Hank staked out a house in Waimea where a female suspect wanted for robbery was allegedly staying. After four hours he'd seen no activity and was more than ready when relief replaced him.

It was full dark by the time he got back to the station. He was surprised to find Lono, prominent chin resting on steepled hands, watching a pre-teen girl across from him at his desk. She was cleaning a disassembled handgun.

"Captain?" Hank asked.

"You're running late," Lono said looking up. "This is Renee. Allison's daughter. Renee, this is Officer Hank Lindsey."

The girl nodded, but her concentration stayed on the gun parts laid out on the captain's desk. She'd caught her upper lip in her teeth as she worked. Hank guessed her at maybe eleven or twelve. She was gawky, all knees and elbows, like a foal whose spindly legs weren't yet under complete control. Renee's painfully thin frame looked nothing like the amply cushioned Allison. At the moment, the child was running a brush with solvent through the bore.

Lono turned his attention back to her. "Okay, now let's reassemble it. Start with the recoil spring."

The girl heaved an impatient sigh and rolled her eyes. "I know that, Frank."

Frank? Clearly, these two had done this before.

Allison squeezed past Hank who was half blocking the doorway to Lono's office. Startled that she was still there Hank said, "I'd say everyone is running late."

"Renee and I went bowling this evening. She's getting better than me. Stopped here to see if the captain needed anything before we went on home."

Hank merely nodded. He'd never mention that the whole department had a pool regarding the captain and Allison. Instead, he told them about his trip to the Mauna Kea Meeting Hall. "You were right," he said to Lono. "I found neighbors willing to tell me about Martina Martin's past."

While he talked about his interview with Clara and Clea, all three adults watched the girl reassemble the recoil spring and barrel into the slide and rack it.

Lono said, "I've met those sisters at church. Peas in a pod. Never can keep straight which is which."

Allison went to her computer to track down the most recent address she could find for Martina's brother, Jeffrey Lee, living in the vicinity of the Kona airport. Lono and Hank decided to pay a surprise visit the following evening.

Done with her chore, Renee looked up and considered Hank. "Your gun need cleaned?"

"No, ma'am. Did it just the other day."

She frowned with narrowed eyes like he was probably lying. "You bowl?"

"Some."

"Bet I could take you."

"That a threat?"

"That's a fact." She crossed her arms and stared tough as a stringy homeboy.

Hank refused to let her see that she amused more than intimidated. He kept his face stone still. "Maybe your mom would let me join you two at the lanes one day."

"She's not my mom. She's Allison."

Hank blanched, but Allison smiled. "That's okay, Hank. Renee is my foster kid. We prefer first names to titles."

Hank tried to believe it, but her smile hadn't quite reached her eyes. "Great then," he said with forced cheer. "Guess I'll go finish up. Tomorrow, captain. Nice to meet you, Renee."

"See you, Hank."

Hank? The kid really did ignore titles.

He plopped down at his desk and filled out all the forms relating to his day's activities. He was so buried in the paperwork that he wasn't even aware when the captain, Allison and Renee left. Or whether they all left together.

Looking in the car's mirror on his way home, Hank could see his five o'clock shadow had become a dark smudge by ten. His eyes were moving toward half mast. But he knew he wouldn't sleep. Nani had been too much on his mind today. He wanted to see her, to get things back on track.

It was simple enough. He'd stop by to give her an update on the investigation. He'd been keeping Nani and Kaleo briefed all along, hadn't he? It would be the natural thing for him to do, wouldn't it?

Later Hank realized that if he'd just gone on home, he wouldn't have forced things from bad to worse.

✦   ✦   ✦

Nani said good night to Mrs. Cunningham's limo driver and waited for him to pull the car out of her driveway. She felt a delightful buzz from the bottles of wine she had shared with Mrs. C and Emelina. It wasn't very late, maybe just 10-ish. But this was a neighborhood of working people who bedded down early. The lights were out in the house next door, although she could hear the familiar drone of a TV drama from their bedroom. She could also make out laughter from the guys across the street as they wrapped up their Tuesday poker game.

I wonder if Kaleo joined them tonight. He was often their stand-in if one of the regulars didn't show. She figured his expressive face would make him the perfect patsy. But she could hear his music from the back of the house above the TV next door. If he'd gone to the game, he was home now.

Nani had forgotten to leave her porch light on and stood for a moment in the dark enjoying the soft night. A breeze rustled the thick greenery, and a lovesick cat made his wishes known. Night insects hummed along with distant traffic on the main road. It was warm enough to go without the light silk scarf she'd worn as a shawl in the limo's air conditioning. She took it off as she climbed the wooden steps to her front porch.

She'd made many changes to the interior of her house, but the exterior was just as her parents had left it. Parker Ranch green walls, white trim, red metal roof, a lanai out back and a small wood railed porch to the front. Like all its neighbors, the house was raised on short stilts so air could pass below to combat the insects and moisture that beleaguered all upland dwellings.

Nani put a hand out like a blind woman to find the front door. She followed its wooden surface to the door handle, then inserted her key and entered the dark hall. As she patted the inside wall aiming for the light switch, a weight like a wrecking ball slammed into her. She crumpled, along with the mass on top of her, pinning her to the floor.

The man wasn't big, but he had her down. And she'd knocked her head on the hardwood floor. Black amoeba danced in front of her eyes as she fought to stay conscious. Nausea rose toward her throat. She opened her mouth to scream, but he clamped a hand over her lips. She bucked and twisted, knocking him sideways. His hand lost position, and she bit into the meat of his palm.

"Jesus!" he shrieked pulling the hand away.

"Kaleo!" Nani yelled.

Please let him be here.

The intruder clambered to his knees and tried for the front door, but before he could get clear of her, Nani circled his head with her fluttery silk scarf. When she yanked with both hands as hard as she could, it became a very satisfying garrote. His body odor intensified with fear sweat. She yelled for her brother again as her captive began to gag. He pushed at her face, splitting her lip in the process.

Thunderous footsteps rolled from the back of the house. Lights flashed on, and over the back of the man tearing at the scarf, Nani saw the charging bull that was her brother. Kaleo bodily picked up the intruder and slammed him head first against the door.

"Nani?" he bellowed.

"I'm okay. Don't kill him."

Her order may have been the only reason the second head slam didn't do just that. The intruder fell to the floor with a yelp. Kaleo helped Nani up. And, arms around each other, they both stared down at Mrs. Cunningham's grandson, Packer.

"You bleeding asshole," Kaleo growled. "What the fuck are you doing here?"

"I'm sorry, I'm sorry. I just wanted to pay you back." Packer was at least conscious enough to plead his case.

"How'd you find me?" Nani asked.

"I followed you home from my *tutu's* after I saw you there. You weren't even supposed to be here tonight. She said you were having dinner with her. I just wanted to trash your place, not you."

Kaleo drew back a massive fist to pound it into the side of the addict's head.

Nani grabbed his arm. "No, Kaleo, wait. How'd you get in?"

"Through the front window. I didn't take anything. Really. Let me go and you'll never see me again."

For the first time, Nani looked around the entry which doubled as the office for her business. Packer may not have taken anything, but he'd tossed the room. Her head now swam less from pain and more from the idea of putting all those files back together.

Shit, oh dear.

She needed to get the jerk out of there before Kaleo did him real harm. She made a quick decision. "We're going to let you go. But if we find any real damage, Kaleo will come for you. You'll work off the debt."

"Otherwise, you'll never come near Nani again," her brother growled.

Packer's skinny legs wobbled. "Yes, ma'am. Uh, sir. Yes, both of you."

"Let me escort you to the door, *cockaroach*." He picked Packer up by the seat of the pants and the scruff of the neck once again, walked out the front door and threw the addict off the porch. "Now get the fuck out of here and don't come back."

Packer scrambled away, disappearing under the greenery like a terrified rodent.

That's when Nani looked up and saw Hank getting out of his patrol car, watching brother and sister with an appalled look on his face. At the same time, from behind her, she heard a feminine voice say, "What's going on?"

She looked back into the hall and saw a woman in a bikini with a half-inked tattoo.

CHAPTER SEVENTEEN

Happy Anniversary to Me
By Jackson O'Reilly
Excerpt from the *Keawalani Voice*, 2015

When this reporter was a young man grappling with Chicago winters, the wind locally known as the Hawk would swoop down to freeze my blood in its tracks. If I ventured outside, it was under so many layers that I looked like Bigfoot. That big cold city ground me down and spit me out twenty five years ago today.

I landed here where I was instantly aware of skin. Golden skin, wrinkled to well-toned, ample to otherwise. It was everywhere, nearly naked on beaches or just slightly more clothed in the markets and fruit stands. You Big Islanders have an ease with your bodies. You're so at home with your shapes and sizes.

You were such exotic creatures to me then, a United Nations of faces and cultures. The one tool the Polynesians employed to unite you all was passion. Your inborn ardor must be the natural result of an island formed by volcanic gods with liquid rock and explosive fireballs at their disposal.

You are passionate about all things. You talk story or talk stink with equal zeal. You openly touch or bluster, dance or battle. You are altogether more *attuned* than those shivering on the frozen mainland.

I have come to life here on this volcanic perch in the middle of nowhere. It has made my prose turn purple. My environs are perfumed and taste of lush sweet fruit. Water sings in tumbling falls and pounding surf to accompany tropical birdsong as my soundtrack. I was a broken man when I first arrived. Now I am healed.

You are no longer exotic, but just the faces of my neighbors. And maybe, after another twenty five years, you'll begin to call this haole a Big Islander, too.

"But I don't want to tell you who he is because then you'll arrest him, and his grandmother will find out he's a jackass, after all that Kaleo and I have gone through to keep her from knowing the truth. Ow!" Nani flinched as Hank applied an ice pack to the knob on the back of her head. He sat next to her at the table in the kitchen nook looking grim.

Kaleo had wisely gone back to the lanai to finish his customer's tattoo. "We'll talk about that later," Nani had muttered to him.

She said no to going to the ER with Hank. Instead, she directed him to the aspirin, peroxide and cotton balls in the medicine cabinet. As she daubed at her lip, he'd filled the ice bag and demanded answers.

She gave him a basic overview of what she and Kaleo had done to the addict that motivated his attack on her house. But she left out Packer's name. She just couldn't tell Hank that. Now the cop looked angry with her. His jaw clenched and his eyes were more glacier cold than blue fire hot. All she would confess was that she often helped her clients with personal problems, whether they realized it or not.

"So you're in danger often?" the ice man asked.

"No! Danger? No! Well, almost never. I'm just lending a helping hand. Really."

From the earliest days of her childhood, her mother and Auntie Hakumele had taught her the necessity of service to others. It was the Aloha Spirit. Nani defined herself by it. Looking up at Hank now she needed him to understand this very basic concept about herself. "How could I not help? This village is my home."

The scar on his forehead distracted her. It appeared to be throbbing. Maybe it was infected, hot to the touch. Nani the Therapist reached up to outline it from his hairline to his eyebrow. She massaged the skin ever so gently.

No, not hot. Maybe just stands out when he's upset.

Her tender fingers seemed to soothe Hank. She could feel his face muscles relax as her hand moved from the scar and traced slowly down the side of his face to his strong jaw line. She could see the anger drain from his eyes, softening his gaze as he stared back at her. His arm over her shoulder, the one holding the ice bag, began to feel like a caress. He was so close, so warm. And she was feeling vulnerable to careful handling after the wrestling match with Packer.

Hank put the ice bag down and gingerly replaced it with his hand on the back of her head. He pulled her toward him. Placing a finger on her swollen lip, he traced it to the verge of the split. She did not resist. In fact, she bent toward that finger and gave it the gentlest of kisses. He slowly moved his hand to her cheek as his mouth reached for hers.

It was not so much a kiss as an exploratory touch between two people whose mouths belonged together. He held off any pressure until she could investigate whether he should back off the torn skin. Maybe the swelling had numbed it some, or maybe the softness of his lips was an instant salve. Whatever the reason, she felt much better as she pushed toward him, and he returned the pressure.

"Okay, that's done," Kaleo said, blundering in from the lanai. "Oops, sorry dudes." But the magic was broken.

Then the mood was broken, too, when Hank said in Nani's ear, "I don't want you doing anything this foolish again. Promise me."

Dammit. Why do men think they have the right to order women around?

Nani didn't need told what to do. The ardor of the kiss faded. Now she pouted. He just didn't get it. "I don't consider helping a friend to be foolish. It's what I will always do."

"I have to know you're safe," Hank said, strengthening his hold on her.

Her passion morphed to its first cousin, anger. "And I have to know you don't think I sit and stay on command."

"Guess I'll be going to bed," Kaleo said, moving back toward the lanai.

"Don't go on our account," Nani said, cool as river rock. "Hank was just leaving."

"I was? You're angry because I think what you did was risky?" He looked the part of a man falsely accused.

"It's my decision to make, and I trust my judgment," she snapped. Obviously he wasn't about to apologize.

He pushed away from her muttering, "Son of a ..." Standing, he frowned down at her. But she had no intention of backing down. She waited him out. Finally, he stalked away down the hall, muttering under his breath, "What is more predictable than an unpredictable woman?"

"What did you say?"

"Absolutely nothing." He slammed the front door behind himself so hard it rattled. So did the louvers on the windows around it. Then a brief moment of silence.

"That went well," Kaleo said, flopping down across from his sister who was now holding the ice bag that Hank had dropped. "He's falling for you, you know."

"The hell he is. He's falling for his image of *me*. And that's a long way from me. I won't have a man order me around the way dad treated mom."

It wasn't the first time she and Kaleo had talked about male supremacy. Their father's posturing when angry or drunk had been hard for them all. "Dad could be a real butt, true. But ... don't you think you're a little too brittle on that subject?"

Nobody but Kaleo could talk to her that way. Nani stared at the ball cap with POLICE emblazoned across the front. Hank had left it on the table. Her swollen lip throbbed in rhythm with the knot on her head ... and with the memory of his kiss. The hat smelled of sweat and maleness.

"Give him a chance, Nani," Kaleo added. "He's not the natural smooth mover that some guys are. Guys like me."

He always could make his big sister smile. "Okay, Smoothie. I'll think on it." Once in a great while Kaleo was right in his opinions. Maybe she should reconsider. But for now, she changed the subject. "So how long have you been in business out back?" She indicated the lanai with a cock of her head that caused it to hurt all the more.

"Ouch."

His smile evaporated. "Now don't go getting pissy with me, too, Nani. The judge didn't say I can't tattoo. Just that I can't do it in my shop."

"I'm not getting pissy. In fact I think it's a great idea, at least until you're ready to paint full time. Keeps you too busy to get in more trouble."

She saw the surprise register on his face. "You mean you're okay with it?"

"As long as your clients use the back door while mine use the front, I don't see a problem. And when you can kick in some cash, I'll have Maggie Wilson start doing the laundry again."

"You know, Nani. You're not an easy woman to predict. Hank has his work cut out for him."

"Up yours, little brother."

"Yours, too, big sister." He leaned forward, kissed her cheek, and headed back to the lanai after taking a couple beers from the fridge.

His bed was out there. Nani had offered him his old childhood room when he moved back into the house. But it was upstairs next to hers. She supposed he didn't want to be so close to her space anymore. In fact, she assumed the bikini woman was waiting for him between the sheets on the lanai.

Nani would be going to bed alone once again, with nothing but her temper to keep her company. And that was damn cold comfort. The price of independence was sometimes too dear. Especially when she was pretty sure this time it had just been her own obstinacy.

She looked out into her backyard, lit only by the spotlight on her garage and another off the lanai. She could see the darkened plot of land toward the back of her lot. Akela the busboy had been here working all day, removing the grass from the plot, then digging up the soil. He had taken her up on her plan. She would provide him with the area to garden with any crop he wished. In return, he would do the rest of her yardwork, pruning the shrubs and mowing the lawn. She'd never really liked doing it, and with his help out there, she'd have time to add another client or two.

The Big Island secret keeper had worked things out again. So it was particularly frustrating that she could help everyone else, but when it came to dealing with Hank, she was doing such a crappy job. She had to admit that Kaleo had a point.

Could I be the one in the wrong?

✦　✦　✦

The next morning, Nani was in the waiting area when Hank arrived at the police station. She took his breath away in that filmy skirt. Her sleeveless yellow tee highlighted the bronze of her skin and exposed the soft promise of her voluptuous ...

Jesus!

She'd already cost him another sleepless night and hours of self-questioning. Yet here she was, and his ridiculous heart sang. He must proceed with caution. She was probably here to register a harassment complaint against the unprofessional asshole who ...

"Here he is now, Nani!" Allison said from her reception/dispatch desk. "He's always on time. But goodness, Hank, you're looking a bit rough this morning. Anything wrong?"

He ignored her wicked grin, eyes only for Nani. "Ah, Ms. Palea? You're here to see me?"

"Yes, Officer Lindsey." She opened the colorful sling bag she had cradled on her lap. "I wanted to return this to you. You left it last night."

She pulled out his hat.

Allison snorted.

Hank glared a warning at the receptionist.

"And I had something I wanted to tell you," Nani continued. "In private."

"Let's go to my ... ah, cubicle."

"Conference room's empty," Allison lilted as she merrily keyboarded away.

They called it the conference room or the incident room or the press room, whatever room they needed at the moment. White boards lined one wall, and windows along another let in the morning breeze. It felt cool against Hank's overheated face.

"I want to apologize," Nani began, perching on the edge of a conference room chair.

Holy crap!

"No, no. It was my fault. I was too clumsy. Of course you have good judgment."

She held up her hand, palm facing him in a stop gesture. "If we're going to avoid another fight, you have to let me say what I came to say."

Eyes so deep a man could drown.

He shut the hell up.

"I took it all wrong," she continued. "Kaleo says I can be bristly as a porcupine, and I guess he's right. I realize that it may have been Hank the Cop telling me I'd been foolish, not Hank the Man. And that's a cop's job. To keep his people all safe."

Fuck! That's good! Why didn't I think of that?

"Can I speak now?" he asked.

Warning finger. "One more thing. I liked that kiss. I'd like to try it again some time."

In his head, music crescendoed.

"How 'bout tonight? ... no, dammit, I have a stakeout. What about tomorrow? Dinner at the Big Island Girl? We can practice kissing 'til we get it right."

She smiled and it filled him like a rainbow. She said, "Or there's a sand sculpture festival at Hapuna Beach. I could pack a picnic."

"I work traffic there 'til five."

"Great. I'll meet you then."

"Tomorrow it is." He hoped his smile worked as much magic on her as hers did on him.

Apparently, it did. "'Til then," she said as she stood up and kissed his cheek. "Aloha, cop." Then she left.

He watched through a window that overlooked the parking lot. The way she swayed, he figured she knew he was watching. Her skirt flipped up as she mounted the Vespa and powered it up.

Mother of God.

She turned onto the road and disappeared into traffic on the ridiculous scooter with its surrey top of woven palm.

Wish she had a safer ride.

Then he caught himself. That's just the sort of thing he'd better never say to her.

CHAPTER EIGHTEEN

Cases Grow Cold, But Not Emotions
By Jackson O'Reilly
Excerpt from the *Keawalani Voice*, 2015

Who killed JonBenet? Where's Hoffa buried? Who was Jack the Ripper? A handful of cold cases stay in the public mind. But most melt away, leaving families in pain, seeking answers. The police officers who have devoted years to finding solutions share that pain, often long after even the witnesses have died.

Matters are getting worse for victims of unsolved crimes and their searchers. The current economic slump is forcing law enforcement groups across the nation to shut down cold crime units. Federal grants and state funding are drying up. Even many large law enforcement departments can no longer afford to employ officers and lab personnel to handle such time-intensive investigations as these old puzzles. And that is a hard cold fact, indeed.

Here on the Big Island we used to leave doors unlocked, keys in ignitions, children playing hide and seek on their own. No more. Like communities everywhere, we have our share of butchered bodies with no known perps … hikers last seen heading into forests … drug hits in back alleys and overgrown fields.

News programs and reality shows have tried to fill in for overburdened law enforcement. Cold case groups including people such as retired cops, crime writers, and psychologists have formed in cities nationwide. But the gap is still there.

Except maybe here in Keawalani. Something here is afoot. Questions regarding our most famous cold case are being asked one more time. The child Maile Palea, gone for twelve long years, still lives in our memories.

As the *Voice* learns more, so will you. If you know more, for the love of God, speak up.

Hank was still jazzed from Nani's surprise visit when Lono appeared beside his desk.

"What the fuck's up with you?" the captain asked. "You're humming, for chrissakes."

"Am not."

Lono motioned him up with a jerk of his thumb. Hank grabbed his cap – that sweat-stained soldier which had played its part in bringing

Nani back to him – and followed the boss out to his car.

"Where to?" Hank asked as Lono clambered into the passenger seat of Hank's SUV. "We going to pick up Jeff Lee now?" He was eager to get it done, get the shit off the street if he was the creep Hank believed he might be.

"Newspaper."

"Newspaper? Vending machine or office?"

"I don't want to buy one, butthead. I want to talk to O'Reilly." As Hank drove, Lono explained that the editor of the *Keawalani Voice* had just called. He'd found something in the files he thought they should see.

"Something about Maile," Lono said as Hank parked at the yellow curb in front of the newspaper office. It was a tiny storefront next to Halemano's Heavenly Treats. Lono said, "Maybe we'll stop after for a couple Spam musubis to get us through til lunch." The boss loved the grilled meat, rice and nori seaweed snacks. Personally, Hank would as soon eat dirt.

O'Reilly wasn't much older than the police captain, but Hank thought the newsman looked a lot worse for wear. His coppery hair was streaked with gray, and his skin, in defiance of the island sun, was as pink as a haole baby's bottom. A roadmap of red veins on his hawkish beak bespoke too many nights on a barstool. It was a newsman's schnoz, one that snuffled its way through the chaff to get to the grain. Hank didn't know the man's whole story, only that he'd moved to the Big Island under a dark cloud decades ago, booted off the metro desk of the *Chicago Tribune*. His columns now covered pig roasts, golden anniversaries and local gossip instead of mob busts and vicious politics. Hank figured the *Keawalani Voice* was O'Reilly's last stop before oblivion.

"Whatcha got, Jackson?" Lono asked as the editor led them through the cluttered space that doglegged between four desks and as many computer tables.

Only one work area was occupied at the moment. A harried woman was on the phone, rolling her eyes and quoting rates. She was also wiping up tea from the paper cup overturned on her desk. A sopping tea bag draped itself on her desk lamp, dripping faster than she was mopping.

"That's Sally," O'Reilly said. He picked up a pile of fallen papers and returned them to her desk as they walked past. "Gets jumpy when she's on deadline." The small triangular sign on her desk identified her as the entire Classified, Display and Internet Advertising Department.

The work station nearest to her was clean of clutter. It looked to Hank like the paper might have a job opening. The equipment littering the next desk told him it was the photography department. The final desk, a large wooden dinosaur, had its own sign pinpointing it as the province of the Publisher, Editor and News/Sports/Features Reporters all wrapped in one.

O'Reilly walked them past his desk and into a shabby back room jammed with tall metal file cabinets along one wall. Opposite the cabinets, shelves were stacked ceiling high with office supplies, reference books and newspaper backcopies. The three men squeezed together, with no more standing room than a Hawaiian Air aisle in coach.

"So this is the heartbeat of the organization," Lono said.

"We call it the morgue. Where old newspapers come to die." O'Reilly indicated the stacks of back issues. "Everything pre-computer is kept here."

Hank was uncomfortable tucked between the two heavier men, each with a Samoan-sized belly. He'd been unaware he was claustrophobic until now. Maybe it was just the ever present booze on the editor's breath that was making him edgy. Or his impatience to get on the road to find Jeff Lee.

O'Reilly plucked a file off a shelf, one that had been separated from all the others. "After I saw you at Sunny Daze, I got to thinking about Maile. About a story she wrote for the *Voice*, maybe a year before she disappeared. Thirteen years ago at least. Hell, I'd forgotten about it." He shifted his attention from the captain to Hank. "Before your time, boy. You were still a punk in Puna." Hank had been brought up in that village on the other side of the island. Many Keawalani villagers still considered him the new kid.

"Of course, everything she wrote was from a child's viewpoint. About finding a new candy at the Ono Grinds Market, or the lowdown on school play casts, or the indignities of age restrictions on scary movies. Charming stuff. Never found a kid to replace her. Too sad to do it, I guess."

Maile Palea was written on the folder tab in Magic Marker. O'Reilly opened the file with nail-bitten fingers. He removed a piece of yellowed notebook paper, stared at it a moment before handing it to Lono.

The captain wrestled his new pair of reading glasses out of his shirt pocket. Lono hated to admit his eyes weren't as sharp as they once where ... all nine of the officers who worked for him knew better than to tease him about them. A reference to 'four eyes' had landed one of them on the night shift for two solid months.

Lono scanned the paper, reading the words that were carefully printed in a child's hand. Then he handed it to Hank:

```
        Keeping Secrets for your Friends
                By Maile Palea


    Mom and Dad buy me things and say I love
    you. Even when daddy yells he loves me. I
    think all grownups love children.
```

But my friend says one hurts kids. Her bruddah knows about it, too. I promised not to tell her name. So I will not.

Maybe I am wrong. Maybe grownups only take care of you until they eat you like they do with chickens they raise. Whateva, they are confusing, yeah?

Hank was appalled. "She wrote this?"

Lono added, "And you didn't tell me?"

"Hold your horses, Lono," O'Reilly said. "She wrote it a long time before she disappeared. I asked her about it, and she wouldn't tell me the name of her friend. I even alerted her parents. She told them she'd made it up, that they'd been learning about bad guys in school and that she wanted to warn her readers, too. That made sense to me back then, but I never printed it. Too controversial for a child's column."

"We'll keep it now," Hank said.

"Of course. Anyway, when you got to talking about the Martins I got to remembering. I wondered if – "

" – if Maile had been writing about Lynn and her brother," Hank said.

"Give the boy a gold star. I dug it out of the file. Never printed it, but I kept it."

"If what Sunny told me was true, their Dad wasn't assaulting the children, at least not penal penetration," Lono said.

"All the more reason to question their Uncle Jeff," Hank said.

"You got a story for the *Voice*?" The newsman's nose twitched.

"Not yet, Jackson," Lono said. "The *Voice* stays silent for now. But I'll let you know when."

✦ ✦ ✦

When the two cops got back in the patrol car, Lono said to Hank, "I'd planned we'd go talk to Jeff Lee tonight. But let's catch him at work instead of at home."

Hank looked at his watch. "Be lunchtime when we get there. You still want those musubis for the ride?"

"No time for that now."

Hank was relieved; he didn't want the smell of the damn things in his car. He flicked on the blue dome and grill lights as well as the si ren. Fishtailing once, the Pilot righted itself and set a raucous course to Kona International Airport.

✦ ✦ ✦

The insulated truck featured bento lunches with two scoops of white rice, one of macaroni salad, and a great dollop of teriyaki chicken, kalua pork or poke fish with a choice of a dozen different flavorings. It was parked on a service road behind the airport where luggage handlers and other employees gathered for their lunch breaks.

Allison had emailed the officers a photo of Jeff Lee. It was an old likeness. When they locked in on the current Lee, he was leaner and sported a ridiculous bandito mustache that overpowered his long, narrow face. He was round shouldered, slouching over a picnic table and eating with four buddies.

Lono, flanked by Hank, approached Lee from the rear. The body English of the other men gave his presence away. Their chatter stopped when the captain said, "I'm looking for Jeff Lee."

Bandito Mustache continued to chew, swallowed mightily and sniffed the air. Without turning around he said, "Is that pork I smell?"

Lono knew the case belonged to Hank. But chances were this son of a bitch had tormented his own kin. Who else might he have cornered? He did something far too malicious for an officer of the law ... something he would have suspended Hank for doing. The beefy captain grabbed Lee from behind by both ears. He lifted the shorter man straight up, fast and with full intent to create intense pain. If Lee had resisted, his ears would have been amputated on the spot. Instead, he dangled momentarily in the air, howling in anguish.

After a nanosecond of shocked disbelief, Lee's buddies began to snarl and work themselves into attack mode like a pack of feral dogs.

Hank, hand on his holstered gun, said, "Keep your seats, gents, and eat up. Lunch break is nearly over."

With curled lips and guttural rumbling, the foursome was not backing down. So Lono spoke into Lee's red swollen ears loud enough for them all to hear. "Been sniffin' round too many kiddies, *cuz*. Fiddling with little ones. Think we'll put an end to that right now."

"What the fuck? You crazy?" Lee yelped over his pain.

Lono's words had their desired effect on the others. They froze in place. Was it possible? If so, their buddy wasn't worth shit after all.

Lono let go of Lee's ears. "On the ground, asshole. Face down with the rest of the dirt."

Lee grabbed the sides of his head, cupping his hands over his ears. "I never. What stink you talkin' cop?"

"On your gut. Now. Put your hands behind your back. And shut your yap, or I might kick a guy when he's down."

Lee did as he was told, and Lono cuffed him.

"Okay, Officer Lindsey. I think Mr. Lee is done with lunch now."

"And you gents, back to work. Now." Hank kept an eye on the

tablemates while they picked up their trash and headed back toward the terminal. Then he helped Lono lift their catch to his feet and walk him to the car. In the process, he read Lee his rights.

"Inside." Lono put his hand on Lee's head and shoved him into the back seat.

"What? What I do?" Lee smelled like fear. Snot and dirt formed a paste in his mustache.

"Not another word 'til I give you permission. I won't say it again." Lono loaded himself into the passenger seat. When he nodded, Hank aimed the SUV back toward Keawalani.

Finally, half way home with Lee moaning in the back seat, Lono said, "Suppose I ought to let Kona District know they're short one of their assholes."

"Sir?" ventured Hank. "That ear thing something you learned in the academy before my time?"

Lono kept a straight face. "Nothing you need to tell anyone."

"Then just between us, maybe your eyesight isn't as sharp as it used to be. But your persuasion skills are still first rate."

CHAPTER NINETEEN

My Book of Revelation
Excerpt from the Year 2003

BF thinks I'm *lolo*, says I get crazy ideas. But he is gentle with me. He finally agreed that Maile deserves the best service we can give her under the circumstances.

Try as I might, I could not keep my eyes off that little body. It somehow chastised me to gaze on my sin. I washed Maile once more and shook the dust from her party dress. I straightened each pleat, pressing it with my fingers. Then I rebraided her hair as close to the way she wore it as I could. I even slicked back the frizzy bits around her little face.

BF had an old fruit crate that he used as a stool set on end, the only place in the room to sit other than the wicker chair. He laid the crate flat and removed the lid to make a bed inside from his pillow and the beach towel I'd brought from home. It was the best casket we could manage. Carefully, he placed Maile into it. I folded her arms across her chest like pictures of saints that I've seen. BF bent her knees to one side so her legs would fit. He cried as he tapped down the lid once more, leaving narrow views of Maile visible through the slats and swaddling.

"It's nice," I told him. The palm leaves printed on the beach towels and the rough hewn crate made a comfy looking container. "Like a nest for a little bird. We have honored her, and I'm so grateful to you for your help. Now, we must rest until dark." There was so much to do, but we couldn't risk being seen. We had to wait until Keawalani slept.

Neither of us felt right about lying on the air mattress. Instead, we clung to each other in that old wicker chair until the garage closed and the sun set. I don't think either of us had really slept when I said, "It's time."

People say you can do most anything when you're desperate. I can now say for a fact that's true. That climb down the cliff is hard enough during the day, but nearly impossible at night. Nobody in their right mind would do it, but then, like BF said, maybe we're not. Maybe we're both *lolo*. It's slick underfoot, steep as shit and dangerous with enormous roots to trip you. And I know those trembling leaves hold night creatures just ready to strike.

He may not look very big, but BF is really strong. Still, carrying Maile's body inside an old crate the whole way kept him breathing hard. I led with one flashlight, carrying my backpack. In the steepest places, I took one end of the crate for him. We stopped to rest, blowing like a couple exhausted workhorses. Then we moved on as quietly as we could.

We each slipped and fell, got scratched from branches and bruised from loose rock. By the time we heard the waterfall near our destination, it felt like we'd journeyed across half the island. No wonder it's called *Big* Island.

Criminy.

We climbed into the lagoon at the base of the falls and washed off as much grime as we could. The water was cool, cleansing after the long climb down the cliff. Neither of us wanted to take the next steps, but we had to. No options now, not if we wanted to hide all trace of the accident that had befallen Maile.

We wrapped ourselves in the white sheets I'd borrowed from the Inn. We tied them on like sarongs. This is one of the things that BF thought was crazy. But, we *had* to be in white. It is the color of funerals for real Hawaiians, and I wanted to be as traditional as Maile might have liked. Finally, I slapped away all the crawling things that were attracted to her body. BF picked up the crate again and, with me in the lead, we entered the secret place.

We'd been here before. Sometimes it's nearly dry. Dry enough for our first time together. It was so dark in there that he couldn't see my body, and I couldn't see his. Now he's seen every inch of me. Virgin-to-Jezebel in next to no time.

When we reached the cubbyhole, he crawled in first. He pulled the crate and I pushed. It just fit through the tunnel. I set some candles on a flat rock along with a cross. In case Maile is Christian, she needs to have those things. I hope she's not Catholic because I didn't have a rosary. But in case Maile preferred the old ways, I'd brought a lei made of maile leaves to honor her and the Hawaiian gods.

After lighting the candles, we prayed. I said the Twenty-Third Psalm and asked that Jesus accept this child as His own. Together we sang *What a Friend We Have in Jesus.* When we finally turned to go, a piece of our souls stayed behind in that forlorn tomb with Maile.

At the pool, we removed the sheets and put our dirty clothes on again. I was exhausted, but the work wasn't done. Together we gathered a pile of rocks. They were plentiful all along the waterfall so the chore was possible with the beams from our flashlights. BF will return over the next few nights to piece them together into a lava wall. His granddad taught him the skill years ago ... that old man would spin in his own grave to know how this boy will use his knowledge.

By the time we were done, we were both sick. Maybe it was exhaustion, but I'm pretty sure it was shame. I felt crippled with despair, but I couldn't stop and I couldn't let BF bottom out either. When we climbed back up that cliffside, I clung to his hand as much as I could. I told him I loved him and that our secret bonded us. Nobody else would ever know. The death of this child would always hold us together. Our lives were entwined forever by the size of our love ... and our crime.

When we reached the road where he had to go one way and I another, we embraced in fatigue and silence. There was nothing left to say. It was a good thing. Because my Father had nothing to overhear when he turned on his light and growled, "Stop there, whore."

We'd been gone too long. The Bad Ass had come out to watch the road in search of me.

He beat BF, I think nearly to death. I couldn't pull him off. He swung the cane again and again, his aim accurate from so much practice. BF didn't fight back. Maybe he felt like a beating was due, that guilt had a price to pay. When he was too bloodied to rise, Father had at it with me. For a good Christian man, he sure knows how to damage the parts that hurt the most.

His last words, as I huddled in the ditch beside the road – insects crawling across my bleeding legs – were, "You are no longer a daughter of mine. God Almighty shuns you from this day forth. You'll never be looked upon by your family, your church again. You are dead to us all."

The whole thing had been feeling unreal to me for the last few days since Maile hit her head on that rock. Like I was watching me in a movie from afar, both observing and acting. But it felt plenty real now. When the Bad Ass was gone, we shivered there in the mud with our wounds. There'd be no returning to normal life now. No brother and sister to raise. No Ma. No school.

Finally, BF asked, "Does he know about Maile?"

"No," I said. My throat was so dry I rasped. "Fucking is sin enough. He'd have killed us for murder." The thought struck me as funny. "Kill us for murder!" I began to howl at the moon. Hysteria.

BF crawled to me and held me tight until I wound down. Together we shivered in pain. There was only one place to go. When we could both stand, we limped back to his room above the shop. We almost didn't make it up the rickety old stairs. The wicker chair and the floor were just too hard for our bruised bodies. So we collapsed on the air mattress where Maile had died.

From now on it will be the three of us locked together. Forever.

CHAPTER TWENTY

Hapuna Beach Sand Sculpture Festival
This Weekend
By Jackson O'Reilly
Excerpt from the *Keawalani Voice*, 2015

For most of us, our first sand sculptures began with a pail and a spoon on a beach. We'd pack in wet sand, turn it over, tap it out and bingo! The castle was underway. It would last until the first wave tsunamied it or the local beach bully stomped it.

Back then, we didn't consider it an art form, just good clean fun. But now professional artists worldwide are playing for prizes. The trick, I'm told, is a low-cost selection of equipment including buckets, ladders, shovels, trowels and other garden tools. Plus the perfect sand, of course, with fine angular grains that adhere to each other when wet.

There's sure to be plenty 'adhering to each other when wet' among the fans and

the sculptures alike this weekend at the
Hapuna Beach Sand Sculpture Festival. The
theme this year is 'At the Movies' so come
root for your favorite flick.

Kaleo wiped his brow. "Kona wind today," he said as he threaded
his longboard between the seats of the Volvo wagon from front to back.

Nani agreed. The sticky southwest breeze prevailed when the
cooling tradewinds were dormant. It was as hot and wet as a steam
room. "Supposed to change later."

"Better surfing if it does," Kaleo said. "'Course bikinis look good
either way."

"You always look on the bright side, *bruddah*."

"Chicks always brighten my day." Kaleo had rented Pink Floyd
to carry his board. He intended to spend the afternoon and night
partying at the Hapuna Beach Sand Sculpture Festival. Nani had
surprised him by hitching a ride.

"Certain cop gonna be there?" asked Mr. Innocent.

Nani ignored the question. "Too much to carry on the Vespa,"
she said as she loaded a picnic, styrofoam cooler, beach blankets, her
paddle board, towels and a sun umbrella. While waiting for Hank
to get off duty, she planned to enjoy the afternoon talking story with
neighbors and playing in the waves.

Pink Floyd chugged out of the highland greenery and descended
toward the ocean. Color spread out before them, a wide rim of brown
then a hazy turquoise horizon that went on forever. Just the ghost
of Maui appeared; the distant island would be clearer if the wind
changed. They crossed the brown rim, a desert where years of drought
had transformed the lava field into a forest of mesquite skeletons.

The parking lot at the state park was high above Hapuna Beach. It
was filled already, but an officer saw them and motioned them onward.

"It's Hank," Nani said, sitting a little straighter in the passenger seat. "He must have recognized Floyd."

"You look like a bird dog on point," Kaleo said, casting a sideways glance at his sister.

"I have no idea what you're talking about."

"And that sarong covers very little that your bikini doesn't."

Nani gave up on playing dumb. "Well, little brother, you said to give him a chance."

"Dressed like that, you'll give him a heart attack."

Hank moved a sawhorse that was next to his Honda Pilot. He motioned them forward onto a scrap of burnt ground. Kaleo maneuvered the Volvo with the care of a cruise captain wedging his ship into the Hilo harbor. After Kaleo dropped anchor, Hank leaned down to Nani's open window. He smiled and touched her shoulder. Her skin tingled, an electrical reaction from the most primitive part of the brain.

Ono. Delicious.

His police cap and dark glasses hid his eyes but she had a marvelous view of the square jaw, white teeth, and tawny throat above the deep blue of his uniform. "I'll find you when I'm off duty," he said, then went back to traffic control. She watched him walk away, enjoying his reverse angle every bit as much as he appeared to enjoy hers.

It took two trips for Kaleo and Nani to carry everything from Pink Floyd down the long path to the beach, past green metal-roofed shelters under mesquite and ironwood trees. Points of lava rock to the far left and right contained white sand between strips of black. The bay was busy with waders, swimmers and boarders, and the beach was pocked with family gatherings of laughing adults, tag playing children and soggy toddlers with shovels and pails. None of them got close to the soft needles beneath the ironwood trees.

Concessionaires of shave ice, bento, burgers and more lined the beach where sand met the tree line, although none parked on those soft needles either. Many past customers had received nasty bites on their bare feet from the centipedes that burrowed there. Only tourists made the mistake of placing their towels in such inviting shade, and this event had very few tourists.

Sand sculptures were in front of the lunch wagons, along the oceanfront just out of reach of the tides. Their builders had worked for days in advance with a slurry of wet sand to create them. This year's festival theme was "At the Movies" and from a distance, Nani could see a recreation of Kauai's Napali Coast – complete with helicopter and oversized dinosaur – representing *Jurassic Park*. The contest entry next to it was a sand-sculpted *King Kong* holding either Fay Wray or Jessica Lang or some other damsel in distress. And something like a transformer was in peril from something like an alien.

How Maile the Movie Critic would have loved this. She'd have given en everything a 5-star review in the Voice.

Nani didn't want to cloud the day so she banished any more such thoughts. She decided to wait for a close up view of all the sculptures until she was with Hank.

Kaleo deposited her and her provisions in a sandy spot near one of the lava spurs. Then he stripped off his tee-shirt, grabbed up his board, and headed toward the waves. Nani popped open her beach umbrella to shade the Styrofoam cooler and spread out a blanket. She knew Kaleo would wander back when he got hungry. Until then, she was alone.

But not for long.

During the afternoon, Bethie Kalapana came by arm-in-arm with her neighbor and new BFF, Mrs. Yohay. They paused to chat while Silas Yohay squinted daggers at Nani from behind them. Apparently the Keawalani alliance of women was keeping him on a short leash.

The two hippy sisters, Clea and Clara Fern, shuffled by, able to use their walkers on the hard-packed rim of sand along the water. They called out, waxing poetic about that nice young officer who was courting Nani. Everyone in the vicinity heard them. She sighed. So much for any secrecy for the Big Island secret keeper herself. Nani was once again amazed by the efficiency of the local grapevine.

Between paddle boarding and swimming, Nani stopped by other picnics just to say hello. Old Man Hookano offered her one of the pork sandwiches from his trusty old grill, but she only accepted a bite to be polite, wanting to be hungry for her own picnic with Hank. She saw Packer up to his old tricks making a buy from a couple of *mokes* between two concessions. There was no indication that the little ferret saw her. She even visited Vincent Moi's clan, leaning over to whisper in the old gardener's ear what plans she and Hakumele had made for the very next night. If anyone was watching, they'd have seen that the little man looked alarmed, at least until Nani whispered assurances that his name would never be mentioned.

✦ ✦ ✦

Nani reclined on her beach blanket to read in the shade of her sun umbrella, but soon she turned her e-reader off, closed her eyes and drifted. It wasn't often that she had so much free time to herself. On Saturday afternoons like this, she tried to avoid booking clients in favor of housecleaning, shopping for groceries at the Ono Grinds Market, or a million and one other chores. Today was special, reserved for Hank and the chances of stepping up the relationship. If, in fact, there was to be a relationship.

Thoughts of a potential new romance inevitably forced her back to the miserable day two years before that she had broken off her engagement to the young doctor. Everyone had said it would be a marriage made in heaven. Everyone but Nani.

She'd lost so much. Maile had disappeared, her mother died, her father deserted the family, her Aunt Hakumele was disappointed in her. The old kumu didn't seem to understand that Nani missed the dances of joy, too, that she herself was in mourning as well. Kaleo was all she had left, and he was grappling with his own issues, so she hated to add her load to the one he was already carrying. She lived in terror of losing him, too. She couldn't keep him from the dangers of the surf, the road, the lifestyle he led, in fact she knew better than to even try. But sometimes she wished she could roll him up in Bubble Wrap.

Since it felt like love always led to loss, Nani was gun shy to get kicked in the heart ever again. But if she couldn't commit completely, she wouldn't at all. It wasn't fair. Not to the young intern, not to her. She'd told him that she held too much of herself in reserve to be the right choice for him.

He moved away after that. Doctors were always needed in Honolulu. He'd let her know she could reconsider, but not to wait too long. She'd heard from Mrs. C that he'd married within that same year. Apparently, Nani wasn't the love of his life after all.

It had all been painful, of course. She'd spent many days smiling at clients and crying herself to sleep at night. For a while, she drank too much and listened to the same sappy ballads over and over. She'd stare into the distance in darkened rooms, seeing nothing. Kaleo didn't yet live with her so nobody knew the trouble she was in. Everyone thought Nani was perpetually happy with her sparkling eyes, gentle manner and magnificent smile.

Kaleo changed that. To keep him from seeing his big sister's misery, she'd stopped drinking on her own while he was serving out his sentence. When he moved in, his nearness comforted her, and his spirit soothed hers. From then on, she let him choose the music. It took very little time for the pretense of health to become her reality, and she'd started to climb back out of the black hole.

But with Kaleo, the law breaker, along came the law. No doubt about it, Hank's body was a magnet that drew hers inexorably nearer. After a two year draught, he was cool water. A simple bout of sex would be a delight; a bump and tickle with a willing partner was good for a person. But something in the way she felt was different than pure animal magnetism. It wouldn't be so scary if that was all there was to it.

This Hank. He was different. She was pretty sure sex would come with strings attached. Was she ready for that? Could she commit this time? What made her think it would be any different than her experience with the doctor?

She was grateful that he was looking into Maile's case, but that might only be a measure of his interest in her. She admired his attraction to a puzzle, an unsolved mystery. He dovetailed with her sense of humor and seemed more interested in Kaleo's friendship than his punishment. Hank appeared to respect what she did for a living where the doctor had considered it little more than pampering. She'd loved that one breathtaking flight with Hank in the Mooney and relished the opportunity to fly with him again.

All that had to do with *liking* him, in addition to desiring him. And her desire was strong. Hank's body was long and lean, more suited to a track than a gridiron. He was all sinew and muscle on a six foot armature. The skin on his back was smooth and unblemished as bronze satin. Muscle memory – or whatever the hell it was – made her fingers prickle with the recollection of the touch. Her craving to see him nude made her grin, and she stretched in the heat of the late afternoon sun.

"What's causing that smile, Sleeping Beauty?"

Nani's eyes snapped open at the sound of his voice. Hank was a new shadow, helping the umbrella block the sun. He'd lost his uniform, probably changing in the old lava-walled toilet at the top of the hill. She had her first look at naked legs below his shorts and naked chest above. Her smile widened. The view lived up to her imagination. Maybe even exceeded it.

He set down a gym bag then reached for her hand and pulled her up. "Come on. Jay Samuels finally relieved me. I need to cool off."

For the next hour, they swam and body surfed and tried to stand double on the paddle board, failing again and again in splashing dives and laughing pile-ups. They occasionally sighted Kaleo far out to sea, riding the waves toward land.

Hank told Nani about Lynn and Marty Martin's Uncle Jeff. "We're letting him cool his heels in jail overnight," Hank said. "Niece and nephew still won't come right out and accuse him, so we probably won't be able to hold him, but he smells plenty rotten to me."

"What happens next? I mean, you just let him go? He may be guilty of taking Maile." Nani had trouble caring whether they could prove it or not. She wanted this dreadful waiting for answers to be over.

"Unless he confesses, we'll have to release him soon. But we won't let up. Give us a little more time, Nani. Jeff Lee has some surprises ahead of him. Lono has made a suggestion to Jackson O'Reilly."

They walked the line of sand sculptures, each choosing a favorite. At the final judging, they disagreed when Catwoman attacking Batman won the day. They talked about movies they'd both liked, moved on to books, organizations and candidates they supported, sports they played. They were discovering whether they had common ground beyond Maile, learning how to be a couple.

By seven, families were beginning to leave and concessionaires were packing up. Hank and Nani finally sat on the blanket to eat their picnic salads and chicken. As if on cue, Kaleo showed up with a knock-out named Jasmine. Nani wanted to order her little brother away as no more welcome at this picnic than ants. He was ignoring her stink eye completely. Finally, there was no other way. Nani said there was plenty, if the couple wanted to join them *until they had to leave since Kaleo had that early morning appointment.*

"Appointment? What appointment?" he asked, dark eyes barely containing their amusement. "Ohhhh yes, that appointment."

All four sat on the blanket and shared the wealth, watching the sun set in lurid Technicolor. Kaleo observed that a Hawaiian beach had no shortage of gorgeous girls, but that the two loveliest were now sharing one picnic with the two luckiest men.

Nani started to groan at his remark until Hank leaned over and whispered, "He's right, you know. No one is as lovely as you." He said it in such earnest, his warm breath tickling her ear. She realized her brother's comment hadn't struck him as a line. Hank meant it.

"I think that makes me the lucky one," she whispered back, and he moved closer, putting a long warm arm around her shoulders.

One of the few remaining family groups built a beach fire, and the instruments came out. Ukes and guitars and island songs replaced bird calls as night descended. The tradewinds arrived at long last, sweeping away the Kona weather and turning down the thermostat. The sound of the surf increased although it was getting too dark to see the waves swell before they broke on the sand.

"Before this gets any more *From Here to Eternity*, I guess we gotta go." With a grunt, Kaleo shoved his ample self up then helped Jasmine to her feet. "Have to get Pink Floyd back to the WikiWiki Fix. I'll drop Jasmine on the way. Nani, you coming? Or Hank, can you take her home?"

"He can take me home," Nani said

" I can take her home," Hank said at the exact same time.

"Glad to hear that's settled without another fight." Kaleo kissed the top of his sister's head, then Jasmine and he headed up the steep path, soon disappearing under the darkened trees at the top.

Not long afterwards, the music stopped. The last of the families gathered their belongings and departed, calling alohas and mahalos to each other. Nani could soon see no more than a few stragglers silhouetted in moonlight and moving down the beach away from her little stretch of lava and sand.

This was the moment. The stage simply could not get any more set. *It's Hank's move.*

And move he did. He rose to his knees, facing her. With his hand in her damp, wind-tangled hair, he pulled her head toward him. This was not the sweet exploration of his first kiss three nights ago. Good thing her lip had healed because this kiss was demanding and unrelenting. During his unyielding mouth on mouth reunion, he lowered her urgently down onto the blanket.

Nani responded in kind with her own eager mouth. There was nothing she loved more than a truly world class kiss, one that gave as good as it got. One that started at her mouth, then worked its way down her neck to her breasts.

Hank broke it only long enough to untie the strings of her bikini, first the top then the bottom. He gasped as he looked at her, bathed in moonbeams. "You're some kind of miracle, Nani. Are you protected?"

"You mean birth control? Yes."

"Should I use a condom?"

"I trust you're safe, Officer."

She started to pull down his shorts with a tug on the elastic, but he pushed her hands aside. He stood to strip them quickly then sank back down between her legs. She reached to place her fingers around his erection. He captured her hand, gently brushing her caress away. "No time," he muttered then kissed her again.

He pulled her arms out from her sides, and worked himself inside. She felt the still-warm sand below them give as his weight was added to hers, pelvis on pelvis. Nani locked her legs over his beautiful back and opened herself to accept his first full thrust. She moaned with the stretch, the pleasure. Another thrust and another, slippery and deep. It was soon over. Their craving for each other had rushed things.

Thrilling. Maybe too fast. Wait'll next time.

They lay interlocked while their hearts relaxed. Nani thought about ice bergs and the nine tenths still to explore. Same with bodies. This time was all about heat. Next would include exploring touches and tastes. She needed that to achieve fullest pleasure. And she could tell Hank was nearly ready for next time to begin. As was she.

His gym bag rang.

"Shit."

"Ignore it."

"Can't."

He crawled on all fours, snatched up the bag and dumped it. He pawed the cell phone out of the sand.

"Yeah?"

"Hank?" Allison Costello said loud enough that Nani could hear.

"Yeah?"

"You okay?"

"Yeah."

"Because Jay Samuels radioed in that your cruiser is still at Hapuna Beach."

"Yeah. I'm, ah, swimming."

"Well, he's out looking for you. So if you're swimming nude, you just might want to cover up."

Nani leaped up and grabbed her sarong. She threw Hank his shorts.

"10-4. And Allison? Thanks."

"Fo' shua."

"Shit," Hank said again, as he helped Nani pack up the picnic and evacuate the scene of the crime.

CHAPTER TWENTY-ONE

Predator On the Loose –
Is It Happening Here?
By Jackson O'Reilly
Excerpt from the *Keawalani Voice*, 2015

Reliable sources have fingered Jeffrey Lee as a 'person of interest' to Hamakua District Police. A co-worker of Lee, who is employed as a baggage handler at the Kona airport, reports that Captain Frank Lono and Officer Hank Lindsey took Lee into custody last Thursday. "They came at lunchtime and hauled him away. I heard the captain say he'd been hanging around too many kids. Little ones."

A second co-worker said, "It shook us up. Bad. If Lee is a danger to children, we need to know about it. We all got families."

Lee spent the night in jail, but was released yesterday afternoon following questioning. Captain Lono said, "We've heard rumors of his behavior going back twelve years or more. Allegations of abusive treatment of children in his own family and possibly others, as well. I want to alert the community that Lee has not been proved guilty. But any information you might have should be reported immediately. This is the type of situation where we need every villager's help."

When asked about the accusations against him, Mr. Lee refused to comment in printable language.

The investigation is ongoing, according to Captain Lono. As the story develops, it would be wise to keep a close watch on all children and to report anything suspicious you observe or hear.

When she'd met Kaleo, Jasmine Awana was at Hapuna Beach looking for treasure. She was a beachcomber but not just for the fun of it, although the noise and smell of the surf, the sandpipers and curlews zigzagging ahead of her, the feel of damp sand shifting under her feet, and the thrill of the hunt were always visceral pleasures. Jasmine was a beachcomber because she was an artist.

Her raw material was sea glass polished and etched by decades of salt water and sand, waves and currents. The gem-colored glass from old broken bottles or discarded vases, in nuggets with edges now rounded as jelly beans, was most visible to the keen eye in the afternoons as light shifted to a slanted view of the beach surface. Admittedly, Hapuna Beach wasn't the best place on the island to find glass, but she wanted to see the sand sculptures. She'd combined work with pleasure.

Pleasure for Jasmine included a little bodysurfing closer to shore than the surfers who rode boards, the *he'e nalu*. She felt newly alive with each wave, being this buoyant as she twisted and stroked up to high speed with no more equipment than her swim fins. As she ditched a spent wave, rolling sideways and tumbling forward, she felt like a bit of colorful glass herself, softened and beautified by the ocean.

Others were bodysurfing, too, but Jasmine was suddenly aware of a large presence very near. A dolphin, perhaps, or – *holy shit* – a shark? No, a very large man sharing her wave. His long black hair swirled like seaweed in the water, just like hers. His golden skin glistened just like hers. But there the similarity ended.

She had seen him earlier when he was riding a longboard. He was the real thing. A big Hawaiian like the ancients, tall and muscular, flexible as a dancer. A magnificent tattoo of pikake and plumeria blossoms, deep green maile leaves, and red 'i'iwi birds entwined his right leg. She smiled to herself. Pikake was Jasmine. And so was she.

Surely this beautiful man had been delivered to her as a gift from the spirits. It was no accident when she slid down the face of a wave, stroking hard with her outstretched arms to move diagonally right into him. Like a seabird returning from a very long flight.

✦ ✦ ✦

After leaving Nani and Hank on the beach, Kaleo drove Jasmine to her home above Waimea. The weathered house was a collection of boxes stacked higgledy-piggledy up the rocky hillside. One room had been added to another as former owners expanded into more bedrooms, family spaces, workrooms. It reminded Kaleo of a Swift Family Robinson tree house without the tree.

When Jasmine put the key in the front door, Kaleo heard thundering footsteps approaching from the other side. "Dogs?" he asked as he waited for the door to open. "Friendly dogs?"

"No, not dogs. But friendly most of the time."

Jasmine threw open the door and two little boys tumbled out, flailing and leaping like bodysurfers without the surf. The littlest grabbed for Jasmine's legs. She reached to pick him up as the older boy screeched to a stop to look up, up, up at Kaleo.

"We already have a dad, you know. So don't get any big ideas."

"Evan, be nice. This is Kaleo. And this little love bug is Tony." Jasmine gave the cuddly child in her arms a kiss on the head.

Kaleo held a palm out to older brother Evan. "No big ideas. Promise."

"*'Kay den*," said the boy and returned the high five.

"Guess what, Evan. Kaleo is a tattoo artist. Just look at his leg," said Jasmine as they all inched their way into the house, and she shut the door.

The boy took a look. "Wow! That's awesome. Could you do me one?"

"Well, sure. You look eighteen to me."

"Ma! He said I look eighteen!" Clearly, Kaleo moved into Evan's plus column.

"Yeah, but you're only just eight," said little brother Tony.

"Oh. Then we'll have to wait a decade, *cuz*."

"You'll have to wait until I'm dead and gone," said an old woman standing in the foyer behind all the action.

Jasmine said, "Kaleo this is my mother, Bea Awani."

"My pleasure, Auntie. If you don't want the kids tattooed, then I'll just paint them instead."

"Are you making fun, young man?" Bea raised an eyebrow while folding her arms akimbo.

"No ma'am. I'll airbrush something that will last maybe a week."

"Really?" shrieked Evan.

"Really?" shrieked Tony.

"Really?" asked Jasmine.

"Really," said Kaleo. "Bring them by the shop or, better yet, I'll come back tomorrow and do the job."

"All right then. It's late. Come in now for ice cream before three of us go to bed." Bea led the noisy procession into the large kitchen that was the first box in the row.

Jasmine looked up at Kaleo with a knowing smile and said, "Welcome home."

✦   ✦   ✦

Kaleo liked beach babes with no strings other than bikinis to untie. They liked him, too. On the mornings after, his women didn't feel like conquests so much as adored natural treasures. He was a generous lover who appreciated all sorts of female types and shapes. Because Kaleo truly enjoyed women, he could keep friendships going even after sex had flown the coop. Women had told him that was rare.

He'd thought that's how things would be with Jasmine. But he'd been wrong. It had been fun, Kaleo thought as he drove toward Nani's house, the early morning light already blinding toward the east. A surprise, for sure. He'd anticipated a night for two. But the noisy reception, the party-like atmosphere of the ice cream with a family, had felt good. It had been so long since he'd been part of such a gaggle. Nani's house was great and all, but the only other people there were her clients or his. Not family.

He teased the kids, and they teased him. He taught them some moves for riding a longboard, twisting and bobbing in the second box of the house which was a scruffy living room. They joined him in the gyrations until they looked like a troupe of very bad dancers. Finally, *tutu* Bea had corralled the boys and hauled them off to bed.

Kaleo had still been prepared for a tryst with Jasmine. And he got one, but not of the sexual kind. She'd led him into the third box, a place far more intimate than her bedroom. It was a magical room of glass. Shards were everywhere, some shiny, some frosted. They were in clear glass bowls, sorted by color and size. As the overhead lights shown on them, they flashed and winked like semi-precious gems. A long work table was covered with needle nosed and round spined pliers, spools of gold and silver wire in different gauges, decorative chains, clips and hooks. Unfinished projects waited under a work lamp.

Finished jewelry hung from wall boards covered with ocean blue velvet. It was stunning. The artist in Kaleo responded like a thirsty man to water. This jewelry was unlike any he had seen before. It was contemporary but with design integrity as old as time.

Jasmine combined glass with starfish charms or freeform pearls or bits of fabric or glass of contrasting shades. She created necklaces, bracelets, rings and earrings, of course, plus cell phone lanyards, key chains and anklets. The gold and silver wire work was swirled around the glass stones, like ocean waves or pieces of coral. Nothing was static as each piece recalled the ebb and flow of the waters that had created these beautiful heirlooms.

"Your work. It's staggering." He couldn't find the words to express how the creations bowled him over. And then he couldn't stop.

They talked into the night on the comfortable old living room sofa whose springs had given up long ago. Jasmine told him more about her art and how it had evolved. When she talked about design, she spoke with her hands and eyes almost as much as Nani did when she danced. It was so graceful, so expressive, so beautiful. Kaleo was excited just looking at her. She was an artwork herself.

"I actually studied textiles at the UH, but it turns out I don't have patience for fabric, at least not enough to sell as a living. Love to mix media, though. Fiber with metal or wood, all of it with glass. And it's commercial enough to make a profit." She sold just enough to support her family, along with her mother's social security plus a little child support from the boys' father.

"Where is he? Their father?" Kaleo asked, hoping he was on the other side of the planet.

"In Volcano, on the other side of the mountains. Alan manages a B and B there."

"Is he here much?"

She shook her head. "I won't let him take Evan without Tony, and Tony's too little for him to want to bother with very much. Maybe as he gets older." To Kaleo she hadn't sounded upset, but she went to the kitchen then and came back with two glasses and a bottle of spiced rum.

"I could get you a Coke, too, if you really want to screw up a good thing."

"Wouldn't think of it."

"Let's not think about my ex anymore, either." Instead, she told him how she sold to locals here in her workshop, but exhibited at oceanfront hotels whenever she could in order to sell to *haoles* and international tourists. How she was thinking about opening an actual shop in Waimea or one of the other villages in the area.

He talked about his mother's beach glass designs which had followed a far more traditional path. For the first time in years, he also described his father's leather work. "Manuku was as tough as cowhide himself and damn near as inflexible. But his saddles were sought after. He could create *kapa* designs you'd swear were actual bark cloth instead of carvings in an unforgiving medium like leather."

"Are your parents both dead? You're very young for that."

"Mom is. Dad's as good as. Haven't heard from him in a decade. Got nothing good to say about his personality, but I've never denied the asshole's artistry." He amazed himself how near he was to whimpering like a baby about the fucking deserter. This woman must be some sort of earth mother to get him revealing so much. He'd soon be blubbering about Maile. Didn't want Jasmine to think he was a wimp.

Enough.

"Guess my dad joins your ex in the let's-not-think-about-him department. At least for tonight."

"Deal." She refilled their glasses, and they clinked on it.

He told her how he'd gotten into the tattoo business, and why the Tat Joint was temporarily closed. She even dredged out of him that he loved to paint and evoked a promise that he would show her some samples one day soon. Proof she was a sorcerer ... he didn't usually offer to reveal them to anybody.

By the time he left in the early hours of the morning, they'd not had sex. But they'd started along the path toward making love.

✦ ✦ ✦

Nani bit into a spoonful of ripe papaya, but its juicy sweetness didn't register. She was also trying to read the *Voice*, but her brain kept veering off to the day before. She thought about the tattoo on Hank's chest.

"What a sweet dolphin," she'd said after tracing its outline with her tongue and thoroughly kissing its nose.

"It's supposed to be a shark." He'd sounded as though his feelings were hurt. "A dolphin's kinda tame for a cop, don't you think?"

"Oh. Maybe Kaleo could patch it up for you." The memory made her snicker until she saw her own reflection in the kitchen window.

I have to wipe this goofball smile off my face.

To get herself back in her own game, she consulted her schedule to confirm what clients would be coming when. It would be a packed day and the evening would be spent with her aunt and John Nawahine. She was thinking about how that meeting could go when she heard a familiar engine sputter to a halt behind the house. It must be Kaleo. She'd figured he had beaten her home last night and was still dead to the world out on the lanai. But here he was, opening the screen door.

Oh, little brother. So you got lucky, too, huh?

Kaleo passed through the lanai and into the kitchen. By the time he flopped down across from her in the breakfast nook, she'd filled his Surfer Gecko mug with coffee, cream and sugar. She slid it onto the table in front of him. "Aloha, *bruddah*. Thought you were returning Pink Floyd last night."

"Never made it back to WikiWiki Fix. Guess I'll keep it for the day after all."

"Spend the night with Miss Hapuna Beach, did you?"

"Now, *sistah*. Me? Kiss and tell?" Broad smile. "But I'm thinking I'll be going back later."

Nani was surprised. "You? A *two* night stand?"

He surprised her again by having no flip reply. In fact, he looked bemused by events himself. "Could be. Could be."

"So you like this Jasmine, huh?"

But Kaleo was saying no more about it. He stretched and yawned, then stood. "Whatevas. Is there a cop lurking upstairs?"

"Of course not. You can go shower."

"You play hide the nightstick with Officer Friendly on the beach?"

Kaleo clambered up the creaky stairs toward the bathroom snorting at his own joke.

Nani groaned then went back to her ruminations. She had not asked Hank to stay although his goodnight kiss had been a clear indication he was eager for the invitation. She liked that. But she worried, too. Morning after jitters.

What is Hank thinking this morning? When will I hear from him again? Does he want more than sex? Do I? What the hell ... have I turned fourteen again? Get over yourself, sistah.

Most of all, she worried if he'd be mad about what Hakumele and she had planned for tonight. He'd probably think it could be dangerous.

✦ ✦ ✦

Hank buckled on his ten pound tool belt and headed out the front door. The sun was great, the drive to work was great, life was great. He looked at himself in the rearview mirror.

Cripes. Gotta wipe this goofball smile off my face.

She'd come to him, she'd apologized, she'd fixed him a meal, she'd allowed him to make love to her. She'd been a tawny-skinned, hip switching, sex goddess. One who was suddenly willing to do what he asked. He was winning her over.

Nothing could darken this day. Nothing except his own insecurities about independent women. He'd been attracted before, but they'd proven hard to understand. He had no magic ring to decode them. Nani might be too ambitious for a simple island boy. Maybe she'd leave the island for riches elsewhere. Maybe he should slow down.

But he'd never before felt the way he did about Nani. She was the most breathtaking thing he'd ever discovered about his Big Island home. He was walking in quicksand here, in danger of sinking at any point. By the time he'd gotten to the police station, he'd managed to work a few dark clouds into his sunny morning after all.

He was sulking as he walked in. As usual, Allison was at the reception/dispatch center to one side of the station's waiting room. While the rest of the small area was humbled with mismatched furniture, overheads with a flickering fluorescent and a wall of overlapping wanted posters and safety bulletins, Allison's desk was pristine. Not a file or Post-It was out of square. No matter how frantic the waiting room got – angry citizens lodging complaints or detainees singing bawdy drinking songs – Allison was always in calm control.

What was unexpected this morning was Renee. Allison's youngster was sitting on the floor in front of a shabby leather sofa that was so cracked it appeared to be shedding its skin like a snake. Her scrawny legs were folded beneath her, only knobby knees visible. A pile of D cells and maybe a half dozen flashlights were scattered in front of her.

Hank wondered why she wasn't in school. His furrowed eyebrows lifted into a question. Allison, without a break in her keyboarding, said, "Teacher meetings. All day."

"I see. Hi, Renee."

"Hank," the child answered. Apparently done with pleasantries, she added, "Leave your flashlight with me."

Wiry curls in her topknot bounced in several directions like miniature antennae. *Gidigidis* was the word for cowlicks in the islands. Hank had heard they were the mark of a particularly mischievious child. Funny how often island myths proved prophetic.

Hank smiled at Renee, but beneath the tangle of curls, her eyes squinted and lips clamped like a pugnacious featherweight. Hank switched to deadpan. This kid was a little dictator. It charmed him.

All in all, she lightened his mood.

"Yes, ma'am," he said, removing the Maglite from his work belt and placing it in her outstretched hand. "Looks like you already got enough of these to light up the night."

She sighed as though the weight of the world pressed down on her narrow shoulders. "You officers *have* to keep your equipment in tiptop shape. I worry that you don't do it. Frank is as bad as the rest of you. I have to be sure guns are clean and your batteries are fresh and, oh, just *every*thing." She jutted out her chin. "I'll be a cop one day and will order someone to do it for me."

"Well, on behalf of all us officers, I thank you for your support." As he doffed his cap to her he heard Lono's shout from down the hall.

"That you, Lindsey? When you're ready to begin your day, maybe you could join me. But don't let me rush you or anything. No worries. I got all day. I'm just your boss and all."

Renee giggled. "Frank blows off steam like Kilauea. That's what Allison says when he's ranting around our house about something."

Allison looked up. "Renee. You don't need to repeat everything you hear. And Hank, I'd advise you the same thing."

He gave her a quick salute and went down the hall to the boss's office. "You bellowed?" he asked.

Lono was leaning back, feet up on an open desk drawer. He was cleaning his nails with the edge of a business card, probably belonging to some minor town official. "While you were out at the beach yesterday, I was here talking with Jeff Lee."

"Hey, whose fault is it that I was on traffic duty?"

"Oh? I guess Nani Palea in a bikini *would* stop traffic." Lono didn't even try to hide a smirk.

Hank exploded. "Jesus! I was off duty by then. And why the hell is my business an APB around here anyway?"

"Take it easy, Officer. It's a public beach, and word gets around.

I've already told you I envy you. Happy to hear things are going well with that young lady."

"Well, let's hear less about Nani and more about that scumbag Lee."

"Right." Lono's jowls returned to their customary scowl. "Man says he never touched Maile Palea. Says he was in Afghanistan at the time serving his country. Allison confirmed it for me. Sure enough, the bastard was there."

"Shit. So that lead is dead."

"As a goddamn dodo. Course, that doesn't mean he didn't abuse his niece Lynn and beat on his nephew Marty through the years."

"But they're not talking. Don't want to enlighten their mother about her brother's dirty little secrets."

"Still not going to allow a pedophile to operate on my island. We'll be watching him. One wrong move, and we'll bag his ass. Got to let him go for now, though."

"I see O'Reilly printed an article about him."

"Yep. Don't see any reason for the *Voice* to keep quiet. Want the village to watch him, too. I may not have proof yet, but that kind of mud sticks."

"Guess my cold case is back on ice."

"Officially, yes. Keep working it in your spare time. Unless you're too busy with Maile's big sister."

"Fuck you, boss."

"What I love about you, Lindsey, is how you brown nose."

CHAPTER TWENTY-TWO

Damn Spam Is Everywhere!
By Jackson O'Reilly
Excerpt from the *Keawalani Voice*, 2015

There was a time when, for me, Spam meant those ubiquitous ads in your email regarding erectile dysfunction or preapproved credit or lonely housewives with remarkable skills. And, of course, it was also canned meat eaten by the poor.

Then I moved to the Big Island and discovered that the locals love it.

Spam, short for Spiced Ham, first invaded Hawaii in WWII along with the military. Soldiers called it Special Army Meat when being polite. According to my ex-military Uncle Bob, they also called it Squirrel, Possum and Mouse (I can't print the other names for fear of breaking my own iffy standards of journalism). Soldiers were sometimes forced to eat it three times a day.

They came to hate it not for its flavor but for its ubiquitousness.

But here, Spam is a delicacy, served with pride at gourmet restaurants and fast fooders alike. It's often called Hawaiian Steak. Hawaiians crave it so much we eat three pounds per year per capita. That far out-consumes the rest of the nation.

We celebrate it in musical Spam Jams. We sculpt it in competitions taken as seriously as sand sculpture. We don't discuss its nutritional value. In Hawai'i, it's not the cheap version of anything … in fact, other canned meats are considered the cheap version of Spam.

It's pink, it's soft, it's an acquired taste. And I'm told I can't be a real Hawaiian until I acquire it. So Daya, next time I'm in the Big Island Girl, make it a Spam musubi and a shave ice, please.

After his shower, Kaleo crawled into his bed on the lanai and slept. When he awoke later in the morning, Nani was working so he made his own breakfast of rice, eggs and grilled Spam without anyone around to criticize.

He did a couple tattoos for clients, one a simple butterfly on a woman's ankle and the other a more complex repair on a stars and stripes scroll that had been poorly done years ago. Just before three in the afternoon, he packed up stencils, ink and an airbrush then drove Pink Floyd to the precarious house of boxes above Waimea.

He arrived just after the school bus unloaded Tony and Evan. Jasmine was beside the road waiting for the boys, and Kaleo dared to think, maybe for him, too. Even the shapeless shift she wore could not hide what a stunner she was, tall and solid with shoulders as broad as an Olympic swimmer. Her hair was in one thick braid that hung down to her mid back. Wisps around her face curled in the humidity. Kaleo decided that pretty wasn't the right word for her. Striking, maybe. Or statuesque. The structure of her face brought to mind the plains Indians whose pictures he'd seen in history books, faces that were noble with sharp features and high cheekbones. In a poi dog, any mix was possible.

They gathered at a game table in the living room, and Kaleo laid out drawings for the boys to look through. He'd brought the matching stencils with him. Tony chose a gecko on a surfboard. Evan, older and worldlier, wanted a dagger or sword dripping blood, but Jasmine nixed it. He settled on a stingray with evil slanted eyes. Kaleo pulled out the stencils, and lined up the right color inks. He rubbed Evan's bicep with an alcohol pad, held the stencil tight to it, and started the airbrush. In no time, the ray swam across the little arm. Next, the gecko waved a shaka from Tony's forearm.

As a final step, Kaleo sprinkled the stenciled tattoos with baby powder. "It'll help them keep from peeling off for little while," he explained. "And when you wash, be gentle."

Jasmine muttered, "They won't wash them at all."

The boys were over the moon.

"Anyone here know how to say thanks?" Jasmine asked.

Kaleo heard shouts of gratitude as the boys tore outdoors to find friends who needed to be lorded over.

"You know, maybe I'd like one of those stencils, too," said Jasmine. She cocked her head and gave him a knowing smile that would have made the Mona Lisa jealous.

"Sure. Where?"

"Come to my bedroom. I'll show you."

While the kids were out playing and Bea was wherever old ladies went in the daytime, Jasmine and Kaleo shared an afternoon delight. Then another.

The kids weren't the only ones who were over the moon.

✦ ✦ ✦

Nani had done five client sessions in a row, and she was feeling it. No doubt about it, a massage that was good for the client could be bad for her hands if the work was deep tissue manipulation. But she still had a phone call to make before Aunt Hakumele picked her up for their evening appointment.

The call was hard. It was to Lynn Martin. The girl sounded wary, but at least she didn't hang up. Their greeting was awkward enough that Nani dispensed with polite small talk and got on to the reason for her call. "I know the police have interviewed your uncle, and that you don't want to talk about that," she said.

Lynn sounded cold. "I *can't* talk about it. My mother would die if her brother was accused of anything by Marty and me. Can't you people understand that?"

Nani hoped nobody sent Martina Martin the morning's *Voice* article. "Believe me, Lynn, I understand the need to keep secrets. But I want to pass on an idea."

Lynn's voice thawed some, but Nani still heard suspicion. "I don't know what you mean."

Here goes.

"I have clients who have suffered abusive backgrounds similar to yours. They have men in their lives that they thought were dependable, and people who would deny the truth if they made public accusations. But, Lynn, some of these women have found a lot of comfort in talking to each other. With a counselor. They tell me it helps to know they're not alone."

"This is too private to talk about, Nani. I know you mean well, but it scares me."

"I get that. But if you ever need the name of a group, call me. I'll find you a good one in Honolulu, and I'll never mention your name to anyone in the process."

There was a pause before Lynn answered. She sounded perplexed. "Why would you do that for me?"

This girl wasn't used to kindness. Nani hoped it wasn't too late for Lynn to discover how much of it was ready and willing to circle around her. The Spirit of Aloha was a code of ethics many islanders used to interact in the world, a joyful spirit of sharing life's troubles and triumphs. Lynn Martin had apparently never been touched by it. Nani said, "We all are here to help each other. The Aloha Spirit, and all that. I believe in it. Helping you is not just my obligation ... it's my pleasure."

"Okay. But I'm not ready yet. Maybe one day. Maybe. And Nani?" Lynn's voice cracked then she lowered it as if afraid of being overheard. "I'm not accusing anyone of anything, but Marty and I are both glad that the police have spoken to Uncle Jeff."

Nani the Secret Keeper had done what she could to open a door. It was up to Lynn to walk through it or not.

✦　✦　✦

"Hank? It's Kaleo Palea."

The call caught Hank just as he was pulling into his driveway. He'd monitored his cell all day hoping for a call or text from Nani. This wasn't it, but her brother was better than nothing. "Howzit?"

"Got a problem, *brah*. I'm in Waimea, and Pink Floyd crapped out. Motorhead musta slipped up. Engine won't turn over."

Hank was surprised to be the person Kaleo contacted. Didn't a guy as friendly as a golden retriever have plenty of buddies? But he was pleased to be on the big man's call list. It wouldn't hurt the cause if Nani's brother could count on him. "You need help? I can come get you."

"A ride, no. Help, yes. Wonder if you'd check on Nani for me?"

Alarm bell.

"Check on her? What's wrong?"

Kaleo explained what Nani and their Aunt Hakumele were up to. They believed the plumeria grower, John Nawahine, was poisoning his workers and his grandson with tainted fungicide. They intended to chat with him about it tonight.

"I planned on following them, but Floyd's breakdown screwed that up. Not that I think there's any real danger. I'm sure Nawahine will hear them out. But, just to avoid any kind of pissing match between them, I thought I should be nearby. Could you go for me? And, maybe not say that I was going to follow them? That I'm the one who called you?"

As Kaleo talked, Hank's emotional temperature climbed skyward. Liking Nani – maybe even loving her – was hell on his system.

He tried to call her. As her cell rang, he practiced how to say, "Are you out of your mind?" without offending her.

Confronting the much respected John Nawahine to accuse him of poisoning people? Can she possibly be right that he's doing such a thing? Would she do such a thing if she wasn't sure?

When the phone routed him to voice mail, all he could spit out was, "Call me! Now!" then he powered up the car, tore out of his drive and off toward the Nawahine farm on the lower slope of Mauna Kea.

CHAPTER TWENTY-THREE

Rack n' Roll Ready to Bowl
By Jackson O'Reilly
Excerpt from the *Keawalani Voice*, 2015

After a two month closure for restoration, Rack n' Roll Lanes re-opens this week. All signs of the grease fire that started in the grill and gutted most of the interior are now a thing of the past. A new snack bar, pin setters, maple lanes, and lobby are awash with retro colors, graphics, and blow molded plastic seating. The rehab looks like a return to the future world of George and Jane Jetson.

New leagues are asked to sign up now. Those that do will receive a 25% discount on snacks, ball and shoe rentals, and lane fees for their first night of league bowling. Let the pins fall where they may.

Hakumele picked up Nani and drove toward John Nawahine's home in her little yellow Scion. It was not far, just outside the next village. Nani had never been to the farm nor met the plumeria grow-er before. The evening was cool, made more so by the ongoing chill between aunt and niece. Nani wrapped her shawl tightly around her shoulders even though Hakumele seemed cozy enough in a volumi-nous sleeveless muumuu.

Hakumele believed John Nawahine would never knowingly use a substandard chemical that endangered his employees. And he cer-tainly wouldn't imperil Kala, his grandson. The kumu said that if a bad product was poisoning the farm, Mr. Nawahine was unaware of it. All Nani had to do was to explain it to him, and he would imme-diately remedy the situation.

But was it really that simple? If he did know what was happen-ing, he'd be plenty angry to find them ready to expose his secret. He might kick them out. Refuse to listen. Call the cops to report slan-der. Continue to use substandard chemicals. Fire Vincent Moi if he figured out who blabbed. Fire up a chainsaw and bury their bloody remains in the fields where no one ...

Oh, quit it.

"What does Mr. Nawahine think our visit is about?" Nani asked, clamping down on her imagination.

"I told him we were coming on an issue involving his grandson. Nothing more."

"You didn't mention the fungicide at all?"

"Of course not. You're the professional about this, and it's your the-ory. It's your job to explain it. I will be there merely to see that he listens to you."

Nani looked sideways at her aunt, a woman who never took a back seat to anybody. She caught a ghost of a grin on the older woman's lips. Hakumele had certainly never called her a professional before, not for anything other than dance. Was it possible her aunt was proud of her massage ability, too? Or just distancing herself in case

Nani was wrong about Kala's infection?

Hakumele's seat was pushed far back in the tiny Scion, but her breasts and belly still just cleared the steering wheel. Nani remembered nestling into that soft spot herself, the ample lap that had comforted her so often in her childhood. Nani hated doubting her aunt like this.

The road to the Nawahine farm angled through ancient mango trees whose limbs formed a canopy over the patchy surface. When they came out of the forest there was still enough twilight to see fields of small plumeria trees. The home itself was worthy of a *House Beautiful* spread on the way things used to be. It had the sprawling grandeur of a nineteenth century sugar cane plantation house. The sharply pitched roof peeked through the surrounding gardens, and a wide porch encircled the whole facade. Nani imagined long days of reading in a wicker chair with tradewinds blowing through the rails, scented with a thousand flowers. Someone named James or Ochoa would appear with tea, or possibly stronger stuff, even before she requested it.

They pulled through an open gate into the driveway of the magnificent home. Even the tall fence was a work of art with birds of paradise forged from iron for beauty as well as protection. Hakumele parked her yellow clown car next to a dark windowed Escalade.

Nani's nerves began to tingle as they climbed the wide front steps together. Hakumele held up the hem of her billowing dress so she wouldn't trip, and Nani was vaguely aware the aging woman wasn't as agile as she used to be. Auntie rang the bell which chimed somewhere deep within the house. Like two trick or treaters, they stood on the front porch, ready for whatever happened next.

The enormous koa wood doors, intricately carved with plumeria leaves and blossoms, dwarfed both women which was no easy feat in the case of Hakumele. Nani thought the homeowner must be some sort of giant to need a double portal like this. Or at least the size of Kaleo.

Wouldn't it be comforting if Kaleo were waiting in the car in case shots explode from inside?

When one of the massive doors swung open, she was taken aback. She had to look down at John Nawahine instead of up. He was an old man, short and soft-looking. If necessary, Nani could wrestle him to the ground as easily as a teacup poodle. Her apprehension drained away. As he rose on his toes to deliver a traditional greeting kiss to Hakumele, Nani observed he was comprised of circles, like a junior Michelin Man. His round head bobbed with no visible neck above his round chest which balanced above an even rounder belly. His soft hands grabbed hers as he leaned forward to kiss her cheek, too.

"You don't look well, John. Are you ill?" Hakumele asked as they entered his home. John Nawahine's face was wrinkled as a newborn and nearly as red.

"Just a touch of flu, *Kumu.* I'll survive."

It's not flu season. Maybe he is suffering from the fungicide, too?

Nani followed her aunt as Nawahine escorted them into a sitting room that nearly sang with island fabrics and art. One wall panel was a stained glass masterpiece with the same pattern as the front door recreated in brilliant colors. Nani recognized a fabulous collection of wooden bowls, hand turned from mango, monkey pod, and ironwood. The craft – as well as many of the trees and the creators – was nearly extinct on the island now. Kaleo would love to see the art treasures in this room. The fact that Nawahine was preserving them made Nani like him. But she cautioned herself.

History is full of bad guys with good taste.

A tea service already graced the low glass coffee table. After he poured them each a cup and assured himself of their comfort, Nawahine turned to business. "So, tell me, *Kumu,* what do you have to say regarding my grandson?" His round face puckered with worry.

"Your grandson is a wonderful dancer, John," Hakumele said. "No doubt he has the potential of championship in his spirit and heart. He is a credit to the Nawahine name. But lately, his feet have not moved him quite so cleverly."

Nawahine's almond shaped eyes opened just the least bit wider. "Is the boy sluffing off? Not practicing enough? Lacking in attitude?" He sounded genuinely concerned to Nani. *He must take hula as seriously as the other island arts.*

She covertly observed his soft fingers as they tightened on the fragile teacup handle. This man did not do the hard physical jobs of farming himself. Maybe that's why he was unaware of a problem with his field workers.

He's innocent just like Hakumele says he is. He will gladly listen.

"It's not the boy, John. Kala is a diligent student. It's something else, something in his environment. And it is curable, according to my niece. She is a past champion of hula as well as a brilliant therapist for bodies under stress. She has examined the boy and can help him now. Nani is here tonight to explain it to you."

Brilliant therapist? Wow, Auntie.

Nawahine turned his attention toward Nani. "I'm eager to hear your advice."

How could this homely little man be the patriarch of a family that produced Kala? At that moment, the answer walked into the room. The newcomer was the image of how Kala would look as an adult. Tall, elegant, incredible.

"Ah, Pierce," said Nawahine. "Ladies, this is Kala's father. My son-in-law is home from the mainland to learn management of the Nawahine operation until Kala is of age."

Pierce took Hakumele's hand and bowed to the *kumu*. "My father-in-law is a consummate salesman. I'm still deciding between the

SECRETS OF THE BIG ISLAND

family business and teaching botany at USC. Both have their advantages." Next he took Nani's hand and stared into her eyes. "But the scale may be tipping toward Keawalani."

Nani had met the type before. Smooth and slippery as a shark. "And your wife? Is she here, too?" She allowed a hint of a smile to cross her face.

A hint of a frown crossed his. "Iolani is in the Florida Everglades counting samples of the rare Fakahatchee Beaked Orchid. We're both botanists, you see. Our travel schedules keep us away so much of the time, it is better for our son to be with his grandfather for now."

Pierce sat opposite the women and rested one slender ankle over the other as he extended his long legs. He had the lithe body movements of the most beautiful males of their species, be they stallions or stags. Nani wondered about Nawahine's daughter. Assuming she resembled her father, how had she attracted this man to the family? She must be a pretty rare orchid herself. Did John Nawahine trust his son-in-law or worry about him? Was family money the real reason ...

Stop!

Some Big Island secrets were not hers to explore. Her business was only Kala.

As though he heard her thoughts, John Nawahine said, "Hakumele and Nani are here regarding the recent regression in Kala's dancing."

Pierce rolled his eyes. "His dancing? You mean he's still playing around with that hula stuff? Might be time to start him in football, don't you think?"

Oh oh.

Nothing got to Hakumele like a slur against hula. The old warrior drew herself up like an unfurling fern. "Young man. The hula carries the Aloha Spirit of these islands, and your son has the chance to become one of the greats. I know because I am the teacher of his halau, a grand champion in my own time as my neice was in hers."

John Nawahine looked flustered. "Now *Kumu*, I'm sure that my son-in-law – "

"To excel, Kala must work harder, build a stronger, more flexible body with better balance and far more cunning than any man who merely carries a ridiculous ball from one spot to another. Be assured that no one except the uninformed questions the discipline, commitment and degree of masculinity such a dance takes."

Nani saw the delight in Pierce's cold eyes as her aunt huffed and puffed. And that pissed her off. How dare he disrespect her Auntie? She turned her back on Pierce and spoke only to his father-in-law as she described the internal infection she had discovered in one of the plantation gardeners, an infection that felt to her like a slow-but-steady toxin fighting the overall health of his system.

Nawahine further wrinkled his wrinkled brow. "And this worker's name? We must help him."

"Not an essential part of the story. He's in good care. It is a confidentiality issue, really."

"So you are a *medical* therapist?" Pierce asked.

She heard the slight in his voice, condescending to her as he did to her aunt. "Well no, but as an educated, trained and experienced *massage* therapist, I have a code of ethics, as well. And I have discovered the beginnings of similar problems in Kala's feet."

Nawahine gasped. "We must consult a doctor right away!"

Nani raised a hand to stop him. "I agree, but it is too soon for a doctor to be aware of the infection that I can feel. It's more advanced in your employee than in Kala. It's as yet a matter of communication between the boy's limbs and my hands, a recognition of bubbles no bigger than those in foam, beneath the skin but threatening with pain to come. It is too soon to manifest as the shortness of breath or headaches or digestion issues that will become noticeable in medical exams if left unchecked."

Her audience stared at her with expressions of concern.

Concern for Kala or that I'm nuts?

"And I believe I know the cause." Nani soldiered on. She explained that she had learned the Nawahine operation recently switched to a new fungicide, one with chemicals from China. She believed this may be the problem, that the purity of the chemicals were in question. Nawahine should stop using them immediately.

"Oh, really." Pierce rolled his eyes again. "We will have a doctor examine Kala, of course. But switch products based on the say of a hula instructor and a masseuse?"

The grandfather ignored him and asked, "Can you fix the boy?"

"Yes, with a bit of time, I can help repair the damage."

"So you *do* practice medicine?" Pierce challenged.

Nani's fuse was running short. "No. I help the nerves and muscles repair themselves." She turned back to Nawahine. "But the biggest help would be for you to go back to your original chemicals while you test the new fungicide. Otherwise, your employees and your family may get worse over time. You, too, if that is not really flu that you are suffering."

"The *biggest* help would be a doctor examining the boy immediately," Pierce repeated. "And he's my son."

Hakumele spoke more calmly this time. "Of course. Have your tests. On the boy and on your chemicals. But, my Nani is right. I can feel it. And until you test, I will no longer teach Kala for fear of damaging him further." She rose to leave.

John Nawahini gasped.

Pierce opened his mouth to speak, but his father-in-law leapt up to his full shortness. "Now, *Kumu*, of course we will test. I cannot have my workers or my family imperiled. Kala plays in those fields and greenhouses while I work here in a lab. He's exposed more than I am.

More than his father. But Pierce is an excellent botanist. He will order the proper tests." He shot a look at his son-in-law.

"Of course I will, John," Pierce said. "Safety, not economics, is our primary concern." He also stood and gave Hakumele a gracious little bow.

It was time to go. The family was upset but willing to resolve the problem. Hakumele and Nani had received the promise they had come for. All four moved toward the massive front doors. As they swung one open, they were surprised to see a patrol car in the drive. An officer was leaning against its front door.

Nani's mouth dropped open in an O as perfect as a Cheerio.

"What on earth?" sputtered Nawahine.

"You mean you called the cops on us?" asked Pierce. "I hardly know whether to be irritated or amused."

"Nani," said Hakumele, the only one on the scene who appeared calm. "I believe your ride is here."

CHAPTER TWENTY-FOUR

Sea Glass: Trash to Treasure
By Jackson O'Reilly
Excerpt from the *Keawalani Voice*, 2015

Around lakes and rivers, it's called beach glass. Along the ocean, you might hear it called sea glass. It's much the same thing although experts will tell you that ocean saline etches in a different way.

Experts also say the real McCoy looks quite different from glass polished in a rock tumbler. Many artists consider the latter to be 'cheating.' They say it looks more gem-shiny while real sea glass is frosted. There's snobbery about the softened shards that are not duplicated artificially.

But the real point of sea or beach glass is this: it turns the throwaway culture of mankind into a thing of beauty. Most of it is found just down the waterfront from factories and dump sites where bottles or dishes or insulators were tossed away two

decades or more ago. Rubbish from ships is
another source. Where beaches are buffeted
by storms and prevailing winds, where glass
can weather from explosive waves and currents and erosion, that's where you'll find
it.

Sea glass is its own minor miracle. It's
one of the very few examples of nature making a silk purse out of a manmade sow's ear.

When Pink Floyd persisted in doing absolutely nothing, Kaleo called
the WikiWiki Fix Garage. The owner said he'd come to Waimea, but
it would be late, probably after ten. He had to go see his kid in a high
school production of *The Music Man*, and his wife wouldn't consider
Kaleo's plight a good enough reason to get out of it, although he'd heard
his kid sing before, and he would have liked any reason not to attend.

Jasmine asked Kaleo to stay for dinner. "Bea does the cooking
around here, and she's great." Kaleo thought of all the aunties and *tu-
tus* he knew who could make magic even with the worst cuts of meat.

How come young women aren't learning those skills?

He figured it was a thought best kept to himself, or he'd have no girl
friend in addition to no car. And no dinner.

"What we having, *tutu*?" Evan asked through clenched teeth as he
wrestled with Kaleo's arm. The boy was pulling down on the massive
hand with both his arms and all his might.

"I thought Hawaiian stew. But I can't find two of my potatoes. I'm
sure I bought them. But who knows where I put them?" The old woman was searching around the coffee maker, the toaster, the cookie jar
and everything else on the cluttered countertop.

Evan suddenly released tension on Kaleo, causing the big man to
pull him all the way over to his other side.

Tony looked worried. His lower lip trembled. "It wasn't my fault, *tutu.*"

"Shut up, *brah,*" Evan muttered, staring daggers at his little brother.

Jasmine squinted a stink eye like the one Kaleo remembered seeing on his own mom ages ago. Maybe it was handed out to them when their children were born. A mother's glare was not to be ignored. "What you two been up to? Where are *tutu's* potatoes?"

It took some time, but it was finally determined that they had somehow magically been rammed up Pink Floyd's exhaust pipe. The two innocents were sent to their room. Kaleo was ordered to quit that snickering. He was also given a barbeque fork and tongs to extract the potatoes. Afterwards, he had no trouble starting up the reliable old Volvo. Then he called Hank, who told him he was at Nawahine's place and, no, Kaleo didn't have to come spell him. All was quiet. Then Kaleo called off the WikiWiki Fix, and Jasmine called for a pizza.

While they waited for dinner to arrive, Kaleo went into the boys' room where they'd been sent for a time out. He sat down on one of the bunk beds. They studiously ignored him, Evan working on a drawing of an intergalactic battlefield, and Tony singing a verse to the ceiling, one that was about worms and puking. Kaleo just barely recalled it from his own childhood.

After a time he asked, "You s'pose somebody could learn at school what a potato in the exhaust pipe can do to a car?"

Little brother stopped singing and said, "Yeah, Arnie told –"

"Shut it," big brother warned.

"Why you s'pose somebody put those potatoes in *my* car?"

"Don't know," Evan said, shrugging his shoulders. He didn't look up from the alien he was drawing.

Tony raised his hand as if in school. "I know! I know! Maybe he didn't want you to leave. He made it so you have to stay here."

"Yeah? How come?" Kaleo asked.

"'Cause he says that the men we like always go away. I mean maybe he said that."

Evan crinkled up the paper and threw the wad at Tony. "Shut up, you little rat."

Kaleo stood, gathered them both up, one under each arm, and swung them in circles. Arms and legs kicked and flailed until they were giggling too much to keep fighting. He then tossed them onto the bed.

"Here's what I think," Kaleo said, writing his cell number in huge letters on Evan's drawing pad. "All the potato bandits have to do is call. I'll be here just as soon as I can. Unless somebody sticks a potato up *my* butt."

Tony hooted. "A potato up your butt!"

"I can't take a seat, I have a potato up my butt," Kaleo said.

Evan leaped up and repeated a surfer move he'd learned the night before. "I'd like to catch a wave, but I have a potato up my butt."

Hysteria erupted in the boxy little room until Jasmine appeared at the door. All three guys looked sheepish as she said, "Thank you, Kaleo, for teaching the *other* children a new phrase. We'd just about gotten past fart jokes, and now this."

Maybe Evan tried to stop himself but couldn't. "Sit down Ma or do you have a potato –"

"Nip it, kiddo. And don't try that with *Tutu* Bea. Now two of you kids wash up for pizza and the third one come with me." She took hold of Kaleo's hand.

As they walked down the hall toward the kitchen, Jasmine stopped, reached up on her toes and kissed him ever so lightly on the lips. "Thank you."

"For what?" Kaleo was puzzled.

"For bringing guy talk into this house once again."

Kaleo knew what it was like to miss a father. But he didn't say such a thing. Instead, he grinned and counted on his fingers. "How lucky can I get? A girl who wants me to be myself. And she's a gorgeous girl. And she's leading me to pizza."

At the end of another family evening, Kaleo spent the night with Jasmine. He was uncertain whether it would happen here in her house, knowing that her kids – and worse yet, her mother – were just a few boxes farther up the hill.

"My mother knows what men and women do," Jasmine said. "And the boys have done what they can to prove they like you here."

"Is your family always part of your dates?"

"Well, so far, I'm not sure we've actually had what I'd call a date."

At the moment, Kaleo was pulling her shift over her head and placing a hand over one lovely breast. He breathed in her ear. "I think we're dating right now."

She began to unbutton his shirt. "It's important that a guy knows what he's getting with me. There's more than one heart on the line here." He pulled her down on top of him. She straddled his chest and slowly worked her way down his body as she continued to speak tough words very softly. "So if you know you're going to break any one of those hearts, do it before this gets too far out of hand."

Holy crap.

This was no Miss Hapuna Beach with nothing but bikini strings. This woman was a whole package wrapped and tied with twine. And he was a man with a big decision to make.

✦ ✦ ✦

Tickled or pissed. Nani didn't know which to feel. She was tickled that Nawahine was going to suspend the suspicious fungicide. But she was pissed at Hank for thinking he had to be there to rescue a damsel who was not at all in distress. She could tell he was pissed at her, too, since his words were few and delivered through clenched teeth. The ride home with Hank was chillier than the ride out with Hakumele.

Damn it all, she was the one who had compromised last time and returned his damn hat to the damn police station. It was his turn to give a little ground, to trust her to handle herself. His presence at the Nawahine home had been an embarrassment. And who the hell did Hakumele think she was, ordering Nani to ride home with Hank? How did she even know that Nani was having a ... a ... *thing* with the cop?

Oh, yeah!

Nani remembered how Daya the Waitress had mentioned Hank in front of her aunt at the Big Island Girl. Implying his whereabouts were of concern to Nani. Hakumele always could read whole novels between the lines. Nani glanced at Hank as he drove, catching him glancing at her. They both quickly looked away.

I won't cry. I won't.

✦ ✦ ✦

I won't apologize. I won't.

Damn it to hell, just because there was no danger after all didn't mean there couldn't have been. Since when did doing the right thing make a guy feel like such a jerkwad? Hank couldn't even tell Nani that he wasn't the one who'd decided she needed to be followed. He should never have made that bullshit promise to Kaleo to keep his name out of it. The whole damn family was driving him nuts. Even the auntie was a tough customer.

Besides, there *had* been danger, just not the kind he'd expected. Hank had seen that jerkwad Pierce guy looking at Nani. The bastard was too rich and too handsome to be fair competition. If that wasn't danger, he'd like to know what was.

They arrived in front of Nani's home. Hank pulled in the drive and shut down the engine. While the car cooled, the couple didn't. Neither of them spoke. But neither of them moved, either. A year passed. Maybe two. Finally Hank pried his jaws open enough to speak. "I thought we had an understanding that you would not do dangerous stunts on behalf of your clients."

"*You* had that understanding, Hank. I didn't. Besides, I had this planned before we went to the beach together. I couldn't go back on my word to my auntie." She crossed her arms and went still again.

They sat. Tick, tock. Okay, she maybe had a point. A promise had been made to her aunt before one was made to him. If she'd actually made that promise which, now that he thought about it, maybe she hadn't. He glanced sideways at her. He couldn't tell if her anger was gearing up or powering down.

Seconds ticked past. Finally, he put exploratory finger tips on her shoulder. She didn't shrug him off. Instead, she leaned a milameter closer to him. Then she said, "Maybe you better come inside."

✦　✦　✦

Kaleo wasn't home when Nani and Hank entered the house. At least he didn't answer when she called to him from the front door. "Must still be at Jasmine's," she said to Hank. "He's setting a record."

A center hall led from the front door back to the kitchen. To the right was Nani's office, then the Keawalani Hands salon. The living room and powder room were on the left and the kitchen to the back.

Nani told Hank to have a seat in the living room. "Would you like a drink?"

"Better not. I'm doing a shift for Jay tonight. Starts at midnight."

"Coffee then?"

"Black and strong. Need the caffeine."

Hank had never been in the living room before. Everything in it was neat and clean, but old. The furniture probably dated back to Nani's parents. All her decorating budget must have gone into creating that tropical atmosphere for the Keawalani Hands salon. Here in the living room, bright yellow throws added color to a dull old wing-back chair and the sofa. A timeworn vinyl recliner in front of a TV had her dad's name on it. Probably Kaleo's now. At least the sprung seat looked like it molded to a backside a lot broader than Nani's.

The amazing thing about the living room was its walls. Two of them formed a dramatic mural. Though an abstract with swirls of red and orange on one wall rushing toward deep blues and greens on the other, Hank could tell it represented waves of lava meeting waves of the night ocean. The two battled for dominion, a collision of elemental forces. It was undecided which was winning, there in the corner where the two walls met. Having seen the mural in the kitchen, Hank knew this was Kaleo's work, too. It was remarkably beautiful and deeply disturbing. Roiling with tension.

He felt more than a little tension himself over Nani. He sat on the sofa and tried to organize his thoughts. He needed to tell her something that could upset her. It was about her father.

At that moment, she swayed into the room with a tray holding two mugs, a coffee pot and a plate of cookies. His thoughts scattered again as he looked at her. Her slacks and shirt were not seductive in the least. In fact, they were close to drab instead of the bright colors she usually wore. Hank guessed she'd toned down for the meeting with Nawahine. But it didn't matter. This woman could be wearing sackcloth and she'd still ooze sex.

"You shouldn't go out in public in a body like that," Hank said.

As she set the tray on the banged up coffee table next to the pile of *Honolulu Calling* magazines, Nani laughed. It was a low effervescent sound he was coming to cherish. It played in his head like a favorite lyric.

He patted the sofa next to him. But she didn't sit beside him. Instead, she lowered herself to her knees on the other side of the coffee table and poured them each coffee. She settled back onto her legs, sitting on her heels. When she straightened her back, her breasts pushed against her shirt. Hank narrowly avoided spilling hot coffee on his crotch.

Mercy.

"You're blushing," she said.

"Cops don't blush."

"And you have something to tell me."

Maybe she was as prescient as her aunt was renowned to be. Crazy family. Crazy.

"It's about your father."

Her posture stiffened.

"I'm going back through Maile's file. With Jeff Lee and Martin Martin out of the picture, we're starting at ground zero again. So I'm still interviewing everyone who was around twelve years ago, just to see if I can flush out another lead. That means finding your father. I just want you to know I'll be searching for him."

Nani listened, face intelligent in repose. She was contained when she was working out a problem, still as a bird hidden in the trees. She said, "Of course you have to look."

"But I don't have to tell you what I find. I mean if I find him, and it's bad. Like he's in prison or dead or, well, anything."

"If you find him, I want to know. Whatever you find. Kaleo needs to know, too."

He nodded. "Okay, then. That's what I thought." She wouldn't want to be sheltered from the worst. Nani was brave. It was part of what drew him, even though he hated knowing he could not always protect her. Nobody could keep anybody safe, not really. It was a helluva thing for a cop to have to admit if only to himself.

"And I apologize for scaring you tonight," she said.

"Now *you're* blushing."

"Women who are trying to apologize often blush."

"Oh, sweetheart. You don't need to apologize. I was wrong. I'm an asshole."

"Yes, you are."

"I won't be if we could have make-up sex."

She laughed that laugh again. "Not when you're about to leave for a midnight work shift. Next time, we take our time. But for now ... how is that shoulder getting on?"

He lifted it in a circular motion. "Oh, it's bad. Boo hoo."

"I take it you'd like me to massage it."

"Oh, yes."

She rose from the floor and sat next to him, beginning to manip-ulate the shoulder. "Is there anything more we need to confess? We seem to be having some problems in the communication department."

"Then it's important for me to say this once and for all." But his thoughts were interrupted as Nani worked the deep tissue where shoulder tension was buried. "Ah, oof, ah."

"It's important for you to say that?"

"It's important for me to say *this*." He pointed at the *Honolulu Calling* magazines. "Would you leave Keawalani for a bigger city? Am I too much of a small town boy to hold you here? You're not thinking of pulling the rug out from under me or anything?"

Nani leaned into him, wrapping her arms around him. "A client passes those along to me. That's all. No force in the world would draw me away from my island for very long. It is my heart. And my heart needs a man who feels the same way about this place."

Hank started to speak, but she put a finger on his lips. As he kissed it, she said, "Now about tasks for my clients. Like I said before, I'll help them when I can. But I won't knowingly put myself in danger without talking to you first. Is that enough of a promise to keep a cop knocking on my door?"

"If that's the most I can get, then I accept the terms. But it frightens me to feel like this when I don't have control of the situation. I get ... unreasonable."

"Fair enough. We'll both work on it. And now, there is one more thing." She pulled away from him.

"Yes?"

She grabbed his hair and gently shook his head. "Who told you where I was tonight?"

She could almost see the panic in his eyes. She let him off the hook. "Never mind. You don't have to rat him out. I can see the hand of Kaleo at work here. He'll be sorry for butting into my business."

"But ... the way things have turned out, aren't you glad he told me? I mean, *if* he told me?"

CHAPTER TWENTY-FIVE

Corruption in Police Department Darkens
Bowling Night
By Jackson O'Reilly
Excerpt from the *Keawalani Voice*, 2015

Thursday was the first league night at the newly restored Rack n' Roll Lanes. Teams included the Firehouse Framers, Mo Betta Mixers (bartenders from the Suck 'en 'em Up Saloon), WikiWiki Washouts, Big Island Gliders (busboy Akela cleaning up the few spares left by Daya the knock-down knock-out), and Sunny Daze Dazzlers of which this reporter is the most dazzling bowler of all. And then there were the Kingpin Kops.

The membership of each team consists of employees or customers of the sponsoring organizations. Except in the case of the Cops. Who expected them to throw in ringers? Hustlers in the pocket, picking up sleepers, knocking over deadwood. I tell you, gentle readers, police corruption is running rampant in Keawalani!

What happened when this reporter questioned Captain Frank Lono regarding the eligibility of Renee, dispatcher Allison Costello's 11-year-old foster daughter? As well as the presence of Nani Palea whose only known connection to the Hamakua Police is her interest in one of the officers and, oh yes, her brother's familiarity with the district hoosegow?

Lono 'deputized' them, that's what happened. The two stand-ins beat the tar out of the rest of us. If that isn't police brutality, I'd like to know what is.

Hank thought this must be love. Up until this point in his life, he'd considered love a battlefield, pretty much like the song lyric. But today, he felt bewitched. Corny as Kansas. His heart was suffering a total eclipse. No lyric he could think of rivaled the real thing.

He was so overbearingly cheery at work that Lono, Allison and his co-workers were sick to death of him. Even his offering of two dozen fresh malasadas didn't appease them for long. Finally, the free-speaking Renee slapped her boney butt down on his desk, dangling her legs over the side. "Officer Hank," she said digging at a grubby anklet that had slipped into the back of her shoe.

"Hi, Sweetie Pie," he said, beaming. "Care for a malasada? Mighty tasty."

"First, I am not Sweetie Pie. That's what Allison calls Frank."

Hank tucked away this little gem. He'd use it on Lono at some totally inappropriate occasion.

"Second, cops shouldn't eat these things." Renee held up one of the crispy lumps of lusciousness. "They're just donuts without holes, and you know what happens to donut-eating cops. They get fat. And slow. They need to stay in good shape. Just like their equipment. I will help you toward that goal." She took an immense bite of the malasada and chewed determinedly like a cow with her cud, until finally gulping the gooey mass down.

"You're so thin, I can see that go through your gullet like a mouse through a snake. Take another. Add a little more flesh to your bones."

She ignored him and continued her lecture. "And third, you're acting dopey. Nobody is intimidated by a cop with a smile like that. You have to look more threatening. You know, more *make my day.*" She gave him a squinty eyed scowl.

"Ah," he said. He rearranged his features into a glower. "I'll try to do better."

"See that you do." She slipped off his desk and walked away, taking the rest of the pastries with her.

As Renee departed, Hank's thoughts returned to Nani. He wanted to do something romantic for her. Find the perfect gift, maybe a flight for two to the stars and back. But for now, he could think of only one thing on the immediate horizon.

This was bowling night. He'd invite her to come root for the Kingpin Cops. She might enjoy watching.

✦ ✦ ✦

No, she didn't enjoy watching, but she loved taking part.

Nani reminded Hank of PBS programs about forces of nature. And son of a bitch if Renee didn't match her point for point. The two of them worked together like Venus and Serena, Torvil and Dean, Bert and Ernie. Hank stared at his 'lady love' open-mouthed, just as Allison watched the child warrior she was raising.

The truth of the matter was that the rest of the team held them back. Hank had never known that Lono, Allison, Jay and he were only mediocre bowlers. Not that the two Terminators so much as implied such a thing. In the parking lot at Halemano's Heavenly Treats after the games, they shared the spotlight of victory with all their teammates. Members of other teams threw insults and jeers at them all. But everyone knew the real truth. Renee and Nani giggled together and high fived with the commoraderie of soldiers who've fought together. They would undoubtedly become fast friends.

Hank did his best to enjoy taking a back seat as he toasted them with his Coffee Crème de Menthe Spiked Shave. But he wasn't the only one who was a little standoffish with genuine enthusiasm. Captain Lono was looking back and forth between the two, an unexpected expression of concentration on his face.

The evening ended with shakas and good hearted barbs about showing them next time. Everyone headed to their cars or bikes. As Hank opened the Honda's door for Nani, Lono strolled over. He leaned down and asked, "Can I borrow my officer for a moment, Nani?"

"Of course, Captain."

Lono and Hank walked a few strides away. Hank noticed his boss's eyes roam, looking for anyone else within earshot. Lono stopped walking and turned to him. "Has Nani ever met Renee before?"

The question surprised Hank. "Not that she's ever said."

"They seem to get along pretty well."

"I'd say it's the thrill of victory although I think Nani gets along with everyone." Hank thought a second then added, "Lots of people trust her with their secrets, or so it seems from the amount of clients who welcome her involvement in their lives."

Lono nodded, before giving an appreciative grunt. He pulled on his lower lip. If he was working on a decision, he'd made it. "You know that Allison and I have a sort of arrangement."

Shit, everyone on the force knows you and Allison have an arrangement.

"An arrangement?" Hank asked, going for innocence.

"Yeah. We, uh, see each other when not in the office. Get my meaning?"

"Yes, of course." Hank smiled. "Congratulations. She's a real handful ... I mean that in a good way."

"Yes, she is. But keep it to yourself, Lindsey. What I need to tell you is that, ah, God knows Allison and I both love Renee. But sometimes the kid can be a bit much to have underfoot. Criticizes me some. Thinks she keeps me in line. You know?"

Hank, well aware of his own orders from Renee, regarding equipment and food, imagined it was like living with a pint-sized drill sergeant on call at all hours. "I can see how that might be."

"So I was wondering if you and Nani would spend some time with Renee. Take her to a movie now and then. Maybe to the beach. Give Allison and me, you know, a little alone time."

Hank didn't have enough of his own alone time with Nani. But this guy was his boss. As well as his friend. Asking a personal favor would have cost Lono, and Hank could see no way to object. "Sure. I'll talk to Nani and if she agrees, we'll come up with some things to do."

He saw the ghost of something in Lono's eye, something that wasn't as expected as a smile or gratitude. If anything, it looked like sadness to him. As he watched the captain amble away toward his own cruiser, Hank had to wonder.

What the hell was that all about?

✦ ✦ ✦

While she cleaned up her breakfast dishes the next morning, Nani was humming a favorite hula, *What About Me?* Hank had told her about Lono's request. She'd made a start at friendship before he'd even gotten back in the car after his talk with the captain. The two bowling buddies had exchanged numbers and a text had already arrived from Renee:

TEACH COPS TO BOWL OR MORE FUN TO WATCH THEM TRY?

Nani smiled and replied: LOL. MORE FUN BUT NO TROPHIES

Renee responded: LOOKS LIKE WE GIVE LESSONS.

It could be fun to spend some time with Renee. Nani could take her on some hikes and teach her about all the plants like her mother Kina had done for her. And they could ride the free *Hele-On* bus over to the Hilo Walmart.

She could do things with Renee that she'd like to be doing with Maile. Of course, Renee was only, what? Eleven or twelve? And Maile would be twenty now. Assuming Maile was still alive.

Nani shook her head, shaking away dark thoughts, the kind that led her to want a drink. She turned on more hot water as she scoured the coffee pot. The physical discomfort to her hands helped her brain skitter back to the here and now.

The lanai's screen door screeched open and slammed shut. Kaleo was home after another night away. Nani grinned to herself. She waited, listening to him drop his clothes, burp and yawn. She heard the springs of his old bed complain as he flopped himself down.

Silence.

"Kaleo!" she then yelled. "I saw a scorpion out there earlier. Before

I could swat the bugger, it disappeared under your pillow."

She heard the immediate outburst: Kaleo slapping at himself, cussing, overturning furniture to locate the nasty little piece of work.

She hadn't really seen one. But her 'Get Kaleo' campaign had begun. As she disappeared into her first client session of the day, she smiled.

Thinks he can get away with having Hank 'save' me at the Nawahine house, does he? He'll be sorry he stuck his big nose into my business.

CHAPTER TWENTY-SIX

My Book of Revelation
Excerpt from the Year 2003

I think about Maile all the time, about what she'd be doing if she was alive. Would she be making paper mache dinosaurs at school? Playing soccer? Learning Hawaiian history?

It's been two months since my boyfriend and I were beaten by the Bad Ass (I refuse to call him Father any more). We healed physically, but we've had a bitch of a time.

BF says I need to let it go, that life is what we made it. He's so, I don't know, resigned. Me, too, I guess. Like there's no reason to try since everything turns to shit anyway. He says I'm mad all the time now. I guess that's an understatement since even I see it in myself. Life isn't a lot of fun. We never make each other laugh like we did.

Anyway, two months. Here are the important bits, the things that have happened, if I can remember them all:

- First, nobody has found Maile. Looks like we're safe from discovery. That doesn't make us any less ashamed, but at least we aren't in prison. Not real prison, anyway.
- I thought Ma might help me behind the Bad Ass's back, but she's chickenshit. She wouldn't take a call from me, wouldn't bring

me my things. Thanks to God I had this notebook in my backpack instead of at home, or they could have read the truth about Maile's death. I guess He provides, but I wish His ways weren't so damn mysterious.

- I saw my little brother and sister in the park playing near the water fountain one day. They turned their backs on me and ran away, and I used to be everything to them. Now I'm nothing. That's what shunning is all about. The hell with them. The hell with them all.

- Ma took back the job at Jacaranda Inn. The Bad Ass probably saw to that, making her do her own work plus the stuff that I did. Her punishment for raising a disappointment like me. He'd take no blame himself. So from the first day of living with BF as a couple, I was out of work and out of money as well as out of clothes. How lucky for him that he chose such a partner.

- The garage owner is a decent man. He's not happy about my staying with BF but feels sorry for us. Nobody who isn't a member of the Bad Ass church likes it very much. So he allows us to keep the space upstairs as long as I stay out of sight (I can only use the bathroom when the shop is closed). In return, BF works long hours on the cars. He quit school so he can do that. The garage pays him minimum wage.

- I found out first hand that nobody wants to hire a kid. Then one of the Inn maids came to find me. She said she knew a lady looking for cleaning help, a lady who wouldn't ask questions about my age and would pay me in cash. I got the job, and that lady recommended me to another lady. So I'm cleaning toilets and windows for people I don't know. I got no right to complain.

- I try to make the place nice for BF. I keep it clean, and I hung some curtains I got at a yard sale. I cook whatever we can get for cheap, whatever the Ono Grinds market has on special. Some nights, it's only rice. And some nights, we hold each other like we used to. But not so much. He says I'm too irritable now. Sex just isn't as sweet as it used to be.

- BF says we brought this on ourselves. I think it was all a dreadful mistake and that after Maile fell, there was nothing we could do. He says we could have tried to get help. I can't agree. I can't ever agree or I will go mad. It's a decision that was made at the time, and that's that. So it's just something we don't talk about or we argue if we do.

- We don't talk about a lot any more. We just continue to *be*. And Maile keeps invading my head.

Well, that all was true for a couple months at least. But things have changed again, from bad to worse. I missed two periods. BF borrowed a junker from the garage and took me to a clinic in Hilo that doesn't ask too many questions. I'm pregnant.

I've worked it out in my head. I probably conceived on the night that Maile hit her head on that rock. A life for a life. You sure can't say that God isn't some kind of jokester.

Criminy.

Nobody but BF knows I'm knocked up. If my ladies knew, they might not let me keep cleaning. I wear muumuus so it'll be easy to hide the baby bump when it appears. Without parental permission, BF and I can't marry because we're too young. Like the Bad Ass is going to agree to that.

I don't know what will become of us. I don't think even Jesus knows.

My Book of Revelation
Excerpt from the Year 2004

Five months have passed. My muumuus got bigger along with my belly. But I'm carrying high, and nobody but BF ever really looks at me anyway. Probably people just think I'm eating too many moco locos. If they think about me at all.

BF found a second job bussing dishes at the Big Island Girl in the evenings. I babysit when I can for the dentist and other people. All together, it doesn't come to much, but at least we get enough to eat. I want the baby to have what she needs while she's growing inside.

I can't see a doctor. Who could afford that? Besides, she might tell authorities about kids having kids. So I read a lot about baby care at the library, hiding the books behind other books on geography or history. I don't check them out, or someone would guess my situation.

I never thought I'd miss my mother, but I do. I saw her alone on the street one day, and I confronted her. I grabbed her shoulders and made her look at me. I asked her for help with her grandbaby, but she told me to get rid of it. That whores like me must know a way. I can't blame her, not really. There's not much she could do without the Bad Ass finding out. He'd beat her, too.

Get rid of it, she said. She's right, of course. What chance does a baby have with just me and BF? Or worse, just me. What if I have it and he leaves us? It could happen. I know he's moody a lot. I hope it's just that he can't be on the soccer team now that he's dropped out of school. But what if it's me, if he hates me? I can't raise a baby by myself. I can't! But I can't be responsible for killing another one either.

What a mess.

My Book of Revelation
Excerpt from the Year 2004

It's over now. BF and I carried out the plan I made. The baby came a month early. I had her on the bathroom floor in the garage. It was night. Nobody but BF was there to hear me cry.

The baby girl was tiny but alive. She looked red but okay. BF told me that. He wrapped her up in the beautiful fluffy yellow blanket, the only thing we'd bought for her that was new. And then he left. He didn't let me see her. I'd told him not to, even if I begged. He took her to the police station and left her in front of the door.

Officer Lono had seemed like a good man to me when he came to the laundry to talk to me. He never found Maile, but maybe he'll find my baby there at the door. He's probably married to a nice lady. They'll do a better job than BF and I can do. I wish I could tell him to name the baby Maile. If they don't raise her, I wonder who will. What name will her new parents choose?

When BF returned, he helped me off the bathroom floor and back up the stairs. He went back downstairs to clean up. I collapsed on the air mattress and have been here a long time. I may float here forever if Maile lets me. She's quiet right now, leaving me alone.

This will be my last entry in my book of revelation. As it says in that other Revelation, the one in the Bible: "*What you see, write in a book ...*"

I've written it down to remember how it really was, no matter what happens from now on. It's my testimony to the things I felt and did. Amen.

CHAPTER TWENTY-SEVEN

The Voice of the Trees
By Jackson O'Reilly
Excerpt from the *Keawalani Voice*, 2015

Old Man Hookano was in his front yard the other night as I walked by on my way home. "If that's fermented grain you got in that bag, cuz, grab a seat," he called. It was. So I did.

For the next few hours we drank whisky and ate tender pork from his ever present grill. In between sips and bites, Old Man took out his guitar and began to play. Soon neighbors showed up to help themselves to everything Old Man had to offer, as well as the foods and instruments they brought themselves.

I asked him what slack-key guitar meant. He looked at me like I was a true doofus and said slack-key meant that some of the strings were loose enough to play multiple chords and slides. It is a method unique to Hawai'i.

The other thing unique to Hawaiian guitars is the sweet music of the koa, a tree at home only here, growing in deep ashy volcanic soil, nurtured by humidity, sun and altitude. It is a tonewood, one used for musical instruments. The voice of koa guitars is crisp and clear but swaddled in warmth.

By the end of the 1800s the Big Island had been stripped of nearly all koa to make room for cattle and crops. Along with it went the two varieties of koa finches. Today, most remaining koa is protected from harvesting. Wood for instruments or bowls or furniture is usually from dead or dying trees. But one day the island will again sustain a magnificent growth because seedlings along the Hamakua coast are now being planted.

The voice of the Hawaiian forest, deep within the wood, is like none other on earth. Old Man Hookano and his guitar can bring tears to your eyes when he plays the haunting songs of things long gone. And that's good. Because we can bring back the forest. But the voice of the koa finch is lost forever.

What Nani needed most was closure. Even if Maile was dead, as Hank believed she must be, Nani had to know for sure. Otherwise, the unknown would haunt her forever.

Like a lot of lawmen, Hank had told families when the deaths of missing loved ones had been confirmed. Their sorrow finally had a release valve. It was as if grief needed a body to grieve over – or if not the body, some other irrefutable proof. It was the only way a fractured spirit could mend.

Hank wanted more than anything to provide Nani this release. It was a dark gift that a cop was uniquely suited to give. He would find her the answers.

He pulled open his lowest desk drawer and dragged out the cold case once again. For the millionth time he read the dog-eared file cover to cover. It had been compiled twelve years ago in the Hamakua police district, largely by young officer Frank Lono. They'd worked with the intelligence they had at the time. Amber Alerts were a new phenomenon back then. In fact, as proof that coincidences *do* happen, Hawai'i's Amber Alerts were renamed Maile Amber Alerts in honor of another little girl. The file contained a *Voice* article from 2005, the year it was renamed.

Amber Alert Now Maile Amber Alert
By Jackson O'Reilly

Maile Gilbert was only six when she was abducted from a family party in the summer of 1985. Her abused body was found the next day in a shallow grave on the Oahu shoreline. An acquaintance of her father was subsequently convicted of the murder and is serving a life sentence in prison.

Many of us remember her abduction and grieved with her family. Now she is memorialized in the newly renamed Maile Amber Alert in Hawaii.

This is an appropriate time to remember
that, here in Keawalani, we have our own
missing Maile. Our Maile Palea has been
gone for over a year from her family and
our village but never from our hearts. According to police, the investigation is ongoing and the case not closed. Anyone with
any information is requested to call Officer
Frank Lono of the Hamakua District Police.

Maile Palea's case remained open all these years later, but it was
stalled. After just so long with no clues – in a police department perpetually undermanned – the trail died in favor of cases whose solutions were more attainable.

Hank set the file aside and went online. He surfed public sites as
well as those available only to law enforcement. Maybe intelligence
available today could provide new direction. He gathered together
bits and pieces.

*Of the 800,000 children reported missing every year, less than ten
percent are actually abducted. And the vast majority of these are tak-
en by family members or friends, not by strangers.*

Hank thought about it. 'Stranger Danger' was nowhere near the
peril that neighbors and buddies were, yet few could believe it of
the people they knew. Lono and his fellow officers had started with
the assumption that Maile did know her abductor. They'd begun a
search immediately and thoroughly examined relatives and neighbors. Just in case they were wrong about Maile knowing her attacker,
they'd also set up road blocks, sent out statewide alerts. On the off
chance that some would-be parents had taken the child not for ransom but to raise as their very own, the local police had even asked for
help from the FBI for any sign of out-of-state involvement. With the

intelligence they had at the time, they'd done the right things, made the right assumptions.

But twelve years ago, Hank reasoned, they'd believed Maile was alive. Now he challenged that assumption. How did that change things? He went back to his monitor.

Abducted children who are murdered are mostly girls. And most are dead within three hours of their abduction.

Just three hours. That's why search parties were frantic. They'd looked everywhere in the immediate area as soon as Maile went missing. Speed is of the essence even if a child isn't adducted but has run away or become lost. The dreadful results of exposure from weather or predators, be they two, four, six or eight legged, increases the longer a child is gone.

In most cases, the murder site is within a quarter mile of the place the child is first contacted by the killer. But the body isn't always there. Half of the murderers conceal bodies to prevent discovery.

Hank could tell from the file that when the searchers found nothing in the early going, they expanded their search. The first time through the immediate terrain, they moved fast and called her name, hoping she'd answer. The second time they slowed their pace, looking under branches, behind dumpsters and within piles of debris – anywhere a little girl could hide or be hidden. But had they searched far enough afield? Had their search gotten less effective as they tired or lost hope?

While abducted children under five are mostly killed by acquaintances, the older the child the more likely a stranger is involved.

Maile was eight. What if the murderer was a stranger? Hank worked on into the late morning, stopping only to handle the daily incidents of shoplifting, car theft and traffic fiascos. Between interruptions he pulled together as much of a profile as he could for a rare killer, a profile based on revised assumptions and information available to him now, but not to Lono back when.

Based on Hank's research, Maile's murderer would have been a male under 29 years old, living alone or maybe with a parent. He'd have been single with prior arrests for violence. He'd have been unemployed or working at a semi-skilled job. Maile's murderer may not have known his victim. He may have killed her and disposed of the body so far from the crime scene it hadn't been found.

Hank knew that some of this profile would be balderdash. But it was better than nothing. He grabbed a copy of it from the printer and headed down the hall toward Lono's office.

When he got there, he interrupted Allison. She turned to him with the same broad smile she'd been using on Lono. "Nani just called to invite Renee to a movie after school. Isn't that a nice thing?"

Allison left Lono's office with a lightness that had been missing lately, now that Hank came to think about it. She'd been less snappy with her comments, maybe even on the somber side. It was nice to see that shit-eating grin on her face again. He hadn't realized that he'd missed it.

Nani sure hadn't waste any time reaching out to Renee. Hank wondered if he was invited to the movie, too.

✦ ✦ ✦

Captain Lono knew that Hank Lindsey was the officer most likely to use his noggin along with his police training and growing experience. He had imagination, something that could send him off in the wrong direction, but just as often it would be right. Hank could be a brilliant investigator with time and support. Not that Lono would tell him that, of course. Compliments just didn't tumble out of his mouth willynilly.

But he sure as hell would support the guy in this Maile search any way he could. He'd never felt at peace about Maile Palea and the hell her family had been through. As a young officer himself, Lono had learned that a trail could just peter out. Losing Maile had made him a sadder but wiser lawman, one who knew endings weren't always happy. Or that sometimes there was no ending at all. It was a lesson that Hank would have to learn one day, but not today, not from Lono. He put his feet up on his desk drawer, laced his fingers over his belly, and said, "Proceed."

For the next few minutes, he listened intently as Hank went through all his research, resting his case like a litigator summing up for a jury. "Twelve years ago, the search parties concentrated on nearby places that were both concealed and reachable within the first three hours. The logic was irrefutable at the time. *But.* Maybe they looked too soon. Maybe Maile was alive a lot longer than that. Maybe we should look again and increase our range."

Lono pursed his lips. It would mean extra hours with no extra pay. The state officials would say he should spend more time on fresh crime and less digging among the ruins. But he took a quick mental inventory and realized he really didn't give a shit about their opinions. "I can't assign a task force to this, Lindsey. Can't get the budget for that. Not on nothing but your gut."

Hank the Hothead said, "Fine. Then I'll do it myself."

Lono held up his hands and said, "Hold your water. I can do some investigating after hours along with you. I'm thinking Allison will help, too."

Hank's face brightened. "I could ask Kaleo and Nani, too, but —"

"Nope. No family members. What we might find, they don't need to see. But you organize a search. Round up that bunch that hangs out at Sunny Daze. They looked twelve years ago with me ... they can look again now."

✦ ✦ ✦

Look again now.

Hank knew it wouldn't be easy. This time, they would be looking for remains, not a living child. The emphasis changed. This time, they would take a less frantic pace, concentrate on hunches and what ifs, move carefully over far flung ground.

To start, he asked Allison to explore computer records for the months following Maile's disappearance. Bones appeared now and again along the coast below the thousand foot high Hamakua cliffs. A child's body might have been dumped into the sea or pitched away in the dense growth that carpeted the steep rock face. Had unidentified human bones been uncovered by dogs in the neighborhood or by gravediggers in churchyards?

Next, Hank called the *Keawalani Voice*. He asked Jackson O'Reilly to publish a time and place for searchers to meet on the following Sunday, the day he figured that the most people could turn out. Word would spread through the village faster than a lava flow. The more help, the better.

As he put down the phone, Allison came up to his desk shaking her head. "No instances of bones suitable for Maile. But put me down for one of the search parties in the field."

He looked with gratitude at this tough, opinionated woman who kept the officers in line, but who gladly took on foster kids like Renee. Wrinkles were beginning to appear in her middle aged face, but they settled in an appealing topography of peaks and valleys. He briefly hoped Allison and Lono made each other feel the way he felt about Nani.

Nani.

His next move was obvious. He needed to let her know what was happening, so he called to ask if she and Kaleo could see him. She suggested he stop by for lunch and stay until Allison dropped off Renee. They could all go to a movie. He was invited after all.

✦ ✦ ✦

Kaleo looked grumpy as a thunder god. "All we have is swill. Skimmed milk, light beer or diet pop," the big man griped, staring woefully into the refrigerator. "Choose your poison, Hank. And I mean that literally."

Nani smiled sweetly. Her eyes twinkled with humor as she glanced at Hank. "Kaleo is upset that I'm taking a serious interest in his overall health. He needs to make some major adjustments to his loco moco intake." She set a lovely fruit salad on the table. "Since he's recently become *so* involved in my welfare, I've decided I should reward him with concern for his."

Hank, sitting on one side of the kitchen nook, felt himself tense. *Oh, crap. Kaleo's gonna think I squealed.* He started to apologize. "Uh, I didn't ... I mean ..."

Kaleo sat opposite him when Nani pushed him out of her way with a switch of a hip.

"No worries," he said, cutting off the apology. "I know you didn't rat me out. How hard was it for her to figure exactly who called in the law? She'll punish me 'til she gets over it. It's a big sister thing." He looked at the sparsely occupied tabletop. "But, Jesus, Nani! Rice cakes? Not even bread and butter?"

She winked at Hank as she set out a basket of crusty rolls and a wheel of warm brie. She took a seat saying, "*'Kay den, bruddah.* No more buttinsky, yeah?"

"Yes, ma'am. From now on, you're on your own."

Hank doubted that would ever be true.

It was with coffee after the meal that Hank finally told them why he wanted to see them both. He explained that a new search for Maile was about to begin.

"You got that to happen?" Kaleo said with genuine surprise. "Mahalo. Guess it takes a lawman to keep the law on the job."

Hank explained that more funds hadn't been appropriated. But that the police were questioning some of the early assumptions they had made. That they wanted to consider the option that Maile's abductor – if indeed there had even been an abductor – was a stranger who had taken her farther afield than originally thought.

"So you believe Maile is dead," Nani said. She said it with that contained calm he'd noticed before, the way she confronted news. Her voice didn't crack, and her eyes didn't look away, but Hank saw the muscles in her throat tense. He took her hand and was grateful that she didn't pull away. "Yes, Nani. This time we are working on that assumption."

She'd told him before that she and Kaleo both liked to think of their sister alive somewhere, living a happy life. This was the fantasy that kept them from healing. The

siblings sat motionless, side by side. Hank saw sadness, of course, and anger. He hoped self-blame was not part of the emotional stew. If either felt guilty to be alive when the little girl was dead, well, that was a craziness that was nearly impossible to overcome.

"That means you are looking for a child's body," Kaleo said. "One dead for many years."

"Yes."

Something unseen, unheard passed between brother and sister, a communication shared by two adults who had depended on each other from a very early age.

"We'll search, too," said Nani.

"No. And this time, it's not *me* giving you an order. It's Frank Lono who said it. You don't need certain images in your head."

"We can take it," Kaleo said.

"No," Hank said, every bit the law enforcer. "The search parties couldn't handle it if you were there. They are grieving, too, or they wouldn't be doing this. It's not right to make things harder for them. When we find anything – if we find anything – I'll tell you immediately. You will have all the information you want."

"And if you find nothing?" Nani said.

"Then I'll continue to look for Maile's trail. I'll never stop. I promise you that."

She sighed. "I've been wrong to avoid it. If she is dead, we need to know. And get on with our lives."

Kaleo nodded. "We need to bury her in our minds so she can live in our hearts."

It sounded like a line of poetry to Hank. Or maybe a lyrical cliché. New words for grief are as hard to come up with as new words for love. Nevertheless, Hank agreed it was the absolute truth.

✦ ✦ ✦

They were still sitting at the table when Allison arrived with Renee.

"Oh dear," said Nani, as she went to the door. "I forgot about Renee. Not sure the mood around here is exactly right at the moment."

When she opened the door, it looked like Renee agreed. She'd crossed her arms over her tiny chest and was peering out from under an uncontrollable mat of curls, a frown on her face.

"What's wrong, Renee? We're going to a movie, yeah?"

Renee continued to frown.

Allison shrugged. "I don't know what happened. She's been so happy about coming."

"We're the two bowling ringers. Right, Renee? We better be buds 'cause we'll be carrying the team all season."

Hank groaned.

Allison groaned.

Renee finally grinned. "Yes, of course. But you should know you have a serious issue here. One to address immediately."

"I do? What could that be?" By now, Hank and Kaleo joined the huddle at the door. Allison took that opportunity to escape, saying she'd be back by seven.

"Just look at that," Renee said, pointing toward the door. "What a shame."

"Ah, you mean those marks in the paint? We had a break in ..." Nani cast a nervous look at Hank, not wanting to bring the subject of Packer up again.

"No wonder. And no, not the paint. Just look at that." She fingered the door lock with disdain. "That is a piece of crap. Older than God. Even a child could pick that." Renee shook her head at Nani. "Really. You should have far better protection."

The movie was forgotten as Nani, Hank and Renee all went to a hardware store in Kona. A top-of-the-line bolt lock was purchased. So was a fast food dinner ... Renee made Nani and Hank share one order of fries. When they got back to the house, Renee installed the new lock with the help of Nani's drill. Hank kept an eye on the process, but the child really didn't need his supervision.

"I might have needed hers," he whispered to Nani as the elfin locksmith went about her business.

By the time Allison came to pick Renee up, the job was done. "You're all still standing around the door?" she said with a quizzical look.

"Yes," Nani said. "I'm so sorry we missed the movie, Renee."

"No worries," the child said brightly. "I've had a ball."

Hank and Nani watched Allison and Renee head down the walk, child chattering to adult about the job she'd completed and oh, boy, how lucky for Nani that she'd fixed that problem.

Nani put an arm around Hank's waist and leaned into him. "I didn't have the heart to tell her that there's no lock on the back door at all."

CHAPTER TWENTY-EIGHT

New Search for Maile Palea: Police
Request Your Help
By Jackson O'Reilly
Excerpt from the *Keawalani Voice*, 2015

Maile Palea disappeared twelve years ago
from a party at the home of Mr. and Mrs.
George Lopaka. She was eight then, and a
beloved reporter for this newspaper. She
was a sunbeam that pierced the darkness in
this tough old newsman's heart. Maybe she
did the same for you. Many of us joined
search parties back then, but no trace of
the child was ever found. Maile's location
remains the Big Island's best kept secret.

The police have compiled a new profile for
an abductor, based on research that has
challenged some of the assumptions made
twelve years ago. They are organizing another search, this time for the child's
remains.

Anyone who can help is asked to join the police outside the station this Sunday. Search parties will be formed throughout the day and taken to assigned areas for a massive grid search. Team leaders will provide search instructions. If you intend to search, please bring with you sunglasses, a waterproof windbreaker or trash bag large enough to wear, drinking water, and if possible, a charged cell phone and a compass. By all means wear comfortable boots.

Maile is the daughter of Kina Palea, now deceased, and Manuku Palea, former resident of Keawalani. Mr. Palea's current location is unknown. Maile's sister is Nani Palea of Keawalani Helping Hands and her brother Kaleo Palea is the proprietor of the Tat Joint, temporarily closed.

When Aunt Hakumele called her to the dance studio again Nani was pleased. She needed a diversion. It was going to be a long week now that the paper had announced a new search for Maile, and it was hard for Nani to stay the hell out of the way. It wasn't in her nature to butt out while Hank handled the whole thing.

She couldn't get it out of her mind. If she forgot for just a moment, another client or well wisher would call. They kept the search at the top of her brain. Of course, they also touched her with their desire to provide therapy to the therapist:

Mrs. C: I can't do the search myself, Nani, but I will support the searchers financially. They'll have the resources they need.

Bethie Kalapana: I no can walk good, but my heart goin stay wit you, girl. I goin be beside you.

Renee via text: YOUR SISTER DISAPPEARED. MY REAL MOTHER DISAPPEARED. WE NEED TO WATCH OUT FOR EACH OTHER.

Jackson O'Reilly: Takes a drinker to know a drinker. I'm just saying. Hope nothing happens to cause anybody to hit the bottle again.

Nani needed a diversion, and the trip to the old school house was just the thing. Besides, she wanted to see Kala dance again for herself. She needed to put a critical eye on his hands and feet in motion, to see if his body tissue was repairing itself now that the suspicious fungicide had been stopped.

For company on the journey, she invited Renee to go along. The behelmeted girl rode behind her on the Vespa, her boney arms wound tightly around Nani's waist. As they sputtered-and-putted along, Renee exclaimed loudly over things they passed, peekaboo views of the blue and jade ocean, a foal challenging them to a race from his side of the wire fence, a man hacking away at mesquite. "Maybe he'll make wood chips for Old Man Hookano's grill." Nani yelled over her shoulder. "Yum."

When they dismounted at the old school, Renee said, "You know, Nani, sounds like your motor could use some help. It's kind of gasping."

The kid was a self-appointed guardian. All the adults around her seemed to be on the brink of perpetual disaster without her intervention. As she opened the front door – not allowing it to slam shut behind them – Nani asked, "You plan on being in law enforcement when you grow up?"

Renee's brow furrowed and her delicate shoulders lifted in a shrug. "Well, I just can't decide. Cop, yeah, maybe. Or a life coach. I don't really know what that is, but it sounds important. Or maybe a veterinarian. People can't be trusted to take care of themselves much less their animals." Another shrug. "It's a serious decision to make."

Nani hid the smile someplace other than her face. Renee was eleven. She'd remake her decision a million times.

They entered the old auditorium, and Renee sat beside her on a metal folding chair. Nani had explained why they were there, and she pointed out Kala. Renee watched with the concentration of a cat at a mousehole.

The boys practiced a hula for warriors. Kala broke form only long enough to smile broadly at Nani, then more shyly at Renee. He quickly went back to the scowls and bends and leaps of a Polynesian about to enter battle. Nani could see no sign of any damage to his young body. She would work with him for a couple more sessions, but then he would be back on the path toward championship.

Yay, Auntie! Yay, Mr. Nawahine! Yay, me!

During the next break, Hakumele came to sit with them on a third spindly chair and part of a fourth. "Who is this beautiful girl?"

"This is Allison Costello's girl, Renee."

"You are ready to learn the dance, Renee?"

"Oh, no ma'am. I don't have time for fun stuff."

Hakumele did not crack a smile. "I see. Then you go out and speak serious things to those silly boys while I speak with Nani, yeah?"

"Of course, Auntie." Renee sprinted toward the door, turning just long enough to call, "Nice to meet you, Auntie. Aloha."

As the girl galloped out of the auditorium, Nani called, "Ah, Renee? Maybe you better keep the boys away from the Vespa. It's our only way home."

"Why is this girl with you?" Hakumele asked.

Well I can hardly tell her that it's to give Lono and Allison time for sex.

"Allison works a full schedule and can use the help. Besides, I enjoy having Renee around. She picks up all the stuff that Kaleo drops on the floor around the house. Nice kid."

"Okay. But in case you have plans, remember: that one will never dance. She has no sense of the music in her soul."

Nani accepted it as sad but true. Her aunt could judge a kid like a horse trainer judging a thoroughbred. If Renee were to dance, it would be for exercise, not for competition.

Now Hakumele folded her hands onto her lap. Nani, with a hitch to her heart, noticed that arthritis was bending those old knuckles out of shape. Fingers must grow weary of handling life for so many years.

Hakumele said, "I have another thing to tell you, Nani. A thing that might widen the divide between us. So it scares me."

Oh shit. Just when it seems like things are getting better. What now?

"This is a thing your lover the cop knows. So he will tell you if I don't."

"My lover the cop?" Nani was so surprised by the phrase that she simply couldn't form any other words.

"He knows that I know where your father is."

"He knows that ..."

"Stop repeating my words and listen. Officer Lindsey suspected that Manuku would not disappear with no contact at all. Apparently people rarely do. So the policeman suspected the contact would be somebody close to him. Like family. Like his sister. Like me."

"You ... you ... "

"Yes, me, me. I have had a contact number for Manuku all these years."

Nani tried to quit sputtering like the Vespa. She drew a deep gulp of air and controlled her breathing as she had when she was a dancer. "Why didn't you tell me this before? And why hasn't Hank said anything to me?"

"Officer Lindsey agreed to let me tell you. He considers it our family business. And he is right. It's my story to tell. He is an understanding man. You should be nice to him." She sighed and spread her hands in a gesture of futility. "I have never used the number because I don't think your father deserves to know about Kaleo and you. I still don't. He lost that right when he left you."

Nani saw Hakumele's anger rise, like a volcano considering whether to release its molten core.

Maybe I should be mad, too. Mad at Auntie and Dad and my lover the cop.

But mostly Nani felt shocked. She became lightheaded, as though she had suddenly become observer instead of participant. She floated like a Macy balloon above the scene, watching how it all would come out.

"Please, hear me out before you decide what to do," Hakumele said. "You and Kaleo were so young. You were without your little sister, then your Father left and then your mother died. Your grief was pure, deep and understandable. You didn't need to know why Dad abandoned you, just that he had. You didn't need to hear his side. Children don't need to know grown up motives for the shit they do, especially when they are in the wrong."

"I take it Hank does not agree with you."

"No. He does not see you as I do. He does not see the broken child, only the accomplished adult. My image of you has grown out of touch. His is accurate. It's time you know the truth. So here it is, as my brother explained it to me." Her frown telegraphed her dissatisfaction with Manuku's explanation. He'd told his sister that after Maile was gone, when he and his wife looked at each other, all they saw was guilt and shame. "They blamed each other for being out of town when Maile needed them. Their shared reproach spiralled them both downward. They were afraid that they'd infect you and Kaleo with their guilt and misery."

"But Kaleo and I have always felt like the guilty ones ..."

Hakumele stopped her with a raised finger and went on. "To-gether, they decided that one had to go while the other raised you. Your father left, and Kina stayed. They thought it would allow you to heal. Instead, your mother just grew weaker by the day so the sit-uation got worse."

Was it possible? Had their father left to protect them ... or was it just an excuse? Had his desertion been for their own good? Nani asked, "Where is he now?"

"I don't know for sure. On Oahu, I think. I only have the phone number, and I gave it to Officer Lindsey. But I can tell you that your father is not well. He quit selling his leather crafts at fairs. Instead, he went to work for a tannery. But tanning agents have formalde-hyde. He now has lung disease."

"How do you know?"

"He calls me every Christmas to ask about Kaleo and you. He makes me promise not to tell you. But Officer Lindsey caused me to break that promise. It is time."

Hakumele stood and removed a small piece of paper from the pocket of her muumuu. She handed it to Nani. "Here is your father's number. Now it is your turn to decide what to do." She put her old palm on Nani's cheek. "Whether or not that includes forgiveness for him, I hope it includes forgiveness for me."

Hakumele stood and walked away, clapping her hands. "Boys!" she yelled. They came running back to continue their lessons.

As Nani walked in a brain fog out the front door of the old school, she saw Kala and Renee bent over the Vespa. A shy smile passed be-tween them before Kala loped back into the school, waving a good-bye.

"It was only a loose sparkplug wire causing the sputtering," Renee said to Nani as they mounted. The Vespa started with a happy hum. "That boy confirmed I had properly replaced the wire. Um, what was his name again?"

✦ ✦ ✦

What will I tell Kaleo about our father? Should I tell him anything?
Nani mentally debated the arguments for keeping her father's secrets versus telling her brother the truth. She was dry mopping the
salon's floor that afternoon when she heard a vehicle pull down her
drive and continue on around to the back of the house. By the time
she got to the kitchen window to peer out, she heard the screen door
slam and saw Kaleo leave the lanai and approach the minivan.

She didn't recognize it, and her brother's broad back blocked most
of her view of the woman who got out of the driver's seat. But when
Kaleo grabbed the woman in a bear hug and delivered a long loving
kiss, Nani figured it sure as hell wasn't Auntie Hakumele.

She was distracted from the clenching couple by two little boys
in swim shorts who toppled out of the backseat and dashed for the
banyan tree. It had three trunks in her yard and several more in her
neighbor's. When she and Kaleo were kids it had been a magnet for
young climbers. Apparently it still was.

She noticed that Akela Onekea was out there pruning an overgrown hibiscus. He came and went so quietly, she often was unaware of his presence. He was watching the kids tackle the tree, too,
and when their eyes briefly met, Akela and Nani both smiled. The
boys were such a rocking and rolling bundle of life that their joy was
as infectious as a litter of pups.

Nani opened the back door and stood on the stoop until Kaleo
came up for air from the kiss. He kept an arm around the woman's
shoulder as he turned to his sister and said, "Nani, you remember
Jasmine Awana." His grin was a smiley button.

Ah. Miss Hapuna Beach. But with kids?

"Hi, Nani," Jasmine said. "I wanted to see some of Kaleo's paintings. Okay with you if my boys play in your yard while he shows me?"

"Of course. Nice to see you again." This must be serious. Kaleo didn't show his paintings to anybody.

There's gotta be more to this woman than that killer bod.

"Evan, keep an eye on Tony," Jasmine called as Nani held the screen door for her.

"Come on through to the kitchen if you'd like to see one of his murals first." Nani led the way.

She heard Jasmine actually gasp as she stared at the emotional abstract soaring above the cabinets in a wild swirl of wings. "Kaleo," she whispered with reverence, the way people do in church. "You have canvasses, too?"

"Some. And watercolors. Sketches, too."

"Please show them to me." The couple went back to the lanai. Eavesdropping from the kitchen where she boiled water for herbal tea, Nani heard her brother opening the large drawers of an art cabinet where he kept his work. The beautiful Jasmine cooed and ahhhhhed, in between shouting "Tony, get off that," and "Evan, don't make me tell you twice."

In time Kaleo yelled, "I'm coming out there to hook me a couple sea monsters. Better swim away fast."

Nani looked out as the kids shrieked with laughter. Akela was hanging upside down from an old banyan limb, tickling them as his arms stretched out with each swing. Clearly, the gardener likes kids. Maybe he'd be willing to work with Renee on a project. They could design a jungle gym or playhouse in the banyan branches where Jasmine's kids could play. Nani imagined how serious Renee would be about proper construction for maximum safety. It would be a perfect undertaking for her.

When Kaleo burst on the scene, Akela dropped to earth and went back to work. Her brother piled her paddle board, the paddle and both kids into the van. Jasmine came in from the lanai to say good-bye. "We're going now. I knew you were a great hula dancer, Nani. I saw you at the Merry Monarch Festival the year you won. But I didn't know your brother was a magnificent artist, too."

Nani shrugged her shoulders. "Almost nobody does, Jasmine. He hides that light under a very large barrel."

"Not for long if I have my way. May I call you later? I have something to discuss."

"Of course. Here," Nani handed her a business card from the stack on the counter. She wondered what was on her mind.

Before she could ask, Jasmine went to another subject. She leaned forward and squinted at Nani's neck. "What a beautiful necklace. It's old, isn't it?"

Nani held her fingers to the heirloom she always wore. "Yes. My mother made it for me when I was little. How did you know it's old?"

"The wrap technique of the gold. You don't see such work much anymore. Artistry runs through your whole family."

Jasmine seemed as sweet as her namesake. Or maybe just smart.

A woman who can give Kaleo a run for his money? This is going to be fun.

✦   ✦   ✦

Jasmine drove along the cliff top highway toward Honolii beach. The minivan's windows were all open. Air scented from endless vegetation billowed through it.

Kaleo felt folded and stuffed into the passenger seat, but he watched the scenery zip by as happy as a big dog with its head out the window. "Not used to being squired around," he said loud enough to be heard over the wind. Then he turned toward Jasmine and admired her profile, another fine specimen of Big Island scenery. "I like it."

"Not to get used to it, my friend. On days you have that heap of scrap metal, you can do all the driving."

"You mean you don't love Pink Floyd?"

"Real men don't drive pink."

"They do if they're my size. Whose gonna laugh at me?"

Jasmine, apparently. The sound of her laugh blended with the crash of the surf, the guitar wailing on the radio, the wind, and the squabbling of the boys in the back.

Kaleo was happy.

It took them some time to find parking, then to jostle down the steep slope to the beach, each of them carrying a portion of their gear. Honolii was one of Kaleo's favorites for surfing, but the deep currents were too dangerous for little boys, especially near the river mouth where it met the bay. He'd brought Nani's paddleboard to show them how to stand up and ride close to shore. Meanwhile, Jasmine planned to hunt for sea glass.

Hawaii's most famous Glass Beach was on Kauai, but Honolii was a draw for the local beachcombers. Amongst the debris of coral, lava rubble, and stones, Jasmine could spot shards of pottery and glass that would make brilliant creations when she wrapped them with wire by hand. She rarely used solder, preferring the technique jewelry makers called cold work to develop heirloom quality pieces.

"Why here?" Kaleo asked, looking at the pebbly beach. "Just looks like stones to me."

Jasmine peered downward for a moment, then reached between the stones and came up with a tiny bit of crockery that might have been the remains of a tea cup or candlestick. "Sugar plantations just up the way," Jasmine answered. "They were all gone forty, fifty years ago. But their trash still lands here after thrashing around in the water all this time."

She cupped the broken morsel in a hand for all three boys to see. When Kaleo leaned down, she kissed his cheek and said, "Now go away, and let me work."

Evan and Tony could both swim. Tony explained it to Kaleo. "Mommy showed us, but she says we must have already known. She says all Hawaiians are little fishes at birth." But neither had tried a paddleboard before.

Today the small swells patted the beach gently. Kaleo took them out past the breaking waves where the water was chest deep for Tony and about to his knees. He held the board by a leash and carried the paddle. When he stopped he said, "This board belongs to my sister. It's lighter than my surfboard but wider. Evan, get up onto the middle and squat down on your knees." He held the board fairly steady while Evan clambered on, then lifted Tony up behind his big brother. Kaleo pulled the board around in big gentle circles while the children got the feel of the rounded deck and how to balance when it turned.

As the board gently bucked and rolled, Tony shouted, "Ride 'em, cowboys."

"Just like the paniolos. Except on seahorses," Kaleo said.

"That's just dopey," said the far more sophisticated Evan.

"Now, raise yourselves up on your knees." The wobbling began in earnest as first Tony slid off, then Evan followed into the drink. With much laughter and lots of spills, the kids got on again. And again. And again until they managed to keep their balance.

"Okay, now Evan, you try to stand."

Wobble ... whoa ... splash! Repeatedly, the older boy tried. The younger was happy staying on his knees, just holding on in the commotion.

When Evan could balance fairly well in a nearly upright position, Kaleo handed him the paddle that had been floating along beside him. It was much longer than one for a kayak or canoe; a paddle-board paddle was meant to be held by a standing adult.

"Nani's pretty short, but her paddle is still too long for you. Try holding it part way down the handle." He showed Evan how to use it on one side of the board then the other.

Still holding the board's leash, Kaleo gave it more and more lee-way. "Look forward, Evan, not at your feet ... Not too far out now ... try to follow the shore ... that's good ... not too far ... Bravo!"

Kaleo plowed along beside them, running through the breaking surf, exhausting himself while shouting encouragement. Like a dad teaching his kid to ride a bike. Well, maybe not like all dads, he thought, when Evan yelped, "This is so cool. Daddy never showed us how to do anything like this."

"Now we're flying fish," Tony added.

Eventually, Kaleo gave the leash to Tony to hold and let the boys go on their own. Other than one near collision with two other pad-dleboarders, they did well. Finally he said that was enough for him for one day. He told them to keep practicing, and he'd be watching from the beach.

He spread out the towels and grabbed a Coke from the cooler, then sat and stared at the kids. He nearly ran for them once as Evan fell, but he held his breath as the boy, wobbly at first but then with authority, got back aboard. "Great job, Evan!" Kaleo yelled with joy. And maybe even a little pride.

What great kids!

But as that thought cheered him, another suddenly swept it away like a footprint under heavy surf. It ripped through his brain and careened off his heart.

The last child I was responsible for is dead.

What the hell was he doing? Were these children mesmerizing him? Was he getting involved with them? He couldn't be trusted with kids. Look what had happened to Maile. Panic attacked. He couldn't draw a full breath. It was as though he had frozen in place when he saw Jasmine kneel down before him. He felt her hands on his shoulders, saw the worry in her eyes. "Kaleo? What is it?"

He struggled for air.

She must have read the fear in his face. She turned to look at the boys playing, then turned back. "They're okay. You taught them to do that."

He gasped, "Yes, but – "

She looked at them again. "They're just playing. What's wrong?"

He choked up but managed to say, "But they could drown."

He saw understanding dawn in her eyes. She smiled at him. "No. You taught them how to do it safely. You've just scared yourself thinking about kids in danger. It's easy to do." She slid forward, settling on his lap and stradding his legs. She pulled his head to her chest and wrapped her strong, lean arms around him. "I don't have a paper bag for you to breathe in. So just slow down. Take deep breaths. That's right. That's right."

He tried, but fear was a tough competitor. "A shark could attack them, a ray could sting them, a surfer overrun them. Before I could get there."

"Then that wouldn't be your fault. It would be life's way of re-minding us of what we can lose. And you don't need any more re-minders." She caught up his big hands and placed them flat in the sand, one on each side of his body. "Feel the ground, the warmth of the sun, smell my perfume. Be here with me. Think about what is, not what could be." She held him and rocked. "Kaleo, it would not be your fault if something happened ... and neither was Maile."

Kaleo moaned. Jasmine hugged him tight as dry sobs racked his body. Catching his breath, he muttered, "I didn't know you knew about Maile."

"Everyone knows about Maile."

"Not everyone knows I was late that day to pick her up."

"Kaleo. Both the Lopakas were there. A dozen other kids were there. Nobody saw her go. And she was gone even before you were supposed to get there."

"But I might have seen – "

"What? A clue everyone else missed? Were you a boy wiser than all the adults, all the neighbors, all the cops? I don't think you were all that special, do you?"

He'd never really thought of it that way.

Damn.

Was his acceptance of blame actually selfish? Was it a mantle he wore to separate himself? To say, 'Look at me. Poor me.'

"I think you've been using guilt to protect yourself," Jasmine said as though she could hear his thoughts.

"But from what?"

"From taking on responsibilities ever again. But my boys broke through your defenses just now."

He fought that realization. "I can't be trusted with children."

"You can be trusted. If only because of what happened to Maile. You'll always be on the alert with children. That's what this panic attack is all about."

He felt a calm try to descend. His hands trembled less. "But what if you're wrong?"

"Kaleo, those are my boys. They are my life. I'd trust you with them in a heartbeat. Long before I'd trust their own father. Or anyone else I know. You are not the free spirit you think you are. You are meant to stand like a rock."

As they watched the boys play, Kaleo cried. Jasmine whispered things about the pain in his art and how easy it was to see his struggles when the colors clashed and collided. Kaleo's tears soon passed like an afternoon rain shower breaking the island heat.

Finally, he could see it: his fear was not just about Maile's disappearance. It was about using guilt to shirk accountability through the rest of his life. He'd cultivated that fear, allowed it to flourish. Kaleo was not the solid, reliable big brother his little sister would have wanted him to become. And it was time he manned up.

CHAPTER TWENTY-NINE

My Book of Revelation
Excerpt from the Year 2015

It's been twelve years since I wrote that swill. *My Book of Revelation*. What a stupid name. I was a histrionic kid too fucked up by religion and circumstance to see the truth. I thought everything was all my fault, poor little idiot me. What rot.

I dragged this out to read after seeing that article in the blat this morning. They're looking for Maile's body again. Shit. Can't they all just leave us alone? Anyway, I think I'll add an entry or two, just to set the record straight. In case anyone ever gives a shit about the way things really were. And are.

First off, I'm Maggie Wilson. And BF is Akela Onekea. There. The Bad Ass is long gone from here, so no more beatings are waiting around the corner. Akela and I have stayed together all these years.

Well, actually, there are three of us all the time now. Akela, Maile and me. She never talks to him because she's in my brain. She sets all of the rules, then I tell them to him. And here's a bombshell: she's not such a sweet child as she always seemed to be. She could give a crap about the misery that Akela and I feel. And it turns out she was jealous of Nani. Nani the champion dancer, Nani the older sister who got to do the most fun stuff, Nani the clear favorite of her big brother Kaleo and her Aunt Hakumele. In Maile's slippahs, I would have hated such a perfect big sister, too.

Maile and me, we're both bitter about the things God had in store for us. Why did our lives, and Akela's, too, turn to such shit?

Even though I've never had a life, Nani Palea still won't leave it alone. She's messing with me just like Maile warned she would. Fucking buttinsky do-gooder bitch. Better than everyone else. It's not bad enough she has Akela eating out of her hand. Now she's got my daughter, too.

Daughter, yeah. Right. Stupid name of Renee like she's all hoity toity Frenchie or something. Maile despises her for stealing her spirit, says Renee is alive because Maile is dead.

I can't hate her though. I know it isn't really Renee's fault. I watch her all the time. Nobody else sees how she looks like Akela if he only had my curls. People are stupid.

That Allison woman isn't raising Renee right. No religion, no discipline. The little snot's getting mouthy. Needs a few hours with the Bad Ass. Or at least with God. That would straighten her out. Time she learned that life is crap no matter what you hope for.

Akela, Maile and I have stayed silent about the whole Maile mess for a dozen years. We were always smart. Nobody ever caught us or even suspected us. Back then, I felt all guilty and shit. But Maile has shown me that nothing was my fault, not really. Bad parents, bad luck, bad guidance from above. Badness everywhere.

Akela stuck with me all these years, and I'm grateful to him, although he's never really grown into a man. Just does what people tell him to do, keeps his opinions to himself. He'll never make decisions or stick up for himself.

Or so I thought. But just lately, he's changing. He's Mr. Popularity. Now *he* has a life. He has friends at the Big Island Girl. Even likes it there. WikiWiki Fix hires him sometimes when Motorhead is backlogged. Now the bugger even works for Nani because he was so simpleminded he lost his job as a landscaper when they found him growing squash.

If you ask me, he's shutting Maile and me out. He's 'happy' or so he thinks. He and Kaleo talk 'old times' about soccer. Nani gives him cold drinks when it's hot. He doesn't see it for what it is: I scrub their dirty laundry and he digs in their dirt.

Dirt. That's all we are. Maile warned me.

Now Nani even has him working with his own daughter to build a kiddies' playhouse or some such shit. Working with Renee! Knowing her, having fun with her.

Crimi-fucking-nuttly.

How dare he? How can he take such a chance? How can he do it to me? And now I read in the goddamn paper that the cops are starting another search.

God help us.

There's a price to pay here. A big price. And I'm not the one who's going to pay it.

CHAPTER THIRTY

Don't Mess with an Angry Woman
By Jackson O'Reilly
Excerpt from the *Keawalani Voice*, 2015

When it comes to smiting and damnation, jealousy and retribution, Pele is one world class goddess. On just your average day, she sends forth *Vog* (a volcanic fog of air pollution consisting of gases such as sulfur dioxide) and clouds of *laze* (acidic lava haze created when molten lava meets the ocean). When you live on the Big Island, you never really forget Pele's right here, right now.

Things get a lot worse when she's really on a tear. Fountains of lava erupt skyward, orange fireballs rain back down, rivers of liquid rock destroy villages as they rush to the sea. Unseen beneath your feet, pockets of methane in the forest floor explode or tunnels of underground lava open and swallow you up. Wild fire, landslide and earthquake follow in the volcanic wake.

This is creation up close and personal, and it is a messy business. Hundreds of acres of land are being added right now as lava sculpts dramatic new formations inland or adds to the coastline when it meets the ocean.

Pele is very busy. And you never want to get in the path of a gal on a mission.

Hank wasn't surprised that villagers would help search for signs of Maile, but come Sunday, he was amazed by how many showed up. Everyone who could, did. He assigned the people who searched twelve years ago to lead parties now; the editor, dentist and barber had all learned the rudiments of grid searches back then, so he used them again.

Hank refreshed all leaders in search requirements and gave each of them a first aid kit, a whistle, sunscreen and a flashlight checked out by Renee. They also carried cameras. Leaders were told to go no faster than their slowest group member, do a head count at regular interviews, not to split the group up, and to stay in one place if the group became lost. If they found anything suspicious, they were to touch nothing and report in immediately.

Eight teenagers from Hakumele's dance school came, spearheaded by Kala. Hank gave them to Allison to organize. Renee chose to go with them. So did Lynn and Marty Martin who had come over from Honolulu just to help. Hank asked Allison to take them out to the flumes in the defunct sugar cane fields. He knew generations of kids had ridden the water through the old concrete irrigation channels after rain storms. If there were suspicious areas around old gates that opened and closed to divert water back in their heyday, the youngsters would know where they were.

Mrs. Cunningham made sure there would be enough money to pay any cop or firefighter who led a group. She also volunteered her grandson Packer to help.

More of Nani's clients pitched in, too. Mr. Nawahine sent a crew of his gardeners, including Vincent Moi. Even that son of a bitch Pierce joined them, but Hank refused to like him anyway. He assigned this group to some of the deepest parts of the forest along the verdant cliff tops, figuring they best knew which plants to avoid for their own well-being. There were old WWII pillboxes and bunkers buried under the overgrown vines up there. Maybe they'd find something besides snakes and rats in those ruins. Hank had to admit he'd be pleased if Pierce came back covered with insect bites.

The Big Island Girl provided food for the searchers. Bethie Kalapana's arthritic feet kept her from searching, but she helped Daya set up tables with loaves, salads and punch while Old Man Hookano manned three grills. The seniors from the Mauna Kea Town Hall, led by the sisters Clea and Clara, kept the food bowls full and the serviceware clean. The WikiWiki Fix donated a couple old vans to the search, one driven by the garage owner and the other by Motorhead. They shuttled teams out to their assigned positions and back again.

Teams examined places further afield than before, cutting their way through undergrowth, inspecting natural occlusions in the ground where a shallow grave might be, checking into caves behind waterfalls. They investigated every derelict building, automotive carcass and abandoned well within miles of the village, scrutinized lava fencerows where rocks may have been moved and replaced. Search parties even poked into the dripping branches of banyan trees, looking for secretive hollows that would have been near the ground twelve years ago.

The last place anyone cared to explore was the same now as

twelve years befoe. Nobody was eager to do it, and they assumed a murderer would have felt the same. They had only done a cursory search at best.

Hank decided it needed more serious consideration now. He saved it for himself. But Frank Lono, not wanting any searcher to work alone, told Hank he would be going, too.

✦ ✦ ✦

Lono was soaked with effort. "Damn belly is getting too big to haul across the damn street much less down this damn cliff," he said between gasps of air. He was hanging onto a sinewy palapalai fern to keep from plunging forward while batting philodendron leaves the size of elephant ears away from his head. Rivulets ran from under his cap down his collar to meet up with the sweat under his arms, and across his back and chest.

Hank wasn't calm, cool and collected either. He was in top condition, sure, what with hours spent running and working out. But this descent through the rainforest was blistering hot. The air was more water than oxygen; sucking in a deep breath was what drowning must be like.

The two cops had, at last, reached their goal, and they stood there to rest for a moment. A thunderous waterfall nearby splashed into a pool throwing enough spray to cool the air just a little. It helped them catch their breath as they stared dead ahead at a hole in the lava wall.

Thickets of undergrowth and skeletal o'hia trees nearly hid the entrance from sight, but Hank knew Keawalani residents could easily pinpoint the taboo location. "I imagine every Big Island kid grows up warned by his mother to stay away from here, that it's *kapu*."

Lono recovered enough wind to reply. "My ma told me it was filled with evil spirits that would deep fry me in a volcanic cauldron and serve me up for dinner. If the evil spirits didn't get me, then the vampire bats would suck me dry. And if not that, then ma herself would give me something to really be scared of."

"Guess that would scare a guy."

"Hell yes. I've still never entered here."

Hank pulled the vegetation apart to reveal more of the hole in the base of the rocky cliff. This was the entrance to a lava tube, one far off any official hiker trail. Tubes existed all over the Big Island like a subterranean honeycomb. Ancient rivers of pahoehoe lava, swift moving liquid fire, had raged toward the sea. They formed banks as their outside edges cooled, banks that built upward as they channeled the molten rock. In time, they crusted over to form ceilings. When the fiery river within finally subsided what remained was a tunnel where the lava had been. Its floor was smooth and swirled, resembling glossy dark chocolate frosting. Walls had striations from the passing flows, and the ceiling solidified with hardened lava drips hanging down like stalactites.

Hank knew all this from his grade school geography days. He hadn't needed a mother's warning to avoid such places. Call it claustrophobia, call it respect for nature gone wild, call it chicken shit cowardice. Whatever, this was no place for a human to hang out. Hank was afraid of this hole in the ground. But the fear that most squeezed his heart was the thought of a lost eight-year-old.

Did Maile run from an evil so dark that it was even scarier than hiding underground? Had she tried to save herself in this hellhole?

Hank knew from the files that searchers had been here and found nothing. Lono, his face grappling with guilt and anger combined, seemed to read Hank's mind. "A search party looked but maybe not well enough. If we fucked up, I'll admit it. I've been haunted by it for twelve years. But it didn't fit the intel we had at the time. This tube is just too damn far away from the point she disappeared. We knew she was most likely taken no more than a quarter mile away from the point of contact, so that's where we concentrated our efforts."

Neither man was eager to encounter the *kapu* inside this tunnel. But they had no other choice. The entrance was a vertical slit with fat solidified rock lips, a hideous mouth that could eat a man alive. It was open just wide enough for Hank to push through, if he bent low and turned his upper body to the side. It would be a tight squeeze for Lono.

"I'll go first so I can push you out if you get stuck," Hank said.

"No argument here. You want the rope?" They'd lugged one down the cliff with them, carrying it from Hank's car where it was parked far above. It was just off the roadway on the narrow shoulder where this unmarked trail began.

"Not yet. Most of these tubes are pretty level. If we need it I'll come back for it."

Hank clicked on his police-issue Maglite, drew a deep breath and wedged his body into the mouth. Moving slow in an awkward crouch, he shoved his way into the gullet. It was an unnerving journey but not very far. He soon broke through and could stand at his full height in the darkness of the tube. The temperature change was dramatic. It had plummeted in here where the sun never shone. A chill went to work on his sweat, producing a shiver deep in his bones.

He flashed the torch to the left and then the right. No movement, no sound. Absolute black without the beam. He gave a silent thanks to Renee for keeping police gear in top notch shape. The tube slanted down toward the sea and up toward the volcano top. This entrance must have only been a vent in the side. Maybe some original entrance had collapsed centuries ago in the wilds above him. Or been cemented over by a more recent flow.

He heard Lono's oomph as the captain squeezed through the portal. "Made it," he said and a second flashlight beam was added to Hank's own. At the same time, he felt the brush of an open wet hand cross his cheek.

Hank jerked his head back with a yelp. "What the ...?" He shot the beam upward and saw the roots of overhead plants hanging down like dripping wet fingers between the stalactites. A dozen blind spiders scurried away from the bright light.

"Jesus! I hate spiders," Lono said. Hank couldn't see his boss, but he'd never heard the man sound frightened of anything before.

"They're gone now," Hank said, trying to keep his own voice steady. "And the wet stuff is just plants, nothing more."

Not life-sucking wraiths wrapping fetid limbs around our necks.

Flipping a mental coin, Hank moved onward. "Let's follow the tube downhill first."

"Choose your poison. I'll bring up the rear."

For a few hundred paces, the walking was easy enough. Both of them could stand at full height. Their beams crossed and flashed in all directions like the outdoor searchlights at a car dealers's grand opening. What sound they made was dead with no reverberation. Hank heard the tinny splash of their feet as they tracked through puddles on the slick floor.

Lono cursed as he nearly slipped then muttered, "Wonder why it's so wet in here."

"The plants. Water gets in where they punch holes through the ceiling. If the lava was too thick for them to do that, it would be dry. Some tubes are." Hank felt the water seep through his shoes into his socks. But that wasn't the worst part. He was just giving thanks for the height of the tube when he realized the ceiling was getting lower.

The walls were getting closer.

Fuck.

The further they went, the more they were forced to crouch. Pain skittered along Hank's hunched back, and he could hear Lono groaning behind him. He thought about Nani's healing hands. Maybe she'd do a couples massage for Lono and him. He snorted at the thought. *Gallows humor.*

"What's so funny?" Lono said, his voice tight with pain.

Hank didn't answer. Suddenly he could see no further. "I think we're at a dead end." He put out a hand and touched the obstructive wall of blackness straight ahead. But it wasn't solid. The tube split, one route no bigger than a crawl space, the other bending away toward the right.

The decision was simple. Neither was eager to crawl. So they went right. But after another fifty yards the tube ended. It was stoppered shut by rock from some long ago collapse of the ceiling.

"Shit," they said in unison.

They retraced their steps until Hank came back to the crawl-space. He flashed his beam across the small opening then ran his hand inside.

"There's an obstruction in here, maybe three feet across."

"Another collapse?"

"I ... I don't think so. It's rougher than the surface around it. Feels too organized for a slide. Jesus, Frank, I think it's a wall. Man made."

Lono wedged his hand over Hank's shoulder bringing the second light into play. The double beams illuminated a barrier about a yard inside the crawlspace. It went side to side, closing off the tunnel. "You're right. Like a fence made with lava rock."

The walls of the tube were smooth but these broken rocks were sharp edged, irregular shapes that fit tightly together like pieces of a jigsaw. "They didn't come from inside here. Somebody gathered them out in the fields." Hank continued to probe at the wall with his hands. "You see mortar? I can't feel any."

"No, but the craftsmen – the good ones – build these walls to last without any."

Hank didn't want to have to say it, but their next step was obvious. It was also terrifying. "We have to see what's hidden in there."

"Yeah, I know."

"I can't dislodge these damn things with my hands." When he tried the jagged edge of one rock delivered a razor cut across his palm.

"I'd get the jack if we had the car. Here, try this." Lono handed Hank his Leatherman. The top of the line multi-tool was a source of machismo for the captain, the kind of thing a real man carried.

Hank took it and, going back and forth between the screwdrivers, the can opener and the short-bladed knife, he slowly dislodged one rock. Then another. A couple of them fell. After that, he could move them with his hands, handing some to Lono to throw aside in the main tunnel and pushing others through into the crawlspace.

When the hole was complete it wasn't much wider than an economy airline seat. "I'll never fit in there," Lono said, peering over Hank's shoulder.

Hank would go. It was too small for him to turn around. If there was no cavern in there, he'd have to back out on his hands and knees. With a shudder, Hank got on all fours. He jammed the flashlight inside his pants, held there by his belt. The beam aimed forward.

He began to crawl.

Lono's beam helped for a few feet until Hank could see it no more. But his boss's voice was some comfort. "It looks like it's drier in there. Higher than the rest of the floor."

"Feels that way," he called back.

"The lava above must be too thick for the roots to pierce it." Lono's voice was receding. "Water can't get in. Probably no vermin in there either."

Hank's shoulders and knees ached but he continued to crawl.

Rock shards cut into his knees. Twenty feet. Thirty. And then he felt the tunnel widen. His shoulders had more room. His hand came down on a wooden structure. It was brittle. He felt splinters as he heard sticks crumble. "There's something here." The cavern was big enough to amplify his voice.

"Can you see it?"

Hank grabbed the flashlight with his other hand and pulled it out of his belt. He aimed the beam as high as he could. "It looks like a ... a crate of some kind. Wood slats. Like a fruit box. Or ... oh, God."

Silence.

"Hank? What is it? Hank?"

He couldn't speak. Behind the wood slats, the tiny bones lay among the remnants of colorful garments. A beach glass necklace that looked like Nani's rested amid the scraps. Tests would tell if the shreds of fabric were the right party clothes, whether the bones were the right age, the right DNA. But Hank already knew this was Maile. And that someone had placed her in this forsaken darkness. He saw what looked like candle wax and shriveled leaves wrapped around a crucifix. Someone had carefully arranged her. And held a ceremony over the body.

Hank felt sick. He had to remind himself to breathe. He turned and crawled out of the crime scene. Lono's beam in his face must have told the boss all he needed to know for now. Together, they labored back out of the tube.

Outside it was inconceivably light and amazingly loud with wind in the canopy, the waterfall, the ocean thrashing miles away and happy songbird chatter. Regardless of the heat, both men shivered. They sat on lava rocks near the pool to rest before getting reinforcements. There was no hurry now.

Neither spoke. But Lono cried for Maile and Hank for the child's sister. And for families of lost children everywhere.

CHAPTER THIRTY-ONE

My Book of Revelation
Excerpt from the Year 2015

Oh, sweet Jesus. They found the body. How could this have happened? The Grim Jokester isn't through with me yet.

They'll poke it and prod it now, looking for clues. Maile is furious at the invasion. I am terrified. What if they discover something that leads right to us? What if they question Akela? What if he breaks, and they come for me? Maile is telling me it will happen, that Akela can no longer be trusted. She says he loves Renee and Nani now more than Maile and me. He wants to be free of even the memory of us.

I'm furious. But it's so hard. He's the only person who has ever given a shit about me. He's the one I've counted on and loved. Without him, what would I have done? Maile says that's all in the past. Akela will destroy us now. She says he must be destroyed first. And that Renee's turn comes next.

Terror and fury war in my brain. The noise is god-awful. I can't think straight. Is this total madness at last?

I wasn't always lolo, you know. People didn't think I was crazy. Keeping silent is where I went so wrong. And nothing was ever right again.

CHAPTER THIRTY-TWO

Omen

By Jackson O'Reilly

Excerpt from the *Keawalani Voice*, 2015

Hawaii's famous weather is a gift of the cooling trade winds which prevail most days of the year. But then there are the rarer days of the Kona winds.

Storm-ladened currents blow over the islands from the southwest. They bring with them the volcanic fog. Muggy, unbreathable air. And rain. Torrents of it. At best, the heat swelters. Children play indoors. Vacationers fan themselves and disbelieve what they've been told about golden Hawaiian days. Horses and cattle huddle together, turning their bottoms to the wind.

At worst, Kona winds drive everyone from the wave-riddled beaches. They damage boats exposed in leeward anchorages. In the mountains, they uproot trees and roofs in downslope blusters over 100 mph.

> This reporter dreads the Kona days. And
> the ill winds that they bring.

Crime scene investigators came to the lava tube in stages, depend-ing on their specialties. In time, the little bones of Maile Palea were respectfully taken away. Long before that, Captain Lono disbanded the desolate search parties, and Hank went to inform the next of kin.

It was sundown when he pulled into Nani's drive. He turned off the engine and sat for a while in the scorching humidity, wishing the weather would break. He could smell his own dried sweat from physical exhaustion and fear in that miserable tube.

He thought about what he had to do. This was the worst of all duties that a policeman faced, especially when he was so involved with the family. Lono had offered to do it, but Hank had promised both Nani and Kaleo that he would keep them informed. Not that the police would ... that he, Hank, would.

He could hear the pinging as his vehicle cooled, but little else. Songbirds had already found beds for the rainy night. It was time for the not-so-fragile hunters to come out, the feral cats, the mongooses and the owls. It was unsafe for a field mouse to skitter from burrow to seed pod.

As he opened his car door, Nani stepped onto her small front veranda, shoulders back and head high, on alert in the dangerous night. She was followed by Kaleo. Hank thought if it had been the other way around, the big man would have eclipsed the small wom-an altogether. Hank nearly chuckled. His brain felt off kilter as he approached them. Shock comes to everyone.

He could see Nani's lovely face even through the faltering light. Hurting her was like eating his own heart. He walked toward the siblings, not even hurrying to escape the rain.

Maybe it was the look he couldn't keep from his face or maybe a dark aura surrounded his whole body, weighing down his shoulders. Whatever gave him away, the siblings knew even as he climbed the steps onto their verandah.

"Maile is dead," Nani said. Her voice sounded like one of those songbirds lost in the dark, an easy target for the night hunters.

"Yes," Hank answered.

"Tell us everything." The big little brother lost his usual jocularity.

"Let's go inside," Hank said, taking Nani under one arm and turning Kaleo toward the house by the shoulder. In silence they gravitated to the kitchen, to the breakfast nook where they'd shared so much.

Hank started to talk. He described the facts of the search, how search parties had spread far and wide, how Lono had stuck by him. He downplayed the cold of the lava tube and the dark and his own fear. Finally he summed it up. "I'd say that Maile's body was placed in a position to look peaceful, cared for. Somebody had honored her with the choice of the position. It was dry in that part of the tube, and the wooden structure around her protected her."

No need to dwell on rats or insects.

"There appeared to be a shrine, part Christian and part island with candles, a cross, dried leis. A kind of memorial, I'd call it. All in all, it looked as though the person who placed Maile there must have felt remorse. But I won't know any more until the CSIs and the labs finish their work."

Kaleo hugged his sister, sighed once and left. Hank hoped he wouldn't wrap Pink Floyd around a tree. "Should I go with him?" he asked.

Nani shook her head. "He'll look for comfort, probably with Jasmine. Then he'll come back here to paint until he exhausts himself."

"It's not his fault that she is dead. Or yours either, Nani."

She attempted a smile for him but failed. It was the saddest thing Hank had ever seen.

"What do I do now?" she asked.

"Tonight, you just hold on to me."

✦   ✦   ✦

In the days that followed, Hank assembled all the information that Lono demanded from other departments and higher ups. But a dozen-year-old murder in a little village off the beaten path was simply not a priority to anyone but them. There were fresh murders to solve and urgencies for the crime labs. Hank knew that. It infuriated him anyway.

His vile mood was compounded by the fact that he couldn't see Nani as much as he wanted. Oh, she was polite and caring and willing to text or call during the workday. But she'd made it clear that she needed time. She didn't want him there every evening to watch her grieve. "It's not pretty. It is something I prefer to do on my own."

It frightened him. He worried that he'd just become a part of a bad memory. He was the one who had pushed and pushed to find that sorry little body. Maybe Nani would rather have the fantasy that her sister lived after all.

"You're an asshole," Lono told him. "Lots of us prefer not to show ourselves at our worst to the people we love. Give her some space."

Forensic reports trickled in slowly, erratically. Amidst his regular duties, Hank doggedly put the data and assumptions together. The investigator in him was driven to solve puzzles and mazes no matter how arcane the clues. Besides, there was that pledge he'd made to Nani that he'd never give up.

She wouldn't chide him if he failed. She wasn't the type to nag if all the answers were never found. She wouldn't hold it against him if the trail ran cold again. But she'd never forgive him if he didn't try.

And he'd never forgive himself. Lono was right. He was an asshole to even think she wouldn't want the whole truth.

With little more than bones and clothing remnants, there wasn't much for the forensic teams to go on. Fabric scraps matched the party dress descriptions given twelve years ago by Maile's family and Mrs. Lopaka, the birthday party hostess. There were also bits of what looked like beach towels. And, of course, the beach glass necklace that matched Nani's. But it took dental records to establish without a doubt that the remains belonged to Maile Palea.

Because there was no soft tissue left on the skeleton, there was no evidence of insect activity. You have to have skin and muscle for that. Hank had asked one of the lab workers if there would be many insects anyway, virtually enclosed as the skeleton was in the nearly air-tight tomb. Her attitude over the phone had been snotty. Like a lot of technicians, she must think of him as an idiot flatfoot, good for nothing but fucking up crime scenes. But she'd explained that there were always maggots if a person was killed in anything but extremely unusual circumstances.

Unusual circumstances. Hank's mind raced. *Underwater? Arctic chasm? Death Valley? What's more unusual than a lava tube?*

The bones showed no evidence of large predators, so rats had been sealed out by the manmade lava rock wall. If that had been the murderer's goal, it had been accomplished. The construction of this wall was one of the primary indicators to Hank that the murderer felt remorse for the actions taken against the child. The quality of the wall indicated that the person who built it was familiar with lava architecture. An islander after all, yes?

Maybe the son of a bitch is sorry it happened. Hope he lives with that festering in hell.

Lab reports showed that there was slight damage to some of the fragile bone ends which would have been spongy in early days. A few of the tiny finger bones had been carried inches away from the rest of the skeleton. Apparently, mice occasionally did get through the barricade; a full-sized mouse could negotiate an opening about the diameter of a pencil. A tunnel or two through the lava rocks – with no mortar to seal them shut – must have been at least three-eighth of an inch wide. That was also why the space was not completely airtight.

Only one large injury appeared on the bones, apparently some kind of fall or blow to the head that cracked the child's soft skull. The pathologist believed that this trauma, based on the location and size of the wound, was enough to have killed Maile. She was most likely dead before her interment. Whatever other terrors she had suffered, she had not been buried alive.

It was an enormous relief to Hank that the little girl had not known she was alone in the dark.

Nothing about the bones told investigators how long Maile had lived between the contact site – where the abductor had seized her – and the murder site or whether it was, in fact, one and the same place. Hank couldn't even be sure that Maile's last known location behind the Lopaka home *was* the contact point – maybe the child had wandered off and crossed the path of a murderer instead of the other way around.

What he did know was that the body recovery site was usually less than two hundred feet from the murder site, but that was almost certainly untrue in this case. Two hundred feet from the lava tube was in the thick of the forest on a steep climb. Hank remembered the scramble down the mountainside that had left Lono and him both short of breath.

Maile's abductor hadn't taken her from the village to the middle of nowhere to do the deed then carry the body down that wicked path.

No. The murder sight was a long way from where the body was

found. It had been placed in the lava tube soon after the murder, because the fluids of decay had soaked into the clothing fabric and porous wood of the box below her. The remains had not had time to get far into the decomposition process before it was placed in its twelve-year resting spot.

Besides, the perp would have wanted it hidden as soon as possible, with no trace back to himself.

Nobody could say how long Maile had actually lived after she disappeared. The skeleton was still small, of course, so at least the girl had not been alive for years. The bones were also noncommittal about how long the body had been in the tube.

Had it been placed there immediately after the abduction? A week? A year?

Even with a body found under normal circumstances – in the open air of a forest, say, versus sealed in a lava tube – the time to become completely skeletonized varied from a couple weeks to many years or even longer in arid conditions. It was a complex equation of temperature, humidity, access by insects and a half dozen other factors. Decay rate was impossible to say.

In this case, decay rate was not very important when all was said and done.

Whether it had taken two years or six or more for the soft tissue to decompose was not vital to know. What was important was that it was gone now, along with any clues about bruising, sexual assault, or other signs of abuse.

What was left of her clothing and the towels was examined. Her cotton panties weren't ripped and did not appear to have semen stains, but they were sent away for DNA testing anyway. Results would take forever, what with the low priority of this case. Maile's dress didn't appear torn, and all the buttons were there. It didn't look like there had been a struggle.

The condition of her shoes supported Hank's belief that she had died before being brought to the cave. They had been new party Mary Janes twelve years ago. There was a partial print on one of them that had been encased in the lava tube all these years. But it was too smudged to match any known person. The soles were clean with minimal scuffing. They had never made the climb down to the lava tube on a living child's feet. Holding the tiny footwear in their plastic evidence bag was enough to shoot bullets through Hank's heart.

The identity of the wooden box that cradled the body was soon confirmed as a fruit crate from the days that pineapple was grown on and shipped from the islands. Probably half the families on the Big Island had at least one such crate in the attic or storage bin. Its slats were mostly intact, and fruit juice appeared along with the dried fluids from the body. The crucifix had been wiped clean of prints, and the candle wax was the type of beeswax widely used by home crafters. The dry remains of the leis were maile leaves of a variety only grown on the Big Island.

Did the murderer know Maile was the child's name? Or that the vine was often given as a sign of love and respect?

If so, the bastard was close by and knowledgeable. Hank's discomfort grew. The murderer was no stranger and might even have been watching for twelve silent years from not very far away.

✦ ✦ ✦

Time was a tortoise, passing slowly. Nani continued to schedule appointments, knowing that routine was the best way to survive these days that crept like weeks. She soothed other people's aches and pains.

The quality of her work never varied although she suspected her clients questioned the quality of her attention. She was distracted, given to long silences. Her conversations with them were well-mannered but concise, revealing nothing personal. That alone was hint enough that she was in turmoil.

They all knew Maile's bones had been found, either through the *Voice* or the village grapevine, and they grieved for Nani. They felt connected to this nurturer who, while touching their physical woes, was capable of soothing their emotional ones, as well. They patiently waited for her return, willing to hold their own issues at bay until the time tortoise passed her by, and Nani was whole again.

Maile was incontestably and undeniably dead. Nani had always fanaticized that she was out there somewhere, happily raising a family of her own. That one bright sunny day, they'd all come together, and the mysterious reasons for the separation would be revealed. In her heart, she'd known it was a pipe dream and had secretly feared the truth for years. The discovery of the body was no more than a period at the end of a paragraph.

Maile is dead.

So why was Nani's grief so bottomless now? Why was she struggling to steer clear of her old bugaboos, sad songs and booze? Even for someone good at self analysis, it took her a long time to see it. Afterwards, of course, it seemed so simple.

Her loss was not just the death of Maile but the death of hope. It was a crock to believe there was a cosmic reason for all things. What reason could there conceivably be for a little girl murdered and left to putrefy in a vast darkness?

And Nani grieved that there was still no "the end." Sure, Maile was dead. But who had killed her? Was it someone they saw every day? Her missing sister could still not rest in her heart.

Will I ever be free?

Kaleo was not a great deal of comfort. Neither wanted to unload on the other. He spent his days creating tattoos and his evenings with Jasmine whose household was teeming with life. The few nights he stayed home, he painted, and that was a lonely pursuit. Nani had no part in it.

As for Hank, well, at the moment all he did was remind her of Maile. Nani knew he was working hard to scavenge any clues from the reports coming in. She had no desire to hear the ugly details. He'd tell her when there was something important for her to know. In the meantime, she preferred not to see him every night. She needed time to be ugly, from her swollen red eyes to her bitter, disheartened spirit. It was not a show she wanted him to see.

In the end, it was the love of four women who brought Nani back.

✦ ✦ ✦

The day of the search, Hakumele stayed in her own home. It was built from weathered scraps of wood bolted to a cliff many decades ago. The structure perched on an ancient lava floe, where liquid rock had hardened while the rest had dropped to the sea. Long before Hakumele's time, observers here had watched for whales to come home or foreign ships to arrive.

Hakumele only trod on the rock floor in her bare feet. She wanted to live directly connected to the earth of her island with no protective layer in between. It made it easier for the ancients to speak with the *kumu*, instilling her feet with the talents of the hula and her heart with the messages of the past. The rock floor told her what mattered.

At the exact moment that Hank broke through the lava wall to discover the body of the *kumu's* smallest niece, Hakumele felt the rock beneath her feet tremble in the way she'd come to recognize as the earth's great sorrow. It took four days of prayer, sacrifice and chanting for Hakumele to translate the desire of the ancients and to do exactly what the rock told her to do.

She descended on Nani's house in the night as fearsome as a wild sow, not stopping to knock on the door. She grabbed the young woman by the shoulders, lifting her from a crumpled position in the living room next to a half empty bottle of bourbon. She shook Nani like a rag doll, causing her own heavy jowls to wobble.

"Listen to me," Hakumele raged. "The gods can just barely accept that you gave up the hula for that lost child. But they cannot accept that you give up your own life for her. You're destroying your present with your past. People need you. I need you. Come back to us."

After her aunt left, a bewildered Nani tracked down Kaleo. "You told her I was in trouble, didn't you?"

"Me? It took Pele to create such fire." For the first time since Hank brought them the news, she saw the fear for his big sister on Kaleo's soft face. After that, they didn't avoid each other so much, were even able to talk about their little sister. It was halting at first, but they soon shared good memories to hold the bad at bay.

Healing began.

✦ ✦ ✦

The second woman to help Nani see what possibilities lay ahead was Jasmine. Back when she had been looking at Kaleo's art, she'd said she wanted to speak with Nani. Now Jasmine sat in the breakfast nook and unwound her plan.

"I have my beach glass business running well enough to support my family, selling to the tourists in the lobbies of hotels. But it could be so much more if displayed in a retail store. And I could work there instead of at home so I could manage the store while I create."

Nani said that was terrific, but she was confused why Jasmine was speaking with her. Was she looking for investors? At a time of mourning like this?

"I want the store to be an art co-op where island artists display our wares and practice our crafts. I now have enough willing artists to begin."

Nani saw Jasmine's excitement dancing in her sparkling eyes. But she still didn't see the connection to herself.

"Old Man Hookano wants to display the wooden bowls and instruments he makes. Some of them could go for thousands of dollars. He's willing to join this art co-op. Clea Fern said she and her sister would create their feather leis in the store ... at least I *think* it was Clea, but it might have been Clara."

Jasmine reached across the table to squeeze Nani's hands. "And Kaleo has agreed to let me sell his paintings."

"What?" Nani exclaimed. "Is it possible?"

"Yes. Both the ones he's already done plus commissions."

"How on earth did you talk him into that?"

A triumphant look appeared on Jasmine's face, a look between sly and smug. "Well, I took some of his paintings with me to one of the hotels. Without his knowledge. A local businessman was lunching there and saw Kaleo's work. He commissioned an oil to be done for eight hundred dollars!"

Nani gasped. "That's wonderful, Jasmine. What is the painting to be?"

"The man who commissioned it is John Nawahine's son-in-law. Pierce is his name. He wants a painting of plumeria for John's collection."

Nani couldn't help but laugh. Like it or not, there's an interconnectness between islanders. She said, "You're a miracle worker."

"Well, no. That will be your job, I'm afraid." Jasmine lowered her chin enough to look a little sheepish as she explained that the only way they could make the co-op work was with a storefront that would cost very little. No upfront fees or triple rents. "That's when I thought about the Tat Joint. It's just there empty. So I talked with the landlord, and he'd like Kaleo back. If Kaleo will advertise inside the space that he still does body art, and gives the landlord a small cut, then we can have the space for the art co-op. I'm thinking the *Art Joint* would be a very good name."

Nani's laugh felt good, as though she were exercising dormant muscles. "Sounds like you're on your way. But how does that make me the one to work miracles?"

"You must go before the judge that sentenced Kaleo. I need his custodian to get permission for Kaleo to go back in business. Maybe Hank could put in a good word, too. Surely part of rehabilitation is to help a guy find better employment."

"Well, I suppose."

"And you also have to agree to let Kaleo continue doing tats out on your lanai since he'll never have the Tat Joint as a place of business again."

"I see."

"And that means my boys may be hanging out around here from time to time. They love your climbing tree. They're a noisy crew, but they'll button their lips when you have clients here."

Kaleo must be falling for the kids as well as the mother.

Commotion and disruption were about to enter Nani's life. All in all, Nani decided, that wasn't such a bad thing. Not a bad thing at all.

✦ ✦ ✦

The third woman to bring Nani back was Allison Costello. The police dispatcher appeared one early morning, without Renee in tow. It surprised Nani because the two women weren't exactly long-time friends. Why was Allison here?

"I dropped Renee at school, and I told Captain Lono I'd be in a little late."

She probably hadn't called it in … just rolled over in bed and told him.

Nani made each of them a cup of tea. Meanwhile, Allison chatted about Renee's teacher, the price of pork at the Ono Grinds Market, the drive for bullet proof vests for police dogs. Not that Keawalani had any police dogs. What really was on the police dispatcher's mind?

Must be about the bowling league.

"I'm sorry I didn't make it to the Rack 'n Roll last night," Nani began. "I've not been – "

Allison interrupted. "Oh heavens, Nani, we all understand. Renee whupped ass for you both. And maybe I shouldn't be here now. I know you're missing Maile, and maybe you don't want to talk about another kid, but I really don't have a lot of time, so I had to come see you once I'd made up my mind." Allison took a break for a gulp of air. Tears threatened, but with near military bearing, she straightened her shoulders and barked, "Goddamn it to hell, I will not cry."

Nani was afraid that the woman's tight grip on her tea cup might shatter it in her hands. For the first time in days, someone else's troubles shoved her own over to make room. Nani the Caregiver was on point. "Allison, whatever is it? How can I help?"

Another deep breath. "Okay, here goes. Frank and I have had a thing off and on for years. Been a couple. You know."

Nani forgot to act surprised, and Allison was quick to notice. "I see it's no secret to you. But Frank likes to keep it quiet around the cop shop because the powers that be would disapprove of the boss dating the dispatcher."

"Oh, I'm sure your secret is safe. I only know it because Captain Lono asked Hank if I'd get acquainted with Renee. I guessed that you two had a special arrangement." The greater part of Keawalani knew about it. Surely that's not what had Allison so worked up now.

"I'm so glad you were willing to get to know her."

"It's certainly been my pleasure. She's a unique child. Easy to love."

"Unique, yes. We literally found her on the doorstep at the station, you know. Poor little thing was putting up a hell of a racket. People do that shit, leave babies. Mostly terrified moms. But Renee had been cared for. She was clean, diapered, wrapped in a soft blanket that was fuzzy as a baby duck. She wasn't a crack baby, showed no signs of fetal alcohol syndrome. A healthy little girl. Who wouldn't want to keep her? So I did the paperwork and took the foster care classes and, well, Renee is now mine."

"She knows her background?"

"She knows she was a foundling. That Frank and I love her to pieces. But she is fascinated with the need to know who her real parents are." Allison made air quotes when she said the word real. "I'm sure it is natural for a kid to want to know her own backstory, and it will get even more important as she gets older."

"I'm sure she knows she is loved."

"Oh yes. But she has such a sense of the proper order of things that it offends her to be missing a piece of her own history. She wants to know her own genetic makeup. I totally understand that. Her need doesn't hurt my feelings ... it just makes me feel bad that the trail is so dead." She sighed. "Now I'll tell you the secret that no one but Frank knows, and that includes Renee. I have cancer." It was an incurable sort that would end her days long before she was ready. And like her foster daughter, Allison had a strong sense of the proper order of things.

"Frank can't care for Renee on his own. She's eleven now, and he wouldn't begin to know how to deal with a teenage girl. We have hopes that you might be willing to step into the roll of mentor. We're not asking you to be a Mom ... just to be sure Renee has an adult woman to go to whenever she needs."

Nani tried to speak, but Allison rushed on. "She really likes you, Nani, and we couldn't ask for a better person to guide her. She'd know that, when I am gone, she still has people around who love her. And she's even crazy about Hank, in case your relationship with him ... ah ... continues."

Nani tried again, but Allison held up a hand. "I know that you are grieving for Maile. But like I say, I don't have much time. And Renee is, well, is another little girl who could use your help."

"Oh, Allison! I – "

" – Frank says if you can keep Kaleo's nose clean, you can sure as hell look after Renee. Besides, he has no real legal claim to her. Renee could disappear into the foster care system. But with you ready to care for her, Frank says we could most likely avoid that. "

Nani understood Allison's desperation, and her heart opened. But this was not a decision to make while emotionally ionized. She needed time. "It's such an honor to be asked. So special. But I have to think."

Allison got up to leave. "Of course. Of course you do. But don't take too long. I must have this piece of the puzzle in the right place before I can move on."

Allison had come during this time of grief to ask for help, not to give it. Or maybe, just maybe, it was one and the same thing. Maybe a distraction was just what Nani needed. But for the love of God. Take on a child after losing another who'd been in her care? A child who'd never known one mother and was about to lose another? Could Renee accept another in that role?

Can I?

✦ ✦ ✦

The fourth woman to save Nani was Mrs. Cunningham even though she didn't make an actual appearance herself. Late one evening, Nani heard a big car engine purr to a halt in her drive. When she looked out front, she saw the long black sleekness of the limousine.

Oh no! Have I forgotten an appointment?

But when she rushed to her door, it wasn't Mrs. Cunningham on the veranda. It was Packer.

"What are you doing here?" Nani snapped at the slouching miscreant.

"Not my choice." He pushed a craft paper bag and a cardboard box forward at her. "My *tutu* told me to give you this. Emelina couldn't bring it because she's allergic. One of the gardeners found it under the hedge. *Tutu* says it will die without help. And that you are the healing hands of Keawalani."

He turned to go.

"Hey! Just a damn minute." Nani said.

The box moved in her grasp. It made a tiny whimper.

"I'd open the bag first if I was you," Packer said with a shrug of his shoulders. "I'm outta here." He climbed back down her steps and into the limo's back seat. The big car prowled off into the night.

Nani carried the bag and the box into the kitchen and set both on the breakfast nook table. A note from Mrs. Cunningham was clipped to the sack:

Nani: I don't know what all maladies this little one has suffered, but she's had a hard time and will never make it on her own. You can see her through if anyone can.

The bag held pre-made formula in a nippled bottle, a couple cans of high grade food, a pan and litter, and a pre-paid card for one appointment at the Keawalani Kritters Veterinary Clinic.

Oh my God.

Nani opened the box. Inside was the smallest kitten she had ever seen. Its ears were still flat but its tail was stiff at attention, and the meatball of a head was too big for the tiny body. The baby wobbled and fell when it tried to step off the blanket that cradled it. Its eyes were open, but its sight was blurry as it tried to fix on Nani.

"Maladies, huh?" Nani said as she picked up the struggling little ball of stripes.

Young as it was, the kitten already knew how to hiss. And it did so at Nani.

✦ ✦ ✦

Nani sighed. The kitten had exhausted her in the last few days. It was possible that caring for a runty furball was harder on you than grieving. It needed fed every few hours so there'd been no more comforting alcohol hazes for her. Ah well, she wasn't sleeping through the night anyway.

She'd visited Keawalani Kritters the day after Packer dumped the bundle on her. According to the vet, the kitten required a boatload of inoculations. It also needed burped like a baby at least in the early going. It stood in its kitten food then dragged it by the pawful across the kitchen floor. It had to be washed constantly – the kitten and the floor both. Worst of all, it cried when it was alone for even a few seconds. It was the gift from hell.

What on earth was Mrs. Cunningham thinking?

From the get go, the baby loved Kaleo. "What's her name?" he asked, holding it against his chest while it cuddled in his massive upturned palm. It had clearly never puked on him.

"After a lot of thought, I believe Malady has won out over Hell Kitty," Nani answered as she spooned a glop of food onto a saucer. "This stuff already smells like shit, and it hasn't even gone through the cat yet."

By the third night, to keep it from yowling, Nani took Malady to bed with her, placing the litter box just inside the bathroom door. Oddly enough, she found that the rhythm of its purring helped her to sleep. And it was such a fragile little thing, after all, what with no adult cat or litter mates. Just keeping it alive gave Nani something new to fret about. Its antics with that string last night had actually reduced Kaleo and her both to laughter.

Maybe Mrs. Cunningham knew what she was doing after all.

Certainly the cat did. By the end of the first week, Malady had squared away the job of every member of the household.

Nani was to care for her like a mother.

Kaleo was to provide her entertainment.

Malady herself would be queen.

CHAPTER THIRTY-THREE

Visitors Are Flying High
By Jackson O'Reilly
Excerpt from the *Keawalani Voice*, 2015

It's possible that the only thing better than being ON the Big Island is being ABOVE it. Tourists can't wait to fork over hundreds of dollars just to have local fly boys (and fly girls, of course) take them soaring over paradise, from the lava floes sizzling into the sea to the wild green cliffs on the other side of the island.

You might think that aviation on the Big Island began with a necessary function. Like the army carrying mail. Or the Parker ranch for commerce (theirs was the first runway to be destroyed by volcanic eruption). But you'd be wrong.

Aviation actually began in 1911 with a visionary who foresaw tourism. He took off in his Curtis Biplane, meaning to demonstrate the joys of flight to the people of Hilo. Instead, he crashed smack into a lauhala tree. While he survived, his plane did not. I can find no historical reference regarding the fate of the tree.

Nonetheless, the idea of flight for the fun of it took root. There's a moral here somewhere. Something about try, try again. Or fortune favors the bold. Or it's never too late to dream a new dream. You can pick your own favorite axiom for success.

Bottom line, whatever made that first aviator want to see the view from the top is still alive and well today. For tourism on the Big Island, the sky's the limit.

Nani invited Hank to the Big Island Girl for dinner. On the phone she said she was ready to come back to life. Maybe they could get on with it together.

Hank wanted to happy dance. More than that, he wanted to look as sizzling hot as he could manage. Nani so often saw him in the somber uniform of the Hamakua cops, wilted at the end of the hot work day and suffering from hat hair (now that his hair was growing back). Tonight, he chose white linen slacks and a new blue-on-blue Aloha shirt. He'd been told blue flattered his eyes.

Whatever works.

He took his time in front of the bathroom mirror, seeking out gray hairs like those that had prematurely attacked his Dad. Fortunately, all strands were still chestnut. He shaved with precision then assessed. Even with that scar over the eyebrow and a slight bump on his once broken nose, he thought he looked pretty damn fine.

A splash of spicy scent. Floss. Mouthwash. And, of course, there was that surprise for Nani that Kaleo had created on his shoulder. He hoped there'd be an opportunity to show it to her. He bid the mirror a satisfied nod before turning out the bathroom light.

Dinner started out brilliantly other than Daya the Waitress gliding around with a grin as knowing as the Mona Lisa. Nani looked great. Far more luscious than anything on the menu. She had the freewheeling style of Hawaii ... those twirly bits of fabric for skirts and the tight tops. Nani's tees were a lot silkier than the ones he owned, and hers didn't have police logos.

The peach colored shirt she wore tonight was as satiny as her skin. He could see one bra strap peeking out where her scoop neck had scooped a little too far to the left. Her breasts and her buttocks had enough size for a man to get an eyeful. Maybe even a handful.

Jesus.

He'd never seen her feet in anything but sandals before, but tonight she was wearing heels. High, high heels. Her legs looked phenomenal even though he was aware only a caveman would keep staring at them the way he did. But when he pulled his gaze away, it was back up to those breasts.

The eyes, idiot, the eyes. Stare into her eyes. Women like that.

Just when he couldn't be happier, Nani brought up Maile. He'd hoped for lighter topics tonight, happier things. Things that could lead to sighs and tastes and scents in the moonlight.

"Do you know when we can get Maile's remains back?" Nani asked, after swallowing a small bite of the grilled mahi-mahi that was a Big Island Girl specialty.

Hank sliced a bite from his steak. "It'll take time, Nani. The lab workers hold on to the bones for quite a while. But I'll get her necklace back to you just as soon as I can." Hank stuffed the grilled morsel into his mouth.

She looked pleased. "I'd like that. Mom made it for her when she made mine for me." Nani fingered the beach glass pendant that hung in the hollow of her throat, right where Hank would like to place a kiss. "We'll go ahead and schedule a memorial without the bones. Kaleo and I wanted to do a ceremony at the mouth of the lava tube. But when we climbed down there, we realized the trail is just too steep for many of the villagers. So Hakumele offered her dance studio."

Hank stopped chewing. The siblings had been to that monstrous hellhole? "When did you go down there?"

"The day after you found the body."

"But you didn't go in, did you?" The thought of Nani inside the lava tube was too harrowing.

She appeared to misunderstand. "No. We didn't disturb the crime scene."

"I didn't mean that, Nani. I just thought it must have been hard for you to go."

She gave a nod of her gorgeous head. "It was. But we had to honor Pele with our prayers. We left leis at the entrance. Maile leaves, of course, and pikake flowers since they were her favorite. Some plumeria branches, too, since it's mine. Kaleo wrote out her name in white coral close to the entrance like they do down near the beach."

"I could have gone with you. I would have liked to."

"Yes, I know. And you can't imagine how much that means, how much your support has mattered through all of this. We wouldn't have our sister back now if you hadn't found her. You've changed our lives more than you can know." She brushed the top of his hand with her fingers. He nearly dropped his fork.

Nani continued. "But we had some private things to say to each other, my brother and I. We talked about accepting our part in Maile's disappearance."

Hank was frustrated by her comment, and this time, set his fork down. He took her hand and gave it a gentle squeeze. "Nani, I've said before that none of it was your fault. The fact that you were the oldest is neither here nor there. You must accept that."

She didn't pull away, even returned the pressure of his grasp. That small caress ricocheted through his body. She said, "I do accept it, Hank. That's what this was about. Letting go. Kaleo told me some things that Jasmine helped him see. That clutching on to guilt forever can be a safety blanket."

"Not sure I get that."

"If people know you feel guilty, they won't criticize you. Guilt allows you to feel sorry for yourself and wallow in the pity of others."

"Harsh."

"Maybe, but it sure can be true. The very idea of dumping guilt has felt sort of disloyal. Like we're abandoning Maile. But Maile wouldn't want us to feel this way. Kaleo and I have agreed to move on."

For a moment, Nani sat a little straighter and announced, "We played no part in it and couldn't have stopped it. There. I've said it right out loud. Now I let it go." She pulled her hand back from Hank and picked up her own fork. "Don't let that steak get cold."

Hank knew he'd look for Maile's murderer forever. But at least for now, there were just the two of them at the table again. He relished the rest of the meal. As they were leaving, he said, "I have something to show you. You could give me a hand. Come for a short drive with me? It's time you met my other girl."

✦ ✦ ✦

The trade winds were back, cooling the evening as they drove, but Nani felt her own heat rising.

His other girl?

Was there someone else she had to deal with? Could be. What did she really know about his love life? He was a handsome man, one that would quicken any woman's pulse. He refused to tell her any more no matter how she tried to wheedle it out of him.

They arrived at the tiny airfield where Hank kept the Mooney. He parked his SUV in front of a hangar that was on the other side of the field from the little terminal. It was one in a long line, like stables in a race horse barn. Each door was nearly as wide as a triple car garage. The metal building was old and battered as if it were WWII issue.

Nani guessed why they were there. She felt an emotion drop from boil to simmer ... a nasty little green-eyed emotion that felt a lot like jealousy. Relief flooded in to take its place. "This is about the airplane you're building, isn't it? I can't wait to see her."

"So much for the surprise. You're just too clever for me."

She took his arm as they walked to the hangar. Hank drew out a ring of keys with a small flashlight attached. Nani held the light as he opened the padlock and hauled back on the hangar door. It screeched like a pissed off banshee, but finally gave way and rumbled along its well worn track. Over the noise, Hank said, "She's awkward now, but she'll be a beaut when she grows up."

Nani stared into the cavernous darkness ahead of her. Darkness.

Hank snapped on the overhead fluorescents. It was like stage lights going up to reveal the airplane inside. "Ta-dah," he sang.

No, not an airplane. A huge dart.

Nani guessed it to be about twenty feet long with a wingspan that was maybe thirty. The wings swept back like a missile except the very tips which curved upward. It didn't look like anything she'd seen before. It was spellbinding, this unhatched Phoenix rising from a pile of aircraft parts.

"It's ... it's ..."

"Yeah, I know. It looks pretty odd. All this still needs to be done."
Hank made a gesture at the stacks of arcane metal shapes and cans
of liquids.

"No! It's magnificent! Oh, Hank!" She touched an unpainted fiberglass wing then walked under it, to peer into the cockpit. "What
kind of plane is it? When will it be done? Will you fly it? Where's the
engine? What's that?"

He laughed, delighted as a boy with a longed for toy. "One question at a time! It's called a Velocity. That's the canard. It's up front to
stabilize her. It replaces a tail on this model."

"No tail?"

"Nope. And the engine will be in the back. The propeller, too, of
course. But right now, the engine is over there."

She squinted into the bowels of the hangar, and in a dark corner,
saw an engine suspended on chains by a shop crane.

"As to when it will be done, well, I build it as I can afford parts.
So it could be years." "What can I do to help? Will you take me with
you when you fly?"

"You'll really go up with me?" His face reflected genuine joy. "Not
just everyone trusts a home built."

"But you're not just anyone building it." As she said it, she realized
she meant it. She trusted this man.

Really? Trust?

The fragile new feeling made her lightheaded, nearly dizzy.

Hank didn't seem to notice that Nani was having an epiphany. He
went on with the business of flying while she grappled with the emotion of it. "Okay then. I need your help with the seats. Watch your
step." He took her hand and walked her to more stacks of parts. In
her high heels, she had to mince carefully around airplane bits and
pieces. She tried to convince herself that was the only reason she was

feeling off balance.

Four tubular metal frames sat side by side, a fiberglass shell attached to each. "These are seat innards?" Nani asked.

"Yep. Without padding and upholstery. Before I do that, I need to cut the frames down to

fit in this model Velocity. Or there won't be room for the padding." He looked down at her. "Would you sit in one for me?"

"Sure, but why?" she said, as she gingerly lowered herself onto the hard fiberglass shell. She had no desire to rip her new skirt. Or fall off the side of these bullshit shoes.

"If you're going to be my co-pilot, I have to know it fits." He got a tape and knelt in front of her, measuring how much the frame overhung the width of her hips.

He isn't just fitting me into a seat. He's fitting me into his life.

She'd have to be very sure that's where she wanted to be, or she'd be lying to him by her actions. The language of love was so full of pratfalls. For now all she said was, "Does this mean I can never gain another inch?"

"If you do, we'll just cuddle closer."

"I don't let just anyone measure me across the beam, you know."

"I've been undressing your beam with my eyes all evening."

"You don't think I know that?"

"I'm sorry."

"I'm not."

✦　✦　✦

Nani was glad that Malady was shut in the bathroom. She was even gladder that Kaleo was nowhere in sight. Before she could get her front door unlocked, Hank pressed up behind her there on the veranda, lit only by moonlight.

She felt the heat as he lifted her hair and kissed the back of her neck. "Mmm. Better than flowers," he murmured. His breath quickened as he ran a slow hand down the curve of her waist to her hip. It continued on to her thigh. Her breath accelerated, too. The scent of him and the feel of those fingers stroking ...

How does this damn lock work again?

She cursed Renee's heightened home security. When she finally got it unlocked, the door banged open. Nani barely had time to turn before Hank encircled her, leaning down and in, pressing her against the wall. Even in the heels she rose on her toes to meet his long, demanding kiss. The perfect mouth, the perfect fit.

"Wait," she said, shaky as she pulled his head back with her hands in his hair. She escaped his embrace and led him toward the stairs. Just as she lifted a foot to begin the climb to her bedroom, Hank picked her up and began carrying her up the stairs.

She felt breathless. Giddy. Like she was taking flight. Half way up the staircase, her heels slipped off her feet and clattered back down.

"Welcome home you two," Kaleo yelled from the lanai. "Do I need to go get the hose?"

"Shut up, Kaleo," Nani yelled.

"Shut the fuck up, Kaleo," Hank yelled.

"To the left," Nani said, a tour guide at the top of the stairs. In all her adult life, no one had ever carried her before. She felt as cherished as a package about to be unwrapped.

Hank settled her gently onto her bed. "I want to do this just right," he murmured in her ear.

"You're making a wonderful start."

They kissed again, their needs stirring each other. Nani pushed upward to meet him, but he pulled her to her feet. "I want to see you," Hank said moving his hands to her shirt and pulling up on the thin silky fabric.

She slid away. "Then watch me. And I'll watch you."

Her hips began to ungulate in the rhythmic motion of the most sensual hulas. She hummed a tune in a voice now husky with desire. Slowly she removed her silky top, revealing the soft contours of her tee-shirt bra. Next, she untied the knot that held her sarong skirt in place. It fluttered to the floor around her like flower petals, exposing the cream colored hi-cuts that matched her bra.

She moved back into his arms. He unhooked her bra then cupped her breasts. As his thumbs touched her nipples, they hardened. "Rosebuds," he said with a smile.

Nani began to undo his shirt buttons, kissing his chest as she exposed each new inch of skin. He trembled then ran his hand under her panties to pull them down. She stepped out of the wisp of fabric and was nude.

"Now you," she said and took a step back. She stayed just out of reach as he pulled off his shirt, then his trousers and his briefs.

"Do you know how stunning you are?" he asked.

But Nani didn't speak. She felt in awe of his sleek sinewy body. She came to him then and they embraced. They were silk on satin, flame to candle. When they tumbled back onto the bed, he responded to her needs, anticipating many, initiating others. Their hands and mouths explored as each whispered, "Touch me here," or "I like it there."

"Velvet glove," he gasped as he slid his full length inside her. Her senses shut down one by one. She heard and saw and felt nothing but pleasure. She climaxed just before him, crying out. Then so did he.

"So this is love," he breathed into her ear when he finally lifted himself away, then gathered her beside him in his arms. In time, he rolled her onto her back and began licking her breasts and abdomen.

His tongue wended its way down her body toward the most intimate of caresses. She felt urgent, wanting him to hurry, but he refused to be rushed.

When it was done, she opened her eyes and began to return the favor. As she started her own journey down his body, she noticed the shark tattoo near his shoulder, on his chest. It had been altered by a particularly artistic tattooist. In fact, it was no longer a shark at all. Kaleo had transformed it into a dolphin leaping for joy.

✦ ✦ ✦

It was late. Nani slept while Hank listened to her low, steady breath. He watched a dream smile cross her beautiful face. She was his. He'd never felt such passion before. And now such peace. But then paranoia raised its ugly head.

What if he lost her now? What if something happened to her? Love is terrifying.

He needed to pee. As gently as he could, he removed his arm from under her neck, then padded barefoot to the bathroom. He shut the door before turning on the light so it wouldn't flash in her eyes. That's when he heard the shriek of the beast and felt claws sink into his ankle. He yelped and pushed the door open. Nani was now sitting up and staring at him, eyes blinking in the harsh light.

"Darling," he said. "Maybe you should have told me you have a cat."

CHAPTER THIRTY-FOUR

Memorial Service for Maile Palea
By Jackson O'Reilly
Excerpt from the *Keawalani Voice*, 2015

A memorial is to be held this Tuesday evening in honor of Maile Palea. According to family member Nani Palea, it will be a ceremony of celebration, filled with the peace, compassion and unity implicit in the Spirit of Aloha.

All villagers are invited to bring their memories of Maile to share with each other. The memorial will take place at the *kumu* Hakumele Silva's Hula Halau in Kona. Mrs. Silva, the aunt of the deceased, will chant while her dancers perform. Old Man Hookano will play the songs of farewell on his slack key guitar.

When John Nawahine heard that plumeria was Nani's favorite flower, he sent an abundant variety of the blossoms to her sister's memorial service. He even created a special arrangement from a miniaturized pink and white variety that no one had ever seen before. He named it *Maile's Spirit*.

Nani gave it pride of place at the front of the congregation, next to a collage of Maile photos that Jasmine had framed for her. She draped leis of pikake and maile leaves over the frame along with the beach glass necklace their mother had made for Maile. Kaleo placed the old plastic flashlight from the Big Island Girl into the plumeria arrangement. The chubby little hula girl was as prominent as an angel on a Christmas tree.

All in all, John Nawahine thought the old school room cum halau studio cum memorial hall looked beautiful enough to honor a little girl's spirit. He felt pleased he could make such an appropriate contribution. At the service, he sat between his grandson, Kala, and his son-in-law Pierce. A youngster whom Kala called Renee had taken the seat next to the boy. What was her last name again?

John had never known Maile. He was here as a tribute to Hakumele and Nani for turning the special boy next to him into a champion. He thought about the fortresses that people try to build around their children and how easily the walls can tumble down. He put his arm around his grandson. And he felt afraid.

✦   ✦   ✦

Mrs. Cunningham and Emelina were escorted by Packer who had managed to get sober for the event. He'd even combed his hair. Mrs. C and Emelina had not yet announced their intended nuptials to the village, but anyone could tell from the way they swayed together like two old palm trees that friendship had been growing here for many years.

Like many of the villagers, they had become used to letting Nani handle their pain. Now they were prepared to handle hers whenever she needed them. The Spirit of Aloha demanded it.

It also demanded that Nani forgive them for gifting her with Malady.

✦　✦　✦

Lynn Martin surprised everyone who knew how shy she'd always been. She stood and told a story from that fateful birthday party when Maile and she were both guests.

"Maile," Lynn said, "was the most popular girl in my class, but she always wanted everyone to have fun. So she invited me, the least popular kid, to twirl the rope with her while the others jumped." Together, they had spun it faster and faster, chanting the old favorite verses that all schoolgirls know.

Mrs. Lopaka had surprised them all by jumping in, too, claiming to be the oldest girl of all. When she tangled herself in the rope – after all, she was so much taller than the rest of the kids – she giggled with the girls who cheered her on.

Lynn didn't notice as she sat back down, that George Lopaka, sitting by himself, began to cry silently. The days when his wife could laugh and play were so very long gone.

✦   ✦   ✦

Nani sat in the front, wearing a light jacket and shift in white, the traditional color for Big Island funerals and rememberances. She was between her aunt and her brother. Hakumele reached out to hold her hand in the middle of the service. Nani looked down at the old fingers, the skin now loose over the multitude of bones. It had been far too long since she had thanked her aunt for being her very own helping hands. She placed her fingers around Hakumele's and gave them a gentle squeeze.

While the various speakers 'talked story' about Maile, Nani allowed her thoughts to roam around this room filled with mourners who were joined by one child's life and death.

Kaleo, next to her, felt solid as a windbreak against a Kona wind. As she'd told Hank, the siblings had already descended together down to the mouth of the lava tube to hold their private ceremony, flowers among the crime tape. Now Nani peeked around her brother to the lovely Jasmine seated at his other side. Her two boys were having great difficulty sitting still, Evan poking at Tony who was kicking back at him when they thought their mom wasn't looking. Kaleo reached one massive hand around Jasmine's shoulder to take Evan by the head and point it toward the front. Peace descended on the rambunctious two. Nani smiled to herself. Kaleo had found a lively group to help him with his grieving. Maybe her beach boy brother was growing up.

Her brain flitted from this new family to the shattered one from the past. She had hoped that her father would come to Maile's service. She'd tried the phone number her aunt had given to her, but it had just rung and rung. She found herself looking for Manuku to stroll through the auditorium doors. Would she know him? Would he know her? In the end, it didn't matter because there was no father, there to seek forgiveness or lend support. There was to be no miracle today.

She looked around at the row of half a dozen officers in dress uniform, representing the Hamakua District police. Hank sat next to Captain Lono at one end of the line-up of dedicated peacekeepers. Nani nodded to Allison, seated at the opposite end. Her eyes went back to Hank and met his looking at her. He smiled and gave her the hint of a salute. Did he also wink? She smiled back at him. He was invading her thoughts now more and more.

Nani listened with half an ear to the eulogies for her sister. She took an inventory of how she felt inside now that Maile was gone forever. The great burden of not knowing whether her sister was dead or alive, that burden had lifted. Sorrow, like a dark bird, had perched in her heart for so long, but Nani felt it depart with a great thrashing of wings. There was now a hole to fill with new joys and commitments. Whether or not the murderer was ever found, Maile had come home for good.

✦ ✦ ✦

The loss of Maile had all but broken Jackson O'Reilly's heart twelve years ago. He'd thought he'd arrived from O'Hare to a dead end back then. But this youngster had helped him discover the charm and harmony of village life. His banishment to the Big Island from the Big City hadn't shattered him after all. It had saved him.

He was relieved that he'd been able to read some of her columns aloud to the congregation without breaking down in tears. Now, although a participant in the memorial, he was also a reporter. He went to work. Jackson wrote notes in his own variety of shorthand using an old fashioned reporter's notebook. He could carry a handier electronic method – a devise that started with the letter *i* or *e* – but he preferred the old ways he'd learned when he was a cub reporter not that much older than Maile had been.

From his location on one side of the dance studio, he could see all of the mourners on the unreliable metal folding chairs, gathered to celebrate one short life. He'd interview as many as he could after the service. Ask them how her loss affected each. Tonight he'd write it up as the lead article for his next edition.

He knew most of them. Like villages across the nation, Keawalani's young often left to find more lucrative opportunities among the skyscrapers. The adults who were there – Old Man Hookano, Clea and Clara, Sunny Daze, Bethie Kalapana, and Mrs. Cunningham – these were the backbone of Keawalani, the teachers who kept the Aloha Spirit alive from one decade to the next.

There were a few young people, too, like Motorhead who had come with his boss's family. The student body of Hakumele's halau, all in traditional hula finery. Maggie Wilson, the seamstress, with Akela Onekea, the busboy from the Big Island Girl. Lynn and Martin Martin with their mother. Mrs. Martin had wept from the first chant of the ceremony and was still going strong as it neared the last.

There were new people, too, fresh blood to keep the village strong. He recognized the Yohays and made a note it was past time to interview them again now that they'd been in the village for a while. Some of the mourners were strangers to him, like the handsome man seated with John Nawahine and his grandson, Kala. Unknown families, young couples, groups who had car pooled from area churches. Lots of fresh stories to keep the *Voice* healthy with news and, of course, gossip.

As he looked across this human ocean, he realized there was likely a murderer among them. One of these people may well be gloating over a deed gone unpunished. Mocking them all. Ah, how the actions of one had affected so many for so long.

Who could have hated a little girl so much?

Jackson felt that the biggest secret had yet to be revealed. He looked down to his notebook, and jotted a note for tomorrow's article:

`Who killed Maile Palea?`

✦ ✦ ✦

It was late afternoon when the last of the mourners exchanged their hugs and alohas, then departed the memorial service at the hula school. Hank was on duty so after a gentle good-bye to Nani, and a paying of respects to Hakumele, he returned to the police station.

Nani and Kaleo dropped Jasmine's brood at her place then aimed Pink Floyd down the verdant hillside, through Keawalani and toward their own driveway. They were both silent most of the way. Nani figured that Kaleo would paint when they got home, his way to wrestle with the vacancy of Maile. Nani thought she might work on a new oil, an aroma therapy blend that would remind her of her sister whenever she used it. It would start with a citrus oil for cleansing. And a bit of clary sage to fix other scents. Star anise for euphoria? No, too fussy. Maybe ylang ylang for sweetness and a basic cheerfulness.

"She's gone. I can let it go," Kaleo interrupted her thoughts. Pink Floyd bumped into their driveway and around to the back of the house. "But I still need to know who did it."

The old Volvo gave a hiccup and sigh as the ignition was switched off. Then all was quiet except a single bird proclaiming that this was his yard. Nani looked at the massive banyan tree where Renee and Akela were building a playhouse for Jasmine's boys.

Renee, Evan and Tony.

"We have other youngsters to look out for now."

"Who the fuck is that?" Kaleo pointed toward the house, his body posture tightening.

Nani followed his sightline to a man sitting on the backsteps. In the descending twilight she could see he was large man, at least tall. He bent over as he sat, supporting his upper body with his arms on his knees. The skin seemed to be dripping off him and for a wild moment, Nani thought he was melting into the old wooden steps. Her mind was grappling with shock as recognition dawned swift as a lightning bolt.

She knew this man! Long ago his body had been all tight muscle where his skin now drooped. This man on her steps was her father, Manuku Palea. Maybe a miracle was happening after all. Or maybe it was an evil apparition.

Either way, Kaleo was having none of it. "Is that who I think it is?"

"I think so. It's our father. Only skinnier. He looks weak."

When Nani had told Kaleo that Hakumele had been in touch with Manuku, Kaleo had made it very clear that he wanted no part of his father anyway. Now they'd just memorialized Maile, said their good-byes to her. And here was this ghost returned from the past. Was he here to hurt them or help them? Surely they had been through enough for one day.

"The fucker is trespassing. I'll run him off." Kaleo opened Pink Floyd's door and began to lurch out, but Nani's hand on his arm restrained him.

"Wait, *bruddah.* I want to hear what he has to say."

Kaleo snorted. "And if he says nothing worth hearing?"

"Then I'll run the fucker off myself."

They got out of the car together and walked toward the lanai. Manuku was far older than his years. He labored to stand as if his joints required time to remember how to mesh together. Nani sensed the ache in those awkward tugs and jerks. A desire to help Manuku's pain threatened to diffuse the years of pain he had caused her.

Dammit. Quit being such a sucker. He's the one on trial here.

The topography of his face was like the Hamakua coast, cheek muscles folded into great soft curves. What had once been handsome now looked as rubbery and veined with red as a Halloween mask.

Like one I should have had to scare Packer. Stop it. Concentrate.

Nani was the first of the trio to speak. "Where you been, Dad? Why are you here now?"

"Yeah. You're like a decade late for dinner, and Ma's too dead to fix it for you." Kaleo spit the words through clenched teeth. The bird that had been singing was startled away by the human commotion.

Nani once again put a hand on her brother's forearm. "Let him talk, Kaleo."

"Talk, yes. I have things to say." Manuku's voice had more gravel in it than Nani remembered. Maybe a smoker's rattle.

"Say it then move on."

Manuku looked at Nani. "You are so like your mother." He turned his eyes, yellowed with sagging lids, to focus on his son. "And you, Kaleo, are a hothead. Just like your father."

"I'm nothing like my father."

In Manuku's voice Nani heard the pain she'd intuited in his body. Her resolve to be tough drained away. Someone or something else had already defeated him. She said, "Let's go inside. I'll make us coffee. Then we can all say what we must."

"Thank you, daughter." Manuku turned and struggled up the

steps. The siblings followed behind as he opened the screen door, cut through the lanai and on into the kitchen, leading the way as though he belonged there. As once upon a time he had.

While Nani prepared the coffee, her father sat in his traditional spot on one side of the breakfast nook. He sighed as he rested his weight on the colorful cushion instead of on his feet. Nani saw his eyes move slowly from place to place in the old kitchen, taking in the cabinets, counters and floor that hadn't changed much since his day. His body quivering ever so slightly.

DTs? The tannery chemicals? Or just anxiety in this home that's no longer his own?

"So much is the same," Manuku finally said as Nani set steaming cups in front of them all. She slipped into the booth beside Kaleo.

Siblings and father on opposite sides. How appropriate.

"So much the same except that," Manuku said, pointing up to Kaleo's color-drenched mural of extinct birds in flight. "That is a gift to this house from a very great artist."

"It's the work of your son." Nani felt the swell of pride for her brother, a boy who'd been self taught. It wasn't like Kaleo ever had a dedicated male role model to teach him much of anything. Certainly this broken carcass across from them didn't qualify.

Manuku slouched further forward, his head now hovering over the table. "Then as a one-time artist myself, I am humbled." He doffed an imaginery hat toward Kaleo.

Kaleo continued to glower like an enraged tiki god. Even so, Nani imagined he was pleased by the unexpected compliment from Manuku. He'd never admit that his father's opinion mattered but, of course, it did. A son always wanted a dad's approval although, as far as Nani could see, Kaleo was already the stronger, better man. She hoped that Manuku's respectful words might soothe her brother at least long enough to allow Manuku to tell his story.

The next thing her father said surprised Nani. Hakumele had told her that her parent's break up was mutual. But Manuku changed that part of his story now. "Your mother blamed me, you know. Never forgave me. Kina said that if I hadn't dragged her off to Hilo for a craft show, we would have been home to watch over Maile. She said I would have found Maile if I'd been here where I belonged."

"But she exhibited at the craft fair, too, didn't she? Her beach glass and jewelry while you showed your leatherwork?" Nani felt confused. "I don't understand."

Manuku sipped his coffee. "That's true. But I allowed her to blame me so that she wouldn't blame herself. Or far worse, blame the two young people we'd left in charge." He glanced from daughter to son, pausing as though awaiting a truth to sink in.

Jesus! Had Mom held us responsible? Had she pointed the emotional figure at us in those years before she died? Is that why Kaleo and I blamed ourselves in the first place?

"So it's Mom's fault you cut out on the family," Kaleo growled. "You couldn't take the heat yourself. You stole our chance to recover. You're no better than a thief."

"Kaleo, I apologize. But I'm not here to find fault. I'm here to tell you what happened if you care to listen." Manuku was not ready to play dead.

Nani felt the testosterone level rise and she needed to tamp it back down. "Please, Kaleo. Let's hear him out."

He sighed and dramatically rolled his eyes. "By all means. Be my guest. Explain away."

Their father continued in a slow-paced monotone, almost as though he'd memorized this recitation. And maybe he had. God knows he'd had plenty of time to invent a story or embellish the real one, to make himself seem less of a culprit and more of a victim. Nani tried to withhold judgment until she heard his whole story.

Manuku explained that when Maile was lost, Kina and he were, as well. They were inconsolable. "It felt as if we'd been gutted like a couple of *opah* fish. Grief hollowed us right out. We just, I don't know, got through the days by following old habits. I'd say in my head things like, 'it's time to take out the trash' or 'it's time to watch the news' or 'it's time to set the table.' We couldn't be a happy couple or responsible parents. Hell, we couldn't even function like ordinary human beings."

"So you threw away two children because you lost a third." This time, Kaleo's spite caused Manuku to flinch as though he'd been punched.

"I can see how it feels like that to you. But that's so far from the truth."

"Yeah? Convince me, old man."

Manuku, unsteady in body and voice, continued. "At first, Kina and I, we struggled to keep the family alive. We kept hoping that Maile would come home and we could go on as before." Manuku shoved his shaggy hair back from his forehead, and cleared the tears out of his throat. "For a couple of months we kept the pantomime going. But Kina was getting more distressed, not less. She'd stopped creating her jewelry, didn't always remember to make dinner, withdrew from me like I was the cause of all this pain. Finally, I couldn't take it."

When he stopped, the silence was deafening. Nani had to fill the air. She said, "So you began to drink for real."

Manuku snorted. "Not just a few beers or a social drink but an endless river of alcohol to wash away the pain. It went for months like that. The bottle is a friend when there's nobody else."

Kaleo wasn't buying. "What bullshit. Just an excuse for losing it."

But Nani felt queasy. She knew what it was like to seek answers in a shot glass. And how that always failed in the end. Her resolve to stay away from it was maybe stronger than her father's at this point in time, but alcohol was always waiting in the wings.

"The day came when Kina finally confessed the real truth of it to me. She said that whenever she looked at me, all she could see was her lost child," Manuku's voice cracked as he touched his own cheeks. "She saw Maile in these features, and she felt desolate. She couldn't forget. I fought it, telling her she'd change one day, that time would cure the wound. But she never changed. Instead, she started turning her back on me. Literally. Wouldn't look at me. Finally, I quit asking and started demanding. God help me, I even struck her. More than once. Booze and rage make that kind of shit seem the right thing."

"Still think it's the right thing? To knock sense into her? Glad I didn't learn about women from you, Daddy Dearest." Kaleo's sarcasm alarmed Nani. Her brother was not often cruel.

"Of course, it wasn't right, Kaleo. Finally, there was no other answer. She demanded I leave her sight so she could recover enough to be a mother to you. She told me to go again and again. So I did. It was only through Hakumale that I learned Kina had failed in her mission. That she had died."

Nani's head reeled with the truth of it. If it was the truth. "So you knew she was dead, but you still didn't return for us."

"Yes, to my great shame. Maybe it was a lousy decision. But I was drinking like never before. Hakumele was watching over you by then. My sister was a better parent to you than I would ever be." Manuku looked straight into Nani's eyes. "I apologize to you, daughter." He turned to Kaleo. "And to you, son."

Until now, he'd mostly looked down like a reprimanded dog. Nani could see encrusted debris in the corners of his eyes and the heightened redness of their rims. She'd seen something similar in her own mirror not so long ago, and she doubled her resolve to be alcohol free.

Another uncomfortable silence. Apparently, Kaleo wasn't ready to accept an apology. Nani wasn't sure how she felt about it. So she ignored the apology for now. "Where were you all this time?"

Manuku, the renowned leather crafter, was too well known to stay locally. He would have been recognized by someone on the island so he hitched a ride on a freighter to Oahu, finding work at a leather tannery there. He no longer created beautiful leathergoods himself, not after that fateful show in Hilo. "My talent disappeared along with my daughter. Now I can prepare skins for others. Over time, too many tanning chemicals have entered my body in my breath, through my skin. That plus all the booze. Well, it's been killing me."

"So we gain a father and lose a father on the same day," Kaleo said. "I've heard enough." His voice was ice. Nani figured that so much anger was a bluff for so much sorrow. But she doubted her father saw it that way when her brother ended with, "Way to go, asshole. Way to fucking go."

Kaleo nearly pushed Nani out of the booth in his haste to leave. He hustled out the back, screen door slamming. Nani could hear Pink Floyd complaining as Kaleo kicked it into life and out of the drive.

Once the car had roared and coughed away, Manuku asked, "Will he forgive me?"

Nani shrugged. "I don't know. Given time, maybe. There are two little boys in his life now. He might think about them, realize that he'd leave them if it were in their best interest, even if it destroyed him. Maybe he'll come to understand why you did what you did. I just don't know."

"And what about you, daughter? Will you accept an apology? And will you forgive me?"

Forgive him? Not if he'd merely come home for his own comfort. Not if he expected her to take care of him now that he was in need.

She'd lost Maile, her father, her mother. Only he had left by choice. Was the story he told excuse enough for his extended absence? Could she forgive him for rejecting her, for stirring up all those abandonment jitters that had riddled her life? Forgive him for teaching her not to trust?

"I don't know that, either. I'll need time."

"I would prefer a yes."

"I'm not ready to give it. But I'm glad you have come back. That's the best I can do for now."

"Fair enough." Manuku rose shakily. "I'll now go ask forgiveness of my sister."

Good luck with that.

As they walked together toward the front door, Nani asked, "Before you go, tell me why. Why have you come back now?"

"Because I heard Maile's body had been found. I stopped drinking that day so I could follow details of the investigation. I've been sober since. I came today to seek forgiveness but didn't want to do it at the memorial. It wouldn't have been right."

"No. It was about her, not about you."

"I'm trying, Nani. Twelve steps and all that. I am without Maile, without my wife, without my home. If I lose Kaleo and you, I have lost everything." His shoulders sagged a little more. "I'm very tired of keeping silent."

It was true that he had lost a great deal. But that did not constitute her need to forgive. Nonetheless, forgiveness was the Aloha Spirit. Nani had always believed that holding a grudge was poisonous to your system. But maybe, just maybe, there was something in between. Maybe you could be unforgiving as long as your anger drained away. As long as it was just a fact of life and didn't damage your spirit. She'd have to think on it for a time.

"Do you need a ride?" she asked. "I only have a Vespa."

"No, I rented a car." Manuku indicated the Focus parked out front. At the door, he turned back to her. "May I hug you, daughter?"

"No. I think not. Not yet."

After he left and she faced the empty house, the loneliness nearly toppled her. "Malady!" she yelled for the kitten. "Get out here and give me some comfort."

But cats do only as they choose.

CHAPTER THIRTY-FIVE

The Things In Between
By Jackson O'Reilly
Excerpt from the *Keawalani Voice*, 2015

When I moved from Chicago I saw something here I never saw there. Maybe it is merely small town vs large. Or maybe it is something more.

I saw wooden boxes out in front of many Keawalani homes. Fruit crates, grocery boxes, even an old drawer from a dresser long since gone.

"Garbage?" I asked Old Man Hookano one day as he was setting out an ancient whiskey crate.

"More like *baggage*," he answered. He indicated the papayas from his burgeoning tree that he'd loaded into his box. "I can't use them all, and I can't let them go to waste. So they are here for any neighbor who can use them."

The wooden box is an open invitation to share things we don't need anymore but that are too good to throw away. The things in between.

It can be hard to recognize when your problem is somebody else's solution. Maybe it is as simple as shoes now too wide for you, but still restrictive enough for someone else. Or maybe it's the beautiful vase that I saw Mr. Lopaka remove from one such box.

"Tell your readers," he said, "that even sad homes can be brightened with flowers."

This writer hopes that the memorial for Maile Palea will lighten the load for many of you. Our village has grieved for twelve long years, and now we can put our child to rest. Her spirit has come back and is waiting for us out front in our emotional wooden boxes. May you exchange her lightness for your heavy load.

For those of us still burdened by the mystery that remains, by the question 'Who Killed Maile Palea," consider this: if only for today, take comfort in what we know, not what we don't. It is the thing in between.

Maile flailed inside Maggie's brain like the beating wings of a Black Witch moth. At first, Maggie was just sane enough to know it wasn't a real demon trapped in there, eternally seeking an exit. Now she believed it was her commanding force, that she was its instrument. She must respond to it in her actions and emotions.

The memorial service had enraged the Maile spirit. It was her time lost, her murder, her premature demise. It was her bereavement, not that of Nani or Renee or any of those other so called mourners. Grief wasn't theirs but hers. And she was Maggie.

Those beating wings finally drove Maggie over the brink of sanity into near perfect madness. The furious child spirit was always there now, fluttering, fluttering. Maggie could no longer tell which of them was in control. But then, she no longer cared. Anger was anger. Revenge would soon be revenge. And it would be sweet for them both.

Leaving the memorial service, the combined force of Maggie and Maile targeted Akela. He was right there next to them. Maggie seethed as he drove toward home in a miserable old crate that he'd borrowed from WikiWikiFix Garage. It had stuck out in the old school parking lot like the ugly duckling among those goddamn swans. Everyone could see how low a life she led.

"Didn't the garage have something nicer?" Her question was a mumble. She knew it would be hard to hear over the cachophanous Britney Spears track that was stuck on perpetual play in the rust bucket's CD slot.

But Akela did hear, and he looked startled. "Something nicer? Not for us to borrow for free."

"Not for us. Never for us." She so seldom complained aloud. It would do him good to know that the existence he provided was far from a picnic, that *he* was a huge disappointment at the end of her rainbow. She'd loved him and supported him all of her life, and now he had turned his back. He was climbing out of the shithole of their life, leaving her to wallow in misery alone.

Black Witch wings thrashed in her head, listing his wrongs in rhythm with the shrill Britney:

Akela had killed Maile. Maggie was an innocent. Innocent.

Akela had never made her bad ass father pay for his treatment of her.

Akela had not taken her away from this fucking village.

Akela was a busboy and a gardener. What kind of man was that? What kind of failure?

Akela now worked for, of all fucking people, Nani Palea. He even liked the bitch.

Akela was bonding with Renee, and that was worst of all. He was getting to know the child who had lived, turning his back on the one who died. The one he had killed. Maile could never, ever allow that. Neither could Maggie.

Thou shalt not.

With all the righteousness of a moral zealot, Maggie knew what must be done. She opened the large tote bag that a seamstress always keeps close at hand. She rummaged through fabric scraps and patterns, bindings and measuring tapes.

Ah. There they were. The scissors. Gleeming surgical steel. Fine strong points for easy snipping.

The wings in her head beat. She lifted the weapon from the bag. *Thy will be done.*

Akela stopped for a turn. Always cautious, he looked both ways. He was facing away when she lunged. With all her considerable strength, Maggie jammed the scissors into her lover's neck. His blood gushed hot onto her hands, her chest and lap. He tried to speak but spit merely bubbled from his mouth. It made her giggle, that noise that sounded like a kid pretending to gargle.

"Judas," she hissed into his ear. "You will never betray me now."

Akela slumped over the wheel. His head hit the horn, one thing in the junker that still worked just fine. It blared as the car rolled gently into the roadside ditch and came to a tilted halt.

Maggie opened her door and said one last thing to Akela. "The next one on our list is your darling Renee. See what you have done?"

Her feet sank into the muddy water at the bottom of the ditch. As she sloshed away, horn and Britney still ringing out, the fluttering in her head didn't stop as she had hoped. Instead, the wings thrashed with such intensity they swept away the last bit of reason trying to tell her how she'd miss Akela so.

✦ ✦ ✦

Racket. Shrieking. A voice? Singing? Car horn? Maybe it was the noise that kept Akela from total blankness.

What had happened? Accident? Was Maggie hurt? No ... wait ... there'd been something so cold then searing hot. Maggie. Had Maggie done this? *His* Maggie? She'd said something about Renee. After she'd cut off his head.

No. His neck was fire, but he could lift his head with help from his hands. The blaring stopped when he took his weight off the steering wheel, but the music played on. And blood, his blood. Slowly he turned toward the passenger seat. He had to help Maggie. But she was gone. All that was on the seat was her sewing bag, spilled on its side.

He tried so hard to focus. Finally, he could see the edge of Maggie's old black school notebook peaking out of her tote, along with snips of flowered fabric. He reached out for the book as the riotous colors in the fabric began to swim. His vision hazed again. His hearing must be going, too, because the singing was sounding more like a siren now.

Darkness.

✦ ✦ ✦

"I'm alone. Kaleo is with Jasmine, I think. My father was here, but then he left. I wasn't kind. Can you come when your shift is done?"

That's what Nani had said on the phone. Hank heard her sadness, of course, but also her need of him. Him. It was a hint, a clue. He was a detective, after all. Maybe he was becoming an essential in her life. The love he was feeling for her, the worry that it would overpower her, maybe it would not be rejected if he offered it.

It was well after midnight before he left the station. Jay Samuels was alone for the rest of the overnight shift. Lono and Allison were long gone; he hadn't seen them since Maile's memorial service. Hank knew they'd be together even though Lono was so sure he was keeping their secret quiet. As long as no one spoke of it aloud, it didn't exist. Their relationship could thrive.

Hank hoped they were thriving at home now, as he was here in Nani's bed. Sex had been slow and gentle. They were lying on their sides, facing each other, speaking quietly even though no one else was there to hear. Their bodies weren't pressed together now, probably because Malady had spread himself lengthwise between them. They managed to hold hands as long as Hank occasionally scratched the kitten's ears.

"He's the only thing in the world that prefers my touch to yours," Hank observed. He then kissed the fresh claw mark on Nani's wrist. "I myself love this wrist and that touch and those, well, all of you. I love all of you."

"I love you, too, Hank," she said.

She loves me!

Conversation waxed and waned through the night, as the two tired people drifted in and out of sleep. Nani told him the story that

Manuku had used to excuse his absence for a decade. Hank wasn't convinced by it, but that wasn't important. He knew Nani needed to make her own decision about her father. He'd left that relationship in Hakumele's hands, trusting the kumu to tell Nani about Manuku. Maybe a little forewarning had eased the surprise of Manuku's reappearance.

Nani had also revealed her own fear of alcohol and her even greater fear of rejection. She told him she'd been so afraid that her fiancé would leave her that she forced him away. She'd never truly committed to him. And she didn't want that to happen again with Hank. "I'm sharing all my secrets so you'll know exactly what you're up against."

In return, he'd expressed not only his love but his worry that he'd push too hard too soon. He would try to give her time to trust him completely. "I'm a cop. I'm hard wired to want answers. But I won't press for commitment. I'll wait until you can make it. And I'll be constant as the tides."

They agreed there was relief in telling their innermost thoughts even though it exposed new nerves that were so tender and raw. It hurt less, it turned out, to speak up than to hold your tongue.

Imagine that.

They told each other their favorite foods and colors and embarrassing moments. She traced the dolphin on Hank's shoulder; Hank touched the cup of her ear. All was well until, at some point in the wee hours, they talked about Renee. Nani told him what Allison had asked of her. Hank was shocked to hear of Allison's condition.

"She wants a woman in Renee's life to help her grow up. I want a child in mine, to replace the life I've lost without Maile."

Through his grief for Allison, Hank listened quietly. But an alarm was sounding. Was his new found twosome about to become a threesome? He really liked Renee, too, but ...

"I think it just makes sense to say yes. Allison needs it, and so does Renee. I think we're getting along pretty well. We text each other between visits. We're saving that sorry ass bowling team. Renee's learning to hula although she really sucks at it."

As she rattled on about Renee, Hank heard the gladness tones in Nani's voice. The alarm bell rang again. He tried to sound casual as he asked, "When Allison ... I mean, when the time comes, will Renee come live with you? Is that how you see it?"

Nani paused. "I guess that would be up to Lono. Allison thinks a teenage girl would be a bit much for him, but that doesn't mean she'd have to live under this roof instead of his. I'd still be her ... her big *sistah*. Either way, you see that as a problem?"

Had she heard it in his voice? Was he already backing off his commitment to her?

"No, no. I just was questioning whether it's fair to think of Renee as a replacement for Maile. She isn't Maile, and it could damage her if you – we – don't take her on own terms."

A touch of steel entered her voice. "I think I can handle that, Hank. I didn't say she'd replace Maile ... just the life I lost without Maile. I know they are very different people. And even if you think that's a stumbling block, the truth is that Allison has few options. Renee doesn't belong in children's services. Lono on his own could lose her to the state. But with me as a backup, we could keep that from happening."

She paused again then asked, "Is that a deal breaker for you?"

That was the crux of it. How he answered would seal the fate of this relationship. The idea of being a couple was so new. He wanted Nani to himself for a while. He felt jealous of a child, even a child he liked. Hank was none too proud of himself for that thought, but it was real. And this was not the time for lies.

"I think I'm not ready to share you. I've only just found you. I know it is the wish of a dying woman, and I know it is a child in need, and I know my boss, my friend needs this help – "

"And you also know there is time. This isn't happening tomorrow. Maybe Allison has more time than she thinks. We have time to prepare. Together." Nani would not plead, he knew that. He heard apprehension in her argument.

And he knew his answer. "It's no deal breaker. In fact, it's tangible proof of my commitment. If Renee will have me in her life as a big brother or uncle or whatever, I will have her in mine."

Nani moved closer, tempting the wrath of the kitten. Hank put his arms around her. "Besides," he said. "Renee would probably put Super Glue in my gun if I said no."

They drifted back into sleep, locked together until Hank's phone rat-a-tatted in the dopey ringtone he had chosen for calls from the station. It took him three bursts of fire before he found it on the nightstand. A hint of early morning light was just showing through the window louvers.

"Yeah, Jay?"

"Got a call from the clinic. Akela Onekea was brought in. He'd been in a wreck, wounded bad in the neck. They've patched him up and think he's gonna make it. The drugs are wearing off, and it's hard for him to talk. But he's asking for you."

✦   ✦   ✦

Maggie, after a long walk home, arrived bloody, muddy and exhausted. Maile had fluttered in her head all the way. Things were hazy. She was unsure where she had been or what had gone on. She only knew she was tired, so tired. She collapsed on the bed she shared with Akela, and time stopped for Maggie. At some point in the hours that passed, her body curled into a tight ball like prey making itself too small to appeal to predators.

... and behold, a pale horse. And the name of him who sat on it was Death ...

The words from Revelation cut through her head, quashing any sweetness that she may have been dreaming. She awoke gasping. Her muscles ached as she stretched and tried to shake the sleep from her brain. It was dark so she turned on a light although she knew she should never waste electricity. She looked down at herself and discovered she was filthy.

Why? What's happened to me?

It scared her. Her heart raced.

She staggered to the kitchen, heated a kettle of water then added the hot to the cold she drew into the sink. It was the closest thing they had to a bath in this miserable shack where Akela and she lived.

Akela. She wondered where he was and when he'd be home. Must be working overtime at the Big Island Girl. Had he told her that? Would he bring home leftovers so they could eat or would it be another hungry night?

She knew it was wrong to be nude in a room as public as a kitchen, although there was a time Akela liked to watch her. Her father would have beaten her for far less, but her parents had moved away from Keawalani long ago. She had no idea where they lived. And she was sure they no longer cared what she did.

... you allow that woman Jezebel ... to commit sexual immorality...I will kill her children with death ...

She pulled her shift over her head and removed her bra. Maggie washed her hair, unruly with curls, then her upper body. Next, she washed her legs and rolled down her underpants. As she scrubbed her privates with a brush until they were nearly raw, she could hear her mother intone from years gone by: "Wash down as far as Possible then wash up as far as Possible then wash Possible." It was the only humor her mother had ever shared and only when Dad was gone from the house.

That was back when the things that were Possible might be exciting and fun. Now all that was Possible looked very bleak. With renewed vigor, the thrashing of wings intensified in her head as Maile reminded her of what she must do. She whimpered.

When she was totally spotless, Maggie felt ready for her next chore. First, she slipped on an old tee-shirt, soft and torn, that belonged to Akela. The logo on the front was so faded all that was legible was 'uck'n'em loon.' She felt herself begin to flag and knew she needed more sleep. But she staved it off. No rest for the wicked, not until she had dealt with Renee. Her child.

... the mother of harlots and of the abominations of the earth ...

Renee. Her very own flesh, ruined by a godless woman who didn't teach her the ways of the Bible as Maggie had been taught. Renee. She was alive because Maile was dead. A reckoning was in order.

It was Renee who must be scrubbed clean, washed of her sins. Maggie had seen the way the whore child had looked at that boy at Maile's memorial. Was it already too late to save the little harlot's soul? Renee must be purified before walking in death with the angels.

... Write the things which you have seen, and the things which are, and the things which will take place after this ...

Write. The words of Revelation reminded Maggie she must write a final entry in her own Book of Revelation. She went to get her sewing bag. It was not next to her nightstand where she always kept it. Next, she sought her journal under her pillow. That's where she often hid it from prying eyes as she slept.

It was gone. Her Book of Revelation was gone. For the first time, her own outrage overshadowed Maile's. Her fury and panic eclipsed the beating wings. Had her book been stolen?

... something like a great mountain burning with fire was thrown into the sea ...

Her brain boiled. Now she knew where she had to go. In the pale light of early morning, she picked up the phone and placed the call.

✦ ✦ ✦

Hank hated the Keawalani Medical Clinic or any hospital facility for that matter. They sounded and smelled like illness which was, of course, the whole point of such places. But now, at the small end of the morning, this one was quiet. Brightly lit but sort of eerie as he had walked down the hall to Akela Oneka's room. Medical equipment lined the walls, arcane and ominous, awaiting a new day of misery. If there was an overpowering odor, it was the carbolic or bleach or whatever the hell they used on the floors.

Akela was a small man but tough and wiry as a bantam weight. Now he looked like a broken doll to Hank, trapped under a blanket tucked around him with military precision and behind a grid of IVs. His skin was pasty white like the bandages and gauze that encased his neck. His eyelids, closed now, were as thin and fragile as rice paper.

Hank looked right at him maybe for the first time ever, although the little gardener had crept around the corners of his life in Keawalani for as long as he could remember. Busing Hank's dirty dishes, changing the oil in his car, pruning the debris in Nani's yard. Akela was one of those service people who exists below the notice of most citizenry. Hank was ashamed to place himself in that category.

The head nurse on duty had told him that the EMTs brought Akela in late the afternoon before. They'd received a call from a driver who'd heard music blaring from the stranded car. Akela had apparently driven into a ditch. Someone had caused a deep wound to his neck. By the time the EMTs delivered him to the clinic, he was nearly a DOA from blood loss. Transfusions, stitches and drugs had stabilized him overnight. His first request had been for water. And his second for Hank.

"Any obvious cause of the wound?"

The nurse squinched up her already wrinkled face. "Well, a weapon wasn't hanging out of the wound, if that's what you mean. Whatever it was, it managed to miss all two hundred and six bones in the human body. Your guess is as good as mine. Or ask Mr. Sleepy when he comes around again."

She appeared ready to go when Hank stopped her. "Anything else you might tell me? Don't mean to be a bother or anything."

She appeared to de-ice. "Sorry, Officer. Been a long night. Yeah, there was one funny thing. The EMTs couldn't pry that out of his hands until the drugs knocked him out. Amazing considering the amount of pain he had to be in." She pointed a gloved finger at a worn looking notebook clutched in Akela's hands. It reminded Hank of the kind he'd had as a schoolboy.

The nurse added, "We put it on his tray table so he'd see it when he came to. He grabbed it up, asked for you, went under again. Now you're here, he's all yours. I got other stops to make." She bustled off, but stuck her head back in the room for a last remark. "Vocal cords weren't cut, but it'll hurt him to talk. Don't interrogate too long, or I'll run you out on a rail."

Why? Why did he ask for me? Mostly I've ignored him all his life.

Why wouldn't he talk to Jay, the duty officer? Or demand Lono, the captain? That's what most people in the village would do. All

Hank could figure was that Akela had seen him often enough with Nani ... and that Nani was the type of person who didn't look through people. She looked at them. Akela might feel safest with a cop that Nani trusted.

As he was staring at those lids, the eyes fluttered open. Hank felt slightly embarrassed to be found peering so close. He straightened and said, "Mr. Onekea? Akela? It's Officer Lindsey. Are you feeling up to talking?"

The eyes unclouded, focused and leaped to panic. "Ay!" Akela yelped as he tried to gasp. He gathered the journal to his chest with one hand and grabbed his neck with the other. It caused him more pain, and he cried out again.

"Easy! Easy, man. Take your time, yeah?" Hank put a hand on Akela's shoulder in hopes of comforting him. "Stay still, and it'll hurt less."

Akela moaned. Hank thought he should call the station to get somebody here for Akela. Somebody the busboy loved. The hospital probably didn't know that he'd lived with Maggie Wilson for years.

"Has someone called Maggie for you?"

Things got instantly worse. Akela tried to form words.

Hank strained to understand.

Akela's mouth opened and closed silently. Then he squeezed out another sound like a desperate cry. Finally, a few tortured words came. "Maggie and me. We kill Maile Palea."

What? What?

"She not her anymore. Maggie not Maggie. Crazy. Save Renee."

Was this some kind of code? What the hell was he saying? Hank said as calmly as he could, "Akela. Are you confessing to a murder? Do you want a lawyer?"

Akela impatiently waved him off with the hand not holding the journal. "You go! Can't speak more."

"Slow down. Try. What about Maggie? Renee who? I don't know

what you're talking about."

Akela opened the worn old notebook with shaking hands. He chose the last few pages and thrust it to Hank. "You read last days. This Maggie."

So Hank read. It sounded crazy. Until it didn't. Rantings began to ring of truth. A story emerged within the crazy talk. How Maggie and Akela had killed Maile. How Maggie had come to believe Maile lived on inside her head. How she was the real mother of Allison's Renee. How she had come to distrust Akela and hate Nani. How she was to punish Renee.

While he read his phone rang, but he ignored it and read on. His world collapsed when he got to the line:

There's a price to pay here. A big price. And I'm not the one who's going to pay it.

Reality hit him like a fist. He knew the two who were going to pay. Hank tightened his grip on Akela's shoulder like a raptor's talons, no desire to comfort now. "Is she going after Nani or Renee first?"

"Her last words to me. Renee."

Crazy or not, pathetic or not, Maggie was about to murder again. That made her Hank's adversary. As he ran out of the hospital, he placed a call to Jay, requesting someone to keep watch on Akela. Next he called Lono at home.

"This better be good, asshole," the boss growled, his voice raspy with interrupted sleep.

Hank yelled into the phone as he maneuvered his car out of the hospital lot. "Renee! Lono, is Renee there?"

✦ ✦ ✦

Long before Hank awakened Lono, Maggie had placed her call to Allison's house and gotten Renee the very first time. She'd thought she'd have to try again and again, hanging up if Allison answered. She took this good fortune as an omen of her righteousness. The Black Witch wings fluttered in excitement.

"Costello residence. Renee speaking."

This was it. She had to sound rational. She couldn't be *lolo*. "Renee," Maggie said in a voice little more than a whisper. "This is your mother, my darling."

"What? Did you say you want to talk with my mother? She's still asleep."

"No, Renee. I am your mother. Your real mother. They've kept me away from you for so long. But I'm close now. And I love you. I've loved you every day."

"But ... I ... I don't believe you." Renee's voice sounded astonished, then in a burst as tough as an eleven-year-old girl could muster, she added, "Liar!"

"It's true, angel. They took you from your real mother and father. But I know you want to know us. To hear the real story. To find out who you really are."

"How do I know you're not lying?" The disbelief was clear in Renee's voice.

"Because I know one of your secrets." Maggie almost snickered. That'd get the little bitch.

Renee was now hesitant. "You do?"

"Yes. You have a strawberry birthmark on your left butt cheek. You hide it, but I know it's there."

"How do you know?"

"I'm your mother. I changed your diapers. Besides, I have a birthmark just like it. That proves you are mine." Maggie knew Renee would hate that birthmark the way she'd hated her own as a little girl. The way she hated her curly hair, the kind she'd seen on Renee as the child grew through the years.

But Renee still wasn't ready to cave. "What color is the blanket they found me in? Allison still has it."

Good, good. Smart girl but she was coming around. Maggie smiled broadly. "It's yellow. Yellow and soft as a duckling."

Maggie heard Renee's quick intake of breath. The child could no longer hide her excitement. Neither could Maggie.

Renee asked in a tentative voice, "Mother? Who are you? I love Allison. She loves me."

"Of course you love Allison, and that's okay. I'm hiding where nobody can find me. I can't stay long so you must be quick. I'll answer all the questions you have when you get here."

"Where are you?"

"Do you know the pool beside the lava tube?" All Keawalani kids snuck down there at some time or other, even with parents who warned them away.

"You mean the lava tube where that kid's body was found?"

"Yes, that's the place."

"I can't go there. It's off limits for me. Why does it have to be so far?"

Maggie nearly yelled at Renee. The kid was being a fucking scaredy cat. But she stayed calm. "Because I'm afraid to come any closer. I have to hide. If you don't come, you'll never know."

"Well ... I guess ..."

"You won't have to go in the cave," Maggie cajoled. "I'll meet you beside the pool where it isn't scary at all. And I'll tell you everything you want to know. But, Renee ..."

"Yes?"

"You must come alone. Otherwise, I won't be here. And you'll never, ever know who you really are."

✦　✦　✦

Hank had left for the Keawalani Clinic. Something about Akela being in an accident. Nani hoped the gardener would be okay. Hank would call her to let her know. She drifted back to sleep.

Her phone awakened her with an incoming text. Probably some client changing an appointment. No ... it was from Renee:

REAL MOM JUST CALLED!!!

WTF, Nani thought. But she texted: WHAT???

GOING TO MEET HER

WHO? WHERE? WHEN?

REAL MOTHER AT LAVA TUBE. NOW!

NO! TELL LONO OR ALLISON

CAN'T OR SHE WON'T BE THERE

THEN WAIT FOR ME

CAN'T. HAVE TO GO ALONE. EXCITED!!!

WAIT

But Renee was gone. Was somebody playing a shitty joke on the kid? Upset, Nani called Hank but couldn't get through. She left a voice message for him, then texted Renee again to say she was coming. But she knew the pugnacious youngster would not listen. Nani threw on her denim shorts and a tee, grabbed up her shoes, then ran out the door.

✦ ✦ ✦

After he called Lono, Hank sped toward Akela's home to look for Maggie. Lono called him back. He'd never heard his boss sound frightened before. "You're right. Renee's gone. Not in her bed, not in the yard. Where is she for God's sake?"

Hank quickly brought Lono up to date. He told him Akela's story and that Maggie was after Renee.

"She's got her, Hank. Maggie's taken our Renee."

"I'm on my way to her house to look for them there."

"I'll call out the rest of the force. And get Jackson to put an alert in the *Voice*."

"I'll let you know what I find."

When he hung up, he noticed the voice mail. He'd ignored it earlier while he was reading Maggie's diary or journal or whatever the hell it was. He played it now:

Hank! I got a text from Renee that she's going to meet her real mother. I don't know who the hell she means. She's going to the lava tube, where you found Maile. I'm pissed, Hank. If this is somebody's joke it's terribly cruel. I'll follow her. Come if you can, and if not I'll let you know when I'm back in cell range.

Nani had promised him she'd stay out of danger. But Nani didn't know about Maggie's madness. Didn't know what she'd done to Maile. Didn't know the danger. He made a noise like a swallowed sob as he slammed on the breaks. No need to go to Maggie's house now. He had to follow Nani. To Renee. To find them both before they died at the lava tube. Maile's final resting place.

Crazy goddamn Maggie.

He tried to call Nani. No answer. Out of cell range. He reversed the big car, nearly backing into the ditch himself, then sped toward the trailhead that led to the lava tube. It wasn't an official trail, not one marked for hikers. All that was there was a spot next to the road where it was wide enough to park.

As he raced on the way, he called Lono again. He couldn't keep the man in the dark, but the call was risky. Lono might tell him to wait for back-up. That's what a captain should do. But if he did, Hank would ignore the order.

Fuck that.

It wasn't a problem. Lono didn't stop him. "I couldn't stand to lose another child, not on my watch. I'll get someone to follow you as soon as possible. But go now, Hank. Go."

As it turned out, Hank received back up after all. When he reached the trailhead Nani's Vespa was already there. Pink Floyd was careening to a stop.

"When she didn't reach you, she called me at Jasmine's place," Kaleo explained.

"Smart girl," Hank said, thrilled she'd showed such discretion. "You got any kind of weapon?"

"Fo' shua. Got my own two hands," the big man answered. "But what's up? Think I'd need them?"

Against those fists, Maggie wouldn't stand a chance. But they had to get down to the tube before she could harm her prey.

"Come on, then." Hank started down the steep, slippery trail with Kaleo right behind him. They were moving fast, too fast for safety, as Hank shouted over his shoulder, "The woman who killed your little sister is stalking your big sister. We gotta move." They plunged ahead at breakneck speed, ignoring the treacherous vines and the loose lava rocks that slid underfoot.

CHAPTER THIRTY-SIX

Cover Up
By Jackson O'Reilly
Excerpt from the *Keawalani Voice*, 2015

Big Islanders are Big People. We're colorful. Fun. We wore baggy shorts long before Home Boys took up the fashion. The slap, slap, slap of flip flops has been our anthem as long as the strum of ukeleles. We weave coconut palm hats and our ladies swirl in the brilliant colors of their muumuus.

Hawaii's most distinctive mode of cover up is the Aloha shirt. Invented as heat resistant business wear in the 1930s, it has become our primary form of dress, from casual to business, from tacky to high class, from subtle colors to eyepopping psychedelics. So many images of Hawaiian culture can be slapped together in one pattern that a designer is quoted as saying, "An Aloha shirt is like a post card you can wear."

Nobody loved Aloha shirts more than soldiers coming home from WWII, and entertainers through the years. Bing Crosby, Burt Lancaster, Arthur Godfrey, Elvis Presley, Tom Sellack … they all had a hand in spreading the word. Aloha shirts are sold now at great expense in gift shops around the world … and in thrift shops to us locals for virtually nothing.

Our Aloha shirts go on easy, hang loose. They're built for comfort (if you ever see one tucked in, you know the wearer is a tourist). They look good on everyone … there might be a hard body under there or maybe a belly that's been to the buffet line too many times. The Aloha shirt is a perfect cover up for whatever shape the flesh is in.

Personally, this writer thinks that's a mighty fine metaphor for life. It may look beautiful on the outside, but a helluva secret can be hidden underneath.

Renee was lucky. She hadn't waited more than a few minutes for the *Hele-On* bus that rumbled through the village on some schedule all its own. It was still early enough in the morning that getting a seat was no problem. And nobody she knew was aboard to ask awkward questions.

She took the bus a few miles down the road before getting off. That left her a very short walk to the trailhead where her hike began in earnest. She'd never actually been down there to the lava tube, but Lono and Hank had done it. If they could handle it, so could she. She'd never admit to being scared or anything. To keep herself moving forward, she thought about her mother, the woman waiting for her just down the way.

I wonder if her hair is curly like mine. Does she hate it, too? Is she or my dad maybe part Chinese? Are they good people? If so, why did they leave me?

Renee knew she was more of a poi dog than Allison who looked pure *haole*. She could see it in the shape of her own eyes and the darker tint of her skin. Maybe she'd grow up to look as beautiful as Nani with all those nationalities written on her face. She thought about it as she picked her way carefully downwards toward the lava tube.

Maybe her mother had been abducted by *kapu* kidnappers or white slave traders and carried off to the mainland where she was forced to build railroads or something. Maybe she'd escaped and was hiding out in the woods until she could get in touch. Renee stopped herself from thinking anymore about that. She was, if nothing else, a realist. Silly fanatasies were kid stuff. She'd know who and what soon enough. Her mother had some explaining to do.

Brave as she was, she wasn't wild about stopping long enough for a black widow or a five-inch centipede to take up residence on her arm and sting her into oblivion. She stopped to rest just once and to take a drink from the water bottle she carried. Streams might look clean but could have the leptospirosis pest that gave you the runs. Renee knew better than to hike without sunscreen, a hat, insect repellant and the like. She considered herself extremely conscientious about such things so she had taken time to pack her gear even though she'd been eager to get out of the house before Allison woke up. As with the cops' equipment she supervised, you couldn't be too vigilant. You were only as prepared as your tools.

A stream braided itself back and forth over the trail. At times it was just a trickle but now, with no shortage of rain, rocks that were stepping stones were often under water, sharp and slippery. Renee tumbled once landing on her knobby knees. They were already bruised and scarred from eleven years of roughhousing. She frowned at the new scrapes. Only recently had she begun to care whether the bits and pieces of her body were looking good. She wondered if she was pretty.

She couldn't help but fantasize a little more as she entered the small clearing in front of the lava tube. Maybe she could introduce her mother to Kala. Maybe ...

She stopped when she saw the crime scene tape still stretched across the entrance to the tube. Vines had been cut back exposing the raw mouth of it, and the grass before it was trampled by dozens of investigators. Dead flowers were near the entrance, left behind as a memorial that someone had held here. And the name 'Maile' was written in white coral amongst the blackest of the lava.

She felt a shiver as she thought about that little girl who'd been entombed there for so many years. Nani's sister. When she'd died, she was younger than Renee was now. Renee had little concept of immortality, just that it wasn't good to be a zombie or anything.

"Hello, Renee," said a woman's voice from behind her. It was soft, muffled by the sound of the waterfall plunging through walls of ferns into a lagoon near the entrance to the lava tube.

My mother!

Renee swirled around expecting to see maybe a spectacular princess in a rainbow of light. Instead, a woman in an old tee-shirt was sitting on one of the lava boulders that rimmed the natural pool.

Renee realized immediately that this woman wasn't her mother. It was just Maggie Wilson. What a disappointment. Renee didn't know her well, mostly just that she was Akela's wife (although Allison had once said that wasn't quite the right word for it).

"Hi, Mrs. Wilson. What you doing way out here?" She walked

over to the woman, in no fear at all. "I'm meeting my mother. Oh! But that's supposed to be a secret." Renee rolled her eyes at her own slip up, and put her hands over her mouth.

Maggie Wilson struck as fast as an island mongoose. She leapt forward, grasping Renee's bony shoulders. "I *am* your mother, you little idiot. No more secrets now!" Maggie gave the child a vicious squeeze then moved her hands to Renee's wild curls. She clutched hold and shook the child with both hands. "Am I so low and horrible that you can't even conceive of such a fate?"

"Hey! You're hurting me." Renee squirmed for freedom, enraged that someone would attack her like this. She'd always believed she could take care of herself, but now ..."You're rattling my brain. Stop it!"

Her anger gave way to pure terror when the voice of this awful woman changed. It suddenly sounded like a petulant little girl. "One of us is going to kill you. Can you guess who? Is it Mommy or Maile?"

Renee had no idea what was happening, but she knew she had to escape fast. She swallowed enough of her panic to make a plan. In the pocket of her shorts she had Lono's beloved Leatherman tool. She'd picked it up from the kitchen counter where he always emptied his pockets at night, adding it her survival gear.

The multi-purpose tool was warranted for life. Renee hoped the stainless steel blade would be especially warranted for her life. While Maggie shook her, Renee dug out the tool and opened it. She'd cleaned it so often for Lono that she knew just where the knife nestled between the screw drivers and wire cutters. She could find it by feel alone.

Maggie was holding her at arm's length, shaking her so hard Renee began to feel woozy. "My brain's shaking loose. Stop! Please stop!" Her own arms were too short to reach Maggie with a deep blow, but maybe she could slash her. Then, when the woman grabbed for her own gut, Renee could run like the wind into the forest to hide with the feral goats and pigs ...

"Whore child!" screamed the Maggie monster.

Renee was sure she would collapse soon. She cried, "Mamas don't do this! Mamas love their babies."

Somehow her words reached Maggie. She abruptly stopped the shaking and released Renee's hair. Instantly, Renee lunged forward with the knife. But she was too dizzy, too slow. Maggie saw it coming and twisted away. Then she grabbed Renee's wrist and snatched the tool from her.

This woman was so much stronger than she looked. Renee was out of breath, out of hope. She began to crumple but wasn't allowed to sag to the ground. Maggie grabbed her shoulders again, this time shoving her backwards, over the boulders down to the smaller, sharper rocks at the pool's edge. Renee felt her head hit the ground as Maggie shrieked in alarm. "No, Maile, not yet. She can't die until she's baptized. Then you can batter her head the way you were killed. You can bury her in there. It's only fair."

Renee felt the water closing over her legs, then her bottom, then her chest, as she was dragged into the pool.

✦   ✦   ✦

Nani was slick with sweat from hurrying down the trail. The stitch in her side had becoming a whole seam of fiery distress. Her breath and heartbeat pounded in her ears so loudly, she wasn't sure what she'd heard above the sound of cascading water.

A woman yelling? A child? Two children?

Nani burst into the clearing. She looked first at the lava tube then over to the waterfall. Shock washed over her. Maggie Wilson was standing in the lagoon, talking crazy about killing and Maile and baptizing.

Is she lolo? Maggie?

Was Maggie wrestling with a big fish, yelling at it? No ... that couldn't be ... the fish turned and materialized into the tortured face of Renee.

"Maggie!" Nani roared as she dashed toward the pool.

Maggie froze, holding the child's body by a shoulder. Renee's head lolled sideways just above water. Blood trickled down her cheek.

Nani saw an ice cold smile cross Maggie's face. "Well, well, well. If it isn't the big *sistah*. Maile, look who's here."

Nani continued forward but Maggie hissed, "Stop right there." She froze on the brink of the pool, struggling for footing on the rocks.

"Maggie, let Renee go." Nani tried to sound calm, even gentle. "You don't want to hurt anybody."

"Nani the beautiful, Nani the good, Nani the sister who got to live. But not for much longer. Should I kill her for you now, Maile?" Maggie's voice took on a child-like tone once more. "Nani was always the better one. I was just a shadow."

It was a freak show. Was Maggie pretending to be Maile? Did she think she was Maile? How dare she? Rage ignited Nani. Maybe she'd kill the bitch with her own two hands. But first, she must save Renee.

Keep rage in control. Be calm.

"M ... Maile? Maggie? Please let Renee go so you and I can sit and talk. I want to understand it all. I want to listen to your story. Tell me what's happened."

"Too late, too late. You want to trick me. Maile's in me now. She knows your ways. We'll get to you when the whore child is pure." Then she shoved Renee all the way under the water and began, "I baptize thee in the name – "

Nani launched herself. From the corner of her eye, Maggie must have seen her coming. She lifted the Leatherman knife. As Nani fell onto the seamstress, the knife skittered across the denim of her cut-offs, then cut into her thigh.

Crazy pain.

Nani closed her hands on Maggie's arm and shook it loose from Renee. As the child floated away, the two women locked together, dragging each other into the deeper water farther into the lagoon.

✦ ✦ ✦

Hank, faster than Kaleo, arrived first. He rapidly assessed. He was faster, but Kaleo was bigger. And a swimmer. So Hank, trained not to panic, went with his head instead of his heart. He yelled at Kaleo to help Nani while he dove to save Renee.

Nani was bleeding but she held onto Maggie like a sand burr. Maggie outweighed her, was taller and should win in a fight. But she couldn't compete with Nani's hands. The hands that had grown so strong massaging away the villages aches and pains. Those hands pulled Maggie down. Maggie kicked and thrashed her way up just once then they both went under again. Time stopped as they tangled. Air squeezed out of Nani's lungs. They began to burn, like hot lava searing water.

Nani couldn't tell if Maggie stopped struggling before or after Kaleo reached her. Either way, she had no intension of letting go. But Kaleo pulled his sister loose and pushed her to the top. She gasped and sputtered, then went back down. There was Kaleo. He had the knife now, in his teeth. But he was near Maggie's feet, not her hands. Was her foot caught on an underwater snag? Had it been wedged there before Kaleo shoved her away?

Kaleo headed up for air and grabbed her once again. "Nani, Nani, stop your fight. Maggie killed Maile. Maggie and Akela together. All those years ago."

Nani's sob sounded more animal than human even to herself.

Hank yelled from the bank where he had carried Renee from the water. "Kaleo? Is Nani all right? Is she hurt?"

Nani said weakly, "Kaleo, Maggie is – "

"She's not coming back up. Come away with me now."

"I wanted to – "

"Come away now."

They left the pool, Kaleo giving Nani a hand up and over the rocks. They sat near Hank, huddled together to recover their breath. The officer's CPR was just bringing the child around.

Renee spit out water, sobbed and looked at Hank. When she appeared to recognize him, she grabbed him around the neck. "Is she? Is she my mother?"

"She thought she was."

Am I *lolo* like her?"

"No, child, no," He put his arms around her and held her tight. "There's nothing like that in your genes. Maggie was a good woman with bad luck. You have no worries at all. You are absolutely perfect."

Hank looked a question at Kaleo. Kaleo shook his head. "Maggie's gone. She's caught on a snag. Or something. Nothing could be done."

Nani saw the look that passed between her brother and her lover. Then Hank said, "It sounds like one of those terrible accidents that just can't be helped. That's how I'll write it up. We can do nothing for Maggie now. And we need to get Renee to a doctor. Nani, too."

She looked down and saw that her thigh was bleeding. In all the excitement, she'd forgotten about her own wound. At least the physical one.

✦ ✦ ✦

Kaleo had been delegated to carry Renee up the trail. "I'll go on now, and you two follow."

Hank had already unbuttoned his police shirt, removed his tee and put the outer shirt back on. He used the Leatherman scissors to snip the seams of the soft material, then tore it into strips. "Handy device to have around," he said as he'd wrapped strips around Nani's wound. "Maybe I'll just keep it."

"Not usually a good idea to steal from the captain. Better job security to give it back."

Hank smiled then helped Nani stand. They took a few trial steps. "Do you think you can make it? We can wait here until help arrives. Lono is sending a team."

"I'll make it if you help." She wanted away from this *kapu* place.

"You sure you want to try?"

"Absolutely. The cut's not that deep." She liked his arm around her. But she winced as she put weight on the leg. "It just stings. I should get to some antibiotic as soon as I can."

Hank and Nani started up the trail behind Kaleo. Nani watched her brother's broad back ahead of them and saw Renee's little hands wrapped around his neck. "He's becoming quite the protector of children," she muttered.

"Yes. Although we have a prior claim on that particular child," Hank answered. "I'd have killed Maggie myself if she'd murdered Renee. Or you." He glanced at her with the same knowing look he'd shared with Kaleo.

Nani diverted the conversation from that particular path. "You said to Renee back there that Maggie was a good woman with bad luck. Explain this all to me. She was the killer, right? She killed Maile?"

As they hobbled up the hill, he told her what he knew from Akela and from reading the last few pages of Maggie's journal. "I didn't have time to read the whole thing. But what I saw was enough to know they killed your sister. Maybe an accident. I'll need to read the rest and interview Akela."

Nani's emotions were on overload. She couldn't feel sorry for Maggie Wilson. The woman had killed her sister, broken her family, taken her money to do the Keawalani Hands laundry. Nani had paid Akela to garden. She let him get close to Renee. *She* put Renee in the same danger that Maile had been in. How dare they play her for such a fool?

She ranted half way up the trail. Hank wisely stayed quiet for the most part. All he said was, "Don't judge too soon, Nani. Wait until we hear what he has to say. And read Maggie's diary. There may be circumstances."

Of course. There were always circumstances. Maybe she'd be sorry for them in the end. But for now, Nani was glad Maggie Wilson was dead.

She'd have killed Maggie herself, never letting her surface. Kaleo had barged in and pushed her away and suddenly Maggie's foot was caught underwater. Nani knew what had really happened out there in the lagoon. Maybe Hank did, too. He'd asked so few questions of Kaleo. She squeezed his hand a little harder.

She winced as she nearly tripped on a lava rock that skidded beneath her foot. Yes, she knew what had happened. And she also knew that, with this unspoken pact among the three of them, she'd be the Big Island secret keeper for the rest of her days.

EPILOGUE

The *kumu* Hakumele was in her office, huffing and grumbling. She shifted her sizable self in her ancient office chair, seeking a more comfortable perch. Her desk was covered with scraps of paper that she shuffled and reshuffled.

So crazy-making, selecting which festivals to attend with which students on which islands. And oh! The two cruise ships that would visit Kona at the same time. Preparing one troup to dance for the passengers onboard was hard enough ... but two at the same time?

"Auweee! So much trouble just to bring art to the world." She removed a pencil that had been stuck in her top knot and tossed it at a cup of pens. It missed.

While she wriggled in the chair again, her brother picked the pencil off the palm mat and put it in the cup. He was in the guest chair in front of the desk. Manuku was staying close to Hakumele these days, like it or not. On the day he went from Nani to Hakumele to seek forgiveness, she had said, "Booze is no longer an option for you, *brudah*. Suck it up." That's how she'd put it in her comforting, sisterly way. "I am now your prison guard. You will not return to your own home until alcohol is no longer your crutch."

He'd asked if that was a life sentence, and she'd nodded. "You will stay with me as long as it takes. Could be forever."

Today, he was reading the article in the *Keawalani Voice*. "Says here the child Renee has been checked out and is fine. She's home with Allison again."

"Humph. Fine physically, maybe. That girl has lost one mother. May soon lose another. Poor Allison. Poor Renee."

Manuku cupped his ear and leaned toward the floor. "The earth trembling? The gods tell you that?"

Hakumele's round face looked like a frownie emoticon. Manuku always could make his sister scowl when he teased her. "No, Nani told me that. She plans to step in for Allison when and if."

"Nani will be there for Renee. Like you were there for Nani when I left her. Not sure I can ever thank you enough for that."

"Make it your life's duty to please me from now on." She rolled her massive shoulders and stretched her back. "Start with making new leather cushions for my chair."

"I don't craft leather anymore. You know that."

"Yeah? Well you do now. No more tanning. No more chemicals. Now you only create patterns again."

"Doubt I have the ability anymore. Booze leaves you shaky. Life leaves you shaky."

She pointed a finger at him. It might as well have been a gun. "You don't waste talent given you by the gods. Take your diazepam and get started with the carving, yeah?"

He rolled his eyes and returned to the *Voice*. "Says that Akela Onekea is now in custody. What you suppose will happen to him?"

Her cheeks sagged like a blood hound. "He'll be gone a long time, I'm afraid. Won't be back to Keawalani in my lifetime. If he and Maggie only spoke up as children, told what happened to Maile, things could have been so different for them. For all of us."

A slamming of the studio door and clatter of metal chairs alerted them that people had entered the studio. It was not unusual for students to stop by just to practice, so the noise didn't alarm Hakumele.

Still, she was surprised when she heard a tape of a hula far too complex for most of her students. It was a song of love, lost and found, the lifting of spirits after long confinement. Its fast pace, intricate body work and infinite grace had made it her own choice when she herself was a champion.

Hakumele felt a glimmer of hope. She hurried out to the studio to see just what was going on. Hank Lindsey and Renee were sitting on two of the rickety chairs next to Frank Lono and Allison Costello. And there was Kaleo with that beautiful Jasmine creature along with her squirming little boys.

It was certainly a surprise to see them there. But they didn't hold her attention for long. Instead, she focused on the front of the studio, on the dance floor beneath the mural by her nephew. Hakumele's bare feet began to move and her body sway as music flooded her spirit with exquisite delight.

Her niece was dancing the difficult hula for this audience. She dipped and swirled, her hands and feet moving with the brilliance and speed of bird wings. The beautiful woman had a look of rapture on her face.

For the first time in years, Nani Paleo was dancing for joy.

THE END

Author's Acknowledgments

At the risk of aging myself past all reason, I must reveal: I made my first visit to the Big Island even before Hawaii became a state. I have loved it ever since.

It took the tutelage and friendship of Sondra AhSam and Claudia Mulder, both residents of the Big Island for many years, to immerse me in the facts and feelings of the island. It's only with their help that I dared write this book about a culture I so admire. For this reason, *Secrets of the Big Island* is dedicated to these two beautiful island women.

For input on criminal statistics, flora and fauna, history, spiritualism and so much more, I am indebted to countless experts, librarians and websites. For her expertise in the practice of reflexology, I thank Carol Richards of Helping Hands Reflexology. For sharing his knowledge of body art, I am grateful to Jeffrey Love, owner of The Tattoo Guy.

For critiques that range from sweet to pit bull in temperament, I am sincerely grateful to my friends Jan Schamberg and Mindy Mailman, my sister Donna Whichello, and to readers of my blog who were cheerleaders when I was flagging.

About the Author

Linda B. Myers won her first creative contest in the sixth grade for her Clean Up Fix Up Paint Up poster. After a Chicago marketing career, she traded in her heels for rain boots and moved to the Pacific Northwest with her Maltese, Dotty. You can visit with Linda on her blog at www.lindabmyers.com or by email at myerslindab@gmail.com.

Check out Linda's other novels:

Lessons of Evil

Fun House Chronicles

Bear in Mind

Hard to Bear

Bear at Sea

Bear Claus: A Novella

The Slightly Altered History of Cascadia

Please leave a review of *Secrets of the Big Island* or Linda's other books on www.amazon.com

Visit with Linda B. Myers at

www.LindaBMyers.com
facebook.com/lindabmyers.author
myerslindab@gmail.com
amazon.com/author/lindabmyers